Where do wizards, bards, and unicorns mingle with murderers, thugs, and thieves? In the city of Sanctuary. The inhabitants spend their time brawling, drinking, conjuring, fishing, making love, and, of course, cheating each other and stealing.

Wings of Omen is the sixth authorized anthology of "Thieves' World" stories, written by today's top fantasy talents. Be prepared to visit the city where everybody carries at least one knife, and even pet birds and cats are trained killers....

WINGS OF OMEN
THIEVES' WORLD™

Don't miss these other exciting tales of Sanctuary: the meanest, seediest, most dangerous town in all the worlds of fantasy....

THIEVES' WORLD
(Stories by Asprin, Abbey, Anderson, Bradley, Brunner, DeWees, Haldeman, and Offutt)

TALES FROM THE VULGAR UNICORN
(Stories by Asprin, Abbey, Drake, Farmer, Morris, Offutt, and van Vogt)

SHADOWS OF SANCTUARY
(Stories by Asprin, Abbey, Cherryh, McIntyre, Morris, Offutt, and Paxson)

STORM SEASON
(Stories by Asprin, Abbey, Cherryh, Morris, Offutt, and Paxson)

THE FACE OF CHAOS
(Stories by Asprin, Abbey, Cherryh, Drake, Morris and Paxson)

WINGS OF OMEN
(Stories by Asprin, Abbey, Bailey, Cherryh, Duane, Chris and Janet Morris, Offutt and Paxson)

THE DEAD OF WINTER
(Stories by Asprin, Abbey, Bailey, Cherryh, Duane, Morris, Offutt and Paxson)

SOUL OF THE CITY
(Stories by Abbey, Cherryh and Morris)

EDITORIAL CLARIFICATION

Recently, there have been various short stories and one novel published involving a *Thieves' World*™ character. While the characters appearing in the stories in these anthologies remain the property of the individual contributing authors, there is just one *Thieves' World* universe. The events which impact the city of Sanctuary are chronicled in these anthologies and *authorized* spin-off products only. Do not be confused by the appearance of familiar names or figures in other works.

We are endeavoring to have an authorized *Thieves' World* product banner such as the one which appears on the cover of this book printed on existing and future material relating to the Sanctuary universe. In the meantime, for your information, a full list of tie-in works includes:

Anthologies	THIEVES' WORLD	Ace Fantasy Books
	TALES FROM THE VULGAR UNICORN	Ace Fantasy Books
	SHADOWS OF SANCTUARY	Ace Fantasy Books
	STORM SEASON	Ace Fantasy Books
	THE FACE OF CHAOS	Ace Fantasy Books
	WINGS OF OMEN	Ace Fantasy Books
	SANCTUARY (hard cover)	Science Fiction Book Club
Novels	BEYOND SANCTUARY by Janet Morris (coming in May 1985 as a Berkley Trade Paperback)	
	BEYOND WIZARDWALL by Janet Morris	
	BEYOND THE VEIL by Janet Morris	
Games	THIEVES' WORLD (fantasy role playing)	Chaosium
	TRAITOR (FRP supplement)	FASA
	DARK ASSASSIN (FRP supplement)	FASA
	SPIRIT STONES (FRP supplement)	
	SANCTUARY (board game)	Mayfair Games

CONTENTS

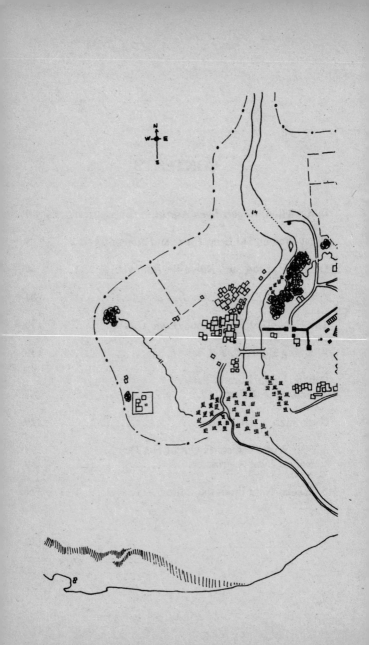

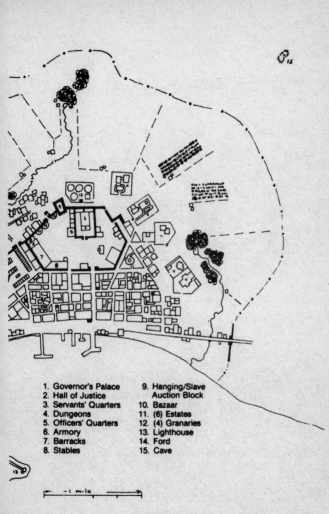

1. Governor's Palace
2. Hall of Justice
3. Servants' Quarters
4. Dungeons
5. Officers' Quarters
6. Armory
7. Barracks
8. Stables
9. Hanging/Slave Auction Block
10. Bazaar
11. (6) Estates
12. (4) Granaries
13. Lighthouse
14. Ford
15. Cave

← – 1 mile →

INTRODUCTION

Robert Lynn Asprin

The birds of Sanctuary are black. From the hawklike predators to the small seedeaters the native birds are black as the heart of a thief.

Hakiem, once the town's leading storyteller, had never paused to reflect on the coloration of the birds before. At moments like this, however, when the business of the Beysa's court was between members of the Beysib clans and conducted in their own incomprehensible tongue, there was little for the Empress's native adviser to do but fidget and reflect. Habits evolved during long years drinking at the Vulgar Unicorn had positioned him with his back to a wall and a clear path to the doors—coincidentally he had gotten himself an equally clear view out a window into the courtyard below. The movement of the birds caught his eye; he found himself watching their antics closely.

When the Beysib arrived in Sanctuary they brought, along with their gold and their snakes, a substantial flock of non-migratory seabirds they called the *beyarl*—as they called their snakes *beynit,* their flowers *beyosa* and their goddess Mother Bey. Every day they threw bread and tablescraps into the courtyard to feed their winged allies. The birds of Sanctuary, who could not tell a palace courtyard from the back door of a Maze slophouse, swarmed to this easy feast and fought savagely among themselves—though the Beysib made sure there was enough for all. Some black birds cawed or shrieked to drive off new arrivals, while others took vengeful pursuit of any bird attempting to make off with a morsel too large to be consumed on the spot.

Two of the white beyarl—the birds for whom the food was intended—soared majestically into the courtyard. In an instant all individual differences among the black birds were forgotten; they rose in a single, dark cloud to drive off the interlopers. No, not quite all, the storyteller observed. A few cleverer birds remained behind, hurriedly bolting food while their comrades and rivals were momentarily distracted.

The storyteller smiled to himself. From high to low everyone in Sanctuary behaved the same—even the birds.

A flicker of white on the roof across from the window caught Hakiem's eye. One beyarl was perched beside a black bird half-again its size. There was an occasional flutter of wings and much head-bobbing, but neither bird was giving ground. The storyteller was no regular bird-watcher; it seemed unlikely that the two could mate—but they certainly weren't fighting. Perhaps—

"Hakiem!"

He jerked his attention back to the court, discovering that the business had been concluded and the parties dismissed. Shupansea, Beysa of the Beysib Empire, had risen onto one elbow from the supine position in which she traditionally conducted state affairs and was staring at him with her large, amber, and inhumanly unblinking eyes. She was young, not past her mid-twenties, slender, and fair-skinned with thigh-length blonde hair that cascaded onto the pillows in a way that only the finest of silks could hope to imitate. Her breasts were bare, in the Beysib tradition, and so firm with youth that even when she moved the dark, tattooed nipples regarded him as steadily as her eyes.

Of course, Hakiem was himself sufficiently advanced in age that such a sight left him unmoved—almost.

"Yes, O Empress?"

He gave a slight bow, cutting his thoughts, and his glance, short before either progressed too far. As a street storyteller he had always been polite to those who gave him a few coppers in return for his entertainments. Now, with the hefty stipend he was receiving in gold, he was a paradigm of courtesy.

"Come, stand beside us," she said, holding out a dainty hand. "We fear we will need your advice in this next matter."

Hakiem bowed again and proceeded to her side with unhurried dignity. As he walked he took secret delight in the jealous stares directed at him from the other courtiers. During his short time at court, the storyteller and the Empress had developed a mutual respect for each other. More importantly, they found they liked each other, a condition which had brought Hakiem favored treatment. Privately he suspected that his elevated status was not so much a compliment to him as it was the Beysa's way of keeping her own clanfolk in line, but he reveled in the attention while he had it.

The next petitioners were ushered in and, dutifully, Hakiem directed his attention to the problems at hand. He did not know the three Beysib in the group save they weren't clan Burek aristocrats and therefore must be Setmur fishermen. The townspeople he recognized at once as the pillars of Sanctuary's fishing community: Terci, Omat, and the one everyone called the Old Man. Usually citizens of Sanctuary appeared at court in the company of Beysib clansmen when one group or the other had a serious grievance to air, but this group radiated no animosity at all.

"Greetings, Monkel Setmur, Clanchief," Shupansea intoned in the singsong pidgin Rankene which passed for a common dialect these days in the city. "Too long have you been absent from our presence. What matter have you brought before us today?"

The smallest, and perhaps the youngest, of the Beysib stepped nervously forward. "Greetings, O Empress. We . . . we have come before you this auspicious day to seek your favor and blessing on a project."

The Beysa nodded thoughtfully, though Hakiem glimpsed puzzlement in her manner. It was clear enough to him: requests for money sounded the same in any dialect. "Tell us more, Clanchief," she requested.

"It is well known that the arrival of our fleet has caused havoc among the local food sellers," the youth said carefully; he had plainly memorized his speech. "As the nearby farmlands were already overworked, it has fallen to the fishing boats to provide enough food to feed not only us, but the townspeople as well. . . ."

"Yes, yes," Shupansea interrupted. "But what of your project?"

Monkel glanced at his colleagues for support, then straightened his shoulders. "We—that is, clan Setmur and the Sanctuary fishermen—wish permission, and financial assistance, for building a boat."

"A boat?" The Beysa swiveled into a sitting position. "We have fifty-odd boats rotting at anchor in the harbor. Use one of them if you need another boat."

The Clanchief nodded; he had expected this response. "O Beysa, our boats were built for long sea voyages and the safe transport of passengers and cargo. They are ill-suited for chasing schools of fish. For months now we have put to sea in our scout-craft beside these native fishermen and learned much of the waters here. Our friends here, with their keelless boats, cannot chase the fish to deep water where they feed in greater numbers; our scout-craft reach the deep water, but have no holds for the fish. We will make a new type of boat—as big inside as a Sanctuary boat and as seaworthy as our scouts. We ask your permission to

4

lay the keel . . . and, er, for your support."

"But why can't the big boats . . . ?"

Hakiem cleared his throat noisily. Shupansea paused and waited for her adviser to speak. "The Beysa will require time to consider your proposal and will consult with Prince Kadakithis before making a decision. Return tomorrow for your answer."

Monkel looked at his Beysa with glazed eyes—totally shocked by the impropriety of a commoner speaking for the Avatar of Mother Bey—but she simply nodded and waved her hand in dismissal. "Thank you, O Empress," he stammered while bowing and backing away from her. The others of his party duplicated his actions.

A short time later, after dismissing all the other courtiers, Shupansea patted the corner of her divan and called Hakiem to join her. "Tell us, Wise One," she said with a smile, "what do you see in this determination of the Setmur to build another boat that we do not see?"

The storyteller sank heavily onto the cushions; formality disappeared, as it usually did when they were alone. "When one reaches my age one learns to appreciate the value of time. One of the few advantages of being an empress, or even a prince, is that you rarely have to make a decision in a hurry. In short, I was afraid that in your haste to determine if the boat were truly needed for fishing you might overlook the greater problems involved here."

"You're speaking in riddles," the Beysa scolded. "We have always been frank with each other. Is this new boat necessary?"

"I haven't any idea, though I suppose I'd trust the opinion of those who make their living catching fish. My point is that, needed or not, the boat should be built if you are to begin solving your greater problems."

"That is twice you have mentioned these greater problems. Speak plainly, Wise One; after a day with our courtiers and subjects we have no patience for riddles."

Hakiem rose and began pacing. "The greatest problem is the friction between our peoples. There is far too much

5

killing and hating going on; every day it gets a little worse, not better. If we are going to live together in Sanctuary without destroying the town and ourselves, there must be peace, and peace must begin somewhere."

Shupansea leaned back, regarding him with hard, staring eyes that were old beyond their years. For a moment she was the Beysa again, the Avatar of the goddess Bey, and not a young woman. "We did not expect garlands and parades when we came here," she explained flatly. "The Setmur have a saying: 'New fish are bought with blood.' We knew there would be hardship, maybe death, wherever we went; Beysib themselves are slow to change and slower to accept change they do not want. That is why we have restrained our retribution when our people have been slaughtered. We had hoped gold would be enough; but if it must be our blood, then it will be—and *theirs* as well."

Hakiem hawked and spat on the polished floor. The Beysa did not threaten often, nor well. "We have a saying too," he retaliated. "'Never pay the asking price—even if you can afford it.' Don't be blind to the first positive sign I've seen wander through this room. Didn't you look at that delegation? Beysib and Ilsig and Rankan, together, proposing a joint action other than slitting each others' throats! Who cares if the boat is necessary—just let them build it!"

The shapely breasts rose and fell in a great sigh. "Ah . . . we see your point. Yes, the boat shall be built regardless of the cost or need."

"Nonsense," Hakiem said with a grin, "*never* pay the asking price. Make them submit an accounting; question every board and nail on it. They'll cheat you anyway, but there's no sense in letting them think you don't care about money; they care very much about it. But you must discuss the matter with the Prince."

"Why?" She was sincere, and that pained Hakiem even more.

"Wood is scarce in Sanctuary, and the building of a new boat will require the felling of trees. For generations the Governor has been the protector of our little forests. If you have truly left Kadakithis as governor, then *he* must issue the edict about the trees—or you should not pretend that he is governor of anything."

The Beysa smiled as she nodded her understanding of the situation, and was about to say something else when the Prince strode into the room.

"Shupansea, I was wondering if... Oh, hello, Storyteller."

"Your Highness," Hakiem responded, bowing as low for the Prince as he did for the Beysa.

The Prince and his entourage were currently living in the Summer Palace, a half-finished rambling structure out beyond Downwind, having surrendered the Governor's palace to the Beysa two days after the fleet arrived. Hakiem tried to close his rumor-sensitive ears to the signs of ever-increasing familiarity between the Prince and the Beysa, but it was almost impossible. The Prince was never at the Summer Palace and never more than a few moments away from Shupansea; his courtesans had been spirited back to the capital, and Molin Torchholder, who should have been above such things, seemed to be encouraging the entire affair.

"Just one little matter, then we can be alone," Shupansea told Kadakithis with a radiant smile. "Tell me, you don't care if a few trees are cut down if it will get the townspeople and my people working together, do you?"

"If trees are what you want, take them all," the Prince said with a casual shrug of his shoulders and an equally radiant smile.

"I think, then, that I should withdraw now, O Empress. The matter seems to be settled now."

Hakiem paused outside the Presence Chamber, trying to control the irritation and, yes, the dread that had been generated by the exchange. Was the Prince so infatuated with Shupansea's overly obvious charms that he had thrown away what little judgment and free will he possessed? Was Sanctuary a Beysib property now, completely and without any recourse? The storyteller liked the Beysa and always advised her honestly, but he was Sanctuary's proudest citizen. It grieved him beyond speech to see what they were doing to his city.

He was suddenly aware that the room behind him was perfectly quiet now; the lovers had escaped. His eyebrows went up as his lips tightened. Perhaps the white bird could mate with the black one. And if they did, what became of all the other birds who were left?

WHAT WOMEN DO BEST

Chris and Janet Morris

From a hunting blind of artfully piled garbage guarded by a dozen fat, half-tamed rats, an Ilsig head, then another, and another, caught the moonlight as the death squad emerged from the tunnels to go stalking Beysibs in the Maze.

They called their leader "Zip," when they called him anything at all. He didn't encourage familiarity; he'd always been a loner, a creature of the streets without family or friends. Even before the Beysib had come and the waves of executions had begun, the street urchins and the Maze-dwellers had stayed clear of the knife-boy who was half Ilsig and half some race much paler, who hired out for copper to any enforcer in the Maze or disgruntled dealer in Down-wind. And who, it was said, brought an eye or tongue or liver from every soul he murdered to Vashanka's half-forgotten altar on the White Foal River's edge.

Even his death squad was afraid of him, Zip knew. And that was fine with him: every now and again, a member was captured by the Rankan oppressors or the Beysib oppressors: the less these idealists of revolution knew of him, the less they could reveal under torture or blandishment. He'd had a friend once, or at least a close acquaintance—an Ilsig thief called Hanse. But Hanse, with all his shining blades and his high-toned airs, had gone the way of everything in Sanctuary since the Beysibs' ships had docked: to oblivion, to hell in a basket.

Standing up straight for a moment in the moon-licked gloom to get his bearings, Zip heard laughter rounding a corner, saw a flash of pantaloon, and ducked back with a hiss and a signal to his group, who'd been trained by Nisibisi insurgents and knew this game as well as he.

The moonlight wasn't bright enough to tell the color of the Beysib males'—Zip didn't think of them as "men"—pantaloons, but he'd be willing to bet they were of claret velvet or shiny purple silk. Killing Beysibs was about as exciting as killing ants, and as fruitless: there were just too damned many of them.

The three coming toward his hunting party were drunk as Rankans and limp as any man might be who'd just come out of the Street of Red Lanterns empty of seed and purse.

He could almost see their fish-eyes bulging; he could hear their jewelry clank. For pussy-whipped sons of snake-women, these were loud and brash, taller than average, and with a better command of street-Rankene: from under their glittering, veil-draped hats, profanity worthy of the Rankan Hell-Hounds cut the night.

There remained nearly the whole Street of Red Lanterns between the two parties. "Pre-position," Zip breathed, and his two young squad members slipped away to find their places.

They'd done this every night since Harvest Moon; the only result of it Zip had seen was a second, then a third wave of Beysib ritual executions. But since those ceremonially slaughtered were hated Rankan overlords and Ilsigs who served the Rankans and the Bey, it wasn't keeping any of the revolutionaries up at night.

And you had to do something. Kadakithis had been a harsh ruler, but the Rankan barbarians were spoken of wistfully and with something bordering on affection now that the Beysib had come: a matriarchy complete with female mercenaries, assassins, magicians more utterly ruthless than men could ever be. It was enough to have brought Zip into the orb of the Revolution—his manhood was something he'd fight to keep. It was going to take more than a few exposed fish-folk titties to make him bow his head or renege on his heritage.

Right now, he was going to kill a couple of Beysib boy-toys and lay their pertinent equipment on Vashanka's Foal-side altar: maybe the Rankan murder-god could be roused to action; Death knew that the Ilsig gods were out of their depth with these women-despots whose spittle was as venomous as the pet snakes they kept and the spells they spoke. The Revolution could use the publicity and Zip could use the money their jewelry was going to bring once Marc melted it down.

Down the street came the Beysib boywhores, laughing in deeper voices than Beysib men usually dared. Zip could make out some words now: "—porking town down on its porking hands and knees with its butt in the air while those porkers pork it—"

Another voice cut in: "I've told you once, Gayle, to watch your mouth. Now I'm making it an order. Beysibs don't— God's balls!"

Without warning, and according to plan, Zip's two cohorts jumped out from concealment as the three Beysibs passed them.

Zip readied his throwing knives: once the Beysibs were herded his way, they were as good as dead. He widened his stance, feeling his pulse begin to pound.

But these Beysibs didn't run: from under their cloaks or out of their pantaloons, weapons suddenly appeared: Zip could hear the grate of metal as swords left their scabbards and the dismayed shouts from his cohorts as they tried to engage swordsmen with rusty daggers and sharpened wooden sticks.

Zip had a wrist slingshot; it was his emergency weapon. He didn't mean to use it; he was still thinking to himself that he was better off not getting involved, that these weren't your average Beysibs—maybe not Beysibs at all—and that he didn't owe the death-squad members anything, when he found himself letting fly once, then again, with his wrist slingshot and making as much noise as he could while running pell-mell toward the fray.

One of his missiles found its target: with a yelp, a pantalooned figure went to its knees. Another turned his head, cursing like a soldier, and something whizzed past Zip's ear. He felt warmth, wetness, and knew he'd been grazed.

Then he realized that neither of his squad members were standing: he slowed to a walk, his breathing heavy, trying to see if the two lying in the dirt were moving. He thought one was; the other seemed too still.

His adversaries, whoever they were, seemed to want to continue the argument: the two with the swords moved toward him, parallel to one another, splitting the street into defensible halves, far enough away from the buildings to avoid any more lurkers in doorways, and from each other to give each room to handle anything that might come his way. Neither spoke; they closed on him with businesslike economy and a certain eagerness that gave Zip just enough time for second thoughts:

These were professional tactics, put into practice by professionals. When times had been easier in Sanctuary and an old warhorse named Tempus had formed a special forces unit of Stepsons and then invited any Ilsigs who dared to train for a citizens' militia, Zip had taken the opportunity to learn all he could about the Rankan enemy: Zip had been taught "street control" by the same book as those now advancing down this particular street toward him.

Two to one against professionals, there was no chance that he could win.

He raised his hands as if in surrender.

The two soldiers-in-disguise growled low to one another in what might have been Court Rankene.

Before they could decide the obvious—to take him alive and spend the evening asking him questions it would be painful, perhaps crippling, not to answer—Zip did what he had to do: let fly with a palmed dagger and then a specially pronged slingshot missile.

Both casts sped murderously true—not into the probably armored chests of the two big men with swords (whose companion was now on his feet and falling in behind them, perfectly and by-the-drill covering every move they made) but into the exposed neck and chest of Zip's own two men: no revolutionary could be captured alive; everyone knew too much; they'd all signed suicide pacts in blood but, in this case, Zip knew he'd better help these two along. Rankan interrogation could be very nasty.

Then as the rear man yelled, "Get the bastard," and the two in front lunged toward him, Zip wheeled and dove for the tunnel entrance, down among the garbage and the rats, pulled the cobble-faced cover in place behind him, and shot the stout interior bolt.

Two days later, Hakiem was sitting on a bench in Promise Park—not one of his accustomed haunts.

He considered himself, as a storyteller, a neutral party in this war between Ranke and the Harka Bey for control of Sanctuary. In his innermost heart he couldn't help but take sides, though, and since his side was the side of the Ilsigi, whose land this once was and whose sorrow he now shared, he'd gotten just a *little* bit involved with helping the Revolution.

This was nothing new for Hakiem: he'd been a *little* involved with Jubal the ex-slaver, a *little* involved with Prince/Governor Kadakithis's Hell-Hounds . . . with everything, if truth be known, that concerned his beloved, benighted town.

He kept telling himself that there was a good story in

whatever it was he shouldn't be getting involved in. The Revolution, which might be the greatest story Sanctuary would ever offer him, was also the most dangerous. Involved in it were Rankans and Ilsigs, fighting together— though some didn't know it and others wouldn't admit it— against the heinous matriarchy of the Beysibs.

But, Hakiem reminded himself as he waited for his contact to appear, he was an old man: he wouldn't have lived to be old if he were too foolish. And Hakiem, who'd been safe on the sidelines, an observer and a certified neutral all his life, was beginning to feel the tug of revolutionary fervor himself—politics, he well knew, was an old man's game: old men sent young men out to lose their lives for principles. He'd have to be careful not to become as deluded as those the Ilsigi populace fought: the Beysibs, the Rankans, the Nisibisi and whoever else wanted to put their stamp on his poor little sandspit of a town.

Whoever had sent him the note which had bade him come here (*Hakiem, for the tale most worth telling this season, meet me at the bench under the parasol pine in Promise Park at midday, two days hence.*) was willing to take outrageous chances: even in daylight, the Beysib discouraged public gatherings. Two, these days, was a public gathering.

Still, this was the first time the rebels had tried to contact him, although it seemed to Hakiem that they should have realized they needed him sooner: without rumor, without the proper stirring stories of heroism and success, without a vision of the Revolution to come, no insurgency could succeed.

Two blond, bare-breasted Bey women went by, their bulging eyes downcast, demurely veiled, Beysib males prancing behind them, and behind those, Ilsig boys carrying sunshades.

When they'd gone, Hakiem took a deep breath. He didn't have any assurances that it was the revolutionaries who'd sent him the note: he'd made an assumption, one that might not be true. Either of the fish-women with their trained

14

serpents who now receded into the distance, their entourage behind, could have sent that note.

Hakiem rubbed his face, bleary-eyed and weary: this final indignity heaped upon luckless Sanctuary was almost too much for him to bear. Daily, the rubble piles grew greater and the bodycount mounted. Orphans now outnumbered parented children, and child gangs as deadly as the Nisibisi-sponsored death squads roamed the town at night when (everywhere but in the Maze, which was impossible to police) the Beysib curfew was in force.

Once, the town of Sanctuary had been sneered at as the anus of Empire—but at least then it had been part of something comprehensible: the Rankan Empire, venal and vicious, was a creation of men and manpower, not of women and sorcery. The Harka Bey and their sorceresses imposed a rule of supernatural terror upon Sanctuary that all priests— Ilsig and Rankan alike—agreed would soon bring down the wrath of the elder gods.

An Ilsigi priest, in his fiery sermons (held surreptitously north of town in the Old Ruins), had warned that the gods might send Sanctuary to the bottom of the sea if the populace did not unite and oust the Bey.

Some had hoped Kadakithis might show his face there last night; but no one in the city had seen the poor Prince/Governor up close since the takeover: sometimes a personage who looked very like Kadakithis appeared at the high window in the Hall of Justice, but the whispers were that this was only a simulacrum of Kadakithis, that the Prince/ Governor languished, all but dead, under the Beysa Shupansea's spell. And the rumors were not so far from the truth, though Kadakithis was held in thrall by love, not magic.

Things were so much worse now than they'd been when the Nisibisi witches had come down from the north preaching Ilsig liberation and prophesying a great upheaval to come that, had the most terrible Nisibisi witch—Roxane, Death's Queen—appeared now before Hakiem and demanded his

15

soul in payment for the opportunity to tell a tale of Sanctuary's freedom, Hakiem would gladly have given it.

Things were so damned depressing, sometimes he wanted to cry.

When he wiped his eyes and took his old, gnarled hands away, a woman stood there before him.

He drew in a shocked breath and almost cowered: was it a witch? Was it dreaded Roxane, come back from the northern war? Roxane, who had all but destroyed the Stepsons and made undead slaves of her conquests? Had he just pacted with a witch? By the mechanism of a thought, just an errant thought? Surely, no one could lose their soul so easily, so offhandedly. . . .

The woman was tall and broad-shouldered, with a firm chin and clear narrow eyes; her hair was as black as a wizard's, her clothes nondescript but cut to facilitate easy movement—her tunic vented, her Ilsig leggings bloused at the knees and disappearing into calf-high, laced boots.

"Hakiem, are you? I'm Kama. Shall we walk?"

"Walk? I'm . . . waiting for someone—my apprentice," he lied lamely. Was this a Bey mercenary? He didn't know they covered their breasts or wore pants. Was he to be arrested? That would be a story— "Inside a Beysib Interrogation Cell"—if only he might live to tell it. . . .

"Walk." The woman's voice was throaty as she chuckled. "It's safer, for this kind of meet. And the someone you're waiting for, I hope, is me." She smiled, and there was something familiar about her eyes, as if an old acquaintance looked out of them. She extended her hand to him as if he were infirm, some old woman to be helped to her feet. Women were getting altogether out of hand in Sanctuary this season.

He brushed her hand aside and got up stiffly, hoping she wouldn't notice.

She was saying, "—your apprentice? That idea's not half-bad. I'd probably qualify, having won first prize at the last Festival of Man, wouldn't you think?"

"First prize? Festival of Man?" Hakiem repeated dumbly. "What did you say your name was?" The Festival of Man was held once every four years, far to the north. It was a festival for kings and armies, a matter of war games and athletic events, and there was a poetry contest for historians of the field and tellers of heroic tales that every storyteller alive dreamed of winning. But even to attend you had to be sponsored by a king, a greatful army, a powerful lord. Who *was* this woman? She'd told him, but he was so melancholy and so depressed—*no, let's face it, fool: you're getting old!*—he couldn't recall what she'd said.

"Can I trust you, old man? Or am I safe because, though I told you once, you've already forgot?" Her mouth twisted in a defensive little grin that definitely reminded him of someone else. But who?

Hakiem said carefully, "You can trust me if your heart is in the right place, Candy." That was what she'd said, he thought—or close enough to make her correct him.

She looked at her booted feet as they scuffed up autumn dirt and when she raised her head she looked right at him: "I'm Kama, of the Rankan 3rd Commando. If *your* heart's in the right place, you'll put me in touch with the rebels. Otherwise," she shrugged, "you folks are going to have a lot of dead amateurs and a stillborn Revolution."

"What? What are you talking about? Rebels? I know no rebels—"

"Wonderful. I like your spirit, old man. You're the ears of this town, and some say the mouth. Tell whomever you *don't* know that I'll be at Marc's Junky Weapons Shop an hour before curfew and thereafter, tonight, to make sure we don't have another little problem like we had on the Street of Red Lanterns two nights ago. If we're going to kick some Beysib pantaloons, we'll need every man we've got."

Hakiem had the distinct feeling that this Kama of the Rankan 3rd Commando had forgotten that she, herself, was a woman. "I can't promise anything," he said politically. "After all, I've only your word and—"

"Just do it, old man; save the talk for those who'll listen. And show up tonight, if you dare, to hear some tales you'll die from telling. Even if you don't, *I'll* be telling everyone I meet I'm your apprentice—do try to remember my name."

She increased her pace, leaving him behind as if he were standing still.

Watching her draw away, Hakiem stopped trying to catch up. There were too many Bey around. If he wanted a story worth dying for, he could drop by Marc's.

He wasn't sure if he would, or sure that *not* going would save him from involvement by implication. But then, she—*Kama*—knew that. He'd been too daunted by her talk of the Festival of Man and her whole bearing to consider much of what she'd said.

Now, walking unseeingly Mazeward, toward the Vulgar Unicorn for the first of many drinks, he did: the Rankan 3rd Commando were rangers with a very bad reputation—since the real Stepsons had left town, filling their ranks with locals, to fight the Wizard Wars in the north, there had been no force on the side of Empire worth rallying round. If the 3rd Commando was here, then the Empire hadn't given up on Sanctuary, all was not lost, and resistance was really possible.

Of course, given the stories about the 3rd's brutality and their provenance—they'd been formed by Tempus long ago to quash just such a revolt as might be brewing in Sanctuary—the cure for Sanctuary's Beysib ills might well be worse than the disease.

Straton wasn't at all sure this was going to work. He hadn't seen Ischade, the vampire woman who lived down by the White Foal, since before the war for Wizardwall, when he'd been an on-duty Stepson, with the whole cadre behind him and Critias beside him, and the only troubles in Sanctuary were sorcery and refractory death squads and the occasional assassination: all standard stuff.

Strat wished Crit was here, then slid off his horse before Ischade's oddly shadowed house and, crossbow at the ready, tethered his big bay horse outside. Crit would be along, one of these days. The whole unit was drifting in, a man here, a pair there; along with Sync's 3rd Commando, they had a good chance of putting things to rights—if they could just figure out what "rights" were. Sync thought they should put every Beysib in town on one big funerary pyre and give 'em to the gods, for starters.

Straton wasn't taking orders from Sync: with Crit still upcountry and Niko in transit with Tempus, Straton was in charge of the Stepsons, who wanted only to kill every idiot who'd made the unit designation "Stepson" a slur and a curse here while they'd been gone.

But Kama had prevailed on Strat to try enlisting the vampire woman's aid. Kama was Tempus's daughter; Strat still respected her for that—not for anything she'd done or earned, just for being his commander's progeny.

So he'd come back here, despite the fact that Ischade the vampire woman was more dangerous than a bedroom full of Harka Bey, to "invite" Ischade to the little party Sync and he were throwing at Marc's.

He'd probably have come anyway, he told himself: Ischade was dangerous enough to be interesting, the sort of woman you never forget once you look into her eyes. And he'd looked into them: deep, hellhole eyes that made him wonder what kind of death she offered her victims. . . .

Nothing for it but to knock on the damn door and get it over with, then.

He pulled on his leather tunic and assayed the walk up to her threshold; as he did, the interior lights flickered and dimmed weirdly. The last time he'd been here, his eyesight had been bothering him. It wasn't, anymore, thanks to a benign spell cast during his northern sortie.

So he'd really see her, this time.

On her doorstep, he hesitated; then he muttered a prayer that consigned his soul to the appropriate god should he die here, and knocked.

He heard movement within, then nothing.

He knocked again.

19

This time, the movement came closer and the lights in her front windows winked out.

"Ischade," he called out gruffly, a dagger in hand to pick the lock or slice its thong or pound upon the wooden door with all his might, "open up. It's—"

The door seemed to disappear before him; off balance, for he'd been about to thump on it hard with his dagger's hilt, he took a stumbling step forward.

"I know," said a velvet voice coming from a wraithlike face cowled in inky shadows, "who you are. I remember you. Have you tired of giving death? Or have you brought me another gift?" Her eyes lifted up to his, her hood fell back, and yet, somehow, backlit in her doorway, her face was still in shadow.

Her eyes, however, were not.

Straton found himself forgetful of his purpose. He wasn't a womanizer; he wasn't an impressionable boy; yet Ischade's gaze was like some drug which made the world recede and all he wanted to do was look at her, touch her, brave the danger of her, and do to her what he was nearly certain none of the sheep she'd fed upon had ever managed to do.

He said, "Invite me in."

She said, "I have a visitor, within."

He replied, "Get rid of him."

She smiled: "My thought exactly. You will wait here?"

He agreed: "Don't be long."

When her door closed, it was as if a bond had broken, a leash been snapped, a drug worn off.

He found that he was shivering, and it wasn't anywhere near as cold in autumnal Sanctuary as it had been on Wizardwall; despite his shaking hands, there was sweat beading on his upper lip. He wiped it and regretted shaving for this court enterprise.

Either he was lucky, and she'd be sated by whatever meat she had in there, so that he could talk to her, convince her, make some sort of deal with her, or he was walking into serious trouble, without Crit or any of his team to get him out if he got in too deep.

About the time he was deciding that no one would ever think the worse of him if he just walked away from this one, left Ischade's stone unturned, and said she hadn't been at home, the door reopened and a delicate, white hand reached out to him:

"Come in, Straton," said the vampire woman. "It's been a long time since one such as you has come to me."

Sync had saved the fabled crimelord Jubal for himself. The Sanctuary veterans he had on staff had warned him about the vicious squalor of Downwind, but he hadn't believed them.

Now he believed, but he believed more in his good right arm and the attractiveness of the offer he had to make.

This Jubal was black and stout as a gnarled tree, older than Sync had been led to believe by half, and sporting a fey blue hawkmask that would have bothered Sync more if the sycophants around the ex-slaver weren't verifying Jubal's identity by every deferential move they made.

The head bootlicker here was named Saliman; the hovel was reasonably commodious once you got inside, but the band of pseudo-beggars ranged around it would give Sync a strenuous afternoon if he had to cut his way through them to get out. He'd unbridled his horse as a precaution: if he whistled, Sync was going to have twelve hundred Rankan pounds of iron hooves and snapping jaws to back him up. 3rd Commando training told him he didn't need more than that: one man, one horse, one holocaust on demand.

Sync wasn't a politician; he was a field commander. But he wasn't in this Downwind potty to fight; he was here to talk.

Jubal, in a flurry of feathered robes, sat down on something very like a throne and said—in a muffled voice through his mask: "Talk, mercenary."

Sync replied: "Get rid of the mask and your playmates,

and we'll talk. This is between us, or not at all."

Jubal responded, "Then perhaps it's not at all. But then you've wasted our time, and we don't like that. Do we?"

Ten scruffy locals made threatening noises.

"Look here, slumlord, are you in the pay of the Beysibs? If not, let's get serious. I didn't come here to give your staff combat lessons. If they need 'em, I've got trainers in the 3rd Commando who specialize in making silk purses out of sow's ears."

Three of the ten were edging forward. Jubal stopped them with a raised hand. From under the mask came what might have been a rattling sigh. "3rd Commando? Should I be impressed?"

Sync said, "I don't know what you're supposed to be, Jubal, in that damn feathered cape and mask. Is everybody in this town in drag?" He crossed his arms, thinking he should have sent a Sanctuary veteran to bring this black man in by the ear. He had to remind himself forcefully not to call Jubal a Wriggly to his face. It was a damned shame, having to join forces with an enemy you'd thoroughly beaten years ago—and on equal terms. The misfortunes of war were neverending.

"Not everybody," Jubal said, leaning forward.

The naked threat in his voice told Sync that he'd pushed just about as far as he could with this ex-gladiator cum slaver cum power player, so he changed tack: "That's comforting. Now, since you won't get rid of your bodyguards, even though it looks to me like you'd be safe enough defending yourself, I'm going to tell you why I'm here and we can have a democratic referendum on how much of a share in the profits your men here get, how much you keep, what everybody's got to do, and who else is—"

"All right," Jubal interrupted. "All right. Saliman, clear the room and make sure no one gets too curious."

"But my lord—" Saliman sputtered.

"Do it!"

Almost as if by magic, the muscle men disappeared.

"Now, what's on your mind, Sink?"

"You must have heard that the 3rd is operating independent of the Emperor—we're on our own."

"Yes?" Jubal purred.

"We're trying to put together a coalition to rid Sanctuary of the Harka Babies and install an interim ruler who suits us—make Sanctuary an independent state: I've got half an army with no place to call home."

"And you'd like to make your home in Sanctuary?"

"Remains to be seen. But if we try this, we'd like you to be a part of it—working with us. Nobody's going to take and hold Sanctuary without your active cooperation, we've heard."

"How do you know the Beysibs haven't heard it too?" Jubal asked cannily.

The old black was sharp, but Sync could feel that he was buying the deal—lock, stock, and misrepresentations. "Because they're having too much trouble, from too many unidentified quarters."

Jubal laughed. The laugh was amplified by his hawkmask and boomed so loud in the small room that its curtains quivered. "That may be, that may be. But flattery won't get you everywhere—just somewhere. Now, let's hear the specifics." The ex-gladiator's arms came out from under his cloak and Sync could see purple scars that told one seasoned veteran of too many wars that he was looking at another.

Sync said honestly: "You can't believe I'd go into that here, with all those ears you've got. I want you to come to a little party we're having, at Marc's Weapons Shop on the Street of Smiths, this evening. Representatives of every faction my Long Recon people think useful will be there. I want to put them together—with your help, of course— in one well-coordinated, working unit."

"Intriguing." Jubal's hawkmask bobbed slowly. "And then what?"

"Then we're going to make this town what it ought to be, what it used to be, what it wants to be: a freehold, a thieves' world, a safe haven where men like you and I don't have to kiss any pomaded pederasts' rings and women do what women do best."

Again, Jubal laughed. When he sobered, he raised his mask—not enough for Sync to see the face beneath; just enough to wipe his eyes. "You, me, and what army?"

"You, me, the 3rd Commando, and Tempus's original Stepsons. Plus, perhaps, the local death squads and revolutionaries, your odd mercenary, the downtrodden Ilsig populace, and the regular army garrison—the ranking officer over there is an old friend of mine. That enough manpower for you?"

"Might be, might be," Jubal chuckled.

"Then you'll come, tonight?"

"I'll be there," Jubal agreed.

Marc's Weapons Shop had a trap door behind the counter, as well as a firing range out back, two display cases filled with blades, and two walls of high-torque crossbows.

Beneath, in the cellar, arcane and forbidden weaponry was kept—alchemical incendiaries, wrist slingshots such as Zip's, instruments of interrogation and of silent kill: poisons and persuaders.

It was early, before the scheduled evening meeting, and Zip and Marc were arguing, alone, while above Marc's blonde and nubile wife minded the store.

"You can't ask me to do this, Marc," Zip said from the corner in which he was hunched, bowstring-taut and feral, his eyes darting from shadow to shadow, looking for the trap he was sure would soon be sprung.

"I've got to ask you, boy, or watch you commit suicide: you can't fight this bunch. You trained with Stepsons; you know that now they're drifting into town again, things are going to change. You stayed out of trouble when they were around last time; now, you can't. They'll tan your hide and use it for a saddle blanket; your polished teeth'll decorate some war-horse's headstall. I don't want to see that happen."

"So you gave them my *name?* I trusted you. I got into

this whole thing by accident. I don't want to be any rebel leader; I don't want to incite any riots or start any twelve-gods-damned revolutions; I just want to protect my own self. *Why* did you do this to me?"

"They're smart. They've had reconnaissance people in town for weeks—they *knew* about you already. If you aren't with them, that bunch assumes you're against them."

"Who? The Buggernauts? The Whoresons? Who cares?"

"*You'll* care, when they make you two inches taller before they make you six inches shorter—mercenaries are a very suspicious breed. I know Strat's Stepsons, and I trust them: they *have* to be trustworthy—it's all they've got: one another and the value of their word. Tempus will be along, Strat says, presently: that means the Storm God—if you still care about Vashanka—is coming home. I'm not good with words . . ." Marc rubbed his beard miserably; his round, brown eyes pleaded with the gutterbred fighter jammed against the joint of two walls as if he were already at bay. "Please just stay and listen to their proposal: without you, the death squads will never give this alliance a chance."

"You're addled. Bewitched. Most of the death squad members got their start with Roxane, the Nisibisi witch. It's a trap: the Stepsons and the 3rd are looking for revenge. Roxane didn't exactly lose gracefully fighting the Stepsons; they lost men; mercs never forget."

"You've got to stay . . . if not for yourself, for me. They've spotted you; they know you're using this place to rearm, to meet, to get in and out of the tunnels. If you don't pretend to join them, I'm having this conversation with a dead man—it's just a matter of days."

"Well, at least you're being honest, now." Zip pushed himself up against the wall. He had a two-day growth of beard and looked a decade older than the years he'd lived. Erect, leaning back in his corner, he said despairingly, "I don't suppose it would do any good to make you promise not to reveal any more of our names? . . ."

"On pain of death? Kill me now, then. And my wife. And everyone else that's helped you. I own, boy, I've seen a lot of action, too many wars to suit me, and I'm telling you: the only way to live through what's brewing in Sanctuary is to make a deal with the 3rd Commando."

"Just so long as it isn't the damn Rankan army—it isn't, you can promise me that, can't you? *Can't* you?"

Marc looked at his big-knuckled hands. The slit-eyed, scruffy youth before him had been orphaned in the Rankan takeover of Sanctuary. He didn't remember his parents and he'd grown up fast and hard, hating Rankans all the way. He'd had no connections, no advantages, no mentors: Marc had known Zip for years, and never dared to get involved—this kind died young and they died unpleasantly.

Now, for some reason known only to the gods, Marc *was* involved: it was a matter of pride, of gut resentment, of life and death.

"No, boy, I can't promise you that. But maybe *they* can. All *I* can promise is that if you don't show up, not me, or my wife, or this shop is going to exist in the morning: they'll level the place and bury us in it."

"Thanks for not pressuring me."

"You're welcome. Thanks for making my shop your favorite haunt."

"I give. Look, tell me who's going to be here."

With a sick feeling in his stomach, fingering an amulet of Shalpa in hopes that the goddess could keep this boy from diving through the open hole by his side into the tunnels and never coming up, Marc began to explain about the vampire woman, Ischade; the crime lord, Jubal; the Rankan 3rd Commando leader, Sync; the storyteller, Hakiem, and the acting garrison commander, Walegrin.

As he did, watching Zip's unbelieving eyes go icy and hostile, Marc couldn't even convince *himself* that tonight's meeting wasn't going to be a wholesale slaughter. Judging by the guest list, somebody could get rid of every trouble-maker in Sanctuary worth mentioning in one cleansing fire—he hoped to hell that "somebody" didn't turn out to be Strat.

The only element missing from the list of invited guests

was a representative of black magic—some honcho from the mageguild, or Enas Yorl, or some Hazard-class enchanter who might be able to keep order through fear of mortal curse.

And if the Stepsons hadn't been allergic to magicians, they'd probably have invited one of them, too.

By the time Sync got to the meeting, the air was already blue with krrf smoke, the packed-clay floor littered with wine dregs.

Kama was presiding, as best she could, over a crowd of thirty-five people who, under any other circumstances, would have been locked in mortal combat by now.

Hakiem the storyteller was the only person in the room who was unarmed, though Sync was well aware that the mouth was mightier than the sword in a situation like this. If things went badly, the rest could be let go, but Hakiem would have to die.

Walegrin, big, blond, and out of uniform, sat in the middle of a half-dozen plain-clothed officers who, by being invited here, would be sufficiently compromised that even if they weren't actively helpful, they wouldn't hinder Sync's progress.

Straton was sitting off by himself in a corner on a winekeg with a woman who must be the vampire, Ischade, else they wouldn't have had that much space to themselves. It was a good thing Critias wasn't in town, or Strat never would have gone after the vampire woman. Sync had to stop himself from looking for signs of vampire-bite on Strat's neck.

The young guerrilla fighter whom Sync, Gayle, and Strat had tangled with on the Street of Red Lanterns—the one who'd killed his own men rather than let them be captured—had the other far corner, a mangy cur scratched fleas by his knee. Sync nodded to Zip and threaded his way to him through the crowd: if there was one single element of this riffraff he needed to secure his tactical advantage, it was this scruffy rebel leader. Reaching him, with all eyes on them, Sync held out his hand and said, "Last time, we forgot to introduce ourselves. I'm Sync. You're?..."

"Zip will do." Eyes slitted, he shook Sync's hand.

"I'm glad you came. When this is over, I'll buy you a meal and we'll compare notes."

He turned and headed toward the table Marc had set up at the front of the room before Zip could ask him what kind of notes or decline his invitation.

Standing beside Kama, Sync waited for Jubal to settle down. Jubal was another one to whom this crowd gave extra room, though he'd come in late with only his first lieutenant—Jubal had been skulking outside in the shadows, waiting for Sync to arrive.

"Now that we're all here," Sync scanned the room, making sure that this was indeed the case; a particular pair of wolfish eyes in a furry face met his and he nodded as he continued, "I'd like to turn the meeting over to our resident expert on covert enterprise, secrecy, and wizardry, Randal, our own ex-Hazard, formerly of the Tysian mageguild."

Mutters broke out; men and women moved away from one another; necks craned, looking for the sorcerer in their midst.

From Ischade's corner, a musical laugh sounded. As all eyes turned to her, the mangy cur, part wolf by the look of it, who'd been scratching fleas near Zip's knee, stretched, yawned, and got to his feet.

The dog, with a sneeze and a sniffle, wandered in seemingly haphazard fashion up to the table, where Kama knelt down, ready with the cloak she'd been wearing, and fastened it around the old dog's neck.

In the back of the room, Zip rose to his feet without a sound; Marc the blademonger put out a hand to stay him.

But no one noticed: the crowd's attention was on the dog before them, changing before their eyes into a man.

It was a smooth transition, smoother than Randal usually could manage. He didn't even sneeze much.

When the mage rose to full man's height, the cloak and the smoke and the shadows thrown by flickering candles in that subterranean meeting room made him seem more imposing than he really was.

For the first time, Sync had that warm feeling in the pit of his stomach that he got when a strategy became reality.

Randal said, "Thank you, Commander."

Sync murmured, "You're welcome," and sat down.

"Good evening, gentle folk," Randal began. "I bring you greetings from Tempus, and from all our friends on Wizardwall. The plight of Sanctuary since the Stepsons left it has come to our attention, and with your help, we're going to set about making things right here—ousting the Beysibs and returning Sanctuary to its former . . . ah . . . glory."

There was a general murmur of agreement.

Randal smiled his boyish, winning smile. The redoubtable mage, his hair grown long enough to cover his too-large ears and too-thin neck, was a born crowd pleaser. When he sneezed concussively, he blamed it on his "lack of suitable garments" and the cold; the crowd bought it. They were so anxious to have the advantage of wizardly aid in fighting the Beysibs that if Randal had talked to them in the shape of a mule or a salamander, they would have listened respectfully, silently, gratefully.

It bothered Sync, just a little, that the credibility of honest fighters wasn't sufficient to satisfy this rabble, but a simple shape-change trick by a fey magician made everybody in the place feel like conquering heroes. He'd counted on that being the case, but it still troubled him: fighters tended to dislike sorcerers, class to class.

If there was one exception, one person not charmed and convinced by Randal's tricks (including the materialization of a topographical map of Sanctuary, a feast fit for the Beysibs in Kadakithis's palace, and "working capital" to the tune of five thousand Rankan soldats), it was Zip.

Marc knew it, and Sync knew it.

When the meeting was over, Marc delayed Zip's exit so that Sync could close in on the youth.

Sync detoured only long enough to ask Strat, in an undertone, "Still got your soul, buddy?" and receive a curt nod in reply before he took the rebel leader by the elbow and suggested they go to the Vulgar Unicorn for a "drink and whatever."

To Sync's relief, Zip agreed, saying: "If we're going to do this, we'd better do it right."

"What's 'right'?" Sync asked, not understanding.

"Right? With One-Thumb's help, soldier. Or are you afraid of Nisibisi magic? It's not like your little baby wizard's, up there." He indicated Randal disrespectfully.

"Magic? I'm afraid of *your* kind of magic—a knife in the back in the dead of night—not theirs," Sync quipped, wondering if this gutterpud wasn't smarter than he looked: no Stepson, no 3rd Commando, and especially no Rankan regular army officer, wanted anything to do with the Nisibisi witch-caste.

When Sync headed for the trapdoor with its stairs leading up into Marc's shop, Zip's hand closed hard on his arm: "Not that way, fool. You want to go to the Unicorn, we go through the tunnels. Smith Street's under curfew, even if the Maze isn't; and, wherever you are these days, two men together rouse suspicion. Come on—that is, unless you're afraid of getting those nice boots wet."

Sync didn't know how Zip could find his way through that dank and slippery darkness. They slogged through sewage, then cleaner water up to their knees, in a phosphorescent green-dark counter-Maze no sane fighter would have entered without ropes, torches, chalk, and reinforcements.

Zip seemed right at home; his voice, at least, was relaxed, though Sync couldn't see his face and was concentrating on holding onto Zip's shoulder, as he'd been instructed, trying not to listen to the part of his brain that kept telling him he'd regret putting himself at the mercy of this sewerlord: Zip could lose him down here and Sync might never find his way out.

But the guerrilla either hadn't thought about treachery, or didn't intend any: Zip's tone was almost friendly as he asked, "Surely you don't expect this so-called alliance of yours to hold?" His last word echoed: *hold, old, ld, d*.

"No," Sync replied, "but before we start warring, we like to introduce ourselves. Anyway, it's good form, and we might pick up a few allies, even if we can't form a coalition townwide."

"In two weeks," Zip said with jocular bitterness, "there'll be twice as many factions fighting, thanks to you: army, death squads, revolutionary idealists, Beysib bitches, your rangers, ersatz Stepsons, real Stepsons—what's the point?"

"That's the point. It doesn't have to happen that way."

"If everyone lets you control it. The chance of that is about even with me marrying Roxane and becoming the reigning Nisibisi warlock."

Right about then, Sync began to wonder if Zip was really taking him to the Vulgar Unicorn. Even the mention of Roxane's name made his skin crawl. He'd had quite enough of wizard wars. That was one of the things Sanctuary had to offer as a winter billet: enough trouble to keep his men from going stale, and no uncounterable magic, just the Beysibs and the weakling sorcerers of Sanctuary's third-rate mageguild in a town that was a war-gamer's paradise.

"Roxane's that good a friend of yours, is she?" Sync took a shot in the dark.

"She's that much of a problem—you'll find out yourself, sooner or later. She's one very big reason why I can't hook up with you. Another is, I can't speak for everybody—hardly for anybody at all."

"Just the Nisibisi-trained and funded death squads?"

"That's right. Take a left turn here; we're going to start climbing stone steps; they're slippery; there's fifteen, then a landing, then ten more."

They climbed in the dark. Sync continued his interrogation: "I've heard that you control most of the territory in Downwind—that you've held it against the Beysibs and that at this point they've given up trying to take it back."

"*Most* of the *territory*? Three blocks? That's what I've got, all I can hold. We don't have drool in the way of arms,

31

or fighters, or anything much but a little Nisibisi support. I'll show my *territory* to you some time. You won't be impressed."

"I'll be the judge of that." Sync had lost count of the stairs; he tried to mount one and his foot thumped down hard through thin air: they'd made the first landing. Three strides, and they were climbing again. With a sinking feeling that had nothing to do with being underground and at the mercy of a boy-guerrilla, Sync asked: "I'd like to meet her, sometime soon—this Roxane. Can you arrange it?"

"Life too dull for you? Just can't wait to lose your soul? Heard that undeads have more fun?"

"I'm serious."

"I wish I wasn't. If you promise me you won't consider it an act of war on my part, I'll hook you up tonight."

"Thanks, I'd appreciate it."

"We'll see about that—maybe you won't be able to appreciate anything, afterward. Any next of kin you want me to notify? At least tell that baby-mage of yours to avenge you?"

Sync chuckled, but he couldn't make it sound convincing. "Randal's going to be introducing himself to Sanctuary, this evening. If Roxane's really here, he won't need to be notified. They've met before."

"Here we are. I'm just going to slide this bolt and then we'll climb up, one at a time—I'll go first. And she's really here. Ask One-Thumb."

There was the sound of wood grating, then a square of blinding light, then a dark silhouette in its midst as Zip levered himself up.

Following, Sync reflected that though this wasn't as harmless an alibi as he'd expected, at least he'd be in public, drinking in the Unicorn when as many of the hundred ruling Beysib women as had accepted an invitation to the opening of "Randal's Pleasure Palace" uptown became wax statues in the exhibit of "Beysib Culture" which was the prime attraction of the mage's Beysib trap.

• • •

This Sync didn't understand what he was getting himself into, Zip knew. The trick was to let the crazy bastard have his way without Zip taking the blame for what became of the 3rd's commanding officer.

Zip hated officers, armies, authoritarian types. He also hated Roxane, when he dared. But not too often—she was more dangerous than three 3rd Commando cadres and she had him by the jewels.

She'd appreciate Sync, all right, if Zip could deliver him. He didn't know why he felt reluctant to do it. Sync was just another murderer, and the worst kind: professional, efficient, charismatic in a Rankan sort of way. The less Rankans in Zip's world, the better. But still, if the Rankans got together and decimated the Beysibs, there'd be less Rankans for the Nisibisi sympathizers to deal with later. Right now, what was good for the Nisibisi-sponsored Revolution was good for Zip.

So he took some chances, letting Sync see how Zip's sort got around in town without being noticed, even showing him where you left your sewer-reeking clothes in One-Thumb's wine cellar and where you got fresh ones before you slunk up the back way and into the Unicorn crowd through the outhouse entrance as if you'd always been there.

One-Thumb wasn't behind the bar; he was probably upstairs with Roxane, or out at the estate—in which case, there'd be nothing Zip could do tonight: you didn't take people to One-Thumb's uninvited . . . not unless you wanted to end up dog meat.

The waitress was one of Zip's people; two hand signals he could only hope Sync didn't see brought him his answer: One-Thumb was in his office upstairs.

Since other things went on upstairs—a bit of whoring and drug-dealing—it was no problem for Zip to go on up, but the man beside him was attracting attention: Sync's sword was too service-scarred, his well-chosen and nondescript garb a little too well-chosen and nondescript for the Unicorn denizens not to mark him as somebody trying not to look like a soldier.

So there were too many eyes on them and the place went too quiet when they settled down in a corner. That was another problem with the mercs: they couldn't stand having their backs exposed; if Sync could have handled a table in the middle of the room, the break in pattern would have relaxed the crowd and Zip wouldn't have felt like he was on display.

But it was like asking a horse to fly. So they sat in a corner, vacated warily by a couple of slitpurses who gave Zip dirty looks for consorting with the enemy, and pretended nonchalance until the girl came back with their ales and a message: One-Thumb would meet them around the back.

Just as they were finishing their draughts and checking their purses, Vashanka's own hell seemed to break loose outside.

The crowd surged toward the door, beyond which the sky was sheeting colored light, then back again as the dreaded Harka Bey—the Beysib mercenary women, assassins in full dress with their damn snakes on their arms—shouldered their way inside, men-at-arms behind them, and backed everyone up against the walls.

"What the frog?" Zip breathed to Sync as the women, who could kill you by spitting on you, if rumor could be believed, starting disarming everyone methodically, then binding their thumbs together behind their backs.

There were ten Bey with crossbows in the middle of the room; Zip kept watch on them under his arms, which were spread above his head like everyone else's.

When Sync didn't respond, Zip whispered, "Well, Ranger, what now? If this is a result of Randal's little 'introduction,' we're standing in an execution coffle: Beysibs don't go after guilty parties, they just round up a bunch of folks at random and slaughter them in the morning. And they don't make it pretty."

Sync shrugged as well as a man can with his hands propped on the wall above his head and his feet spread-eagled: "I'm armed and dangerous; how about you?"

"Close enough, friend. I sure don't want my people to

see me led like a bull to the sacrificial slaughter. And if a woman kills you, your soul never finds its eternal rest."

"I didn't know that," Sync quipped.

"You know it now. Ready? Let's die with our privates intact—it ain't that much to ask."

"Ready," Sync breathed. "On the count of three, we break for the back door." He inclined his head to the right. "To make this work, we'll have to have a couple of those Beysib bitches, so I'm going to start counting when they come to you: as soon as they touch you, grab an arm, jerk it in and grab the bitch, get a choke hold on—"

"Silence!" pealed a deep but assuredly female voice, and the whole place froze.

Zip thought, at first, that it was a Beysib voice, but in its wake came no venomous bite, no snake's fangs, no crossbow bolt through his spine. And in the entire room, nothing so much as moved.

Ducking his head, Zip verified what his ears told him: there was a familiar tread on the stairs—the tap, tap, tap of Roxane's heels. And there was the rustling of One-Thumb's muscular thighs as he descended the staircase beside her, his heavy breathing, and her soft low laugh.

These things could be heard so clearly because, throughout the Vulgar Unicorn, everything else was motionless: the Beysibs stood with mouths agape and weapons at ready, but their eyes were glazed.

Customers in mid-cower were entranced between blinks; tears glittered unshed in serving wenches' eyes.

Only Sync and Zip, of the entire ground-floor crowd, were unaffected by Roxane's spell.

And Sync was already pushing away from the wall, his sword drawn and a half-dozen Bandaran throwing-stars in his left hand. "Pork-all! What's going *on* here? Who the pork is she? What's happening?"

Zip straightened up. "Thanks, Roxane. That could have been dicey." Her beauty didn't affect him as it once had— her sanguine skin and drowning-pool eyes couldn't tempt him; but he couldn't let Sync see that fear had replaced the lust he'd once felt for Roxane. Summoning all his bravado, he continued: "This here's Sync; he wanted to meet you, and One-Thumb too. He wants to join the Revolution. Isn't that right, Sync?"

"Right, right as rain." Sync was just a little bit intimidated, Zip thought. But he'd seen Roxane spellbind a man before, and he knew that Sync wasn't immune: the ranger's eyes never left hers.

Well, Zip thought, he asked for it. Maybe we *will* be allies, after all.

Then Roxane came up, taking both their hands, saying: "Come, gentlemen. I don't want to hold this rabble entranced forever. One-Thumb and I will take you upstairs, and we'll let this slaughter recommence." She licked her lips: she lived on fear, death, and suffering; she was probably having a feast on some psychic plane, just observing the Beysib about their vicious work.

For Sync and Zip, it was a lucky break: she wouldn't feel like teaching them any of her more difficult lessons, Zip was willing to bet—not tonight.

"Zip, my dear little monster, you've outdone yourself this evening." She caressed his face; above her shoulder One-Thumb's eyes met his with what might have been sympathy.

"This?" Zip gestured around, to the Bey and their hapless prey. "I didn't cause this. He did." Zip gestured to Sync. "He's got a mage on staff, and they worked up a little surprise for the Bey hierarchy, across town. This, I'll bet, is the Beysib reaction—or maybe just the beginning of it."

"It is, it is, indeed, just the beginning." Roxane was inebriated with whatever carnage her soul-sucking talents had been treated to this evening. "A half dozen, no less, of the high-ranking Bey bitches are dead, turned to waxen statues in a Tysian mage's museum." She smiled. "And these sheep," her hand encompassed the room, "soon will be dying the slow and horrible death of Beysib retribution."

She caressed Sync's hand, the one with the stars in it;

he looked at her like a starving man at a laden feast-day table. "And," she continued, "since Zip assures me I've you and yours to thank, we'll have a long talk about our mutual future—I'm quite certain, Sync of the Rankan 3rd Commando, that we're going to have one. I may even give you Randal's life, a gesture of appreciation, an indication that we can and will work well together, an introductory gift from me to you."

As if from a dream, Sync roused: "Right. That's very good of you, my lady. I'm yours to command."

"I'm sure you are," Roxane agreed.

Zip knew Sync didn't realize how true what he'd said was likely to be. Not yet, he didn't.

"Would you mind," Sync asked Roxane as they moved among the frozen and the doomed, "if I slit these Beysibs' throats on our way out? It's as fair as the chance the Bey will give these innocents, if I don't." The big soldier's eyes sought Zip's.

Zip said, "It'll give the Revolution credibility."

Roxane paused, pouted, then brightened: "Be my guest. Fillet fish-folk to your heart's content."

Behind her, One-Thumb muttered something about "the right slime for the job."

It didn't take long to slay the unknowing Beysibs. Zip helped Sync while the witch and One-Thumb looked on.

When they were done, they wrote the initials of Zip's "Popular Front for the Liberation of Sanctuary" on the walls of the Vulgar Unicorn in Beysib blood.

By tomorrow, the PFLS's latest kill would be on everybody's lips.

Not bad, Zip thought to himself—not bad at all, for a start.

Then Roxane led the way up the Unicorn's stairs and through a door that had no right to open into the witching room of her Foalside hold, a lot farther than a few steps away from One-Thumb's bar in the Maze.

• • •

Three days had passed since the revolutionaries calling themselves the PFLS had slaughtered too many Beysibs in the Vulgar Unicorn.

Sanctuarites were just daring to go abroad again, pale and haggard from fear and disgust. First the cutthroats and the drunkards, then the vendors and the whores returned to the streets. Then, when it was clear that no Beysib squadrons were waiting to swoop down and scoop them up, others ventured forth, and the town returned to what had become normal: business as usual, with the occasional pitched battle on a streetcorner or sniper in some shanty's eaves.

Hakiem was down on Wideway, selling what tales he could on the dock. Pickings were slim because of his new apprentice, Kama, whose uncannily polished tale of the brave revolutionaries triumphing over the dreaded Harka Bey in the Unicorn drew endless crowds of thrill-seekers, while his own yarns of giant crabs and purple spiders weren't dangerous enough, or newsworthy enough, to compete these days.

Hakiem told himself he didn't really have reason to be piqued: he'd been given money enough at the secret meeting beneath Marc's shop to cover twice what he might be losing.

And Kama, sensitive in her way, dutifully gave him half of all she made.

So Hakiem was watching, paring a bunion where he sat on a splintered keg, while Kama pleased her listeners, when a dark tall youth with a week-old beard and a black sweat-band tied around his head eased toward Kama through the crowd.

It was Zip, and Hakiem wasn't the only one who marked him: Gayle, a foul-mouthed mercenary who'd joined the Stepsons in the north, was lounging between two pilings, as some Stepson always did when Kama was on the streets.

Hakiem saw Kama pale as the scruffy, flat-faced Ilsig caught her eye. She lost her train of thought, polished phrases turned to incoherent clauses, and she skipped to her story's ending so abruptly her gathered clients muttered among themselves.

"That's all, townsfolk—all for today. I've got to leave you—nature calls. And since you haven't had your money's worth, this telling's on the house." Kama jumped down from the crates on which she'd sat, ignoring the rebel leader and heading straight for Hakiem, her hand nervously pulling hair back from her brow.

The youth followed. And so, at professional stalking distance, did the Stepson, Gayle.

"Hakiem," Kama whispered, "is he still there? Is he coming?"

"*He?* They're *both* coming, girl. And what of it? That's no way to build a reputation, cutting half your story out and giving refunds before anybody's asked. . . ."

"You don't understand . . . Sync's gone missing. The last we saw of him, he was with that gutterslime, the one from the meeting—Zip." As she spoke, Kama was tearing open her gearbag, in which metal clanked: this woman never went far from her squadron without her cache of arms.

And up behind her, as she bent over her sack, came Zip, who grabbed her with a crooked elbow around her throat and pulled her back against some bales of cloth before Hakiem could shout a warning or the Stepson, lurking at an appropriate distance, could intercede in her behalf.

"Don't move, lady," Zip said harshly through gritted teeth. "Just call your watchdog off."

Kama gagged and struggled.

Gayle took a half-dozen running strides, then halted, frowning, sword drawn but fists upon his hips.

Zip did something to Kama that made her writhe, then stand up very straight. "Tell him," he said, "to back off. I just want to give your bedmates a message. *Tell him!*"

"Gayle!" Kama's voice was thick, gutteral; her chin, in the crook of Zip's muscular arm, quivered. "You heard him. Stand down."

The Stepson, uttering a stream of profanity built around a single word, hunkered down, his sword across his knees.

"That's better," Zip whispered. "Now, listen close. You too, tale-spinner: Roxane's got Sync. He asked me to set

up a meeting, and I did that. But what happened after—
that's no fault of mine. It might not be too late to save his
soul, if any of you care."

"Where?" Kama croaked. "Where has she got him?"

"Down by the White Foal—she's got a place there, south
of Ischade's. The vets will know where it is. But you tell
'em I told you—that it's not my fault. And that if they
don't get to him fast, it'll be too late. Hit the place in the
daytime—there's no undeads around then, just some watch-
men and a few snakes. Understand, lady?"

Again, he tightened his arm and Kama's head snapped
back. Then he pushed her from him and jumped high, grabbed
the rope on the bales behind him, swung up and over, and
was gone, as far as Hakiem could tell.

Hakiem reached Kama first, coughing and trembling on
the dockside. He was trying to get her up, while she shrugged
off his aid and tried to catch her breath, when he realized
that the Stepson, Gayle, wasn't helping him.

Hakiem looked around just in time to see Gayle vault
the bales after Zip, throwing-stars in hand, and let fly.

Kama saw it too, and screamed brokenly: "No! Gayle,
no! He's trying to help us...!"

"Pork help!" Gayle called back, just before he disappeared. "I hit him. He won't get far—and if he does, the
porker's done for, anyhow." Then Gayle too disappeared.

"Done for?" Hakiem repeated dumbly. "What does he
mean, Kama?"

"The stars." Kama got to her knees, her lips puffy, her
expression unreadable. When she saw that Hakiem didn't
understand, she added: "Those stars are what the Bandarans
call 'blossoms.' They're painted with poison." And, hands
on her knees, bent over, she retched.

Hakiem was still digesting all of that when Kama straightened up, took a handful of sharp-edged metal from her bag,
and started climbing the bales.

"Where are you going, woman? What about the message?"

"Message?" Kama looked down at him from atop the bales. "Right. Message. You take it—tell Strat. He'll know what to do."

"But—"

"Don't 'but' me, old man. That boy's dead if I can't rein Gayle in and get to him in time. We don't kill those who help us."

Like a doused flame, she was gone.

Strat would rather have been anywhere else than in the brush surrounding Roxane's Foalside haunt. He'd had experience with the Nisibisi witch before.

If he hadn't known that Hakiem was trustworthy, that Kama had disappeared, chasing after the street tough who'd brought the message, and that the success of the Stepson/3rd Commando mission into Sanctuary hinged on proving that Roxane couldn't send them running with their tails between their legs, he'd have passed on this particular frontal assault.

As it was, he had no choice.

And he had a good chance of succeeding: he'd asked Ischade to come alone—she had her own bones to pick with Roxane; he'd requisitioned enough incendiaries from Marc's illicit store to send all of Sanctuary up in flames. And his men knew how to use them. The trick was getting Sync out of there before firing up the witchy-roast.

Randal, their Tysian wizard, was sneaking around in mongoose form, right now, taking care of Roxane's snakes and reconnoitering the premises.

When they saw a hawk fly over, right to left, they'd light the horseshoe-shaped fire they'd prepared and rush the place: twenty mounted fighters ought to be able to do the job.

The horses were hooded, their blinders soaked with soda water. The men had bladders of it on their saddles, to wet bandanas if the smoke got too thick.

Ischade was still beside him, in a meditative pose, whatever magic she was going to field unrevealed.

She just waited, tiny and delicate and too pale in the light of day, her claret robe pulled tight about her like a child in her mother's clothes.

"You can still walk away from this," Strat assured her with a gallantry he didn't really feel. "It's not your fight."

"Is it not? It's yours, then?" Up rose Ischade, and suddenly she was terrifying, not small any longer, not the petite, sensual creature he'd brought here.

Her eyes were hellish and growing so large he thought he might be sucked inside them; he recalled their first encounter, long ago, on a dark slum street, when he'd been with Crit and they'd seen those eyes floating over a teenage corpse.

He found he couldn't answer; he just shook his head.

The power that was Ischade bared its teeth at him, the kill-fervor there as sharp as any Stepson's—or any night-mad wolf's. "I'll bring you your man. All of this"—Ischade spread a robed arm, and it was as if night split the day—"that you do is unnecessary. She owes me a person, and more. Wait here, you, and soon you'll see."

"Sure thing, Ischade." Strat found himself squatting down, digging in the sod with his brush-cutting knife. "I'll be right here."

He must have blinked, or looked away, or something—the next he knew, she was gone, and a hawk's baby-cry resounded overhead, and men set their fires and ran for their horses.

Vaulting up on his bay, he wondered if Ischade was right—if he didn't need to risk all this manpower, if magic—hers and Randal's—alone could win the day.

He didn't like to think that way; he was used to letting Crit do his tactical thinking for him; in times like this, a man who was half a Sacred Band pair sorely missed his partner.

And so, thinking more about who was absent than who was present, he urged his horse into a lope and sought the firegate, not realizing until a shape hovered in midair beside him that Randal, on a cloud-effigy of a horse, had drawn alongside.

"In her witching room, he is!" Randal shouted, his face white beneath its blanket of freckles. "And he's yet salvageable, if we can get him out. But it won't be easy—he's totally entranced. I couldn't rouse him in my mongoose form. I'll seek my power globe now and do my best. Fare well, Straton! May the Writ protect us all!"

And his nonhorse thundered away on unhooves.

Craziest damn way to run a war! Strat had come back to Sanctuary to get away from just this sort of thing.

The firewall, around him hot and snapping, gave matters the immediacy of battle, the plain-and-simple truth of life and death.

The fire was just a little out of control, and his horse had to leap hot flames. Within, sod was beginning to smoke and combust, sparks flew, men yelled and squirted water on themselves and their mounts as they let fly with flaming arrows and urged skittish horses toward Roxane's front door.

Strat's plan was to ride roughshod right into Roxane's house, snatch Sync, and get out before she could bewitch them.

It wasn't a plan such as his partner might have made, and he was aware that he might rescue one soldier only to lose another—or others—to Roxane, but he had to do something.

Just as he'd finally convinced his horse of this, and was ready to lead his reformed group up her smoking stairs, an apparition appeared in the doorway:

Ischade stood there, with Sync, his arm over her shoulder, and they walked calmly out onto the veranda and down the steps, onto a lawn spurting sparks and young flames.

Men whooped and raced toward her. Sync, beside her, looked around calmly, his brow knitted as if a slightly amusing problem had him distracted.

Strat, wondering if he was dreaming—if it could really be this easy—got there first, and with Ischade's help pulled

Sync up behind him on the horse.

The fire was loud, and hot, and the horses and men milling around them made talk nearly impossible. But Strat bellowed to the man next to him: "Put her up before you. Let's get out of here!"

The Stepson's mouth formed the word: "Who?"

Strat looked back down, and Ischade was gone.

So he gave the signal to end the sack, and with Sync holding tight to his waist, aimed his sweating horse at a narrowing portal in the flames.

In the thick of Downwind, it was nearly dusk, but the flames from the southeast made a second sunset which wouldn't die.

Zip was in a twilight all his own, stumbling from sewer to alley to dungheap, one hand against his bleeding side, nearly doubled over from the pain.

He'd been stabbed before, beaten often, starved and fevered in the course of life, but never so close to death as this.

He'd pulled the barbed missile out; he didn't understand why it hurt worse now, not less.

He was sick to his stomach and only intermittently did he recall his determination to get home. Home to his own safe haven, or home to Mama Becho's, where someone would tend him, home to...anywhere where he could lie down, where the Beysibs or the Stepsons or the 3rd Commando or the army wouldn't find him.

He was sweating and he was thirsty and he was nauseated. There was a red film before his eyes that made it hard to tell which corner he was on.

If he was lost in Downwind, he was nearly dead: he knew those streets like he knew the tunnels, the sewers...the sewers. If he could find a rat-hole, he could curl up in one; he didn't want to die in public. That thought, and that alone, kept him on his feet just long enough for him to stumble into Ratfall, where people knew him.

He heard his name called, but he was down on his knees

by then, with his head between them. The only thing he could do was curl up before he passed out.

When he woke he was under blankets; there was a cool cloth on his head.

When he could he reached up and grabbed the hand there, held tight to someone's wrist.

He opened his eyes, and a face swam, unrecognizable above him. A voice from that direction said, "Don't try to talk. The worst is over. You'll be all right if you just drink this."

Something was pushed between his lips—hard like clay or metal; it grated on his teeth. Then his head was raised by another's will and liquid spilled down his throat.

He choked, sputtered, then remembered how to swallow. When he couldn't swallow more, someone wiped his lips and then his chin.

"Good, good boy," he heard. Then he slept a sleep in which his side burned and flamed and he kept trying to put the fire out, but it kept starting up from ashes, and his body walked away from him, leaving him invisible and lonely on a deserted Downwind street.

When he woke again, he smelled something: chicken.

He opened his eyes, and the room didn't spin. He tried to sit up, and then it did.

Voices mumbled just beyond earshot, and then a form bent over him. Long black hair brushed his cheek.

"That's a good one; here you go, drink this," said a blurry face.

He did, and well-being surged through him. Then his vision cleared, and he saw whose face it was: the lady fighter, Kama of the 3rd Commando, was tending him. Behind her, the soldier-mage Randal craned his swanlike neck and rubbed his hands.

"Better, you're right, Kama," said the mage judiciously, and then: "I'll leave you. If you need me, I'll be right outside."

As the door closed and he was alone with his enemy, Zip tried to push himself up on his arms. He didn't have the strength. He wanted to run, but he couldn't even raise his head. He'd heard all about Straton's skill at interrogation. He'd have been better off dead in the street than being alive and at the mercy of such as these.

She sat on the bed next to him and took his hand.

He tensed, thinking: *Now it will begin. Torture. Drugs. They've saved me one death to offer me another.*

She said, "I've wanted to do this ever since I first saw you." Leaning close, she kissed him on the lips.

When she sat up straight, she smiled.

He didn't have the energy to ask her what she had in mind for him, or what the kiss was meant to mean; he couldn't find his voice.

But she said: "It was a mistake. Gayle didn't understand what you were trying to do. We're all sorry. You just relax and get better. We'll take care of you. I'll take care of you. If you can hear me, blink."

He blinked. If Kama of the 3rd Commando wanted to take care of him, he wasn't in any condition to argue.

DAUGHTER OF THE SUN

Robin W. Bailey

"Did you miss me?"

Kadakithis whirled away from his window at the sound of that voice and stared in mute disbelief at the young woman in his doorway. She moved through his apartment toward him, aswirl in a summer cloud of dazzling white silks and shimmering sun-drenched hair. Smiling, she reached out to embrace him.

"Cousin!" They squeezed each other until they were breathless, then the Prince held her back at arm's length and laughed. "Gods, how you've changed!" He made her turn while he rubbed his chin with mock-seriousness. "Chenaya, favorite of favorites, you were lovely even before I left Ranke, but you've grown positively exquisite." His fingers traced a thin, pale scar barely noticeable against the deep bronze of her left forearm. "Still playing rough, I see."

47

He clucked his tongue chidingly and sighed. "But what are you doing in Sanctuary, cousin? Did your father come with you?"

It was Chenaya's turn to laugh, and the sound rolled silver-sweet in her throat. "Still my Little Prince," she managed finally, patting his head as if he were a puppy in her lap. "Impetuous and impatient as ever. So many questions!"

"Not so little anymore, my dear," he answered, patting her head in the same condescending manner. "I'm taller than you now."

"Not by so very much." She spun away, her gown billowing with the movement. "Perhaps we should wrestle to see if it makes any difference?" She regarded him from across the room, her head tilting slightly when he didn't reply. A silence grew between them as he studied her, brief but suddenly more than she could bear. She crossed the apartment again in swift strides and seized his hands in hers. "It's so very good to see you, my Little Prince."

Their arms slipped about each other, and they embraced again. But this time his touch was different, distant. She backed off, slipping gently from his grasp, and gazed up at his face, at the eyes that suddenly colored with tints of sadness, or something just as disturbing.

Could he know the news from the capital?

"I smelled a garden when I entered the grounds," she said, tugging his hand, urging him toward the door. It struck her now how dark his quarters seemed, how sparse and empty of warmth or light. "Let's go for a walk. The sun is bright and beautiful."

Kadakithis started to follow, then hesitated. His gaze fixed on something beyond her shoulder; his hand in hers turned cold, stiff with tension. She felt his trembling. Slowly, she turned to see what affected him so.

Four men, guards apparently, stood just beyond his threshold. She had noticed several like them as she passed through the palace—strange, blank-eyed men of a racial type unknown to her. She'd been so eager to see her cousin, she had paid little attention. She'd assumed them to be

48

mercenaries or hirelings. She took note of their garb and the weapons they wore, and hid a private smirk. A man would have to be good with his steel to dress in such a tasteless, gaudy fashion.

One of the four clapped the haft of a pike on the floor stones, needlessly announcing their presence. "The Beysa requests that Your Highness join her on the West Terrace." Then, Chenaya's confusion gave way to a flush of anger as the guard looked directly at her and added with more than a hint of insolence, "At once."

Kadakithis carefully slipped his hand from hers and swallowed. With a shrug of resignation he drew himself up and the tension appeared to melt from him. "Where are you staying, cousin? There are quarters in the Summer Palace if you need them. And I must prepare a party to celebrate your arrival; I know how you love parties." He shot the guard commander a haughty glance as he lingered over this small talk, but he took a first step toward the door.

His expression begged her indulgence; more, it warned her to it. She watched, brows wrinkling, as he moved away from her. "My father has purchased an estate just beyond your Avenue of Temples. The lands reach all the way to the Red Foal River. The papers are being finalized at this very moment." She pushed the small talk, forcing the Prince to defer his exit, studying with a subtle eye the guards' minute reactions. Whoever this Beysa was, these were certainly her men. And who was she, indeed, to command sentries within a palace of a Rankan royal governor?

The Prince nodded, drifting farther away. "Good land can be had cheaply these days," he observed. "How is Lowan Vigeles?"

"Loyal as ever," she said pointedly. *What the hell is going on?* was the message her expression conveyed. *Are you in trouble?* "Though somewhat tired. We made the journey with only eight servants. Protectors, really. Gladiators from my father's school. I handpicked them myself."

Kadakithis pursed his lips ever so slightly to acknowledge her offer. If they were from Lowan's school, better fighters could not be found, and she had placed them at his service. "Go home and give Lowan my well-wishes. I'll need time to plan your party, but I'll send you a message." He turned to join the four guards who barely hid their impatience or their indignation at being made to wait. But he stopped once more. "Oh, have you seen Molin, yet?"

She frowned, then put on a very wide, very forced smile. "I wanted to delay that unpleasantry and visit a friend first."

The smile that spread on the Prince's face was genuine; she'd learned to read his moods in early childhood. "Don't be so hard on the old priest. He's been a great comfort to me, always full of"—he hesitated, and a twinkle sparked in his eyes—"advice."

"Maybe I'll see him," she agreed, running her hands over her bare shoulders, down her arms, feeling somewhat naked and alone as Kadakithis went through the door and out of the apartments.

Two of the fish-eyed sentries remained. "Would you accompany us, please."

Polite words, but she sensed there was no courtesy in them. She shook back her hair, batted her lashes, lifted her nose to a neck-straining angle, and walked over the threshold into the corridor. She was very careful to step on their toes as she passed between them.

Chenaya held her anger in a clenched fist behind her back and regarded the tall, fair-skinned woman who addressed her. Obviously a foreigner like the four guards, she thought, but from what god-cursed land? Painted breasts, indeed! Was that really some kind of webbing between those bare toes? Why, she must be a freak! The woman would be laughed out of any court in Ranke, if only for her garish costume.

Yet, she was also the Beysa, whatever that was, and the guards had bowed when they had presented Chenaya.

The Beysa moved about a room that had to be part of her private apartments. With a short clap of her hands, she dismissed guards and servants all. Only the two of them remained facing each other.

"What did you want with Kadakithis?" the Beysa probed, moving to a chair in the center of the room. Chenaya suspected it had been placed there for just this audience. The foreign woman sprawled there, making a show of appearing at ease.

Chenaya answered slowly, containing herself. There was much to learn here, a secret she had not known when she had come to this city. Now she began to suspect why no word had come to Ranke from Sanctuary in some months.

"The world is a vain collection of private pursuits," she responded vaguely. "By what right do you issue commands in a Rankan governor's palace, or in violation of Rankan law, dare to maintain a personal guard within these walls?"

The Beysa's gaze hardened, fixed on her with a subtle menace. Chenaya lifted her chin and hurled the same cold glare back at the foreign bitch.

"I am not accustomed to rudeness. I could have your tongue ripped out by the root." The Beysa straightened in her chair; the carefully manicured nails of one hand began to tap idly on the chair's carven arm.

Chenaya arched a brow. "You could try," she answered evenly. "But I rather suspect I'd be holding both those marbles you call eyes in the palm of my hand before your guards could answer your summons."

The Beysa stared, but Chenaya could read nothing in those strange eyes. Only a slight twitch of the mouth and those tapping nails betrayed the woman's irritation.

The Beysa spoke again after a long, uncomfortable silence. Her tone was more conciliatory this time. "Perhaps you are not so accustomed to rudeness, either. The regular gate guard who admitted you to the grounds claimed you bore the Imperial Rankan Seal. How is it you have such a thing in your possession?"

Chenaya felt the sigil she wore on her right hand and twisted it. Each member of the Imperial family owned a similar ring by right. Even a Rankan peasant knew that, but she was disinclined to explain it to this woman. Instead, she glanced around the chamber, finely furnished but less lavish than her own in Ranke, and spied a wine vessel and small chalices on a side table. She crossed to it, purposefully ignoring the Beysa, poured a dollop and sipped, not offering to serve. It was sweet liquor, unlike any she had tasted; she wondered if the foreigner had brought it from her own land.

"You are a very rude young woman," her hostess said.

"So are you," Chenaya shot back over the rim of her cup, adding the lie, "only you're not so young."

The Beysa's brow crinkled; a delicate-seeming fist smacked on the chair arm. "Very well, let me be blunt and trade rudeness for rudeness." She rose from her chair, her face clouding over, her finger out-thrust in anger. "Do not come here again. Stay away from Kadakithis. I cannot make myself plainer."

Chenaya nearly dropped the chalice in surprise. Her own cool fury dissolved. She drifted back to the center of the room, the meekest grin blossoming on her lips. Then, unable to restrain herself, she laughed.

"Damn! By the bright lights of the gods, you're in love with my Little Prince!" she accused when she could get her breath again.

The Beysa stiffened. "Kadakithis loves me. I know this, though he says nothing. Mere days after our eyes first met he sent his wife away and all his concubines."

Chenaya felt her brows knit closer. She had not liked Kadakithis's bride; the frail little thing whined far too much. Yet, her cousin had seemed devoted to her. "Sent his wife where?" she persisted.

"How should I know?" the Beysa answered, mocking. "Haven't you reminded me that Rankan business is for Rankans?"

Chenaya studied again those weird brown eyes, the thin pale hair that reached to the waist and lower, the finely boned hands and ivory skin. The Beysa was, perhaps, only slightly older than she. Yet, she gave some impression of age. "You're pretty enough," Chenaya admitted grudgingly. "Maybe, by some god's whim, you have bewitched him."

"Yet, mine is the beauty of the moon, while you shine like the very sun," the Beysa answered harshly, making what could have been a compliment sound like an insult. "I know the ways of men, Rankan, and I know of temptation."

Amazed, Chenaya reassured her. "There is no need for your jealousy. The Prince is my cousin."

But the fish-eyed woman would not be calmed. She answered coldly, "Blood has no bearing on passion. In many lands such a relationship is not only condoned, but encouraged. I do not know your customs, yet. But the thinner the blood, the easier the passion. Cousins you may be, but let us not put temptation in his way. Or there will be trouble between us."

Chenaya clenched her fists; scarlet heat rushed into her cheeks. "On Rankan soil I come and go as I please," she answered low-voiced, moving closer until only an arm's length separated them. Then, she turned the chalice and slowly poured the remainder of her wine on the floor between them. It shone thick and rich on the luxurious white tiles, red as blood. "And no one orders me." Her fingers tightened about the gold chalice as she held it under the Beysa's nose. The gold began to give and bend as she squeezed; then it collapsed under her easy exertion.

Chenaya cast the cup aside and waited for its clattering to cease. She no longer bothered to contain her fury; it found a natural vent in her speech. "Now, you understand me, you highborn slut. You think you're running things around here right now. That doesn't matter a bird's turd to me. If Kadakithis has developed a taste for painted tits, that's between you and him." She raised a finger, and a small, threatening little smile stole over her mouth. "But if I find he doesn't approve of your residence or your high-handed attitude, if he's not a fully agreeable party to your presence in *his* city"—the little smile blossomed into a grin of malicious promise—"then I swear by my Rankan gods

53

I'll hook you and scale you and clean your insides like any other fish sold in the market."

The Beysa's only response was an icy, unblinking stare. Then, a tiny green snake crawled up from the folds of her skirt and coiled around her wrist like an emerald bracelet. Eyes of vermilion fire fastened on Chenaya. A bare sliver of a tongue flicked between serpentine lips. It hissed, revealing translucent fangs that glistened with venom.

"Quite a pet," Chenaya commented, undaunted. She stepped away then and drew a slow breath, willing her anger to abate. "Look," she said. "I've no great desire to make an enemy of you. I don't even know you. If you care for Kadakithis, then you have my good will. But if you're using him, watch out for yourself." She drew another slow breath and sighed. "I'm leaving now. I'm so glad we had this little talk."

She turned her back on the Beysa and strode from the apartment. The guards waited in the hall beyond and escorted her through the palace, across the grounds, and to the main gate. Her litter and four immense and heavily muscled men clad only in sandals, crimson loincloths, and the broad, carved leather belts that were the fashion of Rankan gladiators waited just beyond.

"Dayrne!" she hailed the largest of the four. "Come see the fish-eyes they hire for guards around here!"

Coming to his mistress's side, Dayrne laid a hand on the pommel of his sword. A nasty grin, not unlike the one Chenaya wore, twisted the corners of his lips. He towered head-and-shoulders above the tallest of the Beysa's men. "Not much to them, is there, Lady?"

Chenaya patted the closest Beysib on the shoulder before she stepped through the concealing silks of her conveyance. "But they're very sweet," she replied.

"Shupansea!" Molin Torchholder raged. His normally reserved and passive face reddened, and he shook a fist at his niece. "She rules the Beysib people. When will you ever learn to hold your cursed tongue, girl?"

Chenaya muttered an oath. Her father had brought Molin home after concluding the purchase of the estate, and she'd made the mistake of mentioning her exchange with the Beysa. She hadn't had a moment's peace in the past hour. Not even the sanctity of her dressing room gave her reprieve as he followed her through the house, questioning, berating.

She gave him a blistering glare. If the old priest had the balls to invade her chambers, he was going to get an eyeful. She ripped the silken garments from her body with an angry wrench and cast them at his feet.

Molin sputtered and kicked the shredded clothing aside, ignoring her bare flesh. "Damn everything, you spoiled brat!" He grabbed her arm and spun her around when she started to turn away. "You're not in Ranke anymore. You can't lord it over people as you once did. There are different political realities here!"

"Brother," Lowan Vigeles spoke from the threshold, "you are in my house, and you'll speak civilly to my daughter. And you'd best release her arm before she breaks yours."

Molin gave them both a frosty stare, but he abandoned his grip. Chenaya flashed a false smile and moved to one of many chests pushed against the walls. There had been no time to unpack, but she knew the right one and opened it. She pulled out a bundle of garments, finely sewn fighting leathers, and began to dress.

"Brother," Molin began again in a more moderate tone. "Niece. I beg you to trust my judgment in these matters. You're very new to the ways of Sanctuary." He folded his arms and made a show of pacing about the room. "Your news of the Emperor's murder is terrible, indeed."

"The entire royal family," Lowan Vigeles reminded, "at least those within Theron's reach. Chenaya and I barely escaped, and they may hunt us here. You too, Brother."

Molin frowned; then the frown vanished. "That's why we need the Beysib. They will protect Kadakithis. They are completely loyal to Shupansea, and she seems to dote on the Prince these days."

Chenaya shot her father a look; a barely perceptible nod

of his head silenced her. "What about the 3rd Commando?" Lowan insisted carefully. "They placed Theron on Ranke's throne, and they know Kadakithis is the legitimate claimant to that throne. Did Theron truly exile them, or are they here to commit another murder?"

Molin frowned again and rubbed his hands. "I know nothing about them, except that they were originally formed by Tempus Thales when he served the Emperor."

Chenaya stomped into a boot. "Tempus!" she spat. "That butcher!"

Molin Torchholder raised an eyebrow. "How many have you slain in the arena since I've been gone, child? For Tempus Thales, death is a matter of war or duty." He looked down his nose at her. "For you, it is a game."

"A game that fattened your own purse," she shot back. "Do you think I don't know about the bets you placed on me?"

He chose to ignore that and turned to her father, extending his hands. "Lowan, trust me. Kadakithis mustn't learn about his brother's death. You know what a young, idealistic fool he is. He would ride straight to Ranke to claim his throne, and Theron would cut him down like late wheat." He turned to Chenaya now, genuine pleading in his voice. "Better to keep him here, safe in Sanctuary, until we can formulate a plan that will give him his birthright."

With every word that fled his mouth, Chenaya remembered the small green serpent—the beynit her uncle called it—that wound about the Beysa's wrist. Molin was a snake; she knew that from long experience. He did not hiss so horribly, and he concealed his fangs, but nonetheless, she felt him trying to tighten his coils about her.

"Uncle," she breathed, struggling with the other boot, "you make a big mistake to assume me such a fool. I know my Little Prince far better than you will ever know him. I did not go to the palace to tell him of events in the capital, but to see a friend I've missed." She stood up and began to buckle the straps that were more decoration to her costume than utilitarian. "And to get a feel for the grounds and the palace itself. I plan to spend some time there. Your precious Beysib will not be the only protection Kadakithis has to count on." She took a sword from the chest, a beautifully crafted weapon, gold-hilted with tangs carved like the wings of a great bird and a pommel stone gripped in a bird's talons. She fastened its belt so it rode low on her hip. Lastly, she donned a *manica,* a sleeve of leather and metal rings favored by arena fighters; a strap across her chest held it in place. "Theron will never reach him; I promise you that."

"My niece is confused about her sex," Molin sneered. "Can a common gladiator guard the Prince better than the garrison? Or the Hell-Hounds? Or our Beysib allies?"

She shook back her long blonde curls and set a circlet of gold on her brow to hold the hair from her face. Mounted on the circlet so it rode the center of her forehead was a golden sunburst, the symbol of the god Savankala. "I am no *common* gladiator," she reminded him coldly, "as you well know, old weasel."

Much as she regretted ever telling him, Molin was the only man to share the secret of her dream and the rewards given to her by the chief of the Rankan pantheon, Himself. But she was very young then, only fourteen, and could be forgiven the foolish confidence. He was a Rankan priest; who better to tell about the dream and Savankala's visitation and the three wishes he granted her? Molin had tested her; he knew the truth of her dream.

She ran her hands teasingly over her breasts, reminding him of the first of those wishes. "Did I not grow into a beauty, Uncle? Truly, Savankala has blessed me."

She saw her father frown. To him, her words were mere boastfulness. Though he disapproved, he was used to such from her. He leaned his bulk against the doorjamb. "You're going out?" he said, indicating her dress.

"It's nearly dark," she answered. "I'm going to the temple. Then, there's a lot to learn about this city." She turned that mocking smile on Molin. "Wasn't it you, Uncle, who told me nighttime is best for prying secrets?"

"Certainly not!" he snapped indignantly. "And if you go

out dressed like that you'll find nothing but trouble. Some of the elements in this town would kill just for those clothes, let alone that fancy sword or that circlet."

She went back to the open chest, produced two sheathed daggers, and thrust them through the ornamental straps on her thigh. "I won't be alone," she announced. "I'm taking Reyk."

"Who's Reyk?" Molin asked Lowan Vigeles. "One of those giants you brought with you?"

Lowan just shook his head. "Take care, child," he told his daughter. "The street is a very different kind of arena."

Chenaya lifted a hooded cloak from her chest and shut the lid. As she passed from the room, she raised on tiptoe to peck her father's cheek. She gave nothing to Molin Torch-holder but her back.

It wasn't sand beneath her boots, nor was there any crowd to cheer her on, yet it was an arena. She could feel the prey waiting, watching from the shadowed crannies and gloom-filled alleyways. She could hear the breathing, see the dull gleam of eyes in the dark places.

It was an arena, yes. But here, the foe did not rush to engage, no clamor of steel on steel to thrill the spectators. Here, the foe skulked, crouched, crawled in places it thought she couldn't see: tiny thieves with tiny hearts empty of courage, tiny cutthroats with more blade than backbone. She laughed softly to herself, jingling her purse to encourage them, taunting them as she would not a more honorable foe in the games.

They watched her, and she watched them watching. *Perhaps,* she thought, *if I throw back my hood and reveal my sex. . . .* Yet she did not. There was much she had to do this night and much to learn.

The Avenue of Temples was dark and deserted. She located the Temple of the Rankan Gods easily, a grand structure that loomed above all others. Two bright flaming braziers illuminated the huge doors at its entrance. However, hammer as she might with the iron ring, no one within answered. She cursed. In the capital the temples never closed. She slammed the ring one last time and turned away.

"Father of us all," she prayed tight-lipped as she descended the temple stairs, "speak to me as you did that night long ago." But the gods were silent as the city streets.

She paused to get her bearings, and realized the high wall on her right must be part of the Governor's compound. The park on her left, then, would be the Promise of Heaven, or so she had heard it called earlier as she rode past it to her home. There, men who could not afford a higher class of prostitute haggled for sexual favors from half-starved amateurs. She shrugged, passed the park by, following the Governor's wall until she came to another street she recognized from her day's tour, the Processional.

She stopped again, looked up at the sky, and marveled at how brightly the stars shone over this pit of a city. Though she prayed to Savankala and swore in his name, the night fascinated her. It had a taste and a feel like no other time.

She whistled a low note. A fleet shadow glided overhead, eclipsing stars in its path, and plummeted. She extended the arm on which she wore the manica, and Reyk screeched a greeting as he folded his wings and settled on her wrist. She smacked her lips by way of reply and attached a jess from her belt to his leg.

"Do you feel it, too, pet?" she whispered to the falcon. "The city? The dark? It's alive." She smacked her lips again and Reyk fluttered his wings. "Of course you do." She looked around, turning a full circle. "It seethes in a way Ranke never did. We may like it here, pet. Look there!" She pointed to a shadow that slipped furtively by on the opposite side of the street. She hailed it; it paused, regarded her, moved on. Chenaya laughed out loud as it passed into the gloom.

With Reyk to talk to, she wandered down the Processional, amazed how the few strangers she spied crept from doorway to doorway in their efforts to avoid her. She walked in the middle of the paving, letting the moonlight glint on the hilt of her sword, both a temptation and warning to would-be thieves.

A peculiar odor wafted suddenly on a new breeze. She stopped, sniffed, walked on. Salt air. She had never smelled it before; it sent a strange shiver along her spine. The sea was often in her thoughts. She dreamed of it. Her steps faltered, stopped. How far to the wharves, she wondered? She listened for the sound of surf. In the stories and tales, there was always the surf, foaming, crashing on the shore, pounding in her dreams.

She walked on, sniffing, listening.

At last, on the far side of an immense, wide avenue she spied the docks and the darkened silhouettes of ships in port. Bare masts wagged in the sky; guy lines hummed in the mild breeze that blew over the water. No crashing surf, but a gentle lapping and creaking of wooden beams made the only other sounds. New smells mingled in the air with the salt: odors of fish and wet netting, smoke from fishermen's cook fires or from curing, perhaps. She could not spot the fires if they still burned. Only a dim-lighted window here and there perforated the dark.

Chenaya moved quietly, every nerve tingling, over the Wideway and down one of the long piers. There was water beneath her now: the boards rocked ever so slightly under her tread. Above, the moon cast a silvery glaze on the tender wavelets.

She swept back her hood. The breeze, cool and fresh on her skin, caught and billowed her hair. She threw back her cloak and drew breath, filling her lungs with the briny taste.

A shadow rose unexpectedly before her. Her sword flashed out. Screeching, Reyk took to the sky as she released his jess. She fell back into a crouch, straining to see.

But the shadow was more startled than she. "Don't hurt me!" It was the voice of a child, a boy, she thought. "Please!" It raised its hands toward her, palms pressed together.

Chenaya straightened, sheathed her blade. "What the hell are you doing out here?" she demanded in a terse whisper.

She had never killed a child, but had come damned close just now. "When so few others have the guts for venturing out at night?"

The little figure seemed to shrug. "Just playing," it answered hesitantly.

She smirked. "Don't lie. You're a boy, by the sound of you. Out thieving?"

The child didn't respond immediately, but turned and faced toward the sea. Chenaya realized she had come to the end of the old wharf; if the boy hadn't sprung up when he did, she might have walked off the edge.

"I sneaked out," he said finally. "I sometimes come here alone so I can look out at my home." He sat down again and dangled his feet over the water.

She sat down next to him, giving a sidelong glance. About ten, she judged. The note of sadness in his voice touched her. "What do you mean, *your home*."

He pointed a small finger. "Where I come from."

So, he was a Beysib child. She could not have guessed in the absence of light. He did not look so different; he didn't smell different; and he hadn't tried to kill her—not that he'd be much threat at his size.

She followed his gaze over the water, finding once again that strange chill on the nape of her neck. Then came a rare tranquillity as if she had come home somehow.

"What do you Beysib call this sea?" she asked, breaking the shared silence.

The little boy looked up at her, reminding her with a shock of his foreignness. Those wide, innocent eyes did not blink. They held hers with an eerie, mesmeric quality. The stars reflected in them, as did her own face, with a magical clarity. He said a word that meant nothing to her, a name in a melodic, alien tongue.

She tore her gaze away. "That means nothing to me, but the sound of it is pretty." The whisper barely escaped her lips, so softly did she speak. The moon sparkled on the dancing waves. The dock swayed and moaned beneath her. One hand crept slowly to her breast, and an old dream bubbled unbidden into her unsleeping mind. *Savankala's face hovered, floating on the argent ripples; his lips formed the answer to her third wish. . . .*

"You are not Beysib," the child beside her spoke. "You are not of the sea. Why do you stare so at it?"

The dream left her, and the chill. She smiled a thin smile. "I've never seen the sea," she answered gently, "but we're old friends. Almost lovers." She sighed. "It's very beautiful, just as all the stories said it was."

"So are you," the child answered surprisingly. "What is that you wear in your hair?"

She touched the circlet on her brow. "An ornament," she said simply. "It bears the sign of my god."

He leaned closer; his hand drifted up toward her face. "May I touch it?" he asked. "My parents are poor. We have nothing so pretty. It shines when it catches the light." She felt his fingers touch the metal above her temple; they slid around softly toward the sunburst.

A brilliant flash of white intensity exploded in her eyes, blinding her. She fell backward, the edge of the pier under her spine, her balance tilting toward the water below. Then a strong hand caught hers, helped her to sit again.

But for a swirling host of afterimages, her vision cleared. The Beysib child sat before her, both his hands on hers. On his brow a tiny blaze of shimmering radiance burned, a small sun that illumined the very air around him.

His mouth moved, but it was not his voice. "Daughter." It was acknowledgment, little more.

Chenaya clapped her hands to her eyes, bowed her head in reverent fear. "Bright Father!" she gasped, and could find no more words. Her throat constricted, breath deserted her.

His hands took hers once more, pulled them away from her face. "Do not fear me, Daughter." His voice rolled, filled her ears and her mind, sent trembling waves all through her. "Have you not called me this night?"

She bit her lip, wanting to be free of his touch, fearing to pull away. "I sought your priests," she answered tremulously, "I sought augurs, portents. I never dreamed . . ."

"You did once," the god answered. "And I came to you then to reward you."

She stammered, unable to look upon Him. "And I have worshipped you, prayed to you, but not once since then . . ."

He gently chided. "Have I not favored you more than others of our people? Were my gifts not great enough? Would you have more of me?"

She burst into tears and hung her head. "No, Father. Forgive me, I didn't mean . . ." Words would not come. She shivered uncontrollably, stared at the ambient glow that bathed her hand in his.

"I know what you mean," Savankala spoke. "You called me, not for your own need, but for one we both love. And I will give what little help I can."

"The 3rd Commando," she cried suddenly, blinking back her tears, realizing a prayer was answered. "Strike them down before they harm Kadakithis!"

The god shook his head; the light on his brow wavered. "I will not," he said. "You must defend the last Rankan prince with the skills I have given you. You may not even see the faces of those who would do him injury. But you may know the hour."

She protested, "But Father!"

Those eyes bored deeply into her, fathomless and frightening, more alien than ever. She squeezed her own eyes shut, but it didn't matter. Those eyes burned into her, seared her soul. She feared to cry out, yet her lips trembled.

"When the splintered moon lies in the dust of the earth, then you must fight, or your Little Prince will die and the empire of Ranke fade forever." He released her hands, leaned forward and stroked her hair, shoulder, breast. A sweet radiance lingered wherever he touched her. "Farewell, Daughter. Twice have I come to you. No man or woman can ask more. We shall not meet again."

She opened her eyes as if waking from a long dream. The child stared out toward the sea, swinging his legs over the water. No light gleamed on his brow, nor did he give any indication that anything unusual had transpired. She touched his arm; he turned and smiled at her, then returned his attention outward. "It's very pretty, the sea, isn't it?"

She exhaled a slow breath, reached out and rumpled his hair. "Yes, very pretty." She rose slowly to her feet, fighting the weakness in her knees. "But I really need a drink." She gave a whistle. High atop the nearest masthead, Reyk answered, spread his wings, and glided downward. Chenaya lifted her arm, and the falcon took his perch.

The Beysib child gave a startled cry and scrambled to his feet, eyes widened with awe. "You command birds!" he stammered. "Are you a goddess?"

She threw back her head and laughed, a sound that rolled far out over the waves. Turning, laughing, she left the child, his childish question unanswered.

The streets twisted and curved like a krrf-hungry serpent. The moonlight fell weakly here, lending little light to show the way. Men walked more openly in these streets, but always in twos or threes. The blackened doorways and recesses were full of watchful, furtive eyes.

She began to relax as the awesome dread of speaking with her god passed from her. She stroked Reyk's feathers and took note of her surroundings.

She had not come this far on her morning tour. The air stank of refuse and slop. Invisible life teemed: a muffled footfall, the opening and shutting of a door with no light to spill through, a choked grunt from the impenetrable depths of an alley, mumblings, murmurings.

She smacked her lips at Reyk. If a man glanced her way when she passed, he quickly found another place to turn his gaze when he spied the falcon.

She slipped in something, muttered a curse at the foul smell that rose from beneath her boot. Close by, someone tittered in a high-pitched voice. Purposefully, she exposed half the length of her blade and slammed it back into the scabbard. The rasp of metal on leather gave sufficient warning to any too blind to see her pet. The titter ceased abruptly, and it was her turn to laugh a low husky laugh that scraped in her throat.

She was going to like Sanctuary. She recalled the sun-drenched arenas of Ranke, the glistening sands and cheering throngs, the slaughter of men who held no true hope against her. There had been good men, some excellent; she bore scars that proved their quality. But they could not defeat her. She gave the spectators a show, made an artful kill, and collected her purse.

The game had grown dull.

Here, things would be different, a new kind of game. Sanctuary was an arena of night and shadows. No cheering crowds, no burnished armor, no fanfare of trumpets, no arbitrators. She smiled at that. No appeals.

"Home, Reyk," she whispered to the falcon. "Do you feel it? We have come home."

She prowled the dark streets of the Maze, speaking to none, but studying those she passed, measuring their bearing, meeting their eyes. Truth could be read in a man's eyes, she knew, and all the lies ever told by tongue. The soul resided in the eyes.

"Psst...a few coppers, sir, will buy you the delights of Heaven." A young girl stepped from the gloom, exposing dubious charms through a gaping cloak.

Chenaya pushed back her hood enough to show her own blonde locks. "Stuff yourself, whore." But she reached into the purse she wore on a thong about her neck and tossed a few coins in the dust. "Now, tell me where a drink can be had, and maybe some information."

The little prostitute scurried in the shadows, feeling about for the coins. "The blessing of Ils on you, Lady," she answered in excitement. "Drink? But four doors down. See the lamp?"

As Chenaya walked toward the faint light, a door beneath it opened and slammed. Two burly, cloaked figures retreated up the street to be swallowed by the night.

Above the entrance the lamplight illumined a sign. She

cocked an eyebrow. However mythical the beast embla-
zoned there, she was sure it never did *that* to itself. She
listened to the voices that drifted out to her and nodded to
herself. This was not a place for nobles and gentlemen. Or
ladies either, her father would warn her.

"Up," she said softly to Reyk. The falcon's wings beat
a steady tattoo on the air as it rose, made a slow circle, and
took a new perch on the tavern's sign. She folded the jess
and stuck it through her belt, then pushed open the door.

Conversation stopped. Every eye turned her way. She
peered down through the dingy smoke that wafted from
lamp wicks in need of trimming, from tallow candles placed
high about. She studied hardened, suspicious faces. The
smells of wine and beer and dirty bodies tainted the air.

"It's a door, not a damn viewing gallery!" the barkeeper
bellowed, shaking a meaty fist. "Come in or get out!"

She stepped inside, swept back her hood. The light shone
on her hair as she shook it free.

A grizzled face suddenly blocked her view; fingers brushed
her shoulder. "Welcomest sight I seen in a month," the man
said, breathing stale brew. He winked. "You come looking
for me, pretty?"

She smiled her sweetest smile, slipped her arms about
his neck, smashed her knee into his unprotected groin. He
doubled over with an explosive grunt, clutching himself.
She drove a gloved fist against his jaw, sending him to the
floor, and stepped away. When he made the effort to rise
she seized his belt and collar, ran him headfirst into the
wall. He sagged in a heap and stayed down.

"Happens every time," she said to anyone listening. She
tossed her hair back dramatically, put a wistful note in her
voice. "A lady can't get a peaceful drink anymore." She
flung off her cloak then, making sure they saw the sword
and daggers. But they no longer seemed interested. She
frowned and made her way to the bar.

"A mug of your best," she ordered, slapping a coin down
before the barkeep. He grumbled, swept up her money,
brought the drink. As he set it down she noticed the thumb

of his right hand was missing. Sipping the beer, she turned to survey the other patrons over the rim.

Three men caught her attention at once, and she stiffened; 3rd Commandos, she knew the uniform. These or their comrades had murdered the Emperor and set Theron on the throne—curse his name! They were scum that made even this refuse heap of humanity shine and smell sweet by comparison.

She set down her mug and her cloak. One hand drifted to her sword's hilt as she judged the distance to the three. Then a hand caught her arm. "Stay," a voice murmured in her ear. "They have friends; you never know where a knife might come from."

She turned and met the deepest, blackest eyes she had ever seen. The lashes looked kohlled, almost feminine, beneath brows so thick they nearly met over his nose. The effect was ruggedly mesmeric. "What makes it your business?" she said under her breath, noting that the barkeep had moved within earshot.

That dark gaze ran up and down her body. "Business, is it?" he replied. "Well, let business wait a little. I'd like to buy you a drink."

She indicated her mug. "I've already bought one."

He grinned. "Then join me at my table and I'll buy your next one."

Her turn to look him over. He seemed her own age, and they were a similar height. She might even have a pound or two on him. Yet, there was a kind of rangy strength about him that his shabby tunic could not hide.

"You must be good with knives," she commented, pointing to the several he wore strapped about his person. His only response was a modest shrug. She went on, "I'll buy the drinks; you tell me something about those three in the corner."

His thin lips parted in a brief smile. "You *must* be new around here," he said. "The price of information is more than a drink or two in this town."

She drew a deep breath, looked him straight in the eye.

"I've got a lot more to offer."

He appeared to think about it. "My table, then?" He made a mock bow.

The buzz of conversations had resumed. No one gave her or her young bravo a glance as he pulled out a chair and made a show of wiping the seat. A good table, she decided, positioned to give a view of the entire tavern and its entrance. She set her mug down, draped her cloak on the chair. They sat side by side.

"What's your name?" she asked quietly, leaning over her beer.

He began playing with a small pair of dice that had lain by his own mug. "Hanse," he answered simply. "I never liked that loud-mouthed braggart." He nodded toward the man she'd beaten; the barkeep had him under the arms and was dragging his limp form toward the door.

Chenaya took another drink. "No one else seemed impressed."

Hanse shrugged. The dice skittered over the table; he gathered them up again. "You're Lowan Vigeles's daughter, aren't you?" He rolled the dice between his palms.

She sat back, hiding her surprise. "How did you know?"

He tossed the dice: snake eyes. "Word travels fast in Sanctuary. That's your first lesson."

"Is there a second?" she said, feigning nonchalance.

A barely perceptible nod toward the 3rd Commandos. "People to avoid in Sanctuary." He changed the subject. "Is it true you fought in the Rankan arenas?"

She leaned close so that her shoulder touched his. "When the purse was large enough to interest me." She batted her lashes playfully. "Why should I avoid those dung-balls?"

The dice clattered on the rough surface. "They've got comrades. Lots of comrades."

The barkeep passed them, bearing drinks for another table. Chenaya waited. "How many?" she asked finally.

"Lots. They rode into town some days ago. Already act like they own it, too, though I wager the Fish-Eyes might dispute their claim." He looked up as the barkeep passed

again. "One-Thumb, two more beers here. She's buying."
He smiled at her and drained his mug. "They always go
about in twos and threes. You tangle with one, you tangle
with them all."

She tilted back until her head rested on the wall, and
cursed silently. It couldn't be coincidence that the 3rd Commandos were here. They must be plotting against the Prince.
Of course, that meant danger for her father and herself, too.
And Molin. Theron had spared no energy hunting any who
might claim the crown.

Hanse tapped her arm, and she started. "He wants to be
paid," he told her. One-Thumb loomed over her, looking
surly. Two new mugs had appeared on the table.

Hanse's eyes followed her hand as it dipped into the
purse about her neck and extracted a coin. "You must do
well in the Games," he said.

"Well enough," she answered, dismissing One-Thumb.
"I'm still alive."

"To being alive," he whispered, raising his beer in a
toast. A bit of froth snowed his black mustache. "And if
you want to stay that way, learn to carry a thinner purse
and a plainer sword." He glanced up at her brow. "There
are men here who would slit your throat for that trinket
alone and only afterward worry if the gold was real."

She inclined her chin into one palm and met his gaze.
She liked his eyes, so black and deep. "Since word travels
so fast in Sanctuary, Hanse, you'd best spread this one. It's
a new lesson to learn: don't play with Chenaya. The stakes
are too high."

He regarded her over the rim of his mug. "What's that
supposed to mean?"

She put on that sweet smile again. "It means I never
lose, Hanse. Not at anything." She indicated the dice as he
set his beer down. "How do you play those?"

He picked them up, shook them in a closed fist. "High
number wins," he explained simply. He cast them: six and
four.

She picked them up, dropped them without looking. A

frown creased his forehead. "Two sixes," he muttered and gathered them to throw again.

She caught his hand. "Do you have a taste for Vuksibah?"

His eyes widened. "That's an expensive taste."

She produced two more coins, solid gold stamped with the seal of the imperial mint. She slid them toward Hanse. "I'll bet you can buy anything in this dump. See if old Sour-Face has a couple of bottles stashed away. Do you live nearby?"

He chewed his lower lip thoughtfully, cocked an eyebrow. His head bobbed slowly.

She made a wry face. "The stench in here is overpowering." Her face moved close to his. "I'll bet there are lots of lessons we could teach each other." Her hand slipped under the table, fell to his thigh, encountering quite a surprise.

He caught her look and shrugged. "Another knife," he explained.

Chenaya grinned. "If you say so."

"Really," he insisted, collecting her coins, pushing back his chair. His toe caught the table leg as he rose, sloshing beer from her mug. "Sorry," he mumbled. He shoved through the crowd to the bar, began an urgent conversation with One-Thumb.

Chenaya looked back at the dice, picked them up, dropped them. Two sixes. She cast them again: two sixes. Once more she collected them, then with a sigh she dropped them in the beer.

The night, her seventh in the city, was still. Chenaya paced around her apartment, stared out each of the windows over the broad expanse of her land to the silvery ribbon that was the Red Foal River. It ran to the sea, that river. She could almost hear the sound of it.

She paced and debated if it was worthwhile going into the streets again tonight. All the officers and officials she had bribed the past few days, all the little men she had threatened, all her questioning and seeking had proven fruitless. If there was a plot against the Prince, no word of it had leaked carelessly.

Yet Savankala himself had come to her, told her it would happen *when the splintered moon lies in the dust*. But what did that mean? Thinking that a splintered moon was, perhaps, some astrological reference, she had approached Molin and wound up in a terrible argument. She left her uncle with a string of curses and no more understanding.

She kicked at a stool and threw herself across her bed. Her nails dug into the sheets. When her god was granting wishes, why hadn't she asked for brains?

She rolled over on her side and let go a sigh. Despite her mood a small grin stole over her features as her gaze fell on a table across the room. On it stood a bottle of Vuksibah.

There was a gamble she certainly hadn't lost, she smiled to herself. That handsome little thief taught her a lot, and only a little of it about Sanctuary. After the first bottle of Vuksibah anything he *said* was merest accompaniment to what he *did*. Fortunately, she woke with a clear head able to recall every word. She doubted he could claim the same. She took the remaining bottle, reclaimed her circlet which he had slipped from her brow and secreted beneath a pillow, and left him asleep.

It would be good to see Hanse again, she thought. Why not? Not even her workouts with Dayrne had been able to turn her mind from the danger to her cousin. Yet it served no purpose to continually worry. Perhaps Hanse could find a way to divert her.

She rose, slipped off her gown, and pulled on new leather garments from the chest at the foot of her bed. There, also, were her weapons. She strapped on her fancy sword. As an afterthought, she took up the two daggers. Hanse considered himself good with throwing-knives. It might make exciting play to challenge him.

Dressed, she tucked the bottle of Vuksibah under her arm and left her room. Her father was asleep or reading in his own chambers, and she did not disturb him. He worried when she went out, but never tried to stop her. She loved him most for that.

She descended stairs to the main floor, her boot heels clicking on the stone. Dayrne must have heard her, for he was waiting at the bottom. Two more of her eight gladiators would be prowling about somewhere nearby as well. Kadakithis was not alone on Theron's list; her father had been friend as well as relative to the late Emperor.

"Bring Reyk," she instructed her dark-haired giant. "Then get someone else to stand your watch. You've walked the streets with me these past five nights, and the lack of sleep showed in our workout today."

Dayrne frowned, then quickly hid it. "Let me go with you, Lady. The night is treacherous. . . ."

She shook her head. "Not tonight, my friend." She indicated the liquor she carried. "Tonight, it's a little pleasure I seek."

He seemed about to speak, then thought better of it, turned, and left her alone. The falcons were caged at the rear of the estate, but Dayrne returned promptly with her pet.

Chenaya wrapped the jess around her fingers, then removed Reyk's hood and gave it back to Dayrne. She did not need it to handle her favorite bird; it was a different story for others.

"Now to bed with you." She squeezed playfully at his huge bicep. "And in the morning be prepared for the hardest workout of your life!"

She passed into the warm night, feeling better now that she was free of the confines of her room. She would look for Hanse at his apartment first, at the Vulgar Unicorn if he wasn't home. It might take a little time, but she'd find him. He was worth the effort.

As she crossed the Avenue of Temples a young girl stepped out of the shadows and blocked her path. A small hand brushed back the concealing hood of a worn cloak, exposing dark curls and wide, frightened eyes. "Please,

Mistress," she said timidly, "a coin for a luckless unfortunate?"

Chenaya realized she had forgotten her own cloak. No matter, the street people knew her well by now. She made to pass the girl by.

The girl stepped closer, saw Reyk, and stopped. She chewed the tip of a finger, then said again, "Please, Mistress, whatever you can spare. Otherwise, I must sell myself in the Promise of Heaven to feed my little brother."

Chenaya peered closely at the thin face emaciated from hunger. Those large imploring eyes locked with hers, full of fear and full of hope. Beggars had approached her other nights, and she had kept her coins. Something about this one, however, loosened her heart and her purse strings. Several pieces of Rankan gold fell into the outstretched hand.

It was more wealth than the child had ever seen. She stared, disbelieving, at the gleams in her palm. Tears sprang into her eyes. She hurled herself to the ground, flung her arms around her benefactor's legs, and cried.

Reyk screeched and sprang to defend his handler. Only the jess held him away from the sobbing child. Chenaya fought to control him and to keep her balance as those arms entwined her. The bottle of Vuksibah slipped from under her arm and broke; the precious liquor splattered her boots. She let go a savage curse and pushed the silly beggar girl away.

"I'm sorry, Mistress," she wailed, scrambling to her feet, backing away. "So sorry, so sorry!" She whirled and fled into the darkness.

Bits of glass shone around her feet as Vuksibah seeped into the dust. She sighed, stirred the shards with a toe. Well, another could be gotten at the Unicorn.

Then a tingle crawled up her spine. She kneeled to see better, then cast a glance over her shoulder at the sky. The moon carved a fine, bright crescent in the night, and every piece of glass mirrored its silveriness.

The voice of her god screamed suddenly inside her head.

When the splintered moon lies in the dust.

She released the falcon's jess. "Up!" she cried, and Reyk took to the air. She ran through the streets, her brain ringing with Savankala's warning, until she reached her father's estate. She burst through the doors, breathless.

"Dayrne!" she called out. He had not obeyed her; he came running from a side room still dressed and armed. It was not the time to scold him. "Dayrne, it's now!"

More words were unnecessary. He disappeared and returned with a pack on his shoulders. Four of his comrades followed him, strapping on swords. "Stay and see to my father!" she ordered them.

"Where is Reyk?" Dayrne interrupted.

She raised a finger. "Always close by. I can't run and carry him too."

Together they ran back into the dark and up shadowed streets. The tall silhouettes of temples loomed on their left, and the voices of gods called from the gloom-filled entrances, urging them to hurry. Or, perhaps, it was the wind that rose mysteriously from nowhere, wailed down the alleyways, and pushed at their backs. The moon floated before them, beckoning.

They reached the granaries and stopped. The rear wall of the Governor's grounds rose up on the opposite side of the street, impossibly high and challenging. "The west side," Chenaya ordered.

They had planned this carefully. The gates to the palace were barred at night; only a handful of guards bothered to patrol the grounds. No one was admitted at night except with the Prince's permission. But she and Dayrne had found a way.

Another wall rose around the granaries themselves. It was to the west side of this wall that they ran. Dayrne unslung the pack, removed a grapple and rope. Here the wall was lowest and easy to scale. In no time they were atop it, racing along its narrow surface. Gradually, the wall angled upward to reach its highest point above the granary gate opposite the palace wall. Dayrne prepared the second grapple.

Hanse had bragged how he had broken into the palace. No man was strong enough to hurl a grapple the height of the palace's wall, he claimed. Probably he was right. But the Street of Plenty which separated the granary and the palace was not as wide as the wall was high. Still, for an ordinary man even that was an impossible throw; but not for one possessed of Dayrne's skill and rippling strength.

The night hummed as he whirled the grapple in ever-widening circles. She lay flat to avoid being knocked over the edge. Finally he let fly. Grapple and line sailed outward, disappeared. Then metal scraped on stone. Dayrne tugged the line taut.

They had not rehearsed this part, but she trusted her friend. Feet wide apart, he braced himself; his muscles bulged, and he nodded. She took hold of the rope, stepped into space. Dayrne grunted, but held the line fast. Hand over hand, she made her way to the far wall and over its edge. The line went slack; she could almost see the burns she knew would mark Dayrne's hands and forearms.

Her bribes had paid off in some respects, at least. Directly below her was a rooftop, the servants' quarters. She gathered the line and let it down on the inside, then slipped along its length. She was inside.

But where were the guards? There was no sign of them. Nothing moved within the grounds that she could see. She dropped to the ground, paused in a crouch, began to move from shadow to shadow.

What now? She hadn't planned beyond this moment. Here and there puddles of pallid light leaked from the windows of the palace. Atop the highest minaret, a pennon flapped hysterically in the wind. Far to her right was the Headman's Gate. On impulse, she ran to check it.

A huge, metal-reinforced bar spanned the gate, sealing it. She frowned, turned away, and tripped. She hit the ground hard; the pommel of her sword gouged into her ribs. With a silent curse, she rolled over and found one of the guards. Wide eyes stared vacantly at the moon from under a helmet rim. His flesh was still warm.

Every dark place was suddenly more menacing. No sign of the killer; nothing moved in the darkness. She felt around the guard's body. No blood, no broken bones, no clue to how he was murdered. She shivered. Sorcery?

A low whistle. Soundlessly, Reyk took his perch on her high-gloved arm.

Two more guards lay dead near the Processional Gates. Like the first, there was no trace of a cause. She thought of calling out, of alerting the garrison and the palace residents. Then she remembered the Beysib. One of the dead men was fish-eyed. If the killer heard her shout and made a good escape, if the Beysib found only her with the murdered guardsmen, if they found the grapples by which she broke into the grounds?... Who could blame them for jumping to conclusions?

A sound, metal rasping on stone. She froze, listening, peering uselessly into the blackness. There were only two more gates, both in the eastern wall. She started across the lawn, moving swiftly, noiselessly.

The last gate was the smallest, a private entrance and exit for the governor's staff. There she saw a figure revealed in the small pool of light from an upper residential window. The sound she had heard was a bar of iron that sealed the gate at night. She could not see him well; a cloak disguised his features and his movements.

A gardened walkway led from the gate to a door into the palace itself. He hadn't spotted her yet. Wraithlike, she moved, took a position at the midway point, and waited.

The killer eased back the gate. Five figures slipped inside, indistinguishable, but bared weapons gleamed. The gate closed behind. They started up the walk.

"Still time to place your bets, gentlemen," she said, a grim smile parting her lips, "before the event begins."

In the forefront, the cloaked one who had opened the gate raised something to his mouth. A bare glint of palest ivory, and he puffed his cheeks. *That was how the guards died,* she realized. Her inspections of the bodies were too quick and cursory to discover the venomed darts from the assassin's blowpipe.

"Kill!" she whispered to Reyk. The falcon sprang from her arm, and she threw herself aside as something rushed by her ear. Reyk's pinions beat the air three times, then his talons found the eyes within that dark hood. A chilling scream broke from the man's throat before one of his own comrades cut him down. Reyk returned to her arm. "Up," she told him. "These are mine!"

She laughed softly and drew her sword. She had fought four men once in the arena. Now there were five. The result would be the same, but the game might be more interesting. "Try to make it a good contest," she taunted them, beckoning.

The nearest man rushed, stabbed at her belly. Chenaya sidestepped, kicked him in the groin as her sword came up to deflect the blow another man aimed at her head. She turned it aside and cut deep between that one's ribs. She caught him before he collapsed and hurled him into the way of a third.

She dodged without a hairbreadth to spare as another sword sang by her head. The one she kicked was on his feet again. Four men closed with her, wordlessly, professionally. The ringing of steel, the rasp of hard and rhythmic breathing became the night's only sounds.

Chenaya threw herself into the fight. The force of blows and blocks shivered up her arm. She filled her other fist with one of her daggers; when one of her foes ventured too close, she shoved it through his sternum. It came free with a slick, sucking noise as she kicked him away.

Sweat ran down her face; blood slicked the palm of her right glove. She whirled into the midst of the three remaining attackers, raking the edge of her sword through the eye and cheek of one, planting the smaller blade deep in his throat.

Death hurtled down at her in two glittering arcs. Grasping her hilt in both hands, she caught the blades, intercepting

77

them with her own forceful swing, turning them aside. One lost his grip, and when he dived for his weapon her knee slammed into his face.

The last man on his feet hesitated, finding himself alone, turned and fled for the gate and the streets beyond. Chenaya cursed him savagely, drew the second dagger from its place on her thigh, and hurled. The coward's arms flew up, his sword clattered on the walk, and he fell. One hand flopped, grasping uselessly for the weapon, then was still.

The last man rose slowly, painfully to his feet; blood poured from his broken nose. His eyes were glazed, and the recovered sword was balanced loosely in his weak grip. He stumbled for her.

"You, at least, are no craven," she granted. The edge of her sword cut a swift crimson line beneath his chin, and he tumbled backward.

Chenaya filled her lungs with a deep breath and whistled for Reyk. Together, woman and falcon looked down on the six bodies. They did not wear the uniforms of the 3rd Commandos, she noted with some disappointment. It would have been easy to hang the whole lot of them with such proof, or at least to run them out of Sanctuary.

"That was well done, Lady of Ranke."

She knew the voice at once and whirled. Shupansea herself and a score of Beysib guards blocked the doorway to the palace. Apparently, they had slipped outside while the fight went on. A torch flared to life, then another.

"Don't look so surprised," Shupansea said. She pointed to the body of the cloaked man. "That one entered with the local servants this morning, but did not leave with them, having secreted himself in the stables. My men spotted him, but we wanted to wait and learn his purpose."

Chenaya made no answer, but held her sword and waited to see if the Beysa meant her harm.

"Molin explained your purpose to us, Lady," Shupansea continued. "You need not fear."

Chenaya smirked at that. "My uncle presumes a great deal."

The Beysa finally shrugged. "Perhaps it is just your nature to be rude," she sighed. "Perhaps that will change as we come to know each other. Kadakithis told me he promised you a party when you came to see him. In half a fortnight I, myself, will host an event to welcome you and Lowan Vigeles to our city."

Chenaya forced a tight smile, then kneeled to wipe her blade on the nearest assassin, rose, and sheathed it. "My father and I will of course accept the Prince's invitation." She stroked Reyk's feathers. "I love parties."

The two women locked gazes, and their eyes betrayed their mutual hostility and distrust. However, this night was Chenaya's. Shupansea might have learned about the threat to the Prince, but it was she, a Rankan, who prevented its success. The fish-eyed warriors at the Beysa's back were just so many spectators to admire her kills.

"My thanks and those of your cousin for your exertions on his behalf," Shupansea said stiffly. She waved a hand, and half her guards began to carry the bodies away. "Now, it is a little late to entertain visitors, don't you think? I believe you can find your way out." The Beysa turned away and reentered the palace.

"Keep the grapples," Chenaya said lightly to the guards as she headed down the walkway. "I shouldn't need them again."

A BREATH OF POWER

Diana L. Paxson

"A red one—Papa, I want a red fly now!"

Lalo looked down at his small son, sighed, and picked a crimson chalkstick from the pile. Deftly his hand swept over the paper, sketching a head, a thorax, angled legs, and the outlines of transparent wings. He exchanged red for gold and added a shimmer of color, while Alfi bounced on the bench beside him, a three-year-old's fanatic purpose fixing his gaze on each move.

"Is it done, Papa?" The child squirmed onto the table to see, and Lalo twitched the paper out of the way, wishing Gilla would get back and take the boy off his hands. Where was she, anyway? Anxiety stirred in his belly. These days, violence between the Beysib invaders and a constantly mutating assortment of native factions made even a simple shopping trip hazardous; their oldest son, Wedemir, on leave from his caravan, had volunteered to escort her to the Bazaar. The Beysib honeymoon was over, and every day brought new rumors of resistance and bloody Beysib response. Gilla and Wedemir ought to be back by now....

Alfi jiggled his arm and Lalo forced his attention back to the present. Looking down at the boy's dark head, he thought it odd how alike his firstborn and his youngest had turned out to be—both darkhaired and tenacious....For a moment, the years between were gone; he was a young father and it was Wedemir who nestled against him, begging him to draw some more.

But of course there was a difference to Lalo's drawing now.

"Papa, is the fly going to be able to see?" Alfi pointed at the sketched head.

"Yes, yes, tadpole, just wait a minute now." Lalo picked up his knife to sharpen the black chalk. Then Alfi wriggled, Lalo's hand slipped, and the knife bit into his thumb. With an oath he dropped it and put his finger to his mouth to stop the bleeding, glaring at his son.

"Papa, do it now—do the trick and make it fly away!" said Alfi obliviously.

Lalo repressed an urge to throw the child across the room, sketched in antennae and a faceted eye. It was not Alfi's fault. He should never have started this game.

Then he grimaced, picked up the paper, and shut his eyes for a moment, focusing his awareness until he could—Lalo opened his eyes and breathed gently upon the bright wings....

Alfi stilled, eyes widening as the bright speck quivered, expanded its shimmering wings, and buzzed away to join the jewel-scatter of flies that were already orbiting the garbage-basket by the door.

For a blessed moment the child stayed silent, but Lalo, looking at the insects he had drawn into life, shuddered suddenly. He *remembered*—a scarlet Sikkintair that soared above the heads of feasting gods, the transcendent splendor of the Face of Ils, the grace of Eshi pouring wine...and beside him had sat Thilli, or was it Theba—oh gods, could he be forgetting already?

"Papa, now make me one that's green and purple, and—" A small hand tugged his sleeve.

"No!" The table rocked as Lalo surged to his feet. Colored chalks clattered across the floor.

"But Papa—"

"I said *No*—can't you understand?" Lalo shouted, hating himself as Alfi gasped and was still. He extricated himself from behind the table and started for the door, then stopped short, trembling. He couldn't leave—he had promised Gilla—he couldn't leave the child in the house alone! Damn Gilla, anyway! Lalo brought his hands to his eyes, trying to rub the ache behind them away.

There was a small sniff behind him. He heard the faint clicking as Alfi began, very carefully, to put the chalks into their wooden box again.

"I'm sorry, tadpole—" Lalo said at last. "It's not your fault. I still love you—Papa's just very tired."

No—it wasn't Alfi's fault. . . . Lalo moved stiffly to the window and opened the weathered shutters, gazing out over the scrambled rooftops of the town. You would think that a man who had feasted with the gods would be *different,* maybe have a kind of shining about him for all to see— especially a man who could not only paint a person's soul, but could breathe life into his imaginings. But nothing had changed for him. Nothing at all.

Lalo looked down at his hands, broad-palmed, rather stubby in the fingers, with paint ingrained in the calluses and under the nails. Those had been the hands of a god, for a little while, but here he was, with Sanctuary going to hell around him at more than its usual speed, and there was nothing he could do.

He flinched as something buzzed past his ear, and saw the colored flies he had created spiral downward toward the richer feeding-grounds of the refuse heap in the alleyway. For a moment he wondered wryly if they would breed true, and if anyone in Sanctuary would notice the winged jewels hatching from their garbage; then a shift in the wind brought him the smell.

He choked, banged closed the shutters, and stood leaning against them, covering his face with his hands. In the country of the gods, every breeze bore a different perfume. The robes of the immortals were dyed with liquid jewels; they shone in a lambent light. And he, Lalo the Limner, had feasted there, and his brush had brought life to a thousand transcendent fantasies.

He stood, shaken by longing for the velvet meadows and aquamarine skies. Tears welled from beneath shut eyelids, and his ears, entranced with the memory of birds whose song surpassed all earthly melodies, did not hear the long silence behind him, the stifled, triumphant giggle of the child, or the heavy tread on the stairs outside.

"Alfi! You get down from there right now!"

Dreams shattering around him, Lalo jerked back to face the room, blinking as dizzied vision tried to sort the image of an angry goddess from the massive figure that glared at him from the doorway. But even as Lalo's sight cleared, Gilla was charging across the room to snatch the child from the shelf over the stove.

Wedemir, a dark head barely visible above piled parcels and bulging baskets, stumbled after her into the room, looking for somewhere to set his burdens down.

"Want to make it *pretty!*" Alfi's voice came muffled from Gilla's ample bosom. He squirmed in her arms and pointed. "See?"

Three pairs of eyes followed his pointing finger toward the ceiling above the stove, where the soot was now smudged with swirls of blue and green.

"Yes, dear," said Gilla evenly, "but it's all dark up there, and the colors won't show up very well. And you know that you are not to meddle with your father's colors—you certainly know better than to climb on the stove! Well?" Her voice rose. "Answer me!"

A small, smudged face turned to her, lower lip trembling,

dark eyes falling before her narrowed gaze. "Yes, Mama...."

"Well, then—perhaps this will help you to remember from now on!" Gilla set the child down and smacked his bottom hard. Alfi whimpered once and then stood silently, rubbing his abused rear while the slow tears welled from his eyes.

"Now, you go lie down on your bed and stay there until Vanda brings your sister Latilla home." She gripped his small shoulder, propelled him into the children's room, and shut the door behind him with a bang that shook the floor.

Wedemir slowly set his last basket on the kitchen table, watching his mother with an apprehension that belied the broad shoulders and sturdily muscled arms he had gotten working the caravans.

Lalo's own gaze went back to his wife, and his stomach knotted as he recognized Sabellia the Sharp-Tongued in full incarnation standing there.

"Perhaps that will keep him earthbound another time," said Gilla, settling her fists on her broad hips and glaring at Lalo. "I wish I could fan your arse as well! What were you thinking of?" Her voice rose as she warmed to her subject. "When you said you'd look after the baby, I thought I could trust you to watch him! You know what they are at that age! There are live coals in that stove—would you have noticed when Alfi started screaming? Lalo the Limner—Lalo the Lack-Wit they should call you! Pah!"

Wedemir eased silently backward toward the chair in the corner, but Lalo could not return his commiserating smile. His tight lips quivered with words that twenty-seven years with this woman had taught him not to say; and it was true that ... his vivid imagination limned a vision of his small son writhing in flames. But he had only looked out the window for a moment! In another minute he would have seen and pulled the child down!

"The gods know I've been patient," raged Gilla, "scrimping and striving to keep this family together while the Rankans or the Beysin, or hell knows who, came marching through the town. The least you could do—"

"In the name of Ils, woman—let be!" Lalo found his voice at last. "We've a roof above us, and whose earnings paid—"

"Does that give you the right to burn it down again?" she interrupted him. "Not to mention that if we don't pay the taxes we will not have it long, though Shalpa knows to whom we'll be paying them this year. What have you painted lately, *Limner?*"

"By the gods!" Lalo's fingers twitched impotently. "I have painted—" *a scarlet Sikkintair that soared through azure skies, a bird with eyes of fire and crystal wings*—his throat closed on the words. He had not told her—he would show her the rainbow-hued flies he had drawn for Alfi, and then she would know. He had the powers of a god—what right had she to speak to him this way? Lalo looked wildly about him, then remembered that he had opened the shutters and the insects had flown away.

"I saved your life, and this is all the thanks you have for me?" Gilla shouted. "You'd burn the last babe I will ever bear?"

"Saved my life?" Abruptly the end of his vision replayed in memory—he had been painting a goddess who had wrenched him away from heaven, a goddess who had Gilla's face! "Then it was *you* who brought me back to this dungheap, and you want me to *thank* you?" Now he was shrieking as loudly as she. "Wretched woman, do you know what you have done? Look at you, standing there like a tub of lard! Why should I want to return, when Eshi herself was my handmaiden?"

For one astounding moment struck speechless, Gilla stared at him. Then she snatched and threw a wooden spoon from the pot on the stove. "No, don't thank me, for I'm sorry I did it now!" A colander followed the spoon. She reached for the copper kettle and Lalo ducked as Wedemir got to his feet, protesting.

"You've a goddess to sleep with? Worm! Then go to her—we'll do fine without you here!" Gilla exclaimed.

The copper pot hurtled toward Lalo like a sunwheel,

struck, and clattered to the floor. He straightened, holding his arm.

"I will go—" He fought his voice steady. "I should have left long ago. I could have been the greatest artist in the Empire if you hadn't tied me here—I still could—by the Thousand Eyes of Ils you do not know what I can do!" he went on. Gilla was gasping, her work-roughened hands clenching and unclenching as she looked for something else to throw. "When you hear of me again you'll *know* who I really am, and you'll regret what you said this day!"

Lalo drew himself up stiffly. Gilla watched him with a face like stone and something he could not trouble to interpret in her eyes. A whisper of memory told him that if he let go of his anger he would *see* the truth of her as he had before. He swatted the thought away. The anger burned in his belly, a furnace of power. He had not felt like this since he outwitted the assassin Zanderei.

Silent, he stalked to the door, belted on his pouch, and flung across his shoulder the short cape that hung there.

"Papa—what do you think you're doing?" Wedemir found his voice at last. "It's almost sunset. The curfew will close the streets soon. You can't go out there!"

"Can't I? You'll see what I can do!" Lalo opened the door.

"Turd, slime-dauber, betrayer!" shouted Gilla. "If you leave now, don't think you'll find a welcome home here!"

Lalo did not answer, but as he hurried down the creaking staircase the last thing he heard was the bone-shaking thud as the cast-iron pot hit the closing door.

A rat-patter of feet behind him sent fear sparking along every nerve to clash painfully with the dull anger that had fueled Lalo's swift stride. *Fool!* the lessons of a lifetime dinned in his memory— *Your back is your betrayer. Watch it! Alert is alive!*

In the old days, everyone knew Lalo was not worth robbing, but in the current confusion, running footsteps could mean anyone. Frantically Lalo tried to remember if this block belonged to the PFLS or Nisibisi death squads; to the returning Stepsons or the 3rd Commando; or to Jubal's renascent hordes; or maybe it was to someone else he hadn't heard of yet.

His little dagger glinted in his hand—not much use against anyone with training, but enough perhaps to discourage a man looking for easy pickings before the daylight was gone.

"Papa—it's me!" The shadow behind him came to a halt a safe man's length away. Lalo blinked and recognized Wedemir, flushed a little from his run, but breathing easily.

The lad's in good shape, Lalo thought with a fugitive pride, then unclenched tense muscles from his defensive crouch and jammed the knife back into its sheath.

"If your mother sent you, you might as well go home again."

Wedemir shook his head. "I can't. She cursed me too, when I said I was coming after you. Where were you going, anyway?"

Lalo stared at him, taken aback by his unconcern. Didn't the boy understand? He and Gilla had quarreled finally. His future loomed before him like a splendid, lightning-laden cloud.

"Go back, Wedemir—" he repeated. "I'm on my way to the Vulgar Unicorn."

Wedemir laughed, white teeth bright against his bronzed skin. "Papa, I've spent two years with the caravans, remember? Do you think I haven't seen the inside of a tavern before?"

"Not one like the Unicorn. . . ." Lalo said darkly.

"Then it's time you completed my education—" the boy said cheerfully. "If you're tougher than I am, then knock me down. If not, surely two will walk safer than one through this part of town!"

A new kind of anger tickled Lalo's belly as he stared at his son, noting the balanced stance, the measuring eyes. *He's grown up,* he thought bitterly, remembering the last time he had thrashed the boy—it didn't seem so long ago. *Wedemir is a man. But gods! Did I ever have such innocent eyes? A man, and a strong one. . . .* Even when Lalo had been that age he had not been much of a fighter, and now—the taste of the knowledge that his son could beat him was like bile.

"Very well," Lalo said at last, "but don't blame me if it's more than you bargained for." He turned to move on, then stopped again. "And for Shalpa's sake, take that grin off your face before we go inside!"

Lalo tipped back his tankard, let the last sour wine flow smoothly down his throat, then banged it on the table to call for more. It had been a long time since he had come to get drunk here at the Vulgar Unicorn—a long time since he had gotten drunk anywhere, he realized. Maybe the wine would taste better if he had some more.

Wedemir raised one eyebrow briefly and took another rationed sip of ale, then set his own tankard back down. "Well, I haven't seen anything to shock me so far. . . ."

Lalo swallowed a surge of resentment at the boy's self-discipline. *He's probably despising me. . . .* As the oldest, Wedemir must have known what was happening in the days when Lalo was trying to drink his troubles away and Gilla took in washing to keep the family alive. And during the recent years of prosperity the boy had been away with the caravans. Small wonder if he thought his father was a sot!

He doesn't understand— Lalo held out his tankard to the skinny serving girl. *He doesn't know what I've been through. . . .*

He let the cool, tart liquor ease the ache in his throat and sat back with a sigh. Wedemir was right about the Unicorn, anyway. Lalo had never known such a quiet evening here. The age-polished wooden slats of the booth creaked to his weight as he relaxed against them, looking around the big room, trying to understand the altered atmosphere.

The familiar reek of sweat and sour ale brought back memories; oil lamps set shadows scurrying among the sooty beams overhead and beneath the sturdy tables. Empty tables, mostly, even now, when night had fallen and the place should have been as thick with patrons as a Bazaar cur is with fleas. Not that it was entirely deserted. He recognized the pale, scarred boy they called Zip in one of the booths on the other side of the room, sitting with three others, a little younger and darker than he was, without his protective veil of cynicism to shield their eyes.

As Lalo watched, Zip pounded the table with his fist, then began to draw some kind of diagram in spilled beer. The artist let his gaze unfocus, saw through the masks of flesh a mix of fear and fanaticism that made him recoil. *No,* he thought, *perhaps I had better not use that particular talent here.* There were some souls whose truth he did not want to see.

He forced himself to keep scanning the room. In one corner a man and woman were drinking together, the scars of old fights marking their faces, and of old passions clouding their eyes. They looked like some of Jubal's folk, and he wondered if they were serving their old master again. Beyond them he saw three men whose tattered gear could not disguise some remnants of soldierly bearing—mutineers from the northern wars or mercenaries too dissolute even for the 3rd Commando? Lalo did not want to know.

He took a deep breath and coughed convulsively. That was it; his new senses were at work despite his will, and his nostrils flared with the smell of death and the stink of sorcery. He remembered a rumor he had heard—the tavern-master One-Thumb was somehow mixed up with the Nisibisi witch, Roxane. Perhaps he should gather up Wedemir and get out of here. . . .

But as he started to stand up, his head spun dizzily and he knew that he was in no condition to survive the streets of Sanctuary at this hour. Wedemir would laugh at him, and besides, he had nowhere else to go! Lalo sat back, sighed, and began to drink again.

It was two, or perhaps three tankards later that Lalo's blurring gaze fixed on a familiar dark head and the angular shape of a harpcase humping up the bright cloak its owner wore. He blinked, adjusted his focus, and grinned.

"Cappen Varra!" He gestured broadly toward the bench across from him. "I thought you'd left town!"

"So did I—" the harper answered wryly. "The weather's been too chancy for sailing, so I hooked up with a caravan to Ranke. I was hoping to find someone going from there to Carronne." He shrugged the harpcase from his shoulder and set it carefully on the bench, then squeezed into the booth beside Wedemir.

"To Ranke!" the boy exclaimed. "You're lucky to be alive!"

"My son Wedemir—" Lalo gestured. "He's been working Ran Alleyn's string."

Cappen looked at him with new respect, then went on, "I suppose I am lucky—I got there just after they did the old Emperor in. There's a new man—Theron, they call him—in charge there now, and they say your life's not worth a whore's promise if you're in the Imperial line. So I thought, 'There's Prince Kittycat sitting safe in Sanctuary—things might just be picking up down there!'"

Lalo started to laugh, choked on his wine, and coughed until Wedemir thumped him on the back and he could breathe again.

"You don't have to tell me—" said Cappen Varra ruefully. "But surely there's something to be made from the situation here. Those Beysin women now—do you suppose there's some way I . . ."

"Don't even think about it, Cappen." Lalo shook his head. "At least not the way you usually do! They might like your music, but it's worth your life to even look as if you were offering anything more!"

The harper gave him a speculative look. "I've heard that, but really . . ."

"Really—" Wedemir said seriously. "My sister works for one of their royal ladies, and she says it's all true."

"Oh well!" Cappen saluted them with his tankard. "There's nothing wrong with their gold!" He drank, then glanced at Lalo with a smile. "When I left, you were the toast of the court. I hardly expected to see you here. . . ."

Lalo grimaced, wondering if his vision were going or it was just that the lamps were burning down. "It's the Beysa's court now, and there's no work for me." He saw Cappen's face stiffening into a polite, sympathetic smile, and shook his head. "But it doesn't matter—I can do other things now...things even Enas Yorl would like to know." He reached for his tankard.

Cappen Varra looked at Wedemir. "What's he talking about?"

The boy shook his head. "I don't know. Mother said he'd stopped drinking, but they had a fight and he started talking strange and stormed out. I thought I'd better follow and make sure—" He shrugged in embarrassment.

Lalo raised his eyes from the hypnotically swirling reflections in his tankard and fixed his son with a bitter gaze. "And make sure the old man didn't drown himself? I thought so. But you're wrong, both of you, if you think this is drunken wandering. Even your mother doesn't know—" Lalo stopped. He had come here determined to prove his power, but the wine was sapping his will. Did it really matter? Did anything really matter now?

His wavering gaze fixed on a figure that seemed to have precipitated from the shadows near the door, lean, sullen-browed, with a dark cloak hiding whatever else he wore. Lalo recognized the face he had seen on Shalpa at the table of the gods and thought, *That Hanse, he's another one the gods have played with, and look at the sour face he's wearing now. For all the good it's done either of us, to hell with the gods!*

"Look here, Papa," said Wedemir, "I'm getting tired of all these dark hints and frowns. Either explain what you're talking about or shut up."

Stung, Lalo straightened and managed to focus his gaze long enough to hold his son's eyes. "That time I was ill—" He tried to stop himself but the words flooded out like an undammed stream. "I was with the gods. I can breathe life into what I draw, now."

Wedemir stared at him, and Cappen Varra shook his

head. "The wine," said the harper. "Definitely the wine. It really is too bad...."

Lalo stared back at them. "You don't believe me. I should be relieved. How would you like me to make you a Sikkintair, Cappen Varra, or a troll such as they have fighting in the northern wars?" He shook his head, trying to get rid of the growing ache behind his eyes.

It was not fair—he should not be feeling like this until tomorrow. He had expected the alcohol to deaden his pain, but as his normal vision blurred, he was seeing the truths behind men's veils more clearly than before. That boy across the room—he had killed his own men, and would again.... Lalo winced and looked away.

"Papa, damn it, stop!" said Wedemir angrily. "You sound crazy—how do you think that makes me feel?"

"Why should I care?" muttered Lalo. "If it hadn't been for the lot of you, I would have been free of this wretched town long ago. I'm telling the truth, and I don't give a turd whether you believe me."

"Then, prove it!" Wedemir's voice rose, and for a moment nearby drinkers stared at them. Cappen Varra was looking uncomfortable, but the boy grabbed his arm. "No, don't go! You're one of his oldest friends. Help me show him what nonsense he's talking before he loses what wits he has!"

"All right—" said the harper slowly. "Lalo, do you have anything to draw with here?"

Lalo looked up at him, reading in his face weakness and an extravagant bravery, venality, and a stubborn integrity that even Sanctuary had not been able to wear away, a cynical assessment of women's susceptibility, and devotion to the ideal beauty he had never yet attained. Like Lalo, Cappen Varra was an artist who sought to make songs that would live in men's hearts. What would he think of this? The temptation to impress his old friend and make his cub of a son eat his words was overwhelming. Lalo reached into his pouch, fished among the few coins left there, and brought out a stick of charcoal and a worn piece of drawing lead.

"No paper—" he said after a moment, and sighed.

"Then why not use the wall?" Cappen Varra's eyes were bright, challenging. He gestured toward the scarred plaster, already disfigured by carved initials and scrawled obscenities. "The place will be no worse for some decoration— I'm sure One-Thumb won't mind!"

Lalo nodded and blinked several times, wishing that the blurring before his eyes would go away. Liquor had never affected him like this before—as if he were staring through the harbor's murky waters to a seabed littered with everything the sewers swept out of town.

He struggled up on his knees next to the wall. Cappen Varra was beginning to look interested, but Wedemir's expression was eloquent with embarrassment. *I'll show him,* thought Lalo, then turned his gaze to the wall, cudgeling his imagination for a subject. Lamplight flickered on the bumps and hollows of its rough plaster, sketching a long curve here, and there a mass of shadow, almost like . . .

Yes, that was what he would give them—a unicorn! After all, he had already painted one for the sign outside. He felt the familiar concentration narrow his vision as he lifted his hand; he could almost believe himself at home in his studio, drawing a model for a mural as he had done so many times before.

Lalo let the other part of his brain take over and guide his hand—that hidden part that saw the world in relationships of light and darkness, mass and texture and line, directly recording what it saw. And as his hand moved, his awareness reached out to draw the soul of the subject into the picture, as he also had done so many times before. The unicorn—an imagined unicorn? No, the Vulgar Unicorn, of course—the soul of the Vulgar Unicorn. . . .

Lalo's hand jerked and stopped. He shuddered as unwelcome knowledge flooded in. Here in this booth a man had died not long ago—his lifeblood flowing from the stroke of a deftly-placed blade. He had struggled, and blood had splashed the wall—that smear Lalo had assumed was soot before. Without his volition the charcoal swept around it, incorporating it as a blacker shadow within the whole.

And now other impressions buffeted his awareness, the black, sharp fear of men surprised by the raid of the Beysib, an intricate swirling that resonated with the name of the witch Roxane. But there must be some humor—surely there had also been good times here, enough to give a tilt to the unicorn's head, a sardonic glint to its eye. But there were not many such moments to portray, and no recent ones. . . .

Faster and faster moved the artist's hand, covering the wall with a scrollwork of figures that writhed one into another, contorting the outline that contained them. Here was the face of a woman raped to death in one of the upper rooms, there the desperate clutch of a man robbed of the coppers that would have saved his family. Feverishly the charcoal traced the lineaments of hatred, of hunger, of despair. . . .

Lalo was vaguely aware of others around him, not only Cappen and Wedemir, but the men who had been drinking at the next table, and others from elsewhere in the room, even Shadowspawn, looking over his shoulder with startled eyes.

"That's Lalo the Limner, isn't it—you know, the fancy painter who did all that work up at the Palace," said one voice.

"Suppose One-Thumb's commissioned him to do a little daubing here?"

"Not bloody likely," answered the first voice, "and what's that he's drawing? Looks like a beast of some kind."

Lalo hardly heard. He no longer knew who had left the tavern, who had come in. At one point he felt a tug on his arm; peripheral vision showed him Wedemir's pale face. "Papa—it's all right. You don't have to go on."

Lalo pulled free with a gutteral denial. Didn't the boy understand? He could not stop now. Hand and arm moved of themselves to the next line, the next shadow, the next horror, as all the secrets of the Vulgar Unicorn flowed through his fingers onto the wall.

And then, suddenly, it was finished. The nubbin of charcoal dropped from Lalo's nerveless fingers to be lost in the filth of the floor. He forced cramped muscles to function, eased off the bench, and stepped slowly back to see what he had done. He shivered, remembering the moment when he had stepped back to see the soul of the assasin Zanderei, closed his eyes briefly, then forced himself to look at the wall.

It was worse than he had expected. How could he have spent so much time in the Vulgar Unicorn and never known? Perhaps the normal barriers of the human senses had protected him. But, like a glory-hunting warrior, he had thrown his shields away, and now all the evil that had ever taken place within the tavern was displayed upon its wall.

"Is *this* what you were trying to tell us you could do?" whispered Wedemir.

"Can't you wipe some of it off, or something?" asked Cappen Varra in a shaken voice. "Even here, surely you don't mean to leave it that way. . . ."

Lalo looked from him to the uneasy faces of the others who gazed at what the leaping lamplight revealed, and suddenly he was angry. They had watched, condoned, perhaps participated in the acts from which this portrait was made. Why were they so shocked to see their own evil made visible?

But the harper was right. Lalo had destroyed work before, when it was unworthy. Surely, though his portraiture had never been so true, this picture deserved destruction.

He stepped forward, part of his cape bunched in his hand, and lifted it to the distorted, flat-eared head with its evilly twisted horn.

The eye of the unicorn winked evilly.

Lalo stopped short, hand still poised. How had that happened? A bulge in the plaster or some trick of the light? He peered at it and realized that the unicorn's eye was red. Then his hand throbbed. He looked down and saw new blood welling from the old cut on his thumb.

"Sweet Shipri, preserve us!" muttered Lalo, realizing whose blood was coloring that obscenity on the wall. His hand darted forward, again was stopped before it touched the plaster; for if this was his own blood, what would happen to him if the picture was destroyed? What was he doing, meddling with this kind of power? He needed a professional!

And still the eye of the unicorn mocked him, as Gilla had mocked him when he went through the door, or like a more familiar mockery that he had seen in a mirror once in a face whose mixed good and evil frightened him all the way into the land of the gods. But he had embraced the good, and surely the evil was gone! Desperately, Lalo ransacked his memory for visions of the beauty of the gods.

But there was only darkness and the wicked eye that enticed him more surely than the eyes of the sorceress Ischade, because it was his own.

Closer and closer Lalo came; his right arm hung nerveless at his side. *"I also am your soul,"* whispered the unicorn. *"Give life to me, and you shall have my power. Did not you know?"*

Lalo groaned. The breath of his lungs hissed out and stirred the charcoal dust upon the wall. The red eye of the unicorn began to glow.

Lalo saw and choked, trying to withdraw his breath again. Wedemir clutched at his arm, but Lalo shook free and swiped wildly at the wall, recoiled as a wave of heat blasted him, and fell back into his son's strong arms.

"No!" he gasped, "I didn't mean it! Go back where you came from—this isn't how it's supposed to be!" Men muttered around him; someone swore as a tremor shook the floor.

"Wizard's work!" exclaimed another. Men began to back away. Shadowspawn spat and slipped quietly out the door.

Coughing, Lalo snatched up his tankard and flung it at the wall. Red as blood in the lamplight, the liquid splashed off a solidifying flank and splattered across the floor.

Wedemir made the sign against evil; Cappen Varra's fist closed around the coiled silver of his amulet. "It's only a picture; a picture can't hurt you—" muttered the harper, but Lalo knew that wasn't true. With every second the Thing on the wall gained substance. The trembling in the floor increased. Lalo took a step backward, then another.

One-Thumb launched himself down the staircase, roaring questions, but nobody paid him any attention. He was calling for Roxane, whose powers, if she had cared to exert them, might perhaps have stopped what was happening now. But this night Roxane had other matters in hand. She did not hear.

And then, with a groan that burst at once from Lalo's lips and the wall, the Black Unicorn shuddered free of the plaster that had imprisoned it and leaped to the tavern floor.

Abruptly Lalo remembered the astonished delight with which he had watched his first creation soar through the azure air. That joy was the measure of his horror now.

Alive, the thing was even worse than it had been on the wall—a desecration of the concept of a unicorn. It paused, stamped with hooves like polished skulls, and the posts upholding the upper floors trembled like trees shaken by a wind. It reared, and staggered forward with Minotaurlike lumberings, then dropped back to all fours, and almost casually plunged its horn into the chest of the nearest man.

The victim screamed once. The Unicorn shook its head, and the body flew free to land with a soft sound like a falling sack of meal on the other side of the room. Blood spiraled down the wicked horn. The Unicorn grew.

Its head came around, red eye fixing on the girl who had been serving the ale. She tried to run, but the monster was too quick for her. Her body was still in the air when Wedemir seized his father's arm.

"Papa, quick—we've got to get out of here!"

Cappen Varra was already slipping toward the door. The Unicorn wheeled, herding two men contemptuously across the room. Fresh blood smeared the old stains on the floor.

"No—" Lalo shook his head uncontrollably. "It's mine, my fault—I have to—" He felt his son's strength suddenly as Wedemir seized him, pinioning his arms, and half-dragged, half-carried him away.

Three men pelted after them into the night; then there

were no more, only the screaming from inside the inn that continued as Wedemir dragged Lalo after Cappen Varra, terror lending them its own protection until they reached the harper's dingy room.

The secret hours between midnight and dawn drew on. The Black Unicorn, having finished with the tavern, shouldered out into the street, blotting the night with a deeper darkness, and began to forage through the Maze, emptying the streets more effectively than Imperial order or Beysib curfew had ever done.

On Cappen Varra's dusty floor Lalo dozed fitfully, struggling through dreams of fire and darkness lit by a distant shimmer of crystal wings.

In the luxury of his estate on the east side, Lastel, furious and smarting with pain from a gash across his belly, took a long snort of krrf and waited for Roxane. One death or a dozen in the Vulgar Unicorn did not trouble him unduly, but his alliance with the witch ought to protect him from any other sorcery, and with that Thing that had come off the wall of the Unicorn loose in the city, every mage in Sanctuary would be after his hide. Had the little dauber really done it? Who was using him? Lastel struck at the slave who was trying to bandage him and sniffed at the krrf again. Roxane would know what to do. . . .

The sorceress Ischade lifted herself from silken pillows and the enraptured face of the man beneath her, midnight eyes searching graying shadows. She could feel power eddying in the damp air; the wards she had set between herself and the Nisibisi witch quivered like taut wires in a sudden breeze. Was Roxane moving against her? The disturbance came from the direction of the Vulgar Unicorn, but there seemed no purpose in its meanderings. A word to the black bird perched in the corner sent it heaving into the musky air in a flurry of nightdark wings. "Go," she whispered, "bring back word to me. . . ."

Enas Yorl saw the fragile structure of the spell he was working begin to ripple as the dimensional distortion reached it, and extinguished it with a swift Word. What had happened? The power he sensed was at once alien and shockingly familiar. Automatically he summoned his familiars and sent them scurrying through the twisted streets. Then he began to robe himself, but even as his hand closed on the rich velvet he saw it changing. Swearing in frustrated agony, the sorcerer subsided in a transformation that took from him even the semblance of humanity. By the time Wedemir banged on his brazen door, there was only the blind servant Darous to answer it with the enigmatic assurance that the sorcerer was not at home....

Lythande, lost in timeless contemplation in the Place That Is Not, felt the indefinable tremor and sent her trained awareness winging back to the austere chamber in the Aphrodisia House where she had left her physical form. Yes, there was a new power in Sanctuary, but it was no threat to her, thank the gods. She had already rested here too long, but even as she contemplated her next journey, the Adept of the Blue Star had to suppress a professional curiosity regarding who had created the thing, and why....

And the Black Unicorn, having killed two mercenaries and a beggar at the edge of the Maze, as the sun rose began a destructive foray through the busy streets of the Processional. Terror depopulated them as rapidly as they had filled, and the Unicorn turned, its darkness staining the bright day, and began to slash its way up Slippery Street toward the Bazaar.

"So, you came back...."

Lalo slumped against the doorframe, his cape slipping from strengthless fingers to the floor. "The Unicorn—" he whispered, "they said it was coming here...." Blinking, he looked around him, seeing the kitchen just as he had left it one endless day ago. There were the flaking whitewashed walls, the sloping, well-scrubbed floor, and the bright faces of his children; even Vanda's friend Valira was here with her child, staring at him from their seats about the room....

And Gilla, standing in the midst of them like the statue

of Shipri All-Mother in the Temple of Ils. Shivering, he forced himself to meet her eyes. The apologies he had rehearsed through all the stumbling rush of his run here trembled on his lips, but he could not find the words.

"Well," said Gilla finally, "you don't seem to have enjoyed your debauchery!"

A croak of laughter forced its way from Lalo's chest. "Debauchery! I only wish it had been!" A sudden horror shook him as he looked around the peaceful room. The Unicorn was his—what if it tracked him here? He choked, put his hand on the doorlatch, gathering his strength to go.

"Papa!" cried Wedemir, and at the same moment Gilla's face changed at last.

"There's a monster loose, you fool—you can't go out there!"

Lalo stared at her, hysterical laughter building beyond his ability to control. "I . . . know. . . ." He sobbed for breath. "I created it. . . ."

"Oh, you dear wretched man!" she exclaimed. With a swift step she was beside him, and he looked up fearfully. But already her big arms were enfolding him. He glimpsed Wedemir's astonished face beyond her as his head found the haven of her breast.

And then, for a moment, everything was all right again. He was safe at that still point of rest where he and Gilla were one. He sighed explosively. Tension, fear, unchanneled power flowed from him through her to its grounding in the earth below. Then from the distance came a scream of agony, and Lalo stiffened, remembering the Unicorn.

"I'll go outside—" said Wedemir. "I'm a good runner, and maybe I can lead it off if it comes this way."

"No!" cried Lalo and Gilla as one. Lalo looked at his son, his face shining in the morning light like a young god's, and all his resentment of the night before transformed to agony. In the boy's proud strength there was such awful vulnerability.

He turned to Gilla. "When you looked at that portrait of me, did you see a madman? I have embodied half the evil in Sanctuary and set it free! I tried to get help from Enas Yorl, but he's not there—Gilla, I don't know what to do!"

"Enas Yorl's not the only wizard in Sanctuary, and I never liked him anyway," said Gilla stoutly. But Lalo could feel her fear, and that, more than anything else that had happened, frightened him.

A soft voice stirred the silence. "What about Lythande?"

The reknowned Madam of the Aphrodisia House was no more imbued with civic responsibility than anyone else in Sanctuary, but this Thing that was rampaging through their streets might succeed where curfews and death squads had failed—it might even affect trade. And she knew Valira to be an honest girl—had even offered her a place in the House, though the girl insisted on staying in lodgings with her child. It was enough to gain Valira's friends a hearing, once the little prostitute had poured out her garbled tale. And once Myrtis had heard, to make her their advocate to Lythande.

But Lalo recognized exasperation in the cool voice behind the crimson curtains at the end of the waiting room, and as the Adept pushed through them he saw resistance in every line of the dark robe that concealed Lythande's tall frame. There was silver in the long hair; lamplight limned lean cheeks and a high, narrow brow where the identifying blue star glowed. Lalo looked away, ashamed to meet the wizard's gaze.

How the Adept must despise him, as he would have sneered at a beggar who stole his paints and tried to paint the Prince. But a beggar would only have made himself ridiculous. Lalo's ignorant misuse of power might doom them all.

There was an uneasy silence as the Adept settled into the carven chair. Lalo's nostrils twitched as Lythande lit a pipe and aromatic smoke began to eddy about the room. He twitched nervously, and Gilla, solid as stone on the couch beside him, patted his hand.

"Well?" The Adept's smooth tenor broke the silence. "Myrtis said you had need of me—"

Gilla cleared her throat. "That demon in the shape of a unicorn is my man's doing. We need your help to get rid of it again."

"You're telling me this man is a magician?" Lalo flinched at the scorn he heard. "Myrtis!" Lythande called, "why did you ask me to waste my time with a hysteric and a fool?"

Gilla bristled. "No magician, master, but a man gifted with one power by Enas Yorl and with another by the gods themselves!"

Lalo forced his gaze upward, saw the blue star on Lythande's brow begin to shine as Gilla spoke the other magician's name, casting an eerie illumination on the face below it, a face that was worn by wizardry, with ageless eyes.

His vision blurred. For a moment Lalo saw beneath those austere features a face that was softer, though no less resolute. He blinked, shook his head, and looked again, saw the face of the Adept veiling the other, then both melding together until there was only one face before him, a woman's face whose truth he read as once he had read that of Enas Yorl—

—An implacable and enduring beauty like the blade of a sword, honed and tempered through more years and lands than Lalo could imagine, and the equally endless pain of fulfillment denied and forever voiceless love. The rumor of the Bazaar had only hinted at Lythande's power and had not even suggested the price the Adept paid for it—that *she* paid—for Lalo knew Lythande's secret now.

"But you—" Wonder startled words from his lips and the star on Lythande's forehead blazed suddenly. Lalo's sensitized nerves felt the throb of power, and abruptly he recognized his danger. He squeezed shut his eyes. Powers he might have, but chance memory told him that only another wizard could survive open revelation of the secret of a wearer of the Blue Star.

103

"I see," came the Adept's voice, soft, terrible.

"Master, please!" cried Lalo desperately, trying to let her know, without saying so, that he understood. "I know the danger of secrets—I have told you mine and I am in your power. But if there are any in this city that you love, please show me how to undo the evil I have done!"

There was a long sigh. The sense of danger began to ease. Gilla moved uncomfortably, and Lalo realized that she had been holding her breath too.

"Very well—" There was a certain bitter humor in Lythande's measured tone. "One condition. Promise that you will never paint *me!"*

Dizzy with relief, Lalo opened his eyes, careful not to meet the Adept's gaze.

"But I warn you, help is all that I can give," Lythande went on. "If the creature is your creation, then you must control it."

"But it will kill him!" Gilla cried.

"Perhaps," said the Adept, "but when one plays with power one must be ready to pay."

"What—" Lalo swallowed. "What do I have to do?"

"First we have to get its attention. . . ."

Lalo sat on the edge of one of the Vulgar Unicorn's rickety benches, nervously fingering the edges of the roll of canvas in his arms. *Wedemir—where are you now?* His heart sent out the anguished cry as he visualized his son slipping through dark streets, searching for the Unicorn. The end of Lythande's planning had been this knowledge that the price must be paid by all of them—by Wedemir, walking into danger, and by the rest of them, waiting for him to lead it to them here.

He took a ragged breath, then another, striving for calm. Lythande had told him he must prepare himself, but his stripped nerves kept him nervously aware of the blue pulse of the Adept's presence, as he was aware of Cappen Varra, who sat with hand clasped around his amulet, and of Gilla—

of her more than any, projecting a mixing of strength and fear and love.

Perhaps she simply disliked being in the Vulgar Unicorn. It was the measure of her trust of Lythande that she had accepted the Adept's pronouncement that the Unicorn must leave this dimension by the same Gate through which it had come.

But was this really the Vulgar Unicorn, or only some drunken nightmare? It was so very still. After a brief, explosive interchange between One-Thumb and Lythande, the Adept had expelled the few customers who had braved the birthplace of the Black Unicorn, and cleared away the tables from the booth and the center of the room. Lalo stared at the irregular white space on the wall where his drawing had been, shivered and looked away, found his eyes focusing on the new dark stains that marred the floor, and shut them.

Breathe! he told himself. *For Wedemir's sake—you have to find the strength somewhere!*

"I should never have allowed it—" Gilla's whisper voiced Lalo's fears. "My poor son! How could you let him sacrifice himself? You'd let your baby burn and send your firstborn to be eaten by a demon from Hell—a fine sort of father you are!"

Lalo could feel her gathering steam for another diatribe and found himself almost welcoming the distraction, but Lythande's voice knifed through the pause as Gilla gathered breath to go on.

"Woman, be still! There is more than one life at stake here, and the time for discussion is long gone. Lend some of your anger to your man—he'll need it soon!" The Adept's snapped comment was followed by a half-heard muttering—something about "working with amateurs" that made Gilla's ears burn.

Lalo sighed and tried to formulate a prayer to Ils of the Thousand Eyes, but all that would come to him was a vision of Wedemir's bright gaze.

The door opened.

Lalo jerked around, peering at the shadow that had precipitated itself from the darker oblong of the open door. Wedemir? But it was too soon, and there had been no sound. The figure stepped forward; Lalo recognized the dark cloak and narrow, sullen face of Shadowspawn.

"I got a message——" Hanse surveyed the odd group with disbelief. "I'm supposed to help you?"

His face was eloquent with resentment, and Lalo, realizing abruptly from whom that message must have come, felt a slim stirring of hope. He got to his feet.

"Yes, you can help us," Lythande said quietly beside him. "You saw something get loose here last night. Help us send it home again."

"No." Hanse shook his head. "Oh, no. Once was a time too many to see that thing."

"Shalpa's Son..." Lalo said hoarsely, and saw Shadowspawn flinch.

"Not even for——" he began, then whirled, hands going for his knives. From outside came the sound of feet running, and a deep roaring as if all the sewers in Sanctuary had overflowed.

"Quick, for your life——" snapped the Adept, pointing across the room. "Take your place in the circle, and don't stir!"

For a moment Shadowspawn stared, then he moved.

But Lalo had forgotten him. Bench clattering over behind him, he darted past Cappen Varra to reach his place by the wall, glimpsed Gilla's bulk moving surprisingly quickly to the spot the Adept had assigned to her. As if she had teleported, Lythande was already standing, wand at the ready, at the point between the door and the wall.

Then it crashed open and Wedemir hurtled through, hesitated for a moment as he saw the place he had expected to fill already occupied by Shadowspawn, then stumbled into the middle of the circle, blood from his arm spattering across the floor. Lalo's stomach churned; he reached for the boy and pulled him to his side.

"The blood——" he gasped. "Did the Unicorn get you?"

Wedemir shook his head and touched the knife at his side. Lythande darted them a quick glance.

"I told him to wound himself," the Adept said. "Innocent blood—and your blood, Lalo—the smell of it would be irresistible—"

Then a darkness filled the doorway, deeper than the shadows, in which flamed two glowing eyes. It had grown. Lalo swallowed sickly as the Unicorn forced its expanding bulk through the doorway. The black muzzle bent, snuffling for the blood-trail. Wedemir swayed, and Lalo saw that blood was still welling from between the fingers clenched around his arm to fall smoking to the stained floor. Lalo's altered vision perceived the life-force radiating from each drop. That, then, was what the Unicorn desired.

Ils of the Thousand Eyes, look down and help me! his spirit cried. Gilla's invocation of Shipri vibrated in the heavy air, and beyond her Lalo sensed the blur of Shalpa's power, Lythande's blue glow, and the murmur of Cappen Varra's plea to his northern gods.

The Unicorn reared back: Lalo could not tell whether it went on two legs or four. Did those red eyes see puny human victims, or did it sense the inflowing power of the gods? The monster must not be frightened away, though his every nerve quivered with hope that it would go. Lythande's stern gaze commanded him. Now was the time—the Adept had done her part and he was on his own.

Great Ils! He could not do it; but somehow his feet were carrying him between Wedemir and the Unicorn.

"Unicorn!" Lalo's voice was a crow's croak. He tried again. "Unicorn, come to me! Blood of my blood, here is what you desire!"

The dark form shuddered with thunder and deep laughter. It took a step toward him and then another, contemptuous of the others who stood there. Its gaze was like a horribly intimate touch upon his soul, and Lalo remembered suddenly that it was *his*—his own evil had been joined to that of the rest of Sanctuary in the Unicorn's conception. Lalo's part in the creature yearned for reunion; an answering yearning resonated in the secret depths of his soul. How easy it would be to . . . simply give in.

Lythande poised like a beast of prey, absolutely still. As Lalo wavered, the Unicorn stepped past her; her wand flashed out like a sword of fire, and blue light snapped across the circle to Gilla, back to Cappen Varra, over to Wedemir, occupying Lalo's old place by the wall, up to Shadowspawn and back to Lythande again before the Thing could move.

It roared and whirled, but it was imprisoned by the glowing lines of the pentagram. Lalo realized with horror that he was imprisoned too. Then the Unicorn grew still, senses questing outward to test the barriers. Its darkness pulsed softly; Lalo recognized faces contorted in voiceless torment, blinked away a vision of his own features swirling among the throng, and fumbled to unroll the canvas still clutched in his arms.

The Unicorn heard the rustle of canvas and began to turn.

The results of half a night's labor unrolled stiffly, and Lalo wondered desperately whether it would serve. Taking a deep breath, he closed his eyes, seeking the Face of Ils in memory. Awareness faltered, fixed, and for one timeless moment he was There, but this time he did not look away. The brightness of the Divine Face blinded and burned him, searing that part of him that had responded to the Unicorn. And still the light grew, until Lalo realized that even the Shining Face of Ils had been only a mask for that radiance whose least part burned in the sun and the other stars.

And then he was falling, spiraling dizzily back into the prison of his human body. Still dazzled, Lalo released his pent breath across the canvas in his clenched hands.

The Unicorn shrieked as if it sensed the birth of its enemy. Lalo felt the canvas quiver in his hands. Light shattered and scattered across the floor as crystal wings beat upward into three-dimensionality. He had set out to draw a white bird like something he had once painted for the gods, and Lythande's cool voice and fluttering fingers had tranced him as an aid in recovering the memory.

But he did not recognize the wonder that was emerging

now—it was an eagle, it was a phoenix, it was a swan—it was all of these and none. The great bird opened its bright beak in a piercing cry, talons clutched and unclenched, wings swept wind across the room, and it was free.

Lalo sank back upon his heels, gasping as the Unicorn's darkness gave way before a storm of white wings. The war of fire and ice and darkness sent fierce coruscations of opal light around the room. Roaring, the Unicorn charged against its foe, and Lalo huddled, a still speck at the eye of the storm.

Between one flurry and another he heard someone call his name. Blue light stabbed his eyes. "Lalo—open the Gate!"

Lalo forced his limbs to pull him toward Lythande. The pentagram burned him; then the Adept's wand broke it and he was through. And just in time, for the Bird of Light was driving the Unicorn after him in a tempest Vashanka would have been proud to claim. Lalo struggled upright. Light followed his finger as he traced a line around the pale area on the plaster where he had drawn the Unicorn.

He finished, his hand fell, and the space he had outlined began to shimmer. The plaster thinned, cleared, disappeared to reveal a black gulf that pulsed with sparkling lights. Lalo's ears sang with subliminal vibration, his vision blurred, a strong hand closed on his arm and jerked him out of the path of the bolt of blackness that hurtled past him toward the void, followed by a beam of light.

Lalo thrust out one arm in self-protection as he fell, and screamed as it took the final buffet of the Bird of Light's crystal wing. Then an explosion of radiance dispersed the darkness. The tavern shook as the Gate between the dimensions slammed shut, and both the Unicorn and its opposite were gone.

Two bodies lay in the lee of a wall where Dyer's Alley turned off from Slippery Street. Lythande took a swift step aside to peer at the pallid faces and eyes that stared unseeing at the rising sun, then returned.

"Knifed—" the Adept said. "Nothing unusual. I'll be going now." She nodded abruptly, and began to walk away from them toward the Bazaar.

Lalo stopped rubbing his numbed arm for a moment and stared after her, wanting to call her back. But what could he say? The Adept had favored him with more good advice than he could understand all the way back from the Vulgar Unicorn.

By the time Lalo had recovered consciousness, Shadowspawn was long gone, and Cappen Varra, with voice unsteady and hands that still reached for his amulet at any unexpected sound, had taken his leave as soon as he could thereafter. By the time they got Wedemir's wound stanched and Lalo was able to walk again, the sun was striking gold from the dome of the Temple, and Hakiem was peering through the tavern door. With the tables and benches back in place, only the bare spot on the wall and an unnaturally wholesome atmosphere would have enabled anyone to guess what had happened there; but Lalo supposed that the storyteller would find out. He always did, somehow.

But as Lythande had pointed out, it hardly mattered what the rest of Sanctuary thought of him—it was the wizards he must watch out for now. As the style of a painting proclaimed its creator, so it was with magic, and the Black Unicorn had been signed "Lalo the Limner" for any with eyes to see.

"One way or another they will be after you, and you must learn to use your power..." Lythande's words still rang in Lalo's ears.

He sighed, and Gilla eased more of her arm under his, supporting him. Wedemir, leaning on her other arm, lifted his head, and father and son exchanged apprehensive grins. They knew Gilla's frown, and the twist of lips clamped shut over hard words.

At the foot of their stairs Lalo halted, gathering his strength for the climb.

"All right, O Mighty Magician, do you want my help or can you make it under your own power?" asked Gilla. In the full light of morning he saw clearly for the first time the new lines of anguish by her mouth and the bruise marks beneath her eyes. And yet her body was as steady as the earth below him. It was her strength that had got him this far.

"You are my power, all of you—" His eyes moved from Gilla to Wedemir, meeting his son's steady gaze, accepting him at last as an equal and a man. "Don't let me forget it again."

Gilla's eyes were suspiciously bright. She squeezed his hand. Lalo nodded and began to climb the staircase, and in his labored breathing they heard the whisper of white wings.

THE HAND THAT FEEDS YOU

Diane Duane

The ephemerals have no help to give.
Look at them!
They are deedless and cripple,
strengthless as dreams. All mortalkind
is bound with a chain;
all their eyes are darkened. . . .

The sound of screaming slowly aroused Harran from the mechanical business of pounding out the Stepson Raik's hangover remedy in the old stone mortar. Raik scrambled to his feet, his face ashen, staring toward the gates of the Stepsons' barracks compound. "Just a little more business for the barber," Harran said, not looking up. "More serious than your head, from the sound of it."

"Shal," Raik said, sounding wounded himself. "Harran, that's *Shal*—"

"Knew the damned careless fool would get himself chopped up one day," Harran said. He measured the last ounce or so of grain spirits into his mortar and picked up the pestle again.

"Harran, you son of a—"

"A moment ago you didn't care about anything, including

113

where your partner was," Harran said. "Now you know...
Mriga!"

Over in the corner of the rough stone hut someone sat
in the shadows on the packed dirt floor, hitting two rocks
together—grinding a third rock to powder between them in
a steady, relentless rhythm. The hut's small windows let in
only a couple of dust-dancing arrows of sun; neither came
near the bundle of skinny arms and legs and filthy rags that
sat there and went pound, pound, pound with the rocks,
ignoring Harran.

"Mriga!" Harran said again.

Pound, pound, pound.

Another scream strung itself on the air, closer. From
under Harran's worktable, by his feet, came a different
sound: an eager whimper, and then the thumping of a dog's
wagging tail.

Harran huffed in annoyance and shoved the mortar and
pestle aside. "You start one thing around here," he said,
getting up without looking anywhere near Raik's wild eyes,
"and there's no finishing it. Never fails. —Mriga!"

This time there was a grunt from the pile of rags, though
certainly not in response to anything Harran was saying—
just a kind of bark or groan of animal pleasure in the rhythm.
Harran reached down and grabbed Mriga's hands. They
jerked and spasmed in his grasp, as they always did when
someone tried to stop anything she was doing. "No more,
Mriga. Knives now. Knives."

The hands kept jerking. "Knives," Harran said, louder,
shaking her a bit. "Come on! *Knives*...."

"Nhrrn," she said. It was as close as Mriga ever got to
the word. From under the tangle of matted, curly hair, from
out of the bland, barren face, eyes flashed briefly up at
Harran—empty, but very much alive. There was no intel-
ligence there, but there *was* passion. Mriga loved knives
better than anything.

"Good girl," he said, dragging her more or less to her
feet by one arm, and shaking her to make sure of her attention. "The long knife, now. The long knife. Sharp."

"Ghh," Mriga said, and she shambled across the hut toward Harran's grindstone—oblivious of the disgusted Raik, who nearly kicked her in passing until he saw Harran's eyes on him. "Vashanka's blazing balls, man," Raik said in the voice of a man who wants to spit, "why're you waiting till *now* to do your damned knife-grinding?!"

Harran set about clearing his herbs and apothecary's tools off the table. "Barracks cook 'borrowed' it for his joint last night," said Harran, bending to stir the fire and dropping the poker back among the coals. "Didn't just slice up that chine you were all gorging on, either. He used the thing to cut through the thighbone for the marrow, instead of just cracking it. Thought it'd be neater." Harran spat at Raik's feet, missing them with insolent accuracy. "Ruined the edge. Fool. None of you understands good steel; not one of you—"

Yet another scream, weaker, ran up and down the scale just outside the door. Shal was running out of breath. "Bring him in," said Harran; and in they came—lean blond Lafen, and towering Yuriden, and between them, slack as a half-empty sack of flour, Shal.

The two unhurt Stepsons eased Shal up onto the table, with Raik trying to help, and mostly getting in the way. The man's right hand was bound up brutally tight with a strip of red cloth slashed from Lafen's cloak; the blood had already soaked through the red of it and was dripping on the floor. From under the table came more thumping, and a whine.

"Tyr, go out," said Harran. The dog ran out of the room. "Hold him," Harran said to the three, over the noise of the grindstone.

He pulled a penknife out of his pocket, slit the tourniquet's sodden knot, peeled the sticking cloth away, and stared at the ruin of Shal's lower arm.

"What happened?" Raik was demanding of the others, his voice thick with something Harran noticed but did not care to analyze.

"By the bridge over the White Foal," Yuriden said, his

usually dark face even darker suffused with blood. "Those damned Piffles, may they all—"

"This isn't swordwork," Harran said, slipping the penknife into what was left of Shal's wrist and using the blade to hold aside a severed vein.

The paired bones of Shal's lower arm were shattered and stuck out of the wound. The outermost large bone was broken right at the joint, where it met the many small bones of the wrist which were jutting up through the skin; the smooth white capsule of gristle at its end was ruptured like a squashed fruit. Oozing red marrow and blood were smeared all over the pale, iridescent shimmer of sliced and mangled tendons. The great artery of the lower arm dangled loose, momentarily clotted shut, a frayed, livid little tube.

"No sword would do this. Cart drove over him while he was swiving in the dirt again, eh Yuri?"

"Harran, damn you—"

"Yuri, shut up!" Raik cried. "Harran, what are you going to do?"

Harran turned away from the man moaning on the table, and faced Raik's horror and rage squarely. "Idiot," he said. "Look at the hand." Raik did. The fingers were curled like clenched talons, the torn, retracted tendons making no other shape possible. "What do you *think* I'm going to do? Mriga—"

"But his sword-hand—"

"Fine," Harran said. "I'll sew it up. *You* explain matters to him when it rots, and he lies dying of it."

Raik moaned, a sound of denial as bitter as any of Shal's screams. Harran wasn't interested. "Mriga," he said again, and went over to the grindstone to stop her. "Enough. It's sharp."

The grindstone kept turning. Harran gently kicked Mriga's feet off the pedals. They kept working, absurdly, on the stone floor. He pried the knife out of her grasp and wiped the film of dirty oil off the edge. Sharp indeed; a real hairsplitter. Not that it needed to be for this work. But some old habits were hard to break. . . .

The three at the table were holding Shal down; Raik was holding Shal's face between his hands. Harran stood over Shal for a moment, looking down at the drawn, shock-paled face. In a way it was sad. Shal was no more accomplished than any of the other Stepsons around here these days, but he was the bravest; always riding out to his duties joking, riding back at day's end tired, but ready to do his job again the next day. A pity he should be maimed. . . .

But pity was another of the old habits. "Shal," Harran said. "You know what I have to do."

"Noooooo!!"

Harran paused . . . finally shook his head. "Now," he said to the others, and lifted the knife. "Hold him tight."

The hand gave him trouble. Yuri lost his grip, and the man writhing on the table jerked the arm about wildly, spraying them all.

"I told you to *hold* him," Harran said. He knocked Raik's hands away from Shal's face, took hold of Shal's head, lifted it, and struck it hard against the tabletop. The screaming, which Harran had refused to hear, abruptly stopped. "Idiots," he said. "Raik, give me the poker."

Raik bent to the fire, straightened again. Harran took the poker away from him, pinned the forearm to the table, and slowly rolled the red-hot iron over the torn flesh and broken vessels, being careful of their sealing. The stink in the air pushed Raik away from the table like a hand.

The rest of the work was five minutes labor with a bone needle and catgut. Then Harran went rooting about among the villainous pots and musty jars on the high shelf in the wall.

"Here," he said, throwing a packet to the poor retching Raik. "This in his wine when he wakes up . . . it may be a while. Don't waste the stuff; it's scarcer than meat. Yuri, they're roofing in the next street over. Go over there and beg a pipkin of tar from them—when it's just cool enough to touch, paint the stump with it. Stitches and all." Harran stood, his nose wrinkling. "And when you get him out of here, change his britches."

"Harran," Raik said bitterly, holding the unconscious Shal to him. "You could have made it easier on him. — You and I, we're going to have words as soon as Shal's well enough to be left alone."

"Bright, Raik. Threatening the barber who just saved his life." Harran turned away. "Idiot. Just pray the razor doesn't slip some morning."

The Stepsons went away, swearing. Harran busied himself cleaning up the mess—throwing sawdust on the table to sop up the blood and urine, and scraping Raik's hangover remedy into a spare pot. Assuredly he'd be back for it; if not today, then tomorrow, after Raik had tried to drink his way out of his misery.

The sound of feet thudding on the floor eventually drew Harran's attention. Mriga was still pedaling earnestly away on a grindstone she wasn't touching, holding out to it a knife she didn't have. "Stop it," Harran said. "Come on, stop that. Go do something else."

"Ghh," said Mriga, ecstatically involved, not hearing him. Harran grabbed Mriga and stood her up and shoved her, blinking, out into the sunlight. "Go on," he said at her back. "Go in the stable and clean the tack. The bridles, Mriga. The shinies."

She made a sound of agreement and stumbled off into the light and stink of the Stepsons' stableyard. Harran went back inside to finish his cleaning. He scraped the sawdust off the table, threw the poker back in the fire, and picked up the last remnant of the unpleasant morning from the spattered dish into which he'd thrown it: a brave man's hand.

And lightning struck.

I could do it, he thought. *At last, I could do something.*

Harran sank down on the bench beside the table, speechless, almost sightless. There was a whimper at the door. Tyr stood in the doorway with her big pointed ears going up and down in uncertainty, and finally decided that Harran's silence meant it was all right for her to come in again.

She slipped softly up beside her master, put her nose under one of his hands, and nudged him for attention.

Without really noticing her, he began scratching her behind the ears. Harran wasn't even seeing the walls of the hut. It was both yesterday and tomorrow for him, and the present was suddenly charged with frightful possibility. . . .

Yesterday looked as little like today as could be imagined. Yesterday was white and gold, a marble and chryselephantine glory—the colors of Siveni's little Sanctuary temple, in the days before the Rankans. *Why do I look back on it with such longing?* he wondered. *I was even less successful there than I am here.* But all the same, it had been his home. The faces had been familiar, and if he was a minor priest, he was also a competent one.

Competent—. The word had a sting to it yet. Not that it was anything to be ashamed of. But they'd told him often enough, in the temple, that there were only two ways to do the priestly magics. One was offhand, by instinct, as a great cook does; a whispered word here, an ingredient there, all done by knowledge and experience and whim—an effortless manipulation by the natural and supernatural senses of the materials at hand. The other way was like that of the beginning cook, one not expert enough to know what spices went with what, what spells would make space curdle. The merely competent simply did magic by the book, checking the measurements and being careful not to substitute, in case a demon should rise or a loaf should fail to.

Siveni's priests had looked down on the second method; it produced results, but lacked elegance. Harran could have cared less about elegance. He'd never gotten further than the strict reading and following of "recipes"—in fact, he had just about decided that maybe it would be wiser for him to stick to Siveni's strictly physical arts of apothecary and surgery and healing. At that point in his career the Rankans had arrived, and many temples fell, and priestcraft in all but the mightiest liturgies became politically unsafe. That was when Harran, for the first time since his parents had sold him into Siveni's temple at the age of nine, had gone looking for work. He had frantically taken the first job he found, as the Stepsons' leech and barber.

The memory of finding his new job brought back too clearly that of how he had lost the old one. He had been there to see the writ delivered into the shaking hands of the old Master-Priest by the hard-faced Molin Torchholder, while the Imperial guards looked on with bored hostility; the hurried packing of the sacred vessels, the hiding of other, less valuable materials in the crypts under the temple; the flight of the priesthood into exile. . . .

Harran stared at the poor, blood-congested hand in its dish on the table while beside him Tyr slurped his fingers and poked him for more attention. *Why did they do it? Siveni is only secondarily a war-goddess. More ever than that, She was—is—Lady of Wisdom and Enlightenment—a healer more than a killer.*

Not that She couldn't kill if the fancy took Her. . . .

Harran doubted that the priests of Vashanka and the rest were seriously worried about that. But for safety's sake they had exiled Siveni's priesthood and those of many "lesser" gods—leaving the Ilsigs only Ils and Shipri and the great names of the pantheon, whom even the Rankans dared not displace for fear of rebellion.

Harran stared at the hand. He could do it. He had never considered doing it before—at least, not seriously. For a long time he had held down this job by being valuable—a competent barber and surgeon—and by otherwise attracting no undue attention, discouraging questions about his past. He burned no incense openly, frequented no fane, swore by no god either Rankan or Ilsigi, and rolled his eyes when his customers did. "Idiots," he growled at the god-worshippers, and mocked them mercilessly. He drank and whored with the Stepsons. His old bitterness made it easy to seem cruel. Sometimes it was no seeming; sometimes he enjoyed it. He had in fact gotten something of a reputation among the Stepsons for callousness. That suited him.

And then, some time ago, there had been a change in the Stepson barracks. All the old faces had suddenly vanished; new ones, hastily recruited, had replaced them. In the wake of this change, Harran had abruptly become indispensable—for (first of all) he was familiar with the Stepsons' wonted ways as the newcomers were not; and (second) the newcomers were incredibly clumsy, and got themselves chopped up with abysmal regularity. Harran looked forward to the day when the real Stepsons should come back and set their house in order. It would be funny as hell.

Meanwhile, there was still the hand in its dish on the table. Hands might have no eyes, but this one stared at him.

"Piffles," Lafen had said.

That was one of the kinder of the various nasty names for the PFLS, the Popular Front for the Liberation of Sanctuary. At first there had only been rumors of the Front—shadowy mentions of a murder here, a robbery there, all in aid of throwing out Sanctuary's conquerors, the whole lot of them. Then the Front had become more active, striking out at every military or religious body its leaders considered an oppressor. The pseudo-Stepsons had come to hate the Front bitterly—not only because they had been ambushing Stepsons with frightening success, but for the rational (though unpublishable) reason that most of the present "Stepsons" were native Sanctuarites, and hardly felt themselves to be oppressors. Indeed, there was some supportive sentiment for the Front among them. Or there had been, until the Front had started putting acid in their winepots, and snipers on neighboring rooftops, and had started teaching gutterchildren to smash stones down on hands resting innocently on walls at lunch hour. . . .

Harran himself had agreed fiercely with the aims of the Front, though that wasn't a sentiment he ever allowed anyone to suspect. *Damn Rankans,* he thought now, *with their snotnosed new gods. Appearing and disappearing temples, lightning bolts in the streets. And then the damned FishEyes with their snakes. Miserable wetback mothergoddesses, manifesting as birds and flowers. Oh, Siveni—!* For just a moment his fists clenched, he shook, his eyes stung. The image of Her filled him . . . bright-eyed Siveni, the spear-bearer, the defender-goddess, lady of midnight wisdoms and truths that kill. Ils's crazy daughter, to whom He could never say no: the flashing-glanced hoyden, fierce and fair and wise—and lost. *O my own lady, come! Come and put things to rights! Take back what's yours again—*

The moment passed, and the old hopelessness reasserted itself. Harran let out his breath, looking down at Tyr, whose head had suddenly moved under his hand to look up at the nearer window.

A raven perched in it. Harran stared, and his hand closed on the scruff of Tyr's neck to keep her from chasing it. For the raven was Siveni's bird: Her messenger of old, silver-white once, but once upon a time caught lying to Her, and in a brief fit of rage, cursed black. The black bird looked down at them sidelong, out of a bright black eye. Then it glanced at the table, where the hand lay in its dish; and the raven spoke.

"Now," it said.

Tyr growled.

"No," he said in a whisper. The raven turned, lifted its wings, and flew away in a storm of whistling flapping noises. Tyr got loose from Harran's grip, spun around once in a tight circle for sheer excitement, and then hurtled out the door across the stableyard, barking at the vanished bird.

Harran was so shocked he found it hard to think. *Did it speak? Or did I imagine it?* For a moment that seemed likely, and Harran leaned back against the table, feeling weak and annoyed at his own stupidity. One of the old trained ravens from Siveni's temple, still somehow alive, blundering into his window—

This window? At this moment? Saying that word?

And there was the hand....

The picture of old smiling-eyed Irik, the Master-Priest, came back to him. Fair-haired, graying Irik in his white robes, leaning with Harran and several others over a pale marble table in the students' courts, his thin brown finger tracing a line on a tattered linen roll-book. "Here's another old one," Irik was saying. "The Upraising of the Lost. You would use this only on the very newly dead—someone gone less than twenty slow breaths. It's infallible—but the ingredients, as you see, aren't something you can keep on hand." There was muted snickering and groaning among the novices; Irik was an irrepressible punster. "The charm has other applications. Since it can retrieve anything lost— including time, which the dead lose—you can lay restless ghosts with it; though as usual you have to raise them first. And since it can similarly retrieve timelessness, which mortals lose, the charm's of use as a mystagogue-spell, an initiator. But again, the problem of getting the ingredients comes up—the mandrake, for one. Also, brave men are generally as unwilling as cowards are to give up a perfectly good hand. The spell is mostly valuable nowadays in terms of technique; that middle passage, about the bones, is a little textbook in taxidermy all by itself. If you have to lay ghosts, this next one is usually more useful...."

The white-and-gold memory turned to shadows and mud again. Harran sat and stared at the stained earthenware dish and its contents.

It would work. He would need those other ingredients. The mandrake would take some finding, but it wasn't *too* dangerous. And he would need that old linen book-roll. He was fairly sure where it was....

Harran got up and poked the fire; then poured water from a cracked clay ewer into an iron pot and put the pot on the fire. He picked up his surgeon's knife again and the dish with the hand.

Tyr ran back into the house, stared at him with her big dark doe-eyes, and realized that he was holding a dish. She immediately stood up on her hind legs, dancing and bouncing a little to keep her balance, and craned her neck, trying to see what was on the plate.

Harran had to laugh at her. She was a stray he'd found beaten and whimpering in an alley over by the Bazaar two years ago... when he was new to his job and had considerable sympathy toward strays. Tyr had grown up pretty— a short-furred, clean-bodied, sharp-faced little bitch, brown and delicate as a deer. But she was still thin, and that troubled him. The war on Wizardwall, and then the coming of the Beysib, had driven prices up on beef as on everything else. The pseudo-Stepsons swore at the three-times-weekly porridge, and bolted their meat, when it arrived, like hungry beasts—leaving precious little in the way of scraps for Tyr to cadge. Harran didn't dare let her out of the barracks compound, either; she would end up in someone's stewpot within an hour. So she ate half of Harran's dinner most of the time. He didn't mind; he would have paid greater prices yet. Unlike the old days, when he had constantly been busy administering Siveni's love to her worshippers and so needed very little for himself, Harran now needed all of the love he could get. . . .

He watched her dancing, and became aware of the smell in the room—more than could be accounted for by Shal's pissing on the table. "Tyr," he said, faking anger, "have you been rooting in the kitchen midden again?"

She stopped dancing . . . then very, very slowly sat down, with her ears dejected-flat. She did *not* stop staring at the dish.

He gazed at her ruefully. "Oh, well," he said. "I only need the bones anyway. Just this once, you hear?"

Tyr leaped up and began bouncing again.

Harran went over to the sideboard and boned the hand in nine or ten sure motions. "All right," he said at last, holding out the first scrap of meat for Tyr. "Come on, sweetheart. Sit up! Up!"

Oh, my Lady, he thought, *your servant hears. Arm Yourself. Get Your spear. You'll soon be lost no more. I shall bring You back. . . .*

Preparation occupied Harran for a while thereafter. He kept it quiet. No use alerting the Stepsons to what he was planning, or giving Raik any reason to come after him— Raik, who spat at Harran every time he saw him now, promising to "take care of him" after Shal was better. Harran ignored him. The Piffles were keeping busy out there, and made it easy for Harran to go about his usual routine of stitching and splinting and cauterizing. And in between, when he grew bored, there was always Mriga.

She had been another stray, a clubfooted beggar-child found sitting half-starved in a Downwind dungheap, mindlessly whetting a dull scrap of metal on a cobblestone. Harran had taken her home on impulse, not quite sure what he would do with her. He discovered quite soon that he'd found himself a bargain. Though she seemed to have no mind now—if she'd ever had one—she was clever with her hands. She would do any small task endlessly until stopped; even in her sleep, those restless hands would move, never stopping. You never had to show her anything more than once. She was especially good with edged things; the Stepsons brought their swords to her to sharpen, one and all. Tyr had come to positively worship her—which was saying a great deal; Tyr didn't take to everyone. If Mriga was lame and plain—well, less chance that she would leave or be taken from Harran; if she couldn't speak, well, a silent woman was considered a miracle—wasn't that what they said?

And since Harran was not rich enough to afford whores very often, having Mriga around offered other advantages. He had needs, which, with a kind of numbness of heart, he used Mriga to satisfy. In some moods he knew he was doing a dark thing, again and again; and Harran knew that the price was waiting to be paid. But he didn't need to think of that just now. Payment, and eternity, were a long way from the sordid here-and-now of Sanctuary and a man with an itch that needed scratching. Harran scratched that itch when he felt like it, and spent the rest of his time working on the Stepsons, and the charm.

He would have preferred to leave the hand in a bin of toothwing beetles for some days—the industrious little horrors would have stripped the bones dry of every remaining dot of flesh and eaten the marrow too; but toothwing beetles and clean temple workrooms and all the rest were forever out of his reach. Harran made do with burying the bones in a box of quicklime for a week, then steeping it in naphtha for an afternoon to get the stink and the marrow out. Tyr yipped and danced excitedly around Harran as he worked over the pot. "Not for you, baby," he said absently, fishing the little fingerbones out of the kettle and putting them to cool on an old cracked plate. "You'd choke for sure. Go 'way."

Tyr looked up hopefully for another moment, found nothing forthcoming, and then caught sight of a rat ambling across the stableyard, and ran out to catch it.

Finding the mandrake root was a slightly more difficult business. The best kind grew from a felon's grave, preferably a felon who had been hanged. If there was anything Sanctuary wasn't short on, it was felons. The major problem was that they were easier to identify live than dead and buried. Harran went to visit his old comrade Grian down at the Charnel House, and inquired casually about the most recent hangings.

"Aah, you want corpses," Grian said in mild disgust, elbow-deep in the chest cavity of a floater. "We're havin' a plague of 'em. And the Shalpa-be-damned murderers hain't even got the courtesy to be half-decent quiet about it. Look at this poor soul. Third one in the last two days. A few stones around his feet and into the White Foal with him. Didn't the body who threw him in know that a few cobbles won't keep 'em down when the rot sets in and the bloatin' and bubblin' starts? You'd think they wanted the body t' be found. It's these damn Piffles, that's what it is. Public Liberation Front, they call themselves? Public nuisance, I call 'em. City ought to do somethin'.'"

Harran nodded, keeping his retches to himself. Grian had supplied Siveni's priests with many an alley-rolled corpse for anatomy instruction, back in the white-and-gold times. He was the closest thing Harran had to a friend these days— probably the only man in Sanctuary who knew what Harran had been before he'd been a barber.

Grian paused to take a long swig out of the wine jar Harran had brought for him, "liberated" from the Stepsons' store. "Stuffy in here today," he said, wiping his forehead and waving a hand vaguely in front of him.

Harran nodded, holding his breath hard as the stench went by his face. "Stuffy" was a mild word for the Charnel House at noon on a windless day. Grian drank again, put the jug down with a satisfied thump between the corpse's splayed legs, and picked up a rib-spreader. "No lead in *that*," Grian said with relish, eyeing the wine. "Watch you don't get caught."

"I'll be careful," Harran said, without inhaling.

"You want nice fresh corpses quietlike," Grian said, bending close and forcing his wine-laden growl down to a rumble, "you go try that vacant lot over by the old Downwind gravepit. The lot just north of there, by th' empty houses. Put a few in there myself just the other night. Been puttin' all the bad 'uns in there, all the hangings, for the last fortnight. Ran out of space in the old gravepit. Damn Fish-Faces have been busy 'cleaning up the city' for their fine ladies."

The last two words were pronounced with infinite scorn; Grian might be a corpse-cutter and part-time gravedigger, but he had been "brought up old-fashioned," and did not approve of women, fish-faced or otherwise, who went around in broad daylight wearing nothing above the waist but paint. By his lights, there were more appropriate places for that kind of thing.

"You give it a try," Grian said, hauling out a lung like a sodden, reeking sponge, and tossing it with a grimace into the pail on the floor. "Take a shovel, boy. But you needn't dig deep; we been in a hurry to get all the customers handled; they none of them more'n two foot down, just 'nough to hide the smell. Here now, look at this. . . . "

Harran pleaded a late night's work and made his escape.

The hour before midnight found him slipping through the shadows, down that dismal Downwind street. He went armed with knife and short sword, and (to any assailant's probable confusion) with a trowel; but he turned out not to need more than one of the three. Grian had been wrong about the smell.

The hour before midnight, one death-knell stroke on the gongs of Ils's temple, was Harran's signal. He got to work, going about on hands and knees on the uneven ground, which felt lumpy as a coverlet with many unwilling bedfellows under it—brushing his hands through the dirt, feeling for the small stiff shoot he wanted.

In the corner of the yard he found one. For fear of losing it in the dark (since he might show no light if the root was to work) he sat down by it, and waited. The wind came up. Midnight struck, and with it came the mandrake's swift flower, white as a dead man's turned-up eye. It blossomed, and shed its cold sweet fragrance on the air, and died. Harran began to dig.

How long he knelt there in the wretched stink and the cold, blindfolded with silk and tugging at the struggling root, Harran wasn't sure. And he stopped caring about the time as he heard something drawing near in the darkness— another rustle of silk, not his. The rustle paused. Hard after the silken susurrus came another sort of whisper, the sound of a breath of wind sinking down around him and dying away.

Harran couldn't take off the blindfold—no man may see the unharmed mandrake root and live. By itself, that was reassuring to him; any assailant would not survive the attempt. So, though the sweat broke out on him and chilled him through, Harran hacked away at the root with the leaden trowel, and finally cut through it, pulling the mandrake free. The maimed root shrieked, a sound so bizarre that the huddled wind leaped up in panic and blundered about among the graves for a few moments—then dove for cover again, leaving Harran twice as cold as he had been before.

He yanked off his blindfold, stared around him, and saw two sights. One was the twitching, writhing, man-shaped root, its scream dying to a whisper as it stiffened. The other stood across the cemetery from him, a form robed and hooded all in black. That form stared at him silently from the darkness of the hood, a long look; and Harran understood quite well what had frightened even the cold night wind into going to ground.

The black shape slipped pale arms out of the graceful draping of the robe, raised them to put the hood back. She looked at him—the lovely, olive-skinned, somber face with black eyes aslant, raven-dark hair a second, more silken hood over her. He did not die of the look, as uninformed rumor said he might; but Harran wasn't yet sure this in itself was a good thing. He knew Ischade by reputation, if never before by sight. His friends down at the Charnel House had dealt with her handiwork often enough.

He waited, sweating. He had never seen anything so dangerous in his life, not Tempus on a rampage, or thunderous Vashanka striking the city, lightning-fashion, with testy miracles.

She tilted that elegant head, finally, and blinked. "Rest easy," she said—ridiculous reassurance, delivered in a quiet voice laced with lazy mockery. "You're not even nearly my type. But brave—digging that root here, at this hour, with your own hand, instead of using some dog to pull it for you. Brave—or desperate. Or very, very foolhardy."

Harran swallowed. "The latter, madam," he said at last, "most definitely—bandying words with *you*. And as for the root—foolhardy there too. Yes. But the other way, it's barely a third as effective. I could send away to an herb-dealer or magician for the man-dug root. But who knows when it would get here? And at any rate—in gold or some other currency—the price of the danger would still have to be paid."

She regarded him a moment more, than laughed very softly. "A knowledgeable practitioner," she said. "But this . . . commodity . . . has most specific uses. In this time, this place, only three. There are cheaper cures for impotence—not that your present bedfellow would even notice it. And murder is far more easily done with poison. The third use—"

She paused, waited to see what he would do. Harran

snatched up the mandrake and clutched it in a moment's irrationality—then realized that the worst that could happen would be that she would kill him. Or not. He dropped the mandrake into his simple-bag, and dusted off his hands. "Madam," Harran said, "I've no fear of you taking it from me. A thief you may be, but you're far beyond the need for such crude tools."

"Have a care," Ischade whispered, the soft mockery still in her voice.

"Madam, I do." He was shaking as he said it. "I know you don't care much for priests. And I know you protect your prerogatives—all Sanctuary remembers that night—" He swallowed. "But I have no plans to raise the dead. Or—not dead *men*."

She looked at him out of those oblique eyes, the amusement in them becoming drier by the moment. "A sophist! Beware, lest I ask you who shaves the barber. Whom then are you planning to raise, master sophist? Women?"

"Madam," he said all at once, for the air was getting deadly still again, "the old Gods of Ilsig have been had. Had like a blind Rankan in the Bazaar. And it's their idiot mortal worshippers who've sold them this bill of goods. They've fooled them into thinking that the things mortals do have to *matter* to the powers of gods! Corpses buried under thresholds, necklaces cast in bells or forged into swords, a cow sacrificed here or a bad set of entrails there— It's rubbish! But the Ilsig gods sit languishing in their Otherworld because of it all, thinking they're powerless, and the Rankan gods swagger around and hit things with lightning bolts and sire clandestine children on poor mortal maids, and think they own the world. They don't!"

Ischade blinked again, just once, that very conscious gesture.

Harran swallowed and kept going. "The Ilsigi gods have started believing in *time*, lady. The worship of mortals has bound them into it. Sacrifices at noon, savory smokes going up at sunset, the Ten-Slaying once a year—every festival that happens at a regular interval, every scheduled thing—has bound them. Gods may have made eternity, but mortals made clocks and calendars and tied little pieces of eternity up with them. Mortals have bound the gods! Rankan and Ilsigi both. But mortals can also free them." He took a long breath. "If they've lost timelessness—then this spell can find it for Them again. For at least one of them, who can open the way for the others. And once the Ilsig gods are wholly free of our world—"

"—They will drive out the Rankan gods, and the Beysib goddess too, and take back their own again?..." Ischade smiled—slow cool derision—but there was interest behind it. "Mighty work, that, for a mortal. Even for one who spends so much of his time wielding those powerful sorcerer's tools, the cautery and the bone-saw. But one question, Harran. *Why?*"

Harran stopped. Some vague image of Ils stomping all over Savankala, of Shipri punching Sabellia's heart out, and his own crude satisfaction at the fact, was all he had. At least, besides the image of maiden Siveni, warlike, impetuous, triumphing over her rivals—and later settling down again to the arts of peace in her restored temple—

And Ischade smiled, and sighed, and put her hood up. "No matter," she said. There was vast amusement in her voice—probably, Harran suspected, at the prospect of a man who didn't know what he wanted, and would likely die of it. Nothing confounds the great alchemies and magics so thoroughly as unclear motives. "No matter at all," Ischade said. "Should you succeed at what you intend, there'll be merry times hereabouts, indeed there will. I should enjoy watching the proceedings. And should you fail..." The slim dark shoulders lifted in the slightest shrug. "At least I know where good quality mandrake's to be had. Good evening to you, master barber. And good fortune—if there is such a thing."

She was gone. The wind got up again, and whining, ran away....

131

• • •

Of the greater sorceries, one of the elder priests had long ago said to Harran, in warning, "Notice is always taken." The still, dark-eyed notice that had come upon Harran in the graveyard troubled him indeed. He went home that night shivering with more than cold; and, once in bed, kicked Tyr perfunctorily out of it and pulled Mriga in—using her with something more than his usual impersonal effectiveness. No mere scratching of the itch tonight. He was looking, hopelessly, for something more—some flicker of feeling, some returning pressure of arms. But the lousiest Downwind whore would have suited his purposes a hundred times better than the mindless, compliant warmth that lay untroubled under him or which jerkily, aimlessly wound its limbs about his. Afterward Harran pushed her out too, leaving Mriga to crawl to the hearth and curl in the ashes while he tossed and turned. For all the sleep he found in bed, Harran might as well have been lying in ashes himself, or embers.

Ischade.... No good could come of her attention. Who knew if, for her own amusement, she might not sell to some interested party—Molin Torchholder, say—the information that one lone, undefended man was going to bring back one of the old Ilsig gods in a few days? "Oh, Siveni..." he whispered. He would have to move quickly, before something happened to stop him.

Tonight.

Not tonight, he thought in a kind of reluctant horror. That same horror made him stop and wonder, in a priest's self-examination, about its source. Was it just the familiar repulsion he always felt at the thought of the old ruin on the Avenue of Temples? Or was it something else?

—A shadow on the edge of his mind's vision, a feeling that something was about to go wrong. Some*one*. Someone who had been watching him—

Raik?

All the more reason for it to be tonight, then. He was sure he had seen Raik staggering into the barracks—probably to snore off another night of wineshops. Harran had thought to go back twice to the temple—once to retrieve the old roll-book, and then, after studying it, once to perform the rite. But even that would be attracting too much attention. It *would* have to be tonight.

Harran lay there, postponing getting up into the cold for just a few seconds more. Since that day five years ago when the Rankans served the writ on Irik, he had not been inside Siveni's temple. *For so long now I've been done with temples. Going into one, now—and hers—do I truly want to reopen that old wound?*

He stared at the skinny, twitching shape curled up in the ashes, and wondered. "Every temple needs an idiot," the old master-priest had once said to Harran in creaky jest. Harran had laughed and agreed with him, being just then in the middle of an unmasterable lesson, and feeling himself idiot enough for any twelve temples. Now—in exile— Harran briefly wondered whether he was still living in a temple; whether he had accepted the idiot because she was so like the mad and poor who had frequented Siveni's fane in the days when there was still wisdom dispensed there, and healing, and food. Of wisdom and healing he had little enough. And Mriga never complained about the food. Or anything else. . . .

He swore softly, got up, got dressed. There, in the wooden box shoved under his sideboard, were the bones of the hand, wired and mounted into the correct gesture, with the ring of base metal on the proper finger; there was the mandrake, hastily bound in cord twisted of silk and lead, with a silvered steel pin through its "body" to hold it harmless. Both hairpin and ring had come from a secondhand whore that Yuri had recently brought home for the barracks. Harran, last in line and mildly concerned that the woman might notice when her things went missing, had "considerately" brought her a stoup of drugged wine. Then he swived her until the wine took, lifted ring and pin, and slipped away—first leaving her a largish tip where no one but she would be likely to find it.

So—almost set. He picked up the box, went over to the corner by the table for a few more things—a small flask, a little bag of grain, and another of salt, a lump of bitumen. Then he checked around one last time. Mriga lay snoring in the ashes. Tyr was curled nose-to-tail in a compact brown package under the bed, snoring too, a note higher than Mriga. Harran mussed the meager bedclothes and lumpy bolster more or less into a bodyshape, snatched up and flung over him his old soot-black cloak, and made his way silently through the Stepsons' stableyard.

There was a way over the wall by the corner of the third stall down. Up the shingles, a one-handed grip on a drainpipe, a few moments scrambling to find footholds on old bricks that stuck out just so. Then up to the wall's top, and the hard drop down on the other side. Breathing hard, just before that drop, Harran paused, looking back the way he'd come—and just barely saw the vague shape by the barracks door, standing motionless.

Harran froze. The night was moonless; the torches by the door were burned down to blue. There was nothing to see but the faint flash of eyes catching that light sidewise for a second as the shadow crouched and moved into deeper shadow, and was lost.

Harran jumped, held still only long enough to get his breath, and ran. If he got to the temple in time to do what he intended, no number of pursuers would matter; the whole Rankan Empire, and the Beysibs too, would flee before what would follow.

If he had time. . . .

The Temple of Siveni Grey-Eyes was the second-to-last one at the shabby southern end of the Avenue of Temples. At least, it was shabby now. There had been a time when Siveni's temple had had respectable neighbors: on one side, the fane and priests of Anen Wineface, the harvest-god, master of vine and corn; on the other, that of Anen's associate Dene Blackrobe, the somber mistress of sleep and death. Between them, Anen's polished sandstone and Dene's dark granite, Siveni's temple had risen in its white and gold. There had been a certain rightness to the way they stood together, Work and Wine and Sleep; and Siveni's temple, as was appropriate for a craft-goddess, had looked out over that guilds' quarter. Businessmen made deals on its broad steps, paid a coin or two to buy luck and a cake for Siveni's ravens, then went next door to Anen's to seal their deals with poured libations. Small ones; Anen's wine was generally considered too good to waste on the floor.

Those days were all done now. Anen's temple was dark except for one red light over the altar; his priests' annuity was reduced to almost nothing, and Anen's old patrons, knowing Him out of favor, tended to do their libation-pouring elsewhere. As for Dene's temple, the Rankans, possibly considering Her too contemplative (or too unimportant) to do anything about it, had demolished the building... leaving the merchants and guildsmen to quarrel over the newly available parcel of real estate.

And as for Siveni's temple... Harran stood across from it now, hiding himself in the shallow doorway of a night-shuttered mercantile establishment. He could have wept. Those white columns all smeared with city grime, the white steps leading up to the portico broken, littered, stained.... A slow cold wind swept down the Avenue of Temples toward Ils's fane, a dim shape no more clearly seen than the moon behind clouds. Near it reared up Savankala's upstart temple, and Vashanka's hard by it—both great ungainly piles, and as dark tonight as Ils's. No one walked the street. It was far past the hour for devotions.

Harran held still in that doorway for a long time, unable to shake the feeling that he had been followed. The gongs of Ils's temple rang the third hour after midnight. The sound wavered in the wind like Harran's heart, blowing away down the avenue toward the Governor's Palace and the estates. Something flapped nearby—a sound like a flag snapping in the wind. He jerked around, looked. Nothing but the shadowy shape of a bird on the right, flying heavily in the crosswind, coming to perch on the high cupola of Siveni's temple, becoming another shadow that loomed there among the carvings. A black bird, bigger than a crow. . . .

He unswallowed his courage, looked both ways, and hurried across the street. The strength of the wind, as Harran reached the middle of the avenue, was ominous. If ever there was a night to be home in bed, this was it. . . .

He dashed up the stairs where he had lingered so many times before, tripping now and again over some dislodged stone, some crack that hadn't been there when he was young. On the portico he paused to get his breath and look back the way he had come. Nothing coming, no one passing in the street. . . .

And there, the motion again, something dark; not in the street, but next door in the cloddy, vacant lot that was all that remained of Dene's temple. Harran felt under his cloak for the long knife. . . .

Eyes caught the reflection of the pale stone of Siveni's stairs. Harran found himself looking at the largest rat he had ever seen, in Sanctuary or elsewhere. It was the size of a dog, at least. The thought of Tyr catching up with it made him shudder. As if sensing Harran's fear, the rat turned about and waddled back into the vacant lot, going about its nightly business. Other shadows, just as large, stirred about the pillars of the portico, unconcerned.

Harran swallowed and thought about business. *If I feel I'm being followed, the thing to do is start the spell—draw the outer circle. No one can get through it once it's closed.* He put down the box and the flask and fumbled about his clothes for the lump of bitumen. Slowly he made his way around the great open square of pillars, all of which bore the sledgehammer marks of attempted demolition. The marks were futile, of course—any temple built by the priests of the goddess who invented architecture might be expected to last—but they scarred Harran's heart just looking at them. Right around the portico, as he'd been taught—four hundred eighty paces exactly—Harran went, bent over, his back aching. Dark shapes fled again and again at his passing. He refused to look at them. By the time he came around to the middle of the stairs again and drew the diagram-knot that tied the circle closed, his back was one long creaking bar of iron with smiths working on it; but he felt much safer. He picked up his box again and made his way inward.

The great doors within the portico were long since barred shut from inside, but that would hardly stop anyone who had served Siveni past the novitiate. Harran traced the door's carved raven-and-olive-tree motif just below eye level until he found the fourth raven past the second tree with no olives on it, and pushed in the raven's eye. The bird's whole head fell in after it, revealing the little catch and valve that opened the priests' door. The catch was stiff, but after a couple of tries the door swung open wide enough to admit Harran. He slipped in and swung it silently to behind him.

Harran lifted the dark lantern he had brought with him and unshuttered it. And then he *did* begin to weep; for the statue was gone—the image toward which Harran had once bowed affectionately so many times a day, having eventually learned to see and bow to the immortal beauty behind the mortal symbol. Siveni's great statue in her aspect as Defender, seated, armed and helmed, holding her battalion-vanquishing spear in one hand and her raven perched on the other. The great work, the statue that the artist Rahen had spent five years fashioning of marble, gold, and ivory, afterward putting down his sculptor's tools forever and saying he knew his life's masterwork when he saw it, and would make no other. . . . All gone. Harran could have understood it if they had stripped the gold and ivory off, pried the gems out of the mighty shield. He knew as well as any other Sanctuarite that not even nailing things down could keep them safe here. But he had never thought to have the fact brought home to him so brutally as this. The pediment on which the statue had stood was bare except for bits of rubble, chunks and splinters of shattered marble . . . but those were eloquent even in ruin. Here, a fat pyramidal lump was one corner of the statue's pedestal; there, a long slim shard, smooth and faintly grooved at one end, broken off sharp as a flint at the other—a feather from a raven's outstretched wing. . . . Harran's brain roiled with rage. *Where did they—why—A whole statue, a statue thirty feet high! Stolen, destroyed, lost.*

He dashed the tears out of his eyes, put the lantern down, flung his cloak down on the dusty marble, and picked up his box. One more circle he would need in which to work the sorcery itself. If his back still hurt him, Harran didn't notice it now. Round the vacant pediment he went with the bitumen, not counting paces this time, rather fighting down his bitter anger enough to remember the words that needed to be thought again and again to confine within this inner circle the forces that would soon break loose. It was not easy work, fighting down both his anger and the growing, restless power of the circle-spell; so that as Harran tied the second circle closed he was gasping like a man who'd run a race, and had to stand for some moments bowed over like a spent runner, hands on thighs.

He straightened up as quickly as he could, for there was worse to come. Simple this spell might be, but that wouldn't keep it from being strenuous; and first he needed the rite. Breaking and resealing the circle according to procedure, he went to get it.

Normally the location of the safe-crypt was not information that would have been entrusted to a junior priest, but in the haste surrounding the exile of Siveni's priesthood, quite a few secrets had slipped out. Harran had been one of those conscripted to help old Irik hide away the less important documents, old medical and engineering texts and spells. "We may yet find a use for these, in a better hour," Irik had said to Harran. Just then he had had his arms full of parchments, his nose full of dust, and his mind full of fear; the words had meant nothing. But now Harran blessed Irik as he went around to behind where the statue had been, stepped on the proper pieces of flooring in the proper order, and saw the single block by the rear wall fall slowly away into darkness.

The stair was narrow and steep, with no banister. Harran held up the lantern at the bottom of it and went rummaging, sneezing a lot as he did. Parchments, book-rolls, and wax tablets were piled and scattered every which way. It was the rolls he went for. Again and again Harran undid linen cords, spread a roll out in a cloud of dust and sneezes, to find nothing but a spare copy of the temple's bookkeeping for the third month of such and such a year, or some tired old philosophical treatise, or a cure for the ague (ox-fat rubbed together with mustard and ground red-beetle casings, the same applied to the chest three times a day). This went on till his eyes began to water, rebelling against the poor light, and Harran's mind stopped seeing what he read and kept wandering away to worry about the time. Night was leaning toward morning; this was the time to do the spell, if ever—before dawn, herald of new beginnings—and if he didn't find it soon—

He blinked and read the words again. It wasn't hard; they were beautifully written in an Old Ilsig hieratic script. "... of the Lost, that is to say, an infallible spell for finding the lost and strayed and stolen. The spell needeth first the hand of a brave and living man, the same to be offered up in the spell's working by the celebrant; and it needeth also a mandrake root, called by some peristupe, dug of a night without moon or star, and treated according to the disciplines, also to be so offered; and needeth as well some small deal of salt and wheat and wine, and a knife for blood to propitiate the Ones Below; and lastly those instruments by which the boundary for the spell shall be made.

"First dig your mandrake..."

Harran scrambled to his feet in the dust and the dark, sneezing wildly and not caring. Up the stairs, back into the circle—cutting the knot to let himself in, sealing it shut again behind him. He sat down on the vacant pediment amid the rubble and began to read. It was all here, much as he remembered it, with the little thumbnail sketch of the diagram to be drawn inside the circle, and the rite itself. Part in a very old Ilsig indeed, part in the vernacular. Simple words, but oh, the power in them. Harran's heart began to hammer.

Something moaned, and Harran started—then realized it was only the wind, building now to such a crescendo that he could hear it even inside the temple's thick stone. *Good,* he thought, picking up the piece of bitumen again and rising to his feet, *let it storm. Let them think that something's about to happen. For it is!*

He set to work. The diagram was complex, seemingly a picture of some kind of geometrical solid, though one in which the number of sides seemed to change each time one counted them. The finished diagram made an uneasy flickering in the mind, a feeling that got worse as Harran started setting the necessary runes and words into the pattern's angles. Then came the salt, cast to the cardinal points with the usual purifacatory rhyme; and the wheat—two grains at the primary point, four at the next, eight at the one after that, and so on around the seven. Harran chuckled a little, light-headed with excitement. That particular symbol of plenitude had always been a joke among the student priests; a sixty-four point pattern would have emptied every granary in the world. Nothing left now but the wine, the knife, the mandrake, the hand. . . .

The wind was whining through the pillars outside like a dog that wanted in. Harran shivered. *It's the cold,* he thought, and then swallowed again and silently took it back; to lie during a spell could be fatal. He went to the diagram's heart, feeling as he went the small uncomfortable jolts of power that came of passing over it. Forces besides his were moving tonight, lending what he did abnormal power. *Just as well,* he thought. Harran opened the wine-flask and set it beside the center-point, then put the hand in one of his pockets and the mandrake in the other. In his left hand he held the book-roll, open to the right spot. With the right he drew his knife.

It was his best, Mriga's favorite. He had set her at it that afternoon, and not stopped her for a long while. Now its edge caught the dim lantern-light with a flicker as live as an eye's. He held it up in salute to the four directions and their Guardians above and below, faced northward, and began to pronounce the spell's first passage.

Resistance began immediately; it became an effort to push the words out of his throat. His tongue went leaden. Still Harran spoke the words, though more and more slowly; stopping in mid-spell could be as fatal as lying. The wind outside rose to a malevolent scream, drowning him out. He was reduced to struggling one word out, drawing several rasping breaths, then starting another. Harran had never thought that just fifty words, a few sentences, would seem long. They did now. Ten words remained, every one of them looking as long as a whole codex and as heavy as stone. At the fifth one he stammered, and outside the screaming wind scaled up into an insane yell of triumph. In a burst of fear he choked out two words very fast, one after another. Then the second-to-last, more slowly, with a wrenching effort like passing a stone. And the last, that went out of him like life leaving and smote him down to the floor.

With his falling came the light, blazing in through the temple's high narrow windows like the sky splitting; and the thundercrack, one deafening bolt that reverberated over the roofs of Sanctuary—breaking what glass remained unbroken in the temple's windows, and jolting loose what was already shattered, raining it all down on the marble floor in a storm of razory chimings. Then stillness again. Harran lay on his face, tasting marble and bitumen against his tongue and blood in his mouth, smelling ozone, hearing the last few drops of the glass rain.

I think it's working....

Harran got to his knees, felt around with shaking hands until he found the knife which he had dropped, and then took the skeletal hand out of his pocket. He put it down exactly at the diagram's center-point, palm-up; the outstretched index and middle fingers pointing northward, the others curled in toward the palm, the thumb angled toward the east. Then Harran began the second passage of the spell.

As he read—slowly, being careful of the pronunciation—he became aware of being watched. At first, though he could see nothing, the sensation was as if just one set of eyes dwelt on him—curious eyes, faintly angry, faintly hungry, willing to wait for something. But the number of eyes grew. Harran's words seemed loud as thunder, and his hurrying breath louder than any wind; and the eyes grew more and more numerous. It was not as if he could see them. He could not. But he could feel them, a hungry crowd, a hostile multitude, growing greater by the second, waiting, watching him. And when the silence became so total that he could no longer stand it, then came the sound; a faint rustling, a jostling and creaking and gibbering at the edge of hearing—a sound like the wings and cries of bats in their thousands, their millions, a benighted flock hanging, waiting, hungry for blood.

The sound, rather than frightening Harran worse, reassured him somewhat; for it told him who they were. The spell was working indeed. The shades of the nameless dead were about him, those who had been dead so long that they of all things made were most truly lost. All they remembered of life was what an unthinking, newborn child remembers—heat, warmth, pulsebeats, blood. Harran began to sweat as he picked up the wine-flask and made his way around to the edge of the circle. At the pattern's northern point he took Mriga's favorite knife and cut the heel of his left hand with it, wide but not deep, for the best bleeding. The horror of cutting himself left him weak and shaking. But there was no time to waste. On the northern point, and on all the others, he shed his blood in a fat dollop on the grain, and poured wine over it all, then retreated to the center of the circle and said the word that would let the shades past the fringes of the pattern, though no further.

They came flocking in, crowding to the blood, eyes that he could not see squeezed shut in pleasure, tiny cries withering the silence. They drank their fill, slowly—tiny bat-sips were all they could manage through those parched soul-mouths. And then, satisfied, they milled about gibbering for a little while, forgot why they had come, and faded away. Harran felt slightly sorry for them—the poor strengthless dead, reduced to a shadowy eternity of wistful hunger—but he wasn't sorry to see them go. They would not trouble the spell again; he could get on with the real business now.

He paused just long enough to wipe the cold sweat out of his eyes, then put the book-roll aside, took the mandrake out of his pocket, and started undoing its bindings. When they were off he laid the mandrake carefully in the palm of the skeleton hand, "head" up toward the fingers, and then paused again; the next maneuver was tricky, and he briefly wished for three hands. There was a way to manage it, though. He squatted down, pinned both hand and mandrake securely in place on the floor with the toe of one boot. Then with one hand he plucked the silvered pin out of the mandrake's torso; with the other he squeezed his blood out onto the root's pinprick wound.

Instantly the root began to glow . . . faintly at first; but it would not be faint for long. Harran scrambled to his feet, rolled the book along to the last part of the spell, and began to read. It was in the vernacular, the easiest part of the spell; but his heart beat harder than ever. "By my blood here spilt, and by these names invoked; by the dread signs of deep night inclining toward the morning, and the potent figures here drawn; by the souls of the dead and the yet unborn . . ."

It was getting warm. Harran hazarded a glance, as he read, down at the light growing at his feet. The mandrake was burning such a hue as no one ever saw save while dreaming or dead. To call the color "red" would have been to exalt red far past its station, and insult the original. There was heat in the color, but of a sort that had nothing to do with flame. This was the original shade of heart's passion, of blood burning in a living being possessed by rage or desire. It was dark; yet there was nothing intrinsically evil about it, and it blinded. In that light Harran could barely see the book he read from, the stone walls around him; they seemed ephemeral as things dreamed. Only that light was real, and the image it stirred in his mind. His heart's desire, whose very name he had denied himself for so many years now—and now within his grasp, the longed-for, the much-loved, wise and fierce and fair—

"... By all these signs and bindings, and most of all by Thy own name, O Lady Siveni, do I adjure and command Thee! Present Thyself here before me—" —*in comely form and such as will do me no harm,* said the spell, but Harran would not have dreamed of saying that: as if Siveni could ever be uncomely, or would harm her priest? And then the triple invocation, while he gasped, and everything reeled, and his heart raced in his chest as if he labored in the act of love: "Come Thou, Lady of the Battles, who smites and binds up again. Builder, Defender, Avenger; come Thou, come Thou, O *come!*"

No lightning this time, no thunder. Nothing but a shock that knocked Harran flying in one direction and the knife and book in two others—a hurtless shock that was nevertheless as final and terrible as dreaming of falling out of bed. Harran lay still for quite some while, afraid to move—then groaned softly once and sat himself up on the stone, wondering what had gone wrong.

"Nothing," someone said to him.

The voice made the walls of the temple vibrate. Harran trembled and held his head against the singing in it.

"Well, don't sit there, Harran," said the voice. "Get on with it. We've business to attend to."

He rolled to his knees and looked up.

She was there. Harran staggered; his heart did too, missing beats. The eyes—those were what struck him first: literally struck him, with physical force. Afterward, he realized this should have been no surprise. "Flashing-Eyed," was after all her chief epithet. His best imaginations proved insufficient to the reality. Eyes like lightning—clear, pitilessly illuminating, keen as a spear in the heart—those were Siveni's. They didn't glow; they didn't need to. None of her needed to. She was simply there, so *there* that everything physical seemed vague beside her. A great chill of fear went through Harran then at the thought that perhaps there were good reasons why the gods didn't usually walk the realms of men.

But not even fear could live long, fixed by that silvery regard, that ferocious beauty. For she *was* beautiful, and again Harran's old imaginations fell down in the face of the truth. It was a spare, severe, unselfconscious beauty, too busy with other things to notice itself...definitely the face of the patroness of the arts and sciences. There was wildness in that face, as well as wisdom; thoughtlessness as well as handsomeness in those rich robes—for the blazing under-tunic was tucked casually and hurriedly up above the knee, and the great loose overtunic was a man's, probably Ils's, borrowed for the greater freedom of motion it allowed. The hand that held the great spear she leaned on was graceful as a lady's; but the slender arm still spoke of shattering strength. Siveni as she now appeared was not much taller than mortal womankind. But as he looked at her, and she bent those cool, terrible, considering eyes on him, Harran felt very small indeed. She pushed her high-crested helm back a bit from that coolly beautiful face and said impatiently, "Do get *up*, man. Finish what you're doing so we can get to business." Siveni lifted the raven that perched on her left hand, moving it to her shoulder.

He got up, still very confused. "Madam," he managed to croak, and then tried it again, rather embarrassed at making such a poor showing. "Lady, I *am* finished...."

"Of course you're not," she said, reaching out with that blazing spear and using its point to flick the book-roll up into her free hand. "Don't go lackwitted on me, Harran. It says right here: 'the hand of a brave and living man, the same to be offered up at the spell's end by the celebrant.'" She turned the scroll toward him, showing him the words.

Harran glanced down at the middle of the circle, where in the skeletal hand the mandrake still burned dully bright as a coal. But Siveni's voice brought his glance up again. "Not *that* hand, Harran!" She said, sounding annoyed now. "*That* one!"

And she pointed at the knife, which he had forgotten he

was clutching—and at his left hand, which clutched it.

Harran went as cold all over as he had in the graveyard. "Oh my G—"

"Goddess?" she said, as Harran caught himself as usual. "Sorry. That *is* the price written here. If the gateway you seek to open is to be fully opened—and even as I am not fully here yet, neither would the others be—the price must be paid." She looked at him coolly for several moments, then said with less asperity and some sadness, "I would have expected my priests to read better than *that*, Harran. . . . You *do* read?"

He gave her no answer for a moment. He thought of Sanctuary, and the Rankans, and the Beysib, and briefly, irrationally, of Shal. Then he stepped over to the center of the circle, and the hand. The bones of it were charred. The ring of base metal was a brass-scummed silver puddle on the floor. The mandrake glowed under his glance like a coal that had been breathed on.

He knelt down again and lifted his eyes briefly to the unmerciful loveliness before him; then squeezed his left hand until the blood flowed fresh, and with it pried the mandrake away from the hand's blackened bones.

In the hours that intervened until Harran got up again— a few minutes later—he came belatedly to understand a great deal; to understand Shal, and many of the other Stepsons, and some of the poor and sick he'd treated while still in the temple. There was no describing the pain of a maiming. It was a thing as without outward color as the burning of the mandrake; and even worse, more blinding, was the horror that came after. When Harran stood again, he had no left hand anymore. The stump's scorching pain throbbed and died away; Siveni's doing, probably. But the horror, he knew, would never go away. It would be fed anew, every day, by those who refused to look at the place where a hand had once been. Harran abruptly understood that payment is not later, is never later, but is always *now*. It would be *now* all his life.

He got to his feet and found Siveni, as she had said,

even more *there* than she had been before. He wasn't sure this was a good thing. None of this was working out as it should have. And there were other things peculiar as well. Where was the light coming from that filled the temple suddenly? Not from Siveni; she was striding around the place with the dissatisfied air of a housewife who comes home and has to deal with her husband's housekeeping—poking her spear into corners, frowning at the broken glass. "All this will be put to rights soon enough," she said. "After business. Harran, what are you scowling at?"

"Lady, the light—"

"Think, man," she said, not unkindly, as she stepped over to the circle, examining it, gently kicking a bit of her statue's rubble aside with one sandaled foot. "The spell retrieves timelessness as well as time. The light of yesterday, *and* tomorrow, is available to us both."

"But I—"

"You included the whole temple inside the outer circle, Harran, and you were in the temple. The spell worked on you too. How *not?* It retrieved my physicality—and your godhead...."

Harran stared at her. Siveni caught the look, and smiled.

Harran's heart came near to melting. She might be a hoyden, but she was a winning one.

"*Now* what are you—oh, godhead? Harran, my little priest, it's in your blood. This world isn't old enough for anyone to be removed by more than six degrees of blood from anyone else. Gods included. Haven't you people got far enough in mathematics to have realized that yet? I must do something about that." She reached up with her spear, and somehow, without getting any taller, or her spear getting any longer, knocked down a huge cobweb from a ceiling corner. "So you see as a god sees, for this short while. And permanently, after we do the spell again—"

"Again?" Harran said in shock, staring at his other hand.

"Of course. To open the way for the other Ilsig gods. It's only partially open now, for merely physical manifestation, as I said, and I doubt they've noticed. They're all off feasting beyond the Isles of the North again, getting plastered on Anen's latest batch, I shouldn't wonder." Siveni actually sniffed. "Not an honest day's work in the lot of them. But once I do the spell again, it'll open the gate wholly—and this place will be fit for gods to live in, as it never was even in the old days. Meanwhile"—she glanced around her—"meanwhile, before we do that, we have a few calls to pay. It would be abysmal tactics to give up the advantage of the ground, now we've got it...."

Harran said nothing. This entire encounter was misfiring. "We'll go down to Savankala's high-and-mighty temple," Siveni said, "and have a word with him. A temple bigger than my father's—!" She was indignant, but in a pleased way—like someone looking forward to a good fight. "And after that, we'll stop into Vashanka's place and just kill off that godchild he's got squirreled away in there. Then, afterward—this much talked-about Bey. Two pantheons in one night—save ourselves a lot of trouble later. Come on, Harran! The night's a-wasting, and we need to do the second Opening before dawn." And she swept across the barren inner precinct of the temple and smote the great brazen doors with her spear.

They promptly fell outward and down the steps with a sound that Harran reckoned would wake all Sanctuary—though he much doubted that anyone would be crazy enough to stir out of doors and see what made it. Down the stairs and down the Avenue of Temples they went, the immortal goddess and the mortal man, the goddess leading, peering about her with some interest, and the one-handed man behind, suffering more and more from terrible misgivings. No question that Siveni was all Harran had imagined, and more. It was the "more" that was bothering him. Siveni's wisdom was usually tempered by compassion. Where was that tonight? Had he done something wrong in the spell? Certainly Siveni was an impetuous goddess, resolute, swift when she decided to act. *But somehow I didn't expect this kind of action....*

Harran shivered. There was something wrong with him

too. He was seeing much more clearly than he should have been able to at this time of night. And he felt entirely too fit for a man who had gone digging in a graveyard, screwed himself blind, worked a sorcery, and lost a hand, all in one night. Was this more of what Siveni had mentioned as side effects of the sorcery, the uprising of his godhead in him? It was a distressing thought. Men should not be gods. That was what gods were for....

Harran glanced over at the goddess and found her aspect somewhat easier to bear than it had been before. She was looking over toward the Maze and Downwind in a way that suggested she had no trouble seeing through things. "This place is a mess," she said, turning as she went to look at Harran in reproof.

"We've had some hard times," Harran said, feeling a little defensive. "Wars, invasions..."

"We'll mend that soon enough," said Siveni. "Starting with invasions." They came to a stop in front of the great temple of Savankala. Siveni glared at it, drew herself up to her full height—which somehow managed to be both about three cubits, and about fifty—and shouted in a voice loud enough to rival the thunderstroke, "Savankala, *come out!*"

The echoes repeated the challenge all over the city. Siveni's brows knitted as long moments passed and there was no response. "Come forth, Savankala!" she shouted again. "Or I will tear this ill-built pile of stone down around your ears and reduce your statue to cobbles and stick my spear into an interesting place in the statue of your darling wife!"

There was a long, long silence—followed by a soft rumble of thunder that was more contemplative than threatening. "Siveni," the great voice came from the temple before them—or seemed to, "what do you want?"

"Best two falls out of three with you, Sungod," Siveni shouted triumphantly, as if she had already won the match. "And then you and yours get out of my father's city!"

"Your father. Yes. And where *is* your father, Siveni?"

Harran held quite still, trying to understand what was going on inside him. He hated the Rankan gods, he knew

149

he did. But the sheer slow weight of power stirring around Savankala's voice somehow terrified him much less than the slightly ragged defiance of Siveni's. And there, too, was a problem. *How am I hearing anything but perfection in a goddess's voice? Five minutes ago, ten, she was all beauty, all power, unsurpassable. Now—*

"My father!" Siveni cried. "You leave him out of this! I don't need his permission to use the thunderbolt! I can handle you by myself. I can handle the whole lot of you! For Vashanka Loudmouth is without a grown avatar. You're short a wargod, Father of the Rankans. I shall ruin your temples one by one, if you don't come out and face me, and meet the defeat you've got coming to you!"

The silence might have been long, but Harran was past noticing. *What has happened to my lady? In eternity she should be as she always has been—a calm power, not this cocksure violence. And anyway—why did I call her up, after all? Anger at Ranke and the Beysib? Really? Or something else?*

Love? I—

He dared take that thought no further. Yet, if what she had said to him was true, then he was himself in the process of becoming a god. The thought gave him a moment's wild jubilation. If he could dissuade her from this silliness and get her to do the spell the second time, it would be forever. The very thought of eternity spent in company with this blasting beauty, this wild, daring power—

The memory of soft laughter and of Ischade's voice gently mocking a man who did not know his own heart brought Harran back to his senses, hard. Impulse, impetuousness—that had brought him to this spot, this night, just as it had brought him to the Stepsons long ago. And impulse was blind. Though his body was screaming at its transformation at being dragged into godhead, his mind was now seeing more clearly. He had described the situation to Ischade even better than he knew. Siveni the impetuous, the lightning-swift, had accepted time and its bitterness more thoroughly than any of the other gods. Here in the mortal world, where time was at its strongest, so was her bitterness and rage. She would have no wisdom, no time, no love for him here.

And elsewhere—

Siveni was a maiden-goddess. Elsewhere would not work either.

"Come out!" Siveni was shouting into Savankala's silence. "Coward god, come out and fight me, or I will smite your temple to rubble, and kill every Rankan in this city! Does that mean nothing; are your worshippers so little to you?"

"I hear your challenge," he heard Savankala saying. "Do you not understand that I may not honor it? Destiny has determined that these conflicts among us will be settled by mortals, not by gods. Are you not at all afraid of destiny—of the Power of Many Names that sits in darkness above the houses of all the gods, Rankan and Ilsig and Beysib alike? Will you defy that power?"

"Yes!"

"That is sad. You as a goddess, and supposedly a wise one, should know that you cannot. . . ."

"Wisdom! Wisdom has gotten me nowhere!"

"Yes," Savankala remarked drily, "I can see that. . . ."

Harran was trapped in a terrible serenity, a clarity that refused to admit fear. He knew he would have to sacrifice that clarity shortly. But in the meantime Savankala and Siveni sounded exactly like any two people arguing in the Bazaar, and Harran could tell that Savankala was stalling for time, waiting for Harran to do something. The message had been clear enough. *These conflicts among us will be settled by mortals. . . .*

His hand, or the loss of it, had taught him well and quickly. No hatred was worth pain—not so much as a cut finger's worth. And certainly no hatred was worth death. Not his hatred . . . not Siveni's.

"Then, hide in your hole, old god," Siveni said bitterly. "There's no honor in winning this way, but I can put honor aside for winning's sake. Your temple first. Then your precious people."

She raised her spear, and lightnings wreathed the spearhead.

"No," someone said behind her.

She turned in amazement, stared at him. Harran stared back as best he could, equally astonished that he had spoken and that those ferocious gray eyes didn't blast him down where he stood. *What is she staring at?* he thought, and suspected the answer—while at the same time refusing to think of it. The less memory of his own almost-godhood he carried away with him into either life or death, the better. "Goddess," Harran said, "You are my own good lady, but I tell you that if you move against Sanctuary's *people*, I'll stop you."

Siveni swung on him. "With what?" she cried, enraged, and swung the spear at him. Harran had no idea what to do. Against the first blow he raised the maimed arm, and the lightnings went crackling away around him to strike the paving-stones. But the second blow and the third came immediately, and then more, a flurry of blows that swiftly beat down Harran's feeble guard. And after them came the bolt that struck him to the street—a blow enough like death to be mistaken for it. Harran's last thought as he went down burned and blinded, was that she would have been something to see with a sword. Then thought departed from him, and his soul fled far away.

Somewhere in Sanctuary, a dog howled.

And an odd dark shape that had skulked along through the shadows behind the man and the goddess leapt shrieking out of those shadows, and full onto Siveni.

The sound of crashing in the street was what woke Harran finally. A hellish sound it was, enough to wake the dead, as he certainly reckoned himself; stones cracking, lightning frying the air, angry cries—and a hoarse voice he knew. In that moment, before he managed to open his eyes, it became perfectly plain who trailed him here from the Stepsons' barracks; what dark form had slipped away from him as he drew the circle around Siveni's temple, and had been trapped within the spell—so that it had worked on her as well.

Harran raised himself up from the stones to see the image that, ever after, would make him turn away from companions or leave crowded rooms when he thought of it.

There was the goddess in her radiant robes—but those robes had dirt on them, from falls she had taken in the street; and four hands were struggling on the haft of her spear. Even as Harran looked up, the wiry shape wrestling with Siveni wrenched the spear out of her grasp and threw it clattering down the Avenue of Temples, spraying random lightning bolts around it. Then Mriga sprang on Siveni again, all skinny arms and legs as always—but with something added: a frightening, quick grace about her movements. *Purpose,* Harran thought in fascination and shock. *She knows what she's doing!* And he smiled . . . seeing another aspect of the spell that he might have suspected if he were an artiste rather than merely competent. The spell infallibly retrieved what was lost . . . even lost wits.

The goddess and the mortal girl rolled on the ground together, and there was little difference between them. They both shone, blazing lightlessly with rage and godhead. The goddess had more experience fighting, perhaps, but Mriga had the advantage of a strength not only divine but insane. And there might be other advantages to a life's worth of insanity as well. Mriga's absorption of godhead would not be hampered by ideas about gods, or about mortals not being gods. She took what power came to her, and used it, uncaring. She was using it now; she had Siveni pinned. Their struggle brought her around to where she suddenly saw Harran looking at her. That look *did* strike him like lightning, though he would not have traded the pain of it for anything. Mriga *saw* him. And in four quick, economical gestures, she stripped Siveni's bright helm off, flung it clanging down the avenue, and then took hold of Siveni's head by the long dark hair and whacked it hard against the stones. Siveni went limp.

He never *had* needed to show her anything more than once. . . .

The street fell blessedly silent. Harran sat up on the stones—it was the best he could manage at the moment; his night was catching up to him. More than just his night. For there was Mriga, limping over to him, still halt as before—but there was a kind of grace even to that, now. He wanted to hide his face. But he was still enough of a god not to.

"Harran," she said in the soft husky voice that he had never heard do anything but grunt.

Harran was still mortal enough not to be able to think of a thing to say.

"I want to stay like this," she said. "I'll have to go back with her before dawn, if the change is to take."

"But—it was only supposed to be temporary—"

"For an ordinary mortal, I suppose so. But I'm not ordinary. It will take for me." She smiled at him with a merry serenity that made Harran's heart ache; for it was very like what he had expected, dreamed of, from Siveni. "If you approve, that is. . . ."

"Approve?!" He stared at her—at Her, rather; there was no doubt of it anymore. Moment by moment she was growing more divine, and looking at her hurt his eyes as even Siveni had only at the beginning. "What in the worlds do you need my approval for?!"

Mriga looked at him with somber pleasure. "You are my love," she said, "and my good lord."

"*Good*—" He would have sickened with the irony, had the terrible, growing glory of her presence not made such a response impossible. "I *used* you—"

"You fed me," Mriga said. "You took care of me. I came to love you. The rest didn't matter then; and it doesn't now. If I loved you as a mortal—how should I stop as a goddess?"

"You're still crazy!" Harran cried, almost in despair.

"It would probably look that way," said Mriga, "to those who didn't know the truth. You know better."

"Mriga, for pity's sake, listen to me! I took advantage of you, again and again! I used a *goddess*—"

She reached out, very slowly, and touched his face; then took the hand back again. "As for that business," she said, "I alone shall judge the result. I alone am qualified. If you've done evil . . . then you've also paid. Payment is now, is it not? Would you believe you've spent five years paying for what you were doing during those five years? Or would you put it down to a new goddess's craziness?"

"Time . . ." Harran whispered.

"It has an inside and an outside," Mriga said. "Outside is when you love. Inside is everything else. Don't ask me more." She looked up at the paling sky. "Help me with poor Siveni."

Between the two of them they got the goddess sitting up again. She was in a sorry state; Mriga brushed at her rather apologetically. "She hurt you," Mriga said. "If I hadn't been crazy already, I would have gone that way."

After a few moments ministration, the gray eyes opened and looked at Harran and Mriga with painful admiration for them both. One of the fierce eyes was blackened, and Siveni had a bump rising where Mriga had acquainted her with the cobbles. "The disadvantage of physicality," she said. "I don't think I care for it." She glanced at Mriga, looking very chastened. "Not even my father ever did *that* to me. I think we're going to be friends."

"More than that," Mriga said, serenely merry. Harran found himself wondering very briefly about some old business . . . about the old Mriga's love for edged things, and her strength, and her skill with her hands . . . and her gray eyes. Those eyes met his, and Mriga nodded. "She'd lost some attributes into time," Mriga said. "But I held them for her. She'll get them back from me . . . and lend me a few others. We'll do well enough between us."

The three of them got up together, helping one another. "Harran—" Siveni said.

He looked at her tired, wounded radiance, and for the first time really saw her, without his own ideas about her getting in the way. She could not apologize; apology wasn't her way. She just stood there like some rough, winning child, a troublemaker at the end of yet another scrap. "It's all right," he said. "Go home."

She smiled. The smile was almost as lovely as Mriga's.

"We will," Mriga said. "There's a place where gods can go when they need a rest. That's where we'll be. But one thing remains." She reached out and laid her head on the burned place where Harran's hand had been . . . then slowly leaned in and touched her lips to his.

Somewhere in the eternity that followed, he noticed that her left hand seemed to be missing.

When the dazzle unknotted itself from around him, they were gone. He stood alone in false dawn in the Avenue of Temples, looking down toward where a pair of twisted brass doors lay in the middle of the street. He wondered while he stood there whether some years from now there might be a small new temple in Sanctuary . . . raised for an addition to the Ilsig pantheon; a mad goddess, a maimed and crippled goddess, fond of knives, and possessing a peculiar crazed wisdom that began and ended in love. A goddess who right now had only two worshippers; her single priest, and a dog. . . .

Harran stood there wondering—then started at a sudden touch. His left hand—the hand he hadn't had, and now had—a woman's hand—reached up without his willing it to touch his face.

Payment is now. . . .

Harran bowed ever so briefly to Ils's temple: and with grudging respect, to Savankala's—and went on home.

Elsewhere in the false dawn, a soft, rough cry from the windowsill attracted the attention of a dark-clad woman in a room scattered with a mad profusion of treasures and rich stuffs. Ischade leisurely went to the window, gazed with a slow smile at the silvery raven that stood there, watching her out of eyes of gray . . . and silently considering both messenger and message, took it up on her arm and went to find it something to eat. . . .

WITCHING HOUR

C. J. Cherryh

The room was fine wood and river stone with brocade hangings, and opened onto an entry hall with a winding stair. Fire danced in the marble fireplace and at the tips of a score of white wax candles, and off the gold cups and fine pewter platters and plates; while Moria, at dinner in her hall, gave it all mistrusting glances, not unlike the look she paid her brother at his end of their long table—for none of Moria's life stayed stable. The gold was a dream in which she moved and lived, irony for a thief: she felt constantly she should snatch the plates and run, but there was nowhere to run to and the gold was hers, the house was hers, far too great a possession: she could no longer run at all, and this condition filled her heart with panic. Her brother's face was a dream of a different kind across the candle glow—at one moment familiar; at another, when he shifted slightly or the

159

light fell unkindly on the scars—she felt another wrench of panic, perceiving another thing which she had loved and which had tangled her up like nightmare and held her bound.

One part of her would have run screaming and naked from this place.

"Mistress." A servant poured straw-colored wine into her cup and grinned a gap-toothed grin that shattered other illusions, for the dress was brocade and finest linen, if rumpled from neglect, the hair barbered and immaculate; but the missing teeth, the broken nose, the voice with its Downwind twang—beggars and thieves waited on them. They were clean and fleasless and without lice—she was adamant on that, but on no other thing had she authority with them, except they did their job and did not pilfer.

The Owner saw to that.

There was a shout, a shriek of gutter language from the stairs: Mor-am leaped up and shouted back into the hall in terms the Downwind understood, and her soul shrank at this small sign of fracture. "Out," she said to the servant. And when the servant lingered in his dull-witted way: "*Out, fool!*"

The servant put it together and scuttled out as Mor-am resumed his chair and picked up his wine-cup. His hand shook. The tic was back at the corner of his burn-scarred mouth, and the cup trembled on its way and spilled straw-colored wine. He glowered after he had drunk, and the tic diminished to a small shudder. "Won't learn," he said, plaintive as a child.

A beggar watched the house, outside. Was always there, a huddle of rags; and Mor-am had bad dreams, waked shrieking night after night.

"Won't learn," he muttered, and poured himself more wine with a knife-scarred hand that rattled the wine bottle against the cup rim.

"Don't."

"Don't what?" He set the bottle down and picked up the cup, leaving beads of wine on the table surface, spilling more on the way to his mouth.

"I went out today." She made a desperate attempt to fill the silence, the silence of long hours imprisoned in this house. "I bought a ham, some dates—Shiey says she knows this way to cook it with honey—"

"Got no lousy cook, big house, we got a one-handed thief for cook—"

"Shiey *was* a cook."

"—if she'd done either decent she'd go right-handed. Where'd She *find* that sow?"

"Quiet!" Moria flinched and cast a glance toward the stairs. They *listened,* she knew they listened, every servant in the house, the beggar by the gates. "For Ils's sake, quiet—"

"Swear by Ils now, do we? Do us any good, you think?"

"Shut *up!*"

"Run, why don't you? Why don't you get out of here? You—"

A door came open in the hall, just—opened, with a gust of outside wind that stirred the candles.

"O gods," Moria said, and swung her chair about with a scrape of wood on stone, another from Mor-am, a ringing impact of an overset cup that rolled across the floor.

But it was *Haught* stood in the hallway door, not *Her,* but only Haught, standing there with that doe-soft look in his eyes, that set to his well-formed mouth that betokened some vague satisfaction. A malicious child's satisfaction in startling them; a malicious child's innocence: she hoped it was nothing darker. The door closed. No servant was in evidence.

"New t-trick," Mor-am said. The tic had come back. The cup lay on the floor between them, with its scatter of straw-hued wine.

"I have a few," Haught said, walking to the side of the door where the cups resided on a table. He was well-dressed, was Haught, like themselves; wore a russet tunic and black cloak, fine boots, and a sword like a gentleman. He brought a cup to the table and wine poured with a whisper into the gold cup. He lifted it and drank.

"Well?" said Mor-am. "Well, do you just walk in and serve yourself?"

"No." There was always quiet in Haught. Always the downward glance, the bowed head: ex-slave. Moria remembered scars on his back and elsewhere, remembered other things, nights huddled beside a rough brick fireplace; bundled together beneath rough blankets; convulsed together in the only love there had been once. This too had changed. "She wants you to do that thing," Haught said, speaking to Mor-am. "Tonight." Sleight of hand produced a tiny packet and flung it to the table by the wine bottle.

"Tonight. . . . For Shalpa's sweet sake—"

"You'll find a way." Haught's eyes darted a quick, shy glance Mor-am's way, Moria's next, and flickered away again, somehow floorward: in such small ways he remained uncatchable. "It's very good, the wine."

"Damn you," Mor-am said with a tremor of his mouth. "Damn—"

"Hush," Moria said, "hush, Mor-am, don't." And to Haught: "There's food left—" It was reflex; there were times they had been hungry, she and Haught. They were not now, and she put on weight. She had drunk herself stupid then; and he had loved her when she had not loved herself. Now she was wise and sober and getting fat; and scared. "Won't you stay awhile?"

—Thinking of herself alone once Mor-am went out; and terrified; and wanting him this night (the servants she did not touch—her authority was scant enough; and they were crude). But Haught gave her that shy, cold smile that allied him with Her and ran his finger round the rim of the cup, never quite looking up.

"No," he said. He turned and walked away, into the dark hall. The door opened for him, swirling the dark cloak and whipping the candles into shadow.

"G-got to go," Mor-am said distractedly, "got to find my cloak, got to get Ero to go with me—gods, gods—"

The door closed, and sent the candles into fits.

"Ero!" Mor-am yelled.

Moria stood with her arms wrapped about herself, staring at nothing in particular.

It was another thing transmuted, like some malicious alchemy that left her strangling in wealth and utterly bereft. They lived uptown now, in Her house. And Haught was Hers too, like that dead man—Stilcho was his name—who shared Her bed—she was sure it was so. Perhaps Haught did, somehow and sorcerously immune to the curse attributed to Her. Mradhon Vis she had not seen since the morning he walked away. Perhaps Vis was dead. Perhaps the thing he feared most in all the world had happened and he had met Her in one of Her less generous moments.

"Ero!" Mor-am yelled, summoning his bodyguard, a thief of higher class.

The fire seemed inadequate, like the gold and the illusions that had become insane reality.

There was little traffic on the uptown street—the watcher at the gate, no more than that; and Haught walked the shadows, not alone from the habit of going unnoticed, but because in Sanctuary by night not to be noticed was always best; and in Sanctuary of late it was decidedly best. The houses here had barred windows, protecting Rankan nobles against unRankan pilferage, burglary, rapine, occasional murder at the hand of some startled thief; but nowadays there were other, political, visitors, stealthy in approach, leaving bloody results as public as might be.

It had begun with the hawkmasks and the Stepsons; with beggars and hawkmasks; priests and priests; and gods; and wizards; and nowadays murder crept uptown in small bands, to prove the cleverness of some small faction in reaching the unreachable; and striking the unstrikable; thus fomenting terror in the streets and convincing the terrorized that to join in bands was best, so that nowadays one went in Sanctuary with a mental map not alone of streets but of zones of allegiance and control, and planned to avoid certain places in certain sequences, not to be seen passing safely through a rival's territory.

Haught ignored most lines—by night. There were some foolhardy enough to touch him. Not many. He was accustomed to fear, and, truth, he felt less fear nowadays than previously. He was accustomed to horrors and that stood him in good stead.

He had been prenticed once, up by Wizardwall; and his last master had been gentle, for one of Wizardwall.

"Why do you stay?" his present teacher asked.

"Teach me," he had said that morning, with a yearning in him only the dance had halfway filled: he showed her the little magic that he had remembered. And she had smiled, had Ischade of no country at all: smiled in a very awful way. "Magus," she had said, "would you be?"

He had loved Moria at that time. Moria had been gentle with him when few had been. And he had thought (he tormented himself with the dread that it was not his thought at all, such were Ischade's powers) that it was well to please the witch, for Moria's sake. So he would protect Moria and himself: to be allied with power was safety. Experience had taught him that.

But deep in his heart he had seen that Ischade was necromant, not hieromant; that the lighting of candles and the stirring of winds were only tricks to her.

And he had breathed the wind and sensed the power, and he was snared for reasons that had nothing at all to do with love or gratitude, for he was Nisi and witchery was in his blood.

Tonight he walked the streets and crossed lines and no one dared touch him. And something cramped in him for years spread wings (but they were dark).

He might have lived in the uptown house.

But he took the other way.

The sound of the river was very close here, where the old stones thrust up through newly trampled brush. Squith shivered, blinked, caught something darker than the night itself in this place unequally posed between two houses on the river.

"Squith," a woman said.

He turned, his back to an upthrust stone.

"No respect?" she asked.

He took his hand from the stone as if he had remembered a serpent coiled thereby. Vashanka's. All these stones were; and he would not be here by any choice of his.

"Moruth—Moruth couldn't come. 'S got a c-cold."

"*Has* he?" The woman moved forward out of the dark, dark-robed, her face dusky and all but invisible in the overhang of sickly trees. "I might cure him."

Squith tumbled to his knees and shook his head; his bowels had gone to water. "S-sent me, he did. Respectful, he is. Squith, he says, Squith, you goes and tells the lady—"

"—What?"

"Me lord does what you wants."

"He may survive his cold. It's *tonight*, beggar."

"I go tell him, go tell him." Squith made it a litany, bobbed and held his gut and sucked wind past his snaggled row of teeth. He had a view of a cloak-hem, of brush; he kept it that way.

"Go."

He scrambled up, scrabbling past thorns. One tore his cheek, raked his sightless eye. He fled.

Ischade watched him, and forbore spells that would have urged him on his way. Roxane was at home tonight, not so far away. Thorns regrew. Snakes infested the place. Burned patches repaired themselves with preternatural speed.

A beggar sped toward the beggar-king Moruth. A black bird had landed in Downwind, on a certain sill. And Squith came. Moruth had a cold, and languished in mortal cowardice.

But Moruth had met something one night in a Downwind alleyway that mightily convinced him where his interests lay.

"Go to Roxane," she had whispered in Moruth's unwashed ear. "Go to Yorl, to whatever wizard you choose. I'll know. Or you can promise beggars they'll be safe on the streets again. At least from me. From other things, perhaps. Or at worst they'll be avenged. When a bird lights on your sill—come to Vashanka's altar on the Foal. You know the place."

A nod of a shaggy head. The beggar-king knew, and babbled oaths of compliancy.

Wings fluttered nearby. She glanced up where the dead branches overhead gave rest to other shadows, inky as her robes. A messenger returned.

It was a familiar room, one they had used before and had rather not use again; but it was Vis they had, and Straton operated under certain economies these days—not to let Vis see too much; and not to let Vis be seen.

Vis glared at him, between two Stepsons—real ones— who had brought him to this attic unbruised. So one reckoned. Vis had a ruffled look—smallish and wide-shouldered and dark, and with a look in those dark eyes under that shag of hair that said he had as lief kill as talk to them.

That was well enough. Straton had killed a few of Vis's sort, in this room, after they had been useful. Vis surely had the measure of him and of this place. There was outrage in that stare and precious little hope.

"You had news," Strat said. "I trust you—that it's worth both our time."

"Damn you. I came to *you*. I sent for *you*—I thought I could trust you—if they told you any different—"

"News," Strat said. Outside, on the stairs, a board creaked. But that was the watch he had passed. He sat down in the single chair at the single table which, like the ropes on the wooden wall, had their uses. Mradhon Vis stood there between two guards, all disarranged—they would have found a knife on him, at least; maybe a cord; seldom a penny, though Vis sold himself to at least two sides. Jubal's. Theirs. Gods knew who else. Hence the guard. Hence the forced meetings. The streets were quiet, too quiet. There had been nothing on the bridge but one one-eyed, halfwit beggar. Nothing stirring anywhere on the street outside.

"Get them out of here," Vis said.

"You want to talk this over, or just talk, Vis? You got me here. I've got all night. So have they."

Vis thought that over. So he had run his bluff and made his point. But he was not stupid; and knew where his remaining chances lay. "I get paid for this."

"One way or the other."

"There's rumor out . . . got something coming down."

"What?"

"Not sure." Vis came closer and began to lean on the table. Demas moved to stop him. Strat held up his hand and Vis stayed unmolested. "Something—I don't know what. Nisi squads—they've got a big one brewing. Heard talk about something down at the harbor. Uptown at the same time."

"What's your source?"

"I don't tell that."

"Huh." Strat rocked the chair back, foot braced. "That so?"

"Word's out they've got help. Understand?"

"The Nisi witch?"

There was long silence. Vis stayed where he was. Sweat was on his brow.

"Something got your tongue?"

"I'm Nisi, dammit. She can *smell*—"

"Roxane might help you. Might not. I don't think I'd shelter with *that* one, Vis."

"Word's out she's looking for revenge. The harbor— some move there. *That's* what I heard. Heard someone's going to move there, hit the Beysibs; maybe warehouses. Death squads. I don't know whose. But I know who pays them."

Strat let the chair thump down. "Don't leave town, Vis."

"Dammit, you're going to get me killed—you know what they'll do, with you bringing me in here?"

"You go on making your reports. If anything comes down and we don't find out—understand? Understand, Vis?"

Vis backed away.

"Let him go," Strat said. "Pay him. Well. Let *him* figure how to get himself clear. Tomorrow. Whenever. When I'm clear. When this is proved one way or the other."

"You want a partner?" Demas asked.

Strat shook his head and gathered himself to his feet. "We've got difficulties. Stay here. Vis, mind you remember who pays you *most*. You want more—you tell us . . . right?"

Vis gave him a sullen look—not greedy, no. It was an invitation to a final meeting—more demands. And Vis knew it.

"I'll see to it," Strat said to Demas. "I don't think anything will happen here. Just keep him off the streets." He took a cloak from the peg by the door, nondescript as other clothes they kept here. The horse he rode was the bay, not nondescript, but it would serve.

"You're going to Her."

He heard the upper-case. Turned and looked at Vis, who stood there staring at him.

"You met the one she's got?" Vis asked. "She's finally got a lover she can't kill. Fish-cold, likely. But she's not that particular."

Strat's face was very calm. He kept it that way. He thought of killing Vis. Or passing an order. But there was a craziness in the Nisi traitor. He had seen a man look like that who shortly after set himself on fire. "Be patient with him," he said. "*Don't* kill him." Because it was the worst thing he could think of for a man with such a look.

He left then, opened the door onto the dark stinking stairs and shut it behind.

The footsteps thumped away below, multiplied; and Mradhon Vis stood there in a gray nowhere. Tired. Cold, when the room was far too close for cold.

"Sit down," one said.

He started to take the chair. A foot preempted it. The other Stepson leaned on the table. It left him the floor.

He went over to the corner, liking that at his back more than empty air, braced his shoulders, and slid down against the wall. So they all sat and waited. He did not stare at them, not caring to provoke them, recalling that he had tried that with their chief and recalling why he tried—a dim rage of sympathy for a fellow fool.

She. Ischade. It took no guesswork where the Stepsons would look for help when Roxane was on the move. Where *that* one would look for help, where his thoughts bent. He had kept a watch on Straton—for the pay he got from other sources; and he knew. That was a man infatuated with death, with beating it day by day. He recalled it in himself; until the day he had learned death's infatuation with *him*—and that put a whole different complexion on matters.

Fool, O Whoreson. Fool.

Sanctuary's enemies ringed it round and, with the border northward cracking, Ranke went suicidal as the rest. The very air stank—autumn fogs and smokes; the fevered river-wind found its way through streets and windows, sweet with corruption; and there was no sleep these nights. There was nowhere to go. Part of Nisibis had slipped through the wizards' hands; but Nisi gold, Nisi training still funded death squads throughout Ranke—not least among their targets were Nisi rebels like himself. It was desert folk moving in Carronne; Ilsigi in Sanctuary port; gods knew where the Beysib came from, or what *really* sent them.

He knew too much; and dreamed of nights, same as the Stepson dreamed: the Stepson's cause was tottering and his own was dead. And the river-wind got everywhere in Sanctuary, sickly with corruption, sweet with seduction; and promised—promised—

He had tried, at least. That was the most unselfish thing he had done in half a year. But no one could save a fool.

There were houses in the uptown more ornate than their own. This was one, with white marble floors and Carronnese carpets and gilt furnishings; a fat fluffy dog of the same white and gold that yapped at them until a servant scooped it up. And Mor-am thought hate at the useless, well-fed thing, hate at the servant, hate at the long-nosed fat Rankan noble who came waddling from his hall to see what had gotten past his gate.

"I've got guests"—the noble wheezed (Siphinos was his name)—"guests, you understand. . . . "

Mor-am sucked air and stood taller, with a drawing of one eye, while in the corner of the good one he spied Ero spying out the other hall beyond the archway. "I tell Her that?"

"Out." Siphinos waved at the servants, fluttering Mor-am toward a door, the accounts room: they had been there the last time. Siphinos closed the door himself. Ero stayed outside.

"You were to come after midnight—only after midnight—"

Mor-am held up the packet; and the pig's face and the pig's eyes suddenly had sobriety and a furious red-cheeked dignity, amid all his jowls. Mor-am gave him back his own one-eyed stare and handed it over, watched him examine the seal.

"It'll be coming here," Mor-am said. "That's the word comes with this. They got their eye on you. Death squads move uptown tonight. You hear me, man?"

"Whose? When?" The flush went hectic. A sweat glistened on jowls and brow. "Give me names. Isn't that what we pay you—"

"Word for Torchholder this time. Get the word upstairs. Tell him—look out his window tonight. Tell him—" he tried to recall precisely the words he had been primed with, that Haught had told him a dozen days ago—"tell him he'll understand then what the help we give is worth."

No shrieking, no cursing, not the least cracking of the fat man's fury. *Ilsigi dog,* the look said, wishing him to heel. And fearing the bite he had.

"He knows," Mor-am said, neat and measured, and gods, gods, let the tic stay still. "He can tell the prince-g-governor—" Damn the twisting of his face, the drawing of his mouth. "He'll know where his safety is. He'll pay the cost, whatever we ask. We got our means. Tell Kittycat look out his window too."

Alarms were on their way, plainclothes and moving with deliberation, not panic, word back to the command post, to various places and offices. And Straton rode alone now— imprudence, perhaps; but a full troop of Stepsons clattering up the riverside slow or fast, plainclothes or not—drew too much attention. He slouched like a drunk, kept the bay to an amble, and sweated the entire last block. He had sent his three companions off the other way. Foalside was a mixed kind of street, wide near the bridge and well-used; but higher up the Foal, buildings crowded close and the street became a rough track with only the remnant of ancient stones for pavings. Trees grew untended on the Foalside in a widening lower terrace by the road. Weeds crowded close on that margin. And crouched like some lurking aged beast— a cottage occupied the upper terrace, the northern house on that black river, a tiny place like the southern one—both of which had been singed, both of which had been swept over with fire enough to blacken the brush and kill the trees that grew hereabouts. But nowadays neither showed traces of burning; and both stood just as before, surrounded with brush, and smelling that wet, old smell of places long un- tended in the dark, in the starlight, with old trees lifting autumn (unscarred) branches at the sky.

Ischade maintained a fence and hedge: her house clung to its strip of river terrace and faced beyond its yard and gates a row of warehouses, at a little respectful distance from the ordinary world, distance which the wise re- spected—one of those places in every town, Strat thought, which had that dilapidated look of trouble and contagious bad luck.

Ischade's territory. He had been in it for the length of the solitary ride. And no squad he knew of dared that little strip of street or the warehouses near it.

Strat slid down, looped the reins over the fence, and opened the ridiculous low gate. There were weeds, gods,

everywhere. In so short a time. She grew nightshade like
flowers.

His pulse quickened and his mouth went dry as he came
up to the paint-peeled door and reached out to knock, half-
expecting it to do the thing it had done before and swing
open.

It opened, without his knock, without a sound on the
other side. And he was facing not Ischade but the freedman
Haught, Nisi-complexioned and dressed far too well and
standing there as if he owned the room.

"Where is she?" Strat asked, vexed.

"I don't give out her business."

Something warned him—about that line that was the
threshold. On the brink of hasty invasion, of drawing his
sword and prying it out of pretty-lad, alarms went off. He
stood slouched, hands on hips. "Stilcho here?"—as if that
were what he had come for. He let his eyes focus however
briefly on the dim room beyond. He remembered that place,
that it always had more size than seemed right. And there
was no sign of the man.

"No," Haught said.

The pulse was up again. Strat looked the ex-slave in the
eyes—remarkable: Haught never flinched, and had before.
Rage ticked away, a twitching of his mouth; gods, that he
was reduced to this schoolboy standoff, eye to eye with a
jealous slave who was—dangerous. No wilt, no bluster.
Just a cold steady stare, Nisi and Rankan. And he thought
of Wizardwall, and things that he had seen.

"Try the river," Haught said. "It's a short walk. You
won't need the horse. You're late."

The door shut, with no hand on it.

He caught his breath, swore, looked back where his horse
stood and snorted in the dark.

It was not a place for horses, down on Foalside, beyond
the house, where the brush grew thick along the shore.

Fool, something said to him. But he cursed the voice
and went.

• • •

"Siphinos's son." Molin Torchholder cast a misgiving look at the door and shrugged on his robe with the sense of something gone badly amiss. He waved a hand at the servant who fussed up with slippers while another stirred up the fire. "Move. *Move.* Let the lad in."

"Reverence, the guards—"

"Hang the guards—"

"—want to search the boy, but being nobility—"

"Send him in. Alone."

"Reverence—"

"Less reverence and more obedience. Would you?" Molin drew his lips to a fine-humored line that betokened storms. The servant gulped and fled doorward, returned, and dropped the slippers face-about for him.

"Alone!"

"Reverence," the flunky breathed, and sped.

Molin worked one slipper on and the other, fought off the interventions of the other servant who drew near to fuss with his robe. Looked up suddenly as the fellow desisted. "Liso."

"Reverence." Siphinos's lanky blond son made a bow, all breathless, all courtesies. "Apologies—"

"It should be good, lad. I trust it is."

"It isn't. I mean, not—good." The boy's teeth began to chatter. "I ran—" He raked at his strawthatch hair. "Had my father's guard with me—"

"Can you get to it, lad?"

The boy caught his breath and, it seemed, his wits. "The witch—ours; she says—"

Straton shoved the brush aside, more and more regretting this imprudence. He was not ordinarily a fool. Such was his foolishness at the moment, he reckoned, that he was not even capable of knowing for sure he was a fool; and that alarmed him. But the Nisi witch on the prod—that sent alarms of its own crawling up his back.

You're late, the slave had said—as if Ischade had put it all together long before; as she would if that kind of alarm was ringing, audible to mages, wizards, and those wizardry had set its mark on—gods, that he tangled himself in the like, that he picked Roxane for an enemy or the vampire for an ally. He could not even remember clearly which way around it had been; except Ischade had agreed in Sync's case when there had been no other way, and in doing that, marked every Stepson her ally and Roxane's enemy.

Fool. He heard Crit's voice echoing in his mind.

Vis *knew.* The jolt of that caught up with his befogged wits and he hesitated on the narrow path, hanging by one hand to a shallow-rooted bit of brush, with one foot over black water and empty space. Vis knew where he was going.

Damn.

Down the river, beyond the lights of the bridge, a flash of lightnings showed, and, gods knew, with Roxane stirred up, that lightning-flash set a panic in him. He hauled himself back to balance on the narrow path and kept moving.

Faster and faster. No way to go now but straight on. His messengers were dispersed, alerting what wizard-help they had; one had headed the Prince-Governor's direction, if he got that far. There was no calling back anyone for re-thinking.

Another lightning-flash. A sudden wind swept down the black, light-rimmed chasm of the river, stirring the trees on the terraced shore. Brush cracked beneath his step on the eroded brink, beneath the sickly trees—she would know his presence, Ischade would; she had her ways. Had said once that she would know when she was needed, which intimation he had seized on with the misery and hope of all fools: so he was here, trusting a witch no sensible man would have sought in the first place—ignoring common sense and rules—gods, Crit—Crit would swear him to hell and back—What was wrong with him?

He feared he knew.

He came on an ancient stone, thrust away from it to fight the incline of the path. Hard-breathing, he climbed the treacherous slope and crested the top of it.

And if she had been an enemy, a simple shove could

have pitched him backward into the Foal. He caught his balance and she gave him room there among the autumn-dead trees, on the river-verge with its strange stones. The night went away for him. There was her face, what she wanted, what she might say, nothing else.

"All sorts of birds," she said, "before this storm."

It made no sense to him; and did. "Roxane—" he said. "Word's out she's on the move—"

"Yes," she said. Her face met the starlight within the confines of her hood. There was quiet in her, perilous quiet, and every hair on him stirred with the static in the air. "Come." She took his hand and drew him upslope, following the path. "The wind's getting up—"

"Not your doing—"

"No. Not mine."

"Vis—" He caught his balance against a waist-high stone, recognized where he was, and jerked his hand off it. "Gods—"

"Careful of invocations." She caught his arm to pull him further and he stopped, involuntarily face-to-face with her in the starlight: he saw no detail beneath the shadow of her hood, but only a slantwise hint of mouth and chin; but he felt the stare, felt the smooth cool touch of her fingers slide to his hand. "That's been days gathering. Are you deaf to it?"

"Deaf to what?"

"The storm. The storm that's coming. . . . The harbor, man. What if some great storm should break the seawall, drive those hulking Beysib ships one against the others, stave their timbers, sink them down—Sanctuary'd *have* no harbor. Nothing but a sandbar founded on rotting hulks. And where'd Sanctuary be then?—Death squads, riots, none of these things would matter then. The war's no longer at Wizardwall—no longer leagues away. There are ways to *use* the power for more than closing doors."

He was walking. She had him by the arm and the voice compelled, wove spells, though brush raked his face and he forgot to fend it off.

"I've *interests* here in Sanctuary," said Ischade. "It's been long since I had interests. I like it as it is."

Fool, said Crit's voice at the dim, dim, back of his mind, past hers and the rising sough of wind.

"You didn't have to hire me," she said. "Not for Roxane. That matter's *free.*"

"I can get help." He recalled his wits and his purpose. "Get a message down there, move those ships to open water—"

"She'd eat you alive, Stepson. There's one she won't. One she can't touch. Make a little haste. You're late. Where did you go? The house?"

"The house— *When*—sent for me? *Is Vis yours?*"

"He has bad dreams."

He blinked. Balked. She drew him on. "Damn," he muttered, "could have had a horse—it's the other damn side of the bridge— We've got to pass under the checkpoint, dammit—"

"They won't notice. They never do."

They walked, walked, and the wind whipped the trees to a roar. Thunder boomed. Late, she had said; waiting on him, and late—

"For what?" he asked, out of breath. "For what—waiting on me?"

"I might have used Vis. But I don't trust him any longer— at my back. There'll be snakes. I trust you're up to snakes—"

The brush opened out on the terrace edge that became a rubble slope. The bridge was ahead, the few shielded lights by the bridgehead still aglow on the Sanctuary side of the Foal. Rocks turned, clashed beneath hastening steps— slipped and rattled.

They'll not see us. They never do—

He was out of breath now. He was not sure about Ischade, whose hand held his and urged him faster, faster, while the wind whipped at her cloak and threw his hair into his eyes.

"Damn, we're too late—"

"Hush." Nails bit into his hand. They passed beneath the

bridge. He looked up and looked forward again as a rock rattled which they had not moved, faint in the wind and the river-sound.

A man was in the shadow. Strat snatched his hand toward his sword, but an outflung hand, a black wave of Ischade's cloak was in the way: "It's Stilcho," Ischade said.

He let the sword fall home again. "More help?" he asked. If there had not already been a chill down his back, this was enough: Stepson, this one was...one of the best of the ersatz Stepsons they'd left behind; gods, one he'd well-approved. Haunting the bridge-side. There was something appropriate in that; it was from this place the beggar-king had got him.

Dead, Vis swore. Stilcho had died that night.

Thunder rumbled. "Closer," Ischade said, glancing skyward as they passed out of bridge-shadow, three, where they had been two. Stars were still overhead, but in the south there were continued lightnings and rumblings; winds shivered up the Foal, roared in the trees downriver, on the further, southern, terraces.

Beside him now, a dead man walked. It looked his way once that he caught, with its one remaining eye, its ungodly pallor. It went swathed in black, except the hood; a young man's dark hair—Stilcho had been vain—still well-kept. Gods, what did it want—camaraderie?

He turned his back to it and slogged ahead, up the slope. Ischade drifted wraithlike before him, shadow-black against the shadow of the brush up-terrace, till she was lost in it. He struggled the harder, heard Stilcho laboring behind like death upon his track.

Lightning cracked. He crested the slope and Ischade was there, at his elbow, seizing on his arm.

"Snakes," she reminded him. "Go softly."

In the roar of the gathering storm.

The wind whirled in the window and the room went dark with the death of candles, except the fire in the hearth. "Reverence," the servant said, a small voice, insistent; below, in the perspective from the hill, all Sanctuary had just gone dark, what lights there were whipped out in the face of that oncoming wall; the very stars went out. There was for light only the flicker of the lightnings in the oncoming mass of cloud.

"Reverence."

He turned at the tug on his sleeve, saw in the dim firelight there was left the apparition of a palace guard, disheveled, windblown. "Zalbar?"

"Reverence—two of the patrol came back—someone hit them. Some could have gotten through; they don't know. They lost another man on the way back—"

"Reverence—" Another guard came pelting in at Zalbar's heels, breaking past the servants. "There's fire in the Aglain storehouse—"

"That's one." Kama let fly and missed the sulking figure. Wind carried the shot astray; the dark figure dived past, along the quay where fishing boats rocked and thumped together. The dark hulks of the Beysib ships leaned drunkenly and strained at cables out in the channel, out of reach from this side. "Damn!" She slid down the roof with the wind whipping at her braids and hit the rain-channel with her foot, stopping her descent on the trough of the roof. Lightning cracked. "Too exposed up here. Arrows no good— Get down, get down there."

She slid and bumped down to the stack of boxes, one-handed by reason of the bow, caught herself again, leaped down and came up on her feet—

—face on with a clutch of Beysib.

"Out of here!" she yelled, waving with the bow. "Out, move it—"

They jabbered their own tongue at her. One broke away; the others did, like so many mice before the fire, running down the docks—

A second shadow thumped down beside her, her partner, with an arrow nocked. "Lunatics," he said. Riot on the docks and the Beysib ran straight into the middle of it, fluttering and twittering—

A Beysib dropped. One of the snipers had scored with something; other Beysib reached the water, peeled out of garments like thistledown leaving pods—pale bodies arced toward the water—one, and three, and five, a dozen or more.

"Look at that!" her partner said. For a moment she did nothing but look, thinking it suicide (she was no swimmer, and the water was wild and black).

"Their ships—damn, they're going for their ships—"

They had guts—after all: *Beysib* amazed her; Beysib seamen, risking their lives out there.

The wind roared, making the trees creak. A limb cracked and fell; the smaller debris of old leaves and wind-stripped twigs rode the cold edge of the gusts. Left to right the wind blew here, about the ramshackle dwelling whose lights gleamed balefire red through the murk.

Here they crouched, here in this snake-infested outland, in the wind's howl and the lightning's crack.

"Vashanka's *gone*," Strat protested, his last faith in any logic shredded in the wind. *"Gone—"*

"The *lack* of a god also has its consequence," Ischade said. Her hood had blown back. Her hair streamed like ink in the dark. Lightning lit her face, and her eyes when she turned his way shone like hell itself. "Chaos, for instance. Petty usurpers."

"We going in there?" It was the last place Strat wanted to go, but he had his sword in hand and the shreds of his courage likewise. Inside might be warm. For the moment they lived. And here his bones were freezing.

"Patience," said Ischade; and holding out her hand: "Stilcho. It's time."

There was silence. Strat wiped his tearing eyes and turned his head. The steady flicker of lightnings showed a masklike face set in horror. "—No," Stilcho said. "No—I don't want—"

"You're essential, Stilcho. You know that. I know you know the way."

"I don't want to—" Childlike, quavering.

"Stilcho."

And he tumbled down, facedown, a dead weight that collapsed against Strat's side, utterly limp. Strat flinched aside in a paroxysm of revulsion, held his balance on his sword-hand, and blinked in the sting of wind and leaves. "Dammit—"

But Ischade's voice came to him through the dark: ". . . find him, Stilcho, find him: bring him up—he'll come. He'll come. He'll come—"

He made the mistake of lifting his head, looking up just where a thing materialized—a thing ribboned red and nothing—surely—ever human; but he knew its face, had known it for years and years.

"Janni—"

The murdered Stepson wavered, assumed a more human aspect—Janni the way he had been, before the Nisi witch had him for the night.

"She's yours, Janni." Ischade's distant whisper. "Stilcho. Come on back. Ace—"

His war-name. He had never told her that.

"Get her," Ischade whispered. "I'll hold—hold here. *Get her*. Bring it in on her. . . ."

Janni turned, like an image reflected in brass; moved like one, jerking and indistinct. Another presence stirred, more substantial: Stilcho staggered up, clawed branches for support. Strat moved, stung to be the last. "Janni—dammit, wait!"

But nothing could catch that rippling thing. It paid no heed to winds or brush. Strat thrust out his arm and forced his way through brush, passed Stilcho's efforts—crashed against a projecting branch and broke it on his leather jerkin, a crack swallowed in the wind.

Thorns raked him; the wall of the house loomed in front of him, and Janni was far ahead, diminishing as if he ran some far shore, then vanishing within the dark of that riverstone wall, with its oaken door.

"Janni!" No more need of silence. Janni had lost to the witch before—was *alone* in there, past barriers—gods knew what—*"Janni!"* He hit not the door but the shutters, shattered the rotting wood and plunged through in a roll over shattered pieces, into furnishings—blinding light. Shock lanced through his marrow, flung him flat. His head hit the floor, his sword was—gods, where?—his fingers too numb to feel it; but Stilcho was in, scrambling past him, hacking at something—

Muscle rolled over him, live and round and moving. He yelled and thrust it off and lurched for his knees—*snake*, the motion told him; he yelled and hacked at it, and it looped and thrashed—not the only one. He rolled to his knees and chopped at the looping coils for all the strength that was in him. Stilcho got the head off it: it had begun to scream.

Coils passed through Janni. He just kept moving. And Roxane—the witch Roxane, amid the room—in the midst of that place—stood black in the heart of fire; a pillar of dark, whose hair crackled with the light that came from her fingers and her face. Her hand lifted, and pointed, and the fire leaped. Janni went black himself against that light, a shadow, nothing more. The fire began to wail.

Strat tried; he flung himself forward.

"Get back!" It was Stilcho grabbed him, on some brink he could not see, beyond which was a fall that took them both, down, down, into dark—

But Janni had his arms about the witch, and lightnings wrapped them and crawled up and down the pair of them like veinwork, till the thunder rolled. The light riddled him, shredded his darkness, blew both of them in tatters; and sucked inward then with one deafening clap of thunder.

Darkness then. The stink of burning.

"Janni? Janni? *Stilcho—*"

The wind fell. Fell so suddenly it was like death; with one great crack of thunder that must have hit something near.

The ships started pitching on a sea gone chaotic, no longer heeled by the wind, no longer straining at the cables.

"Gods!" Kama breathed.

"—hit somewhere riverside," the servant said, superfluous as ever. Molin Torchholder clenched the sill and felt his heart start labored beats again.

"I'd say it did."

But where, he could not tell. There was a blossoming of flame in that far dark, not the only one. There were burnings here and there.

None large yet.

And nothing had gotten through.

It was nothing he wanted to remember. It was most of the walk back before he could hear; and most of the long walk he staggered off on his own, reeling this way and that like a drunken man. But sometimes Stilcho had his arm about him, sometimes She had his hand...

...There was fire, another sort of fire, safely in a hearth. The smell of herbs. Of musk.

Ischade's dusky face. She knelt beside his chair, by her fireside, by the tame light. Her hood was back. The light shone on her hair.

"Janni—" he said. It was the first thing he remembered saying.

"Stilcho brought you," Ischade said. She leaned aside. Wine spilled with a liquid, busy sound, the pungency of grapes. She offered him the cup. And he sat still.

The mind took a long time collecting images like that. He sat staring at the fire and feeling the ache in all his bones.

"—Janni?"

"Resting."

"Dead. He's dead, leave him dead, dammit—" thinking of Niko, of Niko's grief, half-of-whole. It would break Niko's heart. "Isn't a man safe dead?"

"I'd have used others. Other souls were—inaccessible. His wasn't. To reach him took very little, in that cause. Stilcho's gotten adept at that two-way trip." A step drew near. Haught's face loomed. "You can go," she said, looking up at Haught. "See to the uptown house. They'll want reassuring."

Haught padded away, took his cloak. There was brief chill as the door opened and closed again. The fire fluttered.

"Roxane," Strat said.

She put the cup into his hand. Closed his fingers on it. "Power has its other side. It's not well to be interrupted— in so great a spell."

"Is she dead?"

"If not, she's uncomfortable."

He drank, one quick swallow after the other. It took the taste of burning from his mouth. She took the cup, set it aside. Leaned her arm and head on his knee like any woman gazing into the fire. And turned her head and looked up at him. A pulse began, the chill about him thawed, but the world seemed very far away.

"Come to bed," she said. "I'll keep you warm."

"How long?"

She shut her eyes. For a moment he was cold. Opened them again and the room grew warm and the pulse grew in all his veins.

"You've always mistaken me," she said. "Vampire I am not. You think it's what I choose. I don't. But some things I can choose."

Her hand closed on his. He leaned down and touched her lips, not caring, not caring to recall or think ahead. It was the way he had gone into that house. Because Ranke might well be through. And he was, soon; and time was, he had learned in his own craft, no one's friend.

"Damnedest thing," Zalbar said, wiping at his soot-streaked face, and a moment's consternation took him. His eyes refocused. "Begging pardon, reverence—"

"Report."

"Got a dozen dead out there we've counted so far, just up and down the streets. Dead men—throats cut, some; stabbed—"

"The ships, Zalbar."

"A few timbers stove, but the Bey's folk, they got to them—the bodies, reverence—a dozen of them."

"In Sanctuary," Molin said with a pitying look at the Hell-Hound, "we notice a dozen bodies come dawn?"

"Two at Siphinos's door; one at Elinos's. Three at Agalin's. . . . They're Nisi. Every one."

"Hey," someone yelled. "Hey—"

He was in the street; his horse under him. He blinked at the sun and the ordinary sights of Sanctuary and caught himself against the saddlebow, staring down at the man who had stopped his horse, a common tradesman. There was a buzz of consternation about. Dimly Strat understood the horse had gotten to some mischief with a produce cart. He stared helplessly at the old man who stared at him in a troubled way; Ilsigi-dark, and recognizing a Rankan lost and prey to anything that might happen to a man by day in Sanctuary streets.

Shingles lay scattered on the cobbles; a tavern sign hung by one ring; debris was everywhere. But trade went on. The bay horse was after apples.

He felt after his purse. It was gone; and he could not remember how. He would have flung the man a coin and paid the damage and forgotten the Wriggly entire; but they were all round him, men, women, silent in mutual embarrassment, mutual hate, and mutual helplessness.

"Sorry," he muttered, and took up the reins and got the horse away, slowly down the street.

Robbed—not of the money only. There were vast gaps in his memory—where he had been; what he had seen.

Roxane. Ischade. He had come back to the river-house. The memory got so far and stopped.

184

He touched his throat on reflex. *You've always mistaken me,* she'd said.

The sun was up. Tradesmen went bawling their wares, the housekeepers were out dusting off the steps.

He would have ridden from the gates and saved himself; but like the bay horse he had learned patterns and was caught in them, kept to the path and to duty.

I promised something, he thought in a chill, half-recovered memory.

Gods—what?

REBELS AREN'T BORN
IN PALACES

Andrew J. Offutt

Offer a prize for the lowest, skungiest dive in Sanctuary, and Sly's Place will win it hands down. That's a good place for hands at Sly's Place, too. Down, near your belt-purse and weapons. Sly's Place is sphinctered in the improbable three-way intersection of Tanner and Odd Birt's Dodge and the north-south wriggle of the Serpentine (near Wrong-way Park). Those are "streets," to those who don't mind a certain looseness or downright ludicrousness in terminology, in that area of town called the Maze. 'Way back deep in the Maze, which is the lowest, skungiest hellhole in Sanctuary and probably on the continent, and let's don't talk about the planet.

Every Maze-denizen and most Downwinders know where Sly's Place is, and yet no one can assign a proper address to it. Its address is not that winding maze-link called the

Serpentine. It isn't given as being on the streetlet called
Tanner. And no one gives Odd Birt's Dodge as an address.
Sly's Place is just *there*, at that sort of three-way corner,
that preposterous intersection where that little Hanse-
imitating cess-head Athavul got his comeuppance a couple
of years ago, and where Menostric the Misadept, hardly
sober and fleeing, slipped on a pile of human never-mind
and actually skidded onto three streets before he came to
an indecorous but appropriate stop in the gutter, sort of
wrapped around the corner so that his head was up against
the curbing on Tanner and his feet were actually in Wrong-
way Park. It is also the area in which welled up so many
disagreements swiftly escalating into encounters, sanguine
fights, brawls, and worse that a physician named Alamanthis
wisely rented space a couple of doors down on Tanner, and
hired a mean ugly nondrinking bodyguard, and made street
calls. He charged in advance, and slept most of each day,
and was getting rich, damn and bless him.

Sly's Place! Name of Father Ils, Sly had taken dropsy
and died three years agone, and the dive was still called
Sly's Place because no one wanted to admit to owning it
or to take responsibility either.

On the other hand, since all that Beyfishfacesin/sorcery
problem in the Vulgar Unicorn and the pursuant edict and
raid—or raid and edict; who in power could be bothered
with niceties where anything in the Maze was concerned?
—business waxed at Sly's like the tide when the moon is
right, like the moon when the heavens are favorable, like
the heavens when the gods are getting along. *Someone* had
to be getting rich off Sly's Place, damn and bless him. Or
her.

Sly's was where a pair of rebels/patriots met, and awaited
the advent of an invited guest. In a town first occupied by
those rank Rankans and then by the much ranker Stare-Eyes
from oversea, rebels/patriots could not, after all, arrange
such a meeting in some fine uptown place such as the Golden
Oasis or Hari's Spot or even the Golden Lizard.

The two had been waiting quite a while and already one knife-fight had played absolute havoc with a winejar, two mugs, an innocent bysitter's pinky, a poorly-made chair, and a kidney.

"Wish that little son-of-a-bitch would hurry up and get here," one said; his name was Zip and he had eyes that would look better on the other side of iron bars.

The other young man frowned, glancing distastefully at the mug on the table before him. "No call to say that—you don't even know who his mother is."

"Neither did his father, Jes."

Jes tried not to smile at that one, and shrugged. "Fine. Call him a bastard, then, and leave slurs to womanhood out of it."

"Lord, but you're sensitive."

"True."

Zip didn't say anything about the reflection on womanhood implicit in the very existence of bastard offspring, because he didn't think of it. His mind was not given to the formulation of such retorts, or much cleverness. He was a rebel and a fighter, not a thinker. On the other hand, he was the very hell of a patriot and rebel. His name was Zip and he had always thought quite a bit of a certain spawn of the shadows and tried to emulate him, until lately. Now he had lost respect for that one, but needed him.

"That's him," Zip said. "A bastard. Both by birth and by nature."

This time Jes went ahead and smiled. "That's pretty good, Zip. Oh—the barkeep's staring at us again." Jes's name was really Kama, and she was nothing at all like Zip except that tonight, like Zip, she was in disguise. Yet she had made one of those astonishing discoveries that come all unsuspected on unsuspecting people who might wish for better: she liked Zip, and she liked him more than somewhat.

"Oh, no. If I have to order another of those rotten cat-urine beers, I'll—ah. Here comes the son of a—the bast— here he comes now," he said, gazing past her. She didn't have to turn much to see the doorway; they had got themselves seated so as to be able to note who came in without seeming to show interest.

A step above the room, the doorway of Sly's Place was graced by thirty-one strands of dangling Syrese rope, each knotted thirty-one times in accord with that superstition. They hung just short of the oiled wooden flooring. Through that unlikely arras had just come a narrow lean wraith of a youthful man of average height, above-average *presence*, and a weening cockiness that showed in face and stance and carriage. Several years younger than Zip he was, and dressed all in black except for the (very) scarlet sash. His hair was blacker than black and seemed trying to decide whether to curl above almost-black eyes to make a person step aside while his own hair tried to curl. The falcate nose belonged on a young eagle. Good shoulders on him, and no hips worth mentioning.

His wearing of weapons was overdone the way a courtesan overdid her gems: as advertisement and braggadocio. Over the sash he wore a shagreen belt; from it a curved dagger swung at his left hip and an Ilbarsi knife, its blade twenty inches long or worse, on the right. The copper-set leather armlet that encircled his right upper arm was more than decoration: it housed a hiltless, guardless, long black lozenge of a throwing knife. So did the long bracer of black leather on that arm. More than one patron of Sly's Place knew that the decoration on his left buskin was the hilt of a knife sheathed within that soft boot. (They were wrong; he'd moved that sticker to the other buskin, and it didn't show.) Maybe he wore other blades and maybe he did not; there were rumors.

From beneath raven's-wing brows he surveyed the place as if he owned it and yet despised it and might turn it into a pet shop or fishmonger's tomorrow morning early. (He didn't own it.) He did own the imperiously Imperial Rankan eagle off the roof of Barracks Three, because he had stolen it for a lark and to use as a pissoir; and for a time he had owned the Savankh, too: the wand of Imperial office and authority of the Rankan governor, which he had stolen from within the very palace (which everyone knew was impossible of clandestine access) and ransomed it back to its rightful possessor, a nice well-meaning blond of about his age.

Quite a fellow, this (calculatedly) sinister-looking youth, who had once told a royal prince of Ranke that killing was the business of princes and the like, not of thieves; and yet who had killed two men one night, his first and his last, on behalf of a fellow he respected but found mighty hard to like. Born in Downwind of casually acquainted parents, he needed pride and any sort of respect badly and was cockily, pridefully sure that he'd risen above Downwind. The Maze might be counted as above Downwind—about a spider's stride above.

Four people in Sly's signed to him or greeted him, two by his name and one by his nickname. None of the four was either of the two awaiting him. He surveyed the place with eyes like chips of anthracite or basalt, and when their gaze touched Zip, Zip pushed a finger into his nose as signal. The newcomer noted, looked on, nodded to someone, made a negligent gesture of greeting to a girl-woman named Nimsy (who winked), noted the two Zip's Boys three tables away from the disguised Zip, and did not change expression. He took a single pace across the little landing and descended the step into the crowded dim-lit alcohol-fumed ambience of Sly's Place.

"Think I'll join those two," he said almost regally to one who had called him by name and nickname both. "Watch that cheap beer, Maldu! Ahdio makes it in the outhouse."

And he passed, Maldu saying, "Aww, Hanse!" loudly and, to his two companions, quietly, "See? I told you. Me 'n Hanse're old buddies. Ever tell you how he actually got the better of ole Shrive the fence-I-mean-changer ha ha?"

Hanse slid down into a chair at the round, three-chair table where Kama and Zip waited. He glanced barward and raised his right hand, half-cupped into a standing right angle, took it higher than his head, then elevated three of the fingers. The bartender nodded and went about drawing three mugs of the good stuff; the brew off which he blew the foam so as to serve an honest measure to those as paid for it.

"Want me to admit I didn't even know you in that black wig and droopo mustache?" Hanse said to Zip. "I didn't even know you."

"Hanse," the normally short-haired and clean-shaven Zip said, "this is Jes." In a much lower voice he swiftly added, "Tonight—name's Kama."

Shadowspawn looked at the soft-faced youth with Zip—also mustached—and was impressed; she was tallish and the disguise was good enough that he hadn't considered her female. Nothing changed in his face, including his eyes.

"Any friend of Zip's," he said affably, "is suspect."

She blinked, recovered, said, "Likewise, I'm sure."

Hanse's black, black, close-nestling brows went up and he blinked. His face looked as if it were seriously considering a smile. He left it at that and flicked his gaze back to Zip.

"We've been waiting awhile," the Downwinder street-lord said.

Shadowspawn said nothing.

Ahdiovizun brought three glazed mugs of beer on a tray; Sly's Place didn't use barmaids because that led to unbelievable stress, strain, strife, and worse. Everyone knew that his gimpy assistant left after closing with only a staff and not a copper. Ahdio was known to be from Twand, in truth was not, and was *large*. He was known to have killed, and had, and known to have felled a Mrsevadan horse with a blow of his fist to the animal's head, and had. The coat of linked chain mail he wore was definitely unusual attire for a taverner. It was considered to be part of the color and ambience of Sly's Place. It was, of course, although that was not its purpose. Its purpose was the same as when its like was worn by a soldier. Ahdio tended bar in Sly's Place and had killed a man or so and felled a horse (a big gray gelding, in fact, with two white stockings) with a single fist-blow to the head, and at times intervened in fights. He also wore a mailcoat and did not leave at closing, alone, but slept upstairs in company with two truly nasty cats, because Ahdio was not stupid.

"Here you go. Three of the best. These two are running a tab."

"Good for them. This round's on me," Hanse said.

Ahdio's smile was easy, open, and amiable. "You, ah, had a good night, Hanse?"

"No," Hanse said, and paused to drink half the contents of the mug Ahdio had just set before Zip. Hanse replaced it, and ignored the way the rebel patriot stared at the sadly depleted container. "As a matter of fact, I haven't. That was last night."

Ahdio, who had never seen Hanse knock back anything that way, thought it best to say, "Ah."

"Ah," Zip echoed, sensing a story. "But . . . you don't drink, Hanse!"

Shadowspawn looked at him. "I just did," he said, while his lean dark hand moved over to Kama/Jes's mug without the aid of his eyes. He glanced up at Ahdio, whose form occluded an incredible number of the tables behind him. "I came here to meet these people, and I'm late. You'll stop fights so I won't have to take them elsewhere?"

Ahdio nodded without changing so much as a single muscle in his face. Shadowspawn nodded in return.

"Ah, that's good, Ahdio," he said, and paused to put a serious dent in the contents of Kama's mug. "No, Ahdio, I'll tell you, tonight has not been a good night. I have just killed a Stare-Eye."

Zip blinked in surprise, then grinned and looked significantly at Kama—whom he found giving him a significant look.

"A good night for Sanctuary!" Zip said with enthusiasm.

"Stairae," Ahdio said. "Don't believe I know him. Her?"

"Stare . . . Eye," Hanse enunciated, and stared, unblinking.

"Ah!" Ahdio smiled again. "One of the froggies! A good

night for us all! I'd better hurry, then. Three more of the same upcoming, on me."

Shadowspawn nodded and came very close to smiling. Ahdio departed. A customer reached out for him *en passant* and jerked back his hand to stare at fingertips instantly bereft of prints. Ahdio's coat of quintuply-linked-and-butted chain was absolutely genuine.

"Shit," the customer said.

"Coming right up," Ahdio threw back.

Amid laughter, Zip leaned forward. "How'd it happen, Hanse?" (He was keeping his hands away from the brew Hanse had ordered and was buying. Shadowspawn was not a killer, had been living high and soft and with a lot of bed-company of late, and obviously had a sincere and monumental thirst this night.)

Hanse seemed to work at relaxing. His shoulders visibly lowered and he sat a bit down in his roundpeg chair.

"The . . . creature accosted me. Like a Lord of the Earth, you know? Arrogant and cocky and expecting me to play sandworm under its feet. I didn't and it got abusive. I endured that awhile, just wanting to be on my way to see what you wanted. It went on with it. Couldn't accept my lack of real response when it wanted foot-licking. It got more abusive. When it finally paused to see if I'd drop dead or start in weeping from all its words, I asked politely enough which had been the fish, its mama or its papa. It took that as an offense, only Ils knows why, and reached for a weapon."

They sat in silence, his table companions staring at him. Hanse noted that somehow he'd emptied his mug, said, "Not thirsty?" and reached over for Zip's mug. He drained it.

A fine sense of drama, Kama thought, *a Rankan and a soldier and a woman in an Ilsig tavern as a man, among Ilsigs only. One of us has to ask; he's forcing us*. And she asked:

"And then, Hanse?"

He leaned forward loosely, elbows thumping onto the

table. "Jes, do not be alarmed when I touch your left shoulder."

Kama/Jes, seated on his left with her right shoulder next to his left, showed surprise and lack of understanding. "All right," she began, and saw a dark blur, felt the touch on her far shoulder, and there was Hanse sitting there with his elbows on the table, looking at her from expressionless eyes the color of the bottom of a well of a moonless midnight.

"You . . ." she began, and aborted that because her voice was going high. She swallowed as unobtrusively as possible and said, "I . . . understand. You are fast."

Zip laughed, exaggeratedly. So did Ahdio, setting down three more.

"You're Rankan," Hanse had said, very quietly. Only Jes/Kama heard, and nodded. She was impressed anew.

"You really take down one of them tonight, Hanser?"

Shadowspawn nodded. "Straight Street, Ahdio, three doors down from Odors."

Ahdio's smile was genuine. "I love it. How? Excuse me— will you tell me now?"

"It attacked." Hanse reached lazily across himself, tapped the leather-and-copper armlet at his right bicep. "In the eye. The right eye. Wiped the blood on its tunic-thing."

Ahdio was grinning. "Mind if I spread the word?"

"Think it's safe?"

"You think they have spies or informants here in the *Maze?*" Ahdio's voice was rich with incredulity.

"I do. Half the people in this room would sell a sister for a good offer, and all of us would spout about anything under torture. I think I'd better say I mind, Ahdio."

The huge man sighed. "My lips're sealed. You three look's if you'd ruther be in the back room."

Zip and Hanse nodded in unison.

A minute later he and Kama were ambling back that way, after having bade Zip good night. The little room beyond the wall behind the bar was plain, with the same flooring, walls adorned only by hanging utensils and pottles and a couple of leathern sacks, full. The table was square and the chairs roughly- and well-made. The room was also occupied by a score or so tuns of beer and a good-sized red cat with a cropped ear, a restless tail, and a mean look. It was looking at Hanse. Hanse didn't like cats overmuch; any animal that could and would stare down a human should be illegal. This one also looked as if it ate large, live dogs for snacks.

"These are friends, Notable," Ahdio told the cat. "Excuse me," he said quietly, and patted Hanse's shoulder, and Kama's. "Friends, Notable. Take a nap."

Notable blinked, long, and didn't say anything. It continued to stare. Kama acted as if it weren't there, while Hanse stared back. They stood still while Ahdio went over and moved a keg that had to weigh several hundred pounds. Next he moved the one behind it. And squatted. When Zip's knock came, the taverner was ready to open the concealed half-door and move back while Zip squat-crawled into the room. Ahdio closed the low door, secured both its locks, and replaced both kegs. He went through the friend-excuse-me-hand-on-shoulder routine with Zip, gestured to the table and chairs, and started to leave.

"Oh," he said, at the door into the main room. "If you want anything, wait awhile. I'll send Throde."

"Who's Throde?" Zip asked, while Hanse was saying, "You telling us not to get up and walk over to that door because of the cat, Ahdio?"

"That's a damned good cat, Hanse. Had a prowler try to get in here one night and Notable screamed loud enough to scare off every prowler from here to Vomit Boulevard. 'Nother fellow followed me back here one night late with his mind on badness and before he had his sticker out of its sheath Notable was eating holes in his knife-arm. Likes beer but won't take it from anyone but me. Zip: Throde is my helper. You know—they call him Gimp. Good boy. From Twand; my cousin's boy."

Since Hanse knew very well that Ahdiovizun was not from Twand, he considered that stuff about Throde or Gimp to be highly unlikely. So what? Ahdio was better than all right, and Throde was his helper, and both Zip and what-was-her-name Jes were in disguise, and—never mind how many lies were being told and lived out in the taproom.

That stuff about Notable the red cat Hanse believed implicitly.

Ahdio departed their company and without a trace of preamble or smile Hanse said, "Let's hear it. You've become leader of a bunch called People's Front for the Liberation of Sanctuary and recently you were very nearly killed. This woman disguised as a man has an accent says she's from Ranke and she knows how to move. An alliance against the Stare-Eyes, then? What's it want with me? I'm not political."

"Popular Front," Zip corrected. "The *P* in PFLS is for Popular, not People's. We don't mind saying you're right about Kama—she's with the Rankan 3rd Commando unit. They're as eager as we are to get rid of the froggies. The Stare-Eyes. It isn't going to happen tomorrow morning or by next Eshday, either. We need more respect, more money, more good people, and even more warm bodies."

Hanse had ceased even touching the mugs of beer or glancing at them either. "Got no money and I'm not good people or interested in joining the *Popular* FLS." He shrugged. "You'll get more respect when you've shown you can do more than write bloody messages on the Vulgar Unicorn's walls and get One-Thumb and a bunch of other people in trouble."

"The PFLS didn't do that, Hanse, and I didn't do it. And you're right—it was a rotten idea. Those froggies that busted in there looking for trouble weren't *official* ones, though. And Hanse...we know how—Kama and I—how we can gain respect and money and more followers all in one operation that won't involve a single death. Not one. Just—"

"You're dreaming."

Kama made a noise, and Hanse didn't glance her way. He did glance at Notable, which was examining its left

197

forepaw with great interest while its tail sort of wandered around the floor behind it.

"Damn it, Hanse—"

"Zip?" Kama waited a moment, and Zip leaned back, trying not to look disgusted. "Hanse," she said, "word is that once someone actually broke into the Governor's Palace and actually stole Prince-Governor Kadakithis's wand of power—the one straight from Ranke as emblem of Empire—and actually got away. Whether it was strictly the thief's idea or not is not for certain and not important anymore. Kadakithis is in hiding or detention and the Beysa sleeps in the governor's suite—alone, presumably—as boss of Sanctuary. Word is also that the thief who pulled off that fantastic piece of work actually ransomed the Savankh back to the prince, and got away with it. Maybe a traitor or two got killed along the way, and maybe not; maybe the prince actually owes a debt to that thief and maybe not. All that doesn't matter."

She paused, waiting, and Hanse decided to outwait her. After thirty seconds or so it got to him and he said, "I've heard that story, or some of it, too. What about it, *Jes?*"

"Call me Kama. What about it is this. What would have happened if it had been noised around that the Savankh was in the hands of the people of Sanctuary—the Ilsigs? Enormous loss of face for the prince and for the Empire he represents, or represented! Lots of laughter in town. And lots of people flocking to join those who had the Savankh. Maybe a few contributions of funds, too. Nowadays things are worse. A lot of people didn't like the Rankan rule of Sanctuary, but *no* one likes these fish-eyed invaders."

"That's for sure," Zip muttered.

"True," Hanse said, and glanced at Notable. As a test, Hanse slapped his leg. Notable put down his paw and took up staring. "I think I like that cat."

"So," Zip said, on an eye-signal from Kama, "if I—if the PFLS had the *Beysin* scepter, *their* symbol of power... and if we spread the word, actually showed it around..."

"You'd have about a million Beys down your throat."

"Maybe about a *hundred*," Zip said, "but they wouldn't be down our throats, they'd be *trying* to find us. Meanwhile just about everyone in Sanctuary would be happily lying to them and misdirecting them, *and* joining us to free Sanctuary for Sanctuarites, *and* contributing services and money and even working deals to get some weapons in here."

"Not me," Hanse said. "I've got a life to live and I'm not political. It's true that I and Prince Kadakithis get along all right as two men, but I'm Ilsig and he's Ranke and the only thing I'd help him do is sneak out of town—provided he was headed away from Ranke."

Kama tapped a finger on the table. "That won't be necessary. Look, Hanse . . . Ranke is in trouble, too. It isn't just the Beysins in Sanctuary. An empire is a lot of land, a lot of people, a lot of Sanctuarys. A united and triumphant Sanctuarite populace who'd got rid of the Beysins would be too proud to let the prince back into the Governor's Palace, and I have to tell you that he wouldn't be strong enough to enforce it." She glanced away. "He couldn't count on any help from Ranke, either. Ranke is busy. Ranke is in trouble."

"Is it true that Vashanka's dead?" Hanse asked.

Both Kama and Zip stared at him and Hanse wondered at their expressions.

"Anyhow," he said, "I'd say that you'll make a lot of noise and get in a lot of trouble and kill some Stare-Eyes and get a lot of our people killed; and then they'll smash you. If you're lucky you'll die in that one, and not have to be tortured to death, Zip. I'll be going about my business, but not with you or your people. I'm just not political, Zip."

Zip's anger had him all ready to blurt "Coward!" but he got control of himself and opted against saying anything so silly, since he wasn't ready to die right now. Instead he said, "Hanse, Hanse . . . you said you killed one just tonight!"

Hanse gave him a look. *"Said* I did?"

Zip gestured and sighed. "Words, words. I wasn't questioning you. The point is—"

"The point is that I did. I had three choices: run, die, or kill. It was that kind of thing. I had to. It wasn't political." Now he, too, sighed and wagged his head. "I didn't say that I *liked* those creepy stare-eyed creatures—I said that I am not political and am not joining any political groups."

Zip slapped the table a bit harder than he should have done, which Notable remarked with a smallish noise in his throat. "We don't want you to join if you don't want to, Hanse, and we don't want any money from you. You have the opportunity to do more for Sanctuary, for your fellow Ilsigi and against *them*, than anybody . . . because only you can break into the palace and steal the Beysa's scepter."

Hanse looked at Zip as if the PFLSer had just asked him to strip and dance through the streets. He jerked at Kama's touch on his wrist—only a touch, he noted, and knew that she was both bright and dangerous; not one to go grasping a touchy man's wrist as just any woman might have done. He looked at her without expression; she had already taken her hand back.

"Hanse . . . only one person in all Sanctuary and probably in the *world* could do it. We—Sanctuary—*needs* you, Hanse."

"And once it's done, we'll swear that we had assistance from inside," Zip said excitedly, "so that they'll suspect their own, see, and we'll never, never tell anyone that Hanse did it."

"That's true," Hanse told him, "because Hanse isn't going to do it. One more time: I am not political. I do love living. You told me that you had this big idea that would do more than anything and no one would have to die. What you *want*, though, absolutely requires the death of one person."

Zip glanced at Kama; looked at the best thief on the continent. "Done," he said, thumping the table. "Who has to die?"

"Me, you damned fool, if I were damned fool enough to try to break into the very *palace* and snatch Her Fishiness's scepter *and* get out again!" And Hanse rose, pushing back his chair, and turned to the door. And looked down into the eyes of the cat that had suddenly got itself to a point two feet from his buskins and was staring up at him with big round black marbles set in green almonds. Showing almost no ears, Notable made a nasty remark.

One dramatic exit blown all to hell by a cat. Hanse sighed and, slowly, eased back down into the chair to await the advent of Ahdio's gimp-legged aide.

"You rotten dam' cat," he muttered, picking up his glazed mug. "I think I like you. Here, have a beer."

Notable hissed.

"I CANNOT BE SLAIN BY WEAPONS OF YOUR PLANE, IDIOT, LITTLE THIEF, POOR DEMI-MORTAL," the god Vashanka had said to Hanse, and then Hanse put the knife into the god, and Vashanka was sore struck and must die, even as He slew Hanse. Yet Vashanka was right: He could not be slain, and so was hurled forever from this plane on which existed Thieves' World, Sanctuary, and Ranke, Vashanka's chosen city and people, and could never return, for here He had been killed.

Since Vashanka had killed Hanse but did not exist on this plane and so could not have killed Hanse, a paradox existed and paradoxes, the god Ils of the Ilsigi said, could not exist. And therefore Hanse called Shadowspawn called Godson was alive and unmarked. And Ils gazed down at him.

"You, beloved son of Shadow, have defeated a God and restored Me to My Own people in Sanctuary. Further, as Vashanka had become the most powerful of the gods of Ranke, that people's power shall wane. Empires die slowly, but it has begun, as of this moment."

And, "For ten circuits of the sun, you shall have what you wish. All that you desire. . . . Then you will face Me again, beloved Hanse, and tell Me what is your desire."

As the weary Hanse, spawn of the shadows and son of the shadow-god Shalpa (and slayer of a God), trudged home that night, he wished that this weariness of battle would go from him; and it was so, and then grinning, he made another wish, and when he entered his room there she was. His wish, awaiting him in his bed all low-lashed and smoky-eyed.

The night was wonderful after that, that night of Hanse's great triumph and Vashanka's death-banishment forever, and in the morning the ships were there. The Beysib had come.

Hanse went down to the dock that day and looked at the ships as they came closer, and closer, and he pondered and considered. Then he went back up to Eaglenest where he had consorted with gods and fought with a god. They were not there. Only the ruins were there. And the well. Hanse sighed. That well had held two horsebags full of silver coin—and a few gold—for many, many months, and the money was his. Without it, strangely, he had been neither better nor worse off. Merely Hanse, thief, thinking about his next theft and his next girl and phantasizing about those he could not ha—

But he could, couldn't he? Ils had sent to his bed Esaria, the beautiful young daughter of Venerable Shafralain. It had been a wonderful night, and no ill had come of it. A shudder took him as he thought that the love goddess Eshi, too, had shared his bed—he thought. And too, She was somehow involved with Mignureal, daughter of Moonflower...who had expressly asked Hanse to stay away from her daughter. He had been willing, but since then—oh, since then, all that had happened!

He walked back down to Sanctuary, pondering. Phantasizing. Along the way a sort of test had arisen: a big accoster had a go at him. Hanse readied himself but took opportunity to wish the fellow would just go to sleep and leave him alone. He watched the man yawn, then crumple up like a falling curtain. Marveling, Hanse checked that crumpled form. Alive, definitely alive. Just asleep. Just like that.

"Why—I have ten days (or months? Surely not *years!*) of this! Whatever I wish!"

In his excitement he spoke aloud in a rising voice, and

danced a few jiggy steps, and joyously entered Sanctuary with a thousand visions and possibilities, a thousand phantasies chasing each other through his mind. He found his beloved Moonflower the seer, and astonished her by hugging her while he wished that she had twice the coinage she thought within the vast cleavage of what she called her treasure chest, and that it was in gold and silver besides. He heard the clinks and saw her look of surprise and some discomfort as that temporary storage vault between the great pillows of her bosom became crowded and heavy, on the instant.

He skipped away laughing, and walked smiling about town so that others wondered what he could possibly be so happy about. Why, people were actually fleeing, with an invasion fleet almost in the harbor! Hanse, however, was become a child with a marvelous new toy, the most marvelous of toys. A block or so later he saw a twice-attractive woman and wished that he might have her, whereupon she looked around and saw him. She came straight to him, all jingle and jiggle and sway of hips and flash of teeth.

"You're beautiful," she assured him. "Take me to bed!"

But by the time they had reached the building wherein he had a second-floor room, he had seen another, and sort of traded in the first, who went away happily with no memory of what she had said and done or rather almost done. He had learned something already! And how cheap lessons were, not as in real life. The second was absolutely beautiful and with a very nice figure indeed, but he soon found that behind closed doors and on a bedsheet she was an absolute dud. He improved that with another wish. . . .

At about dusk he departed, a bit weak in the legs but happy (he'd had to resort to a wish to get her to leave him alone and go away), for he had thought of a wonderful mission for himself: Hanse Godslayer. Along the way his stomach rumbled. He wished he had an apple, so the first vendor he passed called "Hey!" and tossed him a beauty.

Walking along eating with relish, he thought, *I wish that redhead would walk with me; we'd look good together!* She did of course, but that led to some difficulty when her husband appeared and demanded explanation, and Hanse learned something else of this new power. Something prompted him to wish that the couple would forget him and go happily home and be happy ever after and it was the nicest thing any human ever did for another, surely. With the help of Ils, of course. Marvelously attentive god, that Ils!

Arrived at the dock, he found a nervous throng and moved among them. Listening, observing, thinking, seeing their fear and ridiculous hopes. ("Whoever it is, they've come to drive off the Rankans and leave us in peace!" —*Sure,* Hanse thought. "There's always a great profit to be made from newcomers to town!" —*Sure,* Hanse thought, *especially when they come easing up in over a hundred ships.* Oh, sure!)

Then he stood tall and straight and confident, and smiled, and while he gazed at all those approaching sails he wished that they would turn around and go away and never bother Sanctuary.

They came on and Hanse learned something else. Some things, big things, must take longer even for Ils! Tomorrow they'd be gone! That didn't happen either, and Hanse had to accept what he had already known: that not *all* things were possible, and that while Ils was a god, He was not *the* god. Others existed, and the powers of gods had fences and boundaries. (On the other hand, that night he enjoyed a meal beyond mere good, a fabulous meal, in the very house of Shafralain, just because Hanse had seen that wealthy noble and wished that he'd invite Hanse in for dinner.... Naturally he spent the night in the company and arms of Esaria, again. When he awoke before dawn it occurred to him that he was better off leaving now and wishing they'd all forget this whole night. On his way home, he wished that Esaria would know much, much happiness in her life, and again Hanse had done the unlikely: good.

Next day the fascinating but ugly oversea folk landed and tramped into town. It did not take long to discover that they had come to take over, and were expediting that. By afternoon he had tried thirteen several wishes against them. None took. On the other hand, when one of the unblinking creeps accosted him and indicated that Hanse was wanted for something, he wished the ugly never-blinking creep would just start sneezing and continue for a nice long while. That happened, and Hanse went on his way chuckling. Individual Beysibs, obviously, were easy for Ils.

He wandered over to the east side of town, and stood gazing up at a fine lofting mansion he had always admired. He had always wanted to break into that place and see what was there, and remove a few thises and thats. "I wish I could," he muttered, and it was easy, easy. He sold the nice things he removed from the premises, but that seemed silly, somehow, as the coin was counted out to him by a no-questions denizen of the Maze; all this trouble when he could merely wish for money, all he wanted!

Of course he had enjoyed all the passionate kisses and fondling of two lovely slaves of that house, and of course he had wished that on the morrow their master would take a notion to free them and give them a nice departing present, too. Eternal Ils, he had done it again—Hanse had done good!

The money business occupied his mind to a considerable extent. He bethought him of all that Rankan coin down in the well up at Eaglebeak. It was an odd wish he made, then, but he liked the idea: "When I do go for it I wish that it would rise up out of the well to me, and be no trouble—oh! Oh I wish *she'd* just amble right over here and think I'm handsome and want to night with—no, no, offer me a fine wine-red cloak—dark!—to night with her!"

When he and she—her name was Bumgada, but what's in a name?—arose from bed next morning, happy with each other, he thought that something had been forgotten. No, no; she took him right out and downtown and bought him both breakfast and a fine scarlet cloak—a long dark one— and didn't *that* raise eyebrows.

As they were walking along, she said something and

Hanse said something and added, "Oh, and Bumma—I wish you'd just forget everything that happened since just before you saw me yesterday—but not get into any trouble for it at all, and have a nice happy life."

"Excuse me," she said, as if she had just bumped into him, and went on her way, wherever that was. Hanse ambled along, wondering what she *did* remember, and what those slavegirls remembered, and what Esaria and indeed her family and servants remembered, and . . .

He had to find out. It was a dreadfully naughty idea, but he did have to find out, didn't he? He made a wish, involving the awaiting in his bed of a certain person when he reached his room. Next he wished that he could pick ten pockets without being discovered, but that turned out to be stupid and a bore because it was so easy. Besides, he lost count and the eleventh victim grabbed his hand and let out a yell and Hanse had to do some mighty fast wishing. He stopped running after a couple of blocks. After all, it wasn't as if he *had* to, anymore. Just a pleasant habit of long duration.

He found another limit to the power of Ils by wishing that Tempus and his boys would clean up on the Beysibs— maybe that was the way to do it!

Wrong; instead, Tempus and his boys left town and a lot of half-competents and worse began showing up. One gave him trouble and Hanse wished the fool would just fall down on his own dagger, but when it happened he really didn't feel very good about it. After a couple of blocks he turned around and went back. That was how he discovered that he couldn't raise the dead.

As he passed a fine tavern for the wealthy and lordly, he chuckled aloud. Wishing that they'd treat him in manner lordly *and* "remember" that he had paid in advance, and well, he ambled in. An hour later he left, stuffed, with the manager and tableman thanking him and wishing him well and swift return.

He was groaning along, feeling stuffed with more than he should have eaten and far richer fare too, when a thought hit him hard. He immediately expressed the wish that none of the women he had disported himself with had got a child of his. *Nor anyone I happen to find in my bed tonight,* he thought, and smiled a secret smile. And went home.

Her name was Mignureal and she was Moonflower's daughter and she had seen him as no one should see any man, doubly one so cocky and full of needs as Shadowspawn: she had seen him gibbering in sorcery-induced fear one night. She had taken him home with her and tended him with her nervous mother staying close, having seen Mignue's soft eyes admiring Hanse. On another occasion he had been about to set forth on a dreadful mission she did not even know about when a look of strange intensity came over her face. "Oh Hanse—Hanse, take the crossed brown pot with you."

With an eerie feeling, he did that. It was the night on which his mission was to get a pitifully maimed Tempus out of the dripping hands of one Kurd, a man whose occupation bore that which was surely the ugliest word in any language: vivisectionist. Cutter-up of the living—and not as physician, either. As it turned out, the brown pot's contents saved his life that night, and he knew that Mignureal the S'danzo had some of her mother's power of Seeing. And then . . . and then it had been *Mignureal's* form the goddess Eshi had taken, to fetch him to that final dreadful confrontation with Vashanka.

And Eshi seems to love me—at least wants me, he mused, wending his full-bellied, red-cloaked way homeward. *Does Mignureal?*

And after a few steps more: *How old is she, anyhow?*

Ah Gods of Ilsig—what has that to do with anything? I don't even know how old I am!

Yet he knew that he knew, as he walked on all wrapped in his thoughts and new cloak, who and what he was: the son of some woman of Downwind and . . . Shalpa. A god. *Demi-mortal,* Vashanka had called him. That was a phrase that implied another half: demigod. Hanse was a demigod.

How in Ten Hells can I live with that?

How in Eleven Hells can I live with this wishing busi-

ness?! Anything I want—it's well nigh boring already!

He reached home, and his room, and she was there, small and lovely and vulnerable-looking in her nakedness, sitting up in his bed to smile and stretch forth her shapely arms to him as he entered. Mignureal, little Mignureal daughter of the woman Hanse loved but did not even know he wished were his mother.

"Darling! I thought you'd never come home to me!"

He turned to close the door and pretended to have trouble with the latch, keeping his back to her while he frowned and wrestled with thoughts and emotions.

So she slid out of the bed and came to him. She was all willowy and even lovelier, naked and softly lit, for there was only the light of the bright moon that smiled boldly through the window.

Unable to resist her nearness and upraised arms, he stepped into her embrace and as they kissed his hands moved all over the back of her, from nape to sulcus and back. Both of them trembled, and both longed.

"Mignue, Mignue...what are you doing here?"

She smiled, pressed to him, and nuzzled his neck. "You know what I am doing here, Hanse."

"Please...why did you come, Mignue? Why tonight? What prompted you to come—tonight?"

"Because I wanted to be with you, darling—to be yours."

He squeezed his eyes shut. Oh damn, damn. Six more questions elicited similar lovely yet unsatisfactory answers. It was all circular. *She has no idea and probably didn't really want to do this at all,* he thought in growing agony, *she's here because I wished it and Ils sent her, that's all, and I feel...I feel just so, so...rotten!*

She had just unbuckled and removed his belt, both sheaths included, and laid it carefully aside on the old keg he used as nightstand. She turned only her head, to give him an arch look over her shoulder. Hanse swallowed hard, and again. He felt truly evil, truly a monster.

She turned to face him with her hands behind her back and her head partly down, flaunting her breasts, and swung her torso this way and that far more in the manner of a little girl than a temptress. Her eyes and voice, however, were not those of a little girl:

"Want me, Hanse?"

"Ils and Eshi—who could not want you, Mignue? I—"

But that was the wrong thing to say, under the circumstances, which involved his mental state; a joyous smile sunned over her face and she ran to him across two whole feet, her arms whipping around him. Hanse stood stiff, one hand just touching her, while he chewed his lip and wished that he were— *No! I wish that if ever I wish that I were dead, it be not considered a wish!* And *"Oh,"* Mignue said, low, having discovered herself pressing against a very aroused male. And her arms around him clamped the harder, and she pressed in harder.

He stroked her thick and very soft hair. Revelation and inspiration hit him and he said it aloud:

"Ah, Mignue, Mignue . . . I wish that you wanted to wrap yourself in my nice new cloak and just *talk* a while."

"This may sound awful," she said against his chest, "but know what I'd like to do?"

Yes, he did.

She looked unequivocally and downright dangerously fetching in that wine-dark cloak, especially sitting on his bed with her legs drawn up (within the cloak, gods be thanked). Yes, of *course* she remembered telling him to take the crossed brown pot—and hadn't he? —Yes. And had it proven useful? —Yes. And he told her of that night, and she was astonished that *he* had done all that, rescuing the mighty and apparently immortal Tempus. Yet, that she had saved his life did not astonish her.

"It is the S'danzo, Hanse. You must know that a S'danzo never tells a client that she foresees his death. Never. Nor does a S'danzo dare try to interfere with the way of a world and the will of the gods, other than to suggest that that person have a care." She sat with her arms enwrapping her drawn-up legs and her hand clasping her wrist, and she was not looking at the young man who sat on the windowsill with his feet on the floor. He had drawn the drapes almost closed, but the room was as if twilit, not nighted.

"On the other hand . . . with those we love, we S'danzo cannot See as well, because the emotions are involved—you know, darling. *But!* There is a compensation. Sometimes we can See the danger, often without realizing it, and See just what those we love should do to avoid or to, uh, cope with it."

Hanse blinked. *She is telling me that she loves me . . . and has for over a year! Oh! Oh, g—Ils, Ils, god of my fa—hmp!—my mother, God of Gods . . . I wish that I knew whether that were true or not! Or not, I say!*

"There . . . I've said it. Now you know, Hanse, oh, Hanse. Now you know . . . I have loved you, loved you, oh *loved* you for years—ever since first I saw you, surely, although I was only a girl then."

Hanse swallowed. He felt like melting wax and his eyes had gone all blurry. *Me! Shadowspawn! Who ever loved me?! It's all I ever wanted—but I had to pretend, didn't I, so that when it happened, if it happened, I would know it was real . . . but I never would because I've always had to test, to try so hard not to be hurt. . . .*

He tried to be unobtrusive about wiping the damned unmanly embarrassing glistening tear off his cheek. As soon as he had done, the other eye let go. I hope she doesn't see, he thought, and was not even thinking about the power of the wish.

He asked her question after question about the whole Ils/Eshi/Vashanka business. She remembered none of it. She *had* had a horrible dream about his being forever lost to her, beyond her, because he was in the arms of a goddess, and she had wakened weeping. Her mother had held her and held her and crooned and spoken soft words to her and made her see that was silly, not at all logical or likely or possible.

Of course, Hanse thought, and said, "Me! With a goddess? Oh Mignureal!"

"I know," she said, darting a look at him and looking

away just as swiftly. "But we can't control our dreams, and sometimes they're so *real!*"

He steeled himself, and swallowed hard, and said, "This is a dream, of course."

She looked sharply at him. "What?"

"I said," he said, exerting all his strength to look at her and to say the words, "that this is a dream, of course. You could *not* be here in my room. You could *not* have been waiting naked for me, in my bed. It is not S'danzo; it is beneath that great soaring wonderful mother of yours, and your fine and proud old people, and . . . above all, Mignue, it is not you. You would not do such a thing. It is . . . it is *beneath* you. It is not what I want or you want, not in such a way, not now. It is not in accord with your pride or your dignity."

She was staring at him, and tears were flowing in long glistening tracks all down her cheeks and onto his cloak.

"It has to be a dream, don't you see?"

Mignureal raised her eyebrows, and no girl but a woman said, "It is not a dream, Hanse."

Again it hurt, and he had to steel himself and swallow hard and take a deep breath as well, that his voice might hold without breaking: "It is a dream, Mignue. And you will remember every bit of it. I wish that this were a dream for you, Mignureal, dear sweet Mignureal, and that you would remember every bit of it, and that you were at home asleep in you bed."

She said nothing in return, because she was not there. Only the new red cloak was, crumpled on his bed. He could still see the tear-spots, even from the windowsill. The wet darker spots from her tears, and he knew that she was home in bed.

He sat there feeling really stupid and feeling really sorry for himself, and yet after a time he seemed to hear a soft female chuckle in his head, inside his head, and knew that it was Eshi who chuckled and said, inside his head, *And you wondered why I came to you as Mignureal, ass—an ass and lovable being an ass, like all men!*

His purpose had been to spend this night abed with Mig-

211

nureal as he had others, and then to go to her home and learn what her mother and she, what her father and siblings, knew and thought and remembered. Now he would not know, for Hanse had at last discovered that which was not worthy of him. *I wish that I could be worthy of Mignureal and her love,* he thought, without thinking at all of Ils or of the power of the wish, and the entirety of his life was changed in an instant. Without knowing that, he undressed and went to bed.

The torture began.

Nearly an hour later he gave it up and made a wish.

The very very shapely daughter of that customs man and investigator Cusharlain was all soft writhing femininity in his bed and just wonderfully loving and amorous and wonderful to feel and think about and want, but after a while in her arms a poor pitifully surprised Hanse had to make the wish that he cease thinking about Mignureal and get over this very first experience with impotence.

Somewhere Ils smiled. In Hanse's bed, an ultra-shapely young woman did, too. At first Hanse simply sighed in relief, but that was soon replaced by both stronger emotion and stronger physical activity.

After that night a rather befogged Shadowspawn indulged himself in a very great deal of thinking. He could hardly wait for the time to be up and to be summoned again into the presence of the gods!

As it turned out, Ils had meant ten days and nights, not years or months. Then once again the tumbled lightless ruins of Eaglenest were transformed into a dazzling palace of gods, and Hanse of Downwind and the Maze was gazing down that long table at the faceless Shadow that was Shalpa, and the great light that was Ils of the Thousand Eyes, He from whom the Ilsigi had taken their name, and at the most absolutely incredibly beautiful and shapely woman any man ever saw. For that was the form Eshi chose to take this night, and Hanse realized: the *goddess* was showing him how magnificent She could be, how far beyond mortal Mignureal, and a great warmth and pride soared in him.

It occurred to him to ask if his wishes were done with, and the Great God replied that aye, all were done with save only the final lifelong desires, and Hanse said that was too bad, for a diplomat rose up in him and avowed that he'd have wished that the *woman* he loved, Mignureal, could be touched with the beauty and magnificence and sexuality of the *goddess* Eshi, who was beyond him.

"*Fa*ther-r—" Eshi began, and her father silenced her.

"And so you face me again, Hanse," He said. "Tell me that which is your desire."

"My desire is threefold," Hanse said. "First, that neither I nor anyone close to me, dear to me, ever knows the true moment of my *unavoidable* death. Have I expressed that aright?"

"It is specific, and well-expressed," that quiet sonorous voice of Power said, "and it is Done. And?"

"I desire superior ability with weapons, as well as good health and good fortune," Hanse said. "And to forget all that has happened. All that I have done and thought and wished (saving only for a dream that I share with Mignureal, daughter of the S'danzo), since that time when first You did approach me, in the matter of Vashanka."

For a long moment there was silence, and then the Shadow spoke, the living god who was shadow itself and who sat at the right hand of his father. "What? You would forget that you are my *son?!*" The voice was rustly, as befitted that of a shadow among shadows, but the last word boomed.

Hanse looked down. "Yes."

"What?" Eshi demanded. "You would forget all that you have done—forget that you have lain with *me?*"

And again Hanse waxed diplomatic: "I choose to be a human and mortal, O Beauty Itself. How could any man live at peace, when he has seen You and even held You, and knows it? It is too much, Goddess, Eshi. You must not let me remember and be tortured with memory of what was and might have been."

She waxed even more beautiful then, and as irresistible as the word itself, and her smile was sun and moonbeams bathing him in warmth. "Let it be," she said, and became a handsome and shapely woman in white, and no more.

"Your son, Shalpa my son, is touched with genius," He of the Thousand Eyes said. "Yet I would remind you, Hanse, Godson. Much, much of the world is within your grasp. We have conferred; you could even opt to join us, to preside perpetually over the mortals of the earth. Would you *be* one of them instead?"

"I am . . ." (Hanse swallowed hard) ". . . grandfather."

"You might also continue to have your every wish so long as you are within our precincts, or the greatest of wishes: that your every desire and wish be yours."

"That one," Shalpa's voice rustled, "and *then* forgetfulness."

Hanse fell to his knees and his voice shook. *"Let me be Hanse!"*

"It's the damned eternal truth," Eshi said. "Your charming bastard is a damned genius, Shalpa!"

"Yet damned," her brother answered. "Damned by his own tongue and his own wish. The terminator of a god, the savior of his city and toppler of Empire, the son of a god and lover of a god—and beloved of a god, eh?—damned to mortality, humanity, by his own asinine wish!" And the Shadow of Shadows . . . vanished.

"Tell my father," Hanse said very quietly, "that I have known misery not knowing the identity of my father, and now in knowing it. Tell him that . . . that his son is strong."

"True," Ils said, "and I'd never have thought it. Done!"

When Hanse awoke he was in the ruins of Eaglenest and wondered what in all Hells he was doing here. Yet he had had this wonderful joyous dream involving Mignureal, and he felt a glow as he dragged himself to his feet on that pocked, cracked stone floor and, stepping around fallen columns and detritus, left the mansion that had been. He glanced over at the old well but shrugged. It was going to take a lot of labor and gear to get those moneybags up out of there. He sighed and started pacing down the hill toward Sanctuary.

On the day following, Moonflower told him seriously that she might have been mistaken in forbidding him to see Mignureal; perhaps gods were at work, here. That day only three persons were slain, one way or another, by the Fish-Eyed-Folk-From-Oversea, but many more lives were ruined by them and their doings. That evening while three of her siblings peeked and giggled from this vantage point and that, Hanse and the very young S'danzo Mignureal discovered together that they had both had the same dream last night, and that gods must be at work here.

Considerably later a much-bejeweled Beysib amused herself by punishing an Ilsigi offender—never mind the minor offense—by handing the youth a pouch from her belt. When he opened it, the beynit inside bit him at once. The snake's neurotoxin worked swiftly. The Sanctuarite was dead in less than a minute, and the Beysib was not punished. The PFLS burned a wagonload of hay on the Processional. That was the day Hanse received the message to meet Zip in Sly's Place.

(Rumor was that Throde the Gimp was set upon that night after closing, but he was fine next day, limping around Sly's without a mark, and no one took the rumor seriously.)

She had been a fixture of the Maze for a hundred years, or maybe it was a dozen. She sat outside the family home/shop in which her husband sold . . . things, and raised their several children well while keeping her husband happy. And she Saw. She did not charge a great deal of money for her Seeings, this S'danzo named Moonflower. She Saw danger and felicities to come, pain and pleasure to come, and she Saw *linkages*.

She had Seen enough once to let Hanse know that he was involved in a very large plot emanating from Ranke itself; a treacherous governor's concubine had quite charmed Hanse and, with a treacherous Hell-Hound, aided him into the palace one night to steal the Savankh.* Warned by

*Detailed in "Shadowspawn," in *Thieves' World*, 1979

Moonflower, Hanse had wriggled out of that one, and the two plotters paid the supreme penalty. Moonflower had Seen other things for Hanse, whom she could not help liking and thinking of as a good boy even though she knew he was not. And she had Seen many things for many others. Ilsigi and Twanders, Mrsevadans and Rankans, Syrese and Aurveshi... and now Beysibs.

Oh yes, even the newest conquering invaders came to the gross diviner Hanse called "Passionflower" (for he did charm that woman and bring out the kitten in her), sitting just outside the shop on a stool which she overflowed all around, wearing yards and yards of fabrics in divers colors and hues and patterns and more colors. She made a Seeing for the Beysib Esanssu on Anenday, and again on Ilsday, and the following Anenday as well. The fish-folk woman complained about the brevity of the first reading, and then on her return she dared complain of its accuracy even though it did help her rediscover both lost objects she had sought. And so Moonflower gave her another divining at half-rate, and damned if the oversea bitch didn't complain that this time she was not treated with sufficient respect. (An eight-year-old child, Moonflower's, stared at her was all; it was *hard*, not staring at freaks.)

At least she went away all elated after the third session, because the S'danzo had Seen an upturn in Esanssu's love-life. All races had losers, even conquerors, and Esanssu botched it. Naturally she came back to blame Moonflower. She railed and screamed and threatened to such an extent that Moonflower's husband came rushing out, fearful for his wife. Blind with rage, Esanssu hardly saw him as she drew and slashed him. He fell spurting blood.

Moonflower screamed. All huge-eyed, she started to collapse, but caught herself, or perhaps it was adrenaline that caught her and powered her to her feet in a lurch and flaring rustle of skirts and shawls of many colors and hues and patterns. All on automatic she slapped the murderous creature from oversea, with all her considerable weight behind the blow. The Beysib was dashed against the wall of the shop with frightful impact. Her head struck first. She slid down the wall, leaving a bright red smear on the stucco, until she reached a sitting position. Her eyes were open and her legs twitched. To Moonflower's horror (had she not been crouched over her wounded husband, weeping but curbing her wails while she ripped skirts to stem the tide of his blood) Esanssu was dead.

All that was bad enough and everyone knew that Moon-flower was in trouble. Justice was a word, and the Beysib were conquerors. Unfortunately there was more; a Beysib soldier, just insulted by three Ilsigi children who had run and seemingly vanished into a warren of alleys and alley-like streets, came arunning. Already irate, and having lost her head along with having taken on the arrogance of all conquering occupation forces everywhere, she drew her long single-bladed sword from her back and struck, all in a rush. Moonflower's husband would live; Moonflower died there on the street.

Hanse arrived only a few minutes after that flurry of senseless violence and murder. Half in shock, he tried to cope with the weeping of Mignureal and the screams and wails of her siblings, and could not. He was too choked with grief to talk coherently and too blinded with tears even to see. Without even knowing it he ran, blindly and full of the agony of grief. And rage.

Upon turning a corner a couple of blocks away he ran full into a Beysib peacekeeper. He never knew whether it was the same who had murdered Moonflower, beloved Moonflower, mother of Mignureal.

"Here you, what's all this ru—"

"Excuse me," Hanse said sobbing, and buried his dagger in the creature's belly, and twisted it and drew it out and, hardly having paused, ran on. Everyone got out of his way, for Hanse called Shadowspawn seemed to have gone mad.

"Here, you—what the (deleted) are you doing here?—this is Zip's turf, *Mazer,* and you're carryin' an awful lot of sharp metal. Me an' my buddy here will just take—"

That one of Zip's Boys named Jing broke off. He knew this interloper at the edge of the several blocks of Downwind that Zip controlled, and he'd never seen the sinister fellow look so—so sinister. Mean. His black eyes below his black hair and above his russet peasantish tunic looked so *ugly*. His face was working as with a tic and his expression was one of rage barely controlled by mighty effort.

"I don't know you but I know Speaklittle there with you. You reach for one of your weapons and you are deader than the Stare-Eye froggy I ran into a few hours ago. I promise not to use the same knife on you, though—don't want to contaminate the blood of a fellow Ilsig with the cess they have for blood . . . even if you are busy dying at the time." An arm jerked up and pointed. "I'm outside Zip's line. Go and tell him I'm here to see him. Zip and I know each other and he's expecting me. I'll see him but I'll be wearing my stickers when I do, and I expect him and you and his body-guards to be armed, too. Go on, Speaky, *hurry!* Get Zip!"

Jing frowned, made a sneery face, and reached for his sword. That quick, he was looking at a slender throwing knife in the hand poised just above the interloper's left shoulder. It stayed there, ready, and Jing left his short nasty sword where it was. The world knew that the former Down-winder named Hanse knew how to throw a knife, and Jing thought that continuing to live was just what he wanted to do.

The knife went back into its sheath so fast that Hanse might just have flipped it there, except that he hadn't. With an expression of seething and only just-controlled rage, he looked at Speaklittle.

"Speaky, go on and tell Zip. I and your friend will stay right here and make mean-eyes at each other. *Go*, damn it!"

Speaklittle departed at speed while Jing looked at Hanse, mean-eyed. For some reason he said, "You really kill a fish-eyes today, Hanse?"

"A few hours ago. Since then I've been trying to think

and I been grieving. That makes two of 'em I've killed.
I'm ashamed that it hasn't been more, but I'm slow about
some things. And the knife I had out to warn you—believe
that. It's not the one I stuck into the Stare-Eyes. This is the
one that's been into two Stare-Eyes."

"Ahhh. And . . . you say Zip's *expecting* you?"

"Can't imagine why you didn't have the word," Hanse
lied, catching Jing's respectful look. "What's your name?"

A few minutes later Speaklittle came running back, to
escort Hanse to Zip. No one said anything about Hanse's
arsenal. They went about a block and a half, and into a
building and out again, and into a barrel. That led into a
very secret passage, a short one, which led to Zip. He was
flanked by two bodyguards and looked as hungry as ever.

"Hanse. You're presuming a bit, but I go along. What's
so—"

"I'm breaking into the god-damned palace to remove the
Beyswine's god-damned scepter and the heart of any god-
damned Stare-Eye murderer that gets in my way and I hope
some do, Zip. I thought you'd be interested. You want to
help? I could use some good line, silk, and a very good
archer with guts. Decide fast, man—I'm goin' in tonight."

The first time Shadowspawn had entered the governor's
lofting manse he had walked in, with help from Prince-
Governor Kadakithis's traitor-concubine, Lirain. He'd had
only to break out, with the Savankh. The second time had
been on his own and, as he realized only after he was in
the Prince's privy apartment 'way, '*way* up in the palace,
ill-advised. He had stolen nothing, and again he had to break
out.

This time he had no inside help, but he had help. PFLS
members, working hard to look unobtrusive, haunted every
street within blocks. Others were way over on the other side
of town, raising a ruckus and attracting lots of armed Beys.
From the shadowy granary across from the palace's outer
defense wall, Hanse watched while Zip's best archer sent
the arrow up. It whizzed past the spire atop the palace and,

checked by the long line it trailed, swung back. It went around the spire about six times and the archer and his assistant really leaned on the line.

Shadowspawn raised his eyebrows and nodded. "You do good work," he muttered, and nudged himself out of his natural habitat, the shadows.

The PFLSer didn't even flash his teeth. Once Hanse had hold of the silken line strong enough to support two Hanses, the archer did his best to emulate the thief. Into the shadows, with arrow ready for any interfering Beysib—or even nosey fellow Ilsigi, since this mission was more important than individuals. Right now Hanse, not a member of the Front, was the most important person in the Front. Zip had said so. The best archer in Sanctuary figured that made him fourth, after Zip and Kama. Right now Kama was fourth, since she was an archer's assistant.

He watched while the wraith all in black squirreled up onto the roof of the granary, poised, and swung out across the street. Looked like he hit the palace wall hard. Went right on up, though, after just a moment.

He was without that long swordlike knife, but with a leathern pouch boiled to rocky hardness and strapped to his chest, and with a pair of throwing stars, and that strange four-foot staff, too, and of course the prepared arrows and the short bow. Step after step and hand over hand, he went up that wall in an impressive sort of reverse rappel.* Eventually the archer and Kama and the other secretly watching PFLSers lost sight of him, but they continued to wait and to stare upward just as if they could see.

They could not; they could see only shadows. The thing was, any one of those shadows might be Hanse.

It had been weird, really weird. The elated Zip and Kama arranged this and that help, and offered all sorts of other

*For a detailed description of Hanse's entry into the upper precincts of the palace, see "The Vivisectionist" in the third Thieves' World volume, *Shadows of Sanctuary*. No better way in has been found, although having help is nice.

aid that Hanse neither needed nor wanted. Yet as he was returning from Downwind, he had met a person he had never seen before in his life. A skinny ugly girl with warts and a facial birthmark the size of a lemon but the color of dried blood, and a figure so unfortunate that even her mother must wince.

"You are he called Shadowspawn, and you are going climbing. My master bids me give you this wand, and trebly urge you to take it with you. Just push it into your boots or something, and leave it behind when you leave your . . . destination."

"My name is Mudge Kraket," Hanse impatiently said, "and I am not going aclimbing. Heights scare me. Why not find someone else to hand that funny stick? Looks like a good piece; a dune-viper carved from mahogany, isn't it?"

"Because you are Hanse and you are on a mission for all Ilsigi and thus Ils Himself, and because you will need this. It is important. Gods are at work this night, Hanse." She continued to proffer the staff.

"Orders?" he came back, and he was truculent.

"Oh stop being silly." And suddenly she was all aglow, and the glow was *bright,* like Love itself, so that Hanse squinted and shielded his eyes and wished that sorcery would leave him alone. "Take it! Have you really forgot so soon, Godson, lover?"

Since she then vanished utterly, and the stick had got itself somehow into his hand, Hanse decided that it were best to take the damned thing up the wall with him. He *respected* sorcery; only idiots did not. He just didn't like it, any more than did most non-adepts. Definitely hoping he must have to do with no more this night, he went on.

He was swinging down Tanner when the true light appeared—Mignureal, all wan and red-eyed and droopy in her dark red dress of mourning. She ran into his embrace and at once commenced to weep. Hanse, who had sworn off weeping two hours ago, immediately began anew. Meanwhile he hugged her close and stroked her long dark hair.

"I'm about to have to leave this damned town, Mignue,"

he told her very quietly, "and I want you to come with me."

"But," she said, pushing herself back to look into his face, "why—why would you want to 1—" And her eyes went blank while a jerk went through her. Then so stiff that she quivered while she spoke in that strange voice: *"Hanse— take the red cat."*

"What?!"

"When you go up the silken rope for Sanctuary, Hanse, take along the red cat."

Hanse held her automatically while he stared at nothing. *God and gods damn it all, sorcery's all over the place and everybody in Sanctuary knows what I'm going to do and has advice! If this goes on I'll be so laden I couldn't climb into bed!*

Yet he knew that was not so; only two knew, one by sorcery and Mignue by a sudden seizure of her S'danzo Seeing. And he remembered the brown pot, and as she suddenly said, "Oh. What am I doing—I have to go home and get ready," he knew that he had to go to Sly's Place. She whirled and ran. Hanse heaved a great sigh and rubbed his face. He started walking, feeling dizzy.

A short time later he was staring at Ahdiovizun with eyes like dying coals. "Ahdio, I—"

"Hanser! Lord God Ils and Shalpa, Hanser! I've wanted to see you! You'll never believe what happened the other night after you three left! Ole Notable pounced up on the table in back and lapped up every bit of the beer in your mug that he could reach, then cried and pawed for me to help him get the rest!—and he wouldn't *touch* the mugs of those other two! What'd you *do* to that cat, anyhow—you a sorcerer, Hanse?"

"Ahdio," Hanse said as if he hadn't heard and without changing expression, "I need to borrow Notable. Just for awhile, just tonight. Please, Ahdio, don't give me a hard time. I've got to."

"Hanser, that cat wouldn't *ever*—"

Ahdio broke off to watch as Notable came in and started in rubbing Hanse's buskined legs.

And so Shadowspawn bore a cat in a claw-proof, fang-proof pouch on his chest when he went up the wall this night, and a flask, and a (presumably sorcerous) wand-thing and bow and two arrows on his back. The cat was a bit weighty and Hanse was used to climbing light. Still, the junk on his back aided the balance and Notable was still and quiet. The cat was no heavier than a glazed brown pot with a cross on it, Hanse told himself, and up he went. Eventually he peered downside up through the diamond-shaped window, into the luxurious apartment that had been Prince-Governor Kadakithis's and now was the dwelling of the Beysa herself. It was unoccupied.

Hanse swung in. Without even looking around he saw to his egress, as planned. The silken cord dangling from the pinnacle was a loss. The one he'd come down on was bound and braced on the roof-wall above. So was the third one, which was very long. Lacing its end through the pre-pared arrow, he dumped the rest of the cord out the window. Then, awkwardly bracing himself, he nocked arrow to short-bow and took aim as well as he could.

I can do it. Have to. Don't want to have to pull the thing back up and shoot again! You can do it, Hanse! Breathe out, in, out; suck in a good deep one. Pull. Sight. Oops. Now—

The string twanged and the arrow zipped out the window, trailing its line.

Peering out, Hanse saw at once that it was a rotten shot, way wide of the mark, arcing leftward. Oh Thousand-Eyed Ils, and there was someone down there, too, watching. *Suppose it's a Stare-Eye . . .*

That one of many posted PFLS members let the arrow pass, caught the cord, held it aloft and waved it, and started running to where Kama and the archer waited. *Knew I could do it,* Hanse thought smiling. He turned, opening the rocky-hard pouch on his chest. Without a sound Notable emerged and bounced feather-light onto the pillow-strewn, silken-sheeted bed. It sat, examined a paw, and began to lick it.

Oh, really wonderful, Hanse mused, and supposed that

he would just have to accept that Mignureal was a *young* S'danzo and inexperienced, and couldn't be right every time. And he had to get the fool cat back down, too—but thinking of Mignue had reminded him of Moonflower, and that put mist in his eyes. Once he had angrily rubbed them clear, he saw two things.

The first was not the Beysa's wand of office but her *crown*, a coiled snake done in gold with emeralds set as eyes; with markings of coral and of ruby and twinkling bits of glass banding the body again and again. That was the first thing he saw: a golden snake of far more value to the PFLS than a mere wand. The second thing he saw, however, was the real thing.

A beynit, he knew. A nasty-tempered snake with a bite that killed in a minute or less—and no way of stopping or countering that toxin. This one was probably trained—a watch-snake. It was about four feet away on the carpet, and it was staring at him.

Oh my god, Hanse thought, *I'm dead!*

At the very edge of the bed, not two feet directly above the beynit, Notable arched its back and hissed. The snake snapped its head over to stare up at the cat. Notable made a mean sound in its throat. The beynit recoiled just a bit, a sinuous rope, and Notable made another nasty remark. Then it hissed with what seemed to Hanse enough volume to rouse every unblinking sword-backed fish-eyed guard in the palace. Sliding his feet, Hanse moved back and to the side. He moved more slowly than ever he had, as he eased one of the throwing stars off his belt. The beynit caught that motion, and twitched its head to stare . . . and with a low growly sound Notable pounced at its tail. The snake's nerve broke. It rushed into the nearest nice, dark haven—the pouch so recently occupied by Notable.

Hanse whipped the flap over and back up and over again, winding the bag, and fastened it tight. The chances were that not even a worm could have gotten out of that pouch, but Hanse dumped a pillow out of its nice striped satin casing and popped the pouch in. The fit was very snug.

With an azure robe-sash he tied that pillowcase as tightly as he had ever bound anything in his life.

"Remind me to take that with me," he muttered, and hurried to the Ti-Beysa's crown. Notable said nothing, but only stared at the pouch while his tail imitated a nervous snake. Hanse shook another pillow out of its casing, choosing a dark one, and with a smile popped in the crown worth the ransom of a prince—or of a scurvy little town called Sanctuary. He tied that silken package, too, and made it very, very fast to his back.

"Notable," he said, gingerly picking up the pillow casing that housed a bag of boiled leather he kept reminding himself was hard and thick enough to turn a good dagger-blow, "we've got to go. I'm afraid you can't ride in the bag. This snake'll be of some value to Z—to Sanctuary. Got any ideas about your travel arrangements?"

Uncharacteristically, Notable gave him a nice little "mrow."

"That," Hanse said, "is a rotten dumb answer. Here." And he took the little flask from the pouch at his waist, and poured beer into a superbly wrought Rankan bowl that was not Beysib property. After that it was maddening, jittering there by the window while the damned cat lapped daintily as if it had all the time in the world not to mention a sore tongue.

After about a month of that, Notable finished and looked up with eyes like black marbles. He licked his mouth exaggeratedly, and started in on his whiskers.

"I'm impressed," Shadowspawn said. "I am also leaving."

Notable said "mew" in a sickeningly sweet voice and sent his tongue all the way around his yawning mouth again. Hanse made a face, started to swing up into the window, remembered, and turned to toss the snake-carven staff onto the floor. It landed about a foot from Notable and rolled a foot. Notable pounced straight past Hanse to the windowsill and turned back to look.

"Look at you. Bravest cat in the world with the real

thing, and afraid of a little st—"

The staff shimmered, its wriggly carving seeming to wriggle in reality. Then, while a few hundred ants played footrace up Hanse's back, the staff moved. It glided along the floor, and up onto the bed, and to the far end, and into a nice dark sheltering place: under the Beysa's figured silk bedspread.

"I've got to get out of this damned town," Hanse muttered in a voice wavery as the sand-viper, and went out the window. He had to drag himself back up that fulvistone wall on one silken rope so that he could go down another—all the way across the palace grounds and wall and the Processional to where Kama and company would have made the arrow-end of the line fast.

Notable passed him on the way to the roof. Hanse gave him a glare, wishing he could go up walls that way. Maybe with the talons the Stare-Eyes slid onto their fingers when they ate . . .

He was up and on his belly, pulling himself up between two merlons of that toothily crenelated defense-wall around the roof, when he heard the voice. The accent was neither Rankan nor Ilsigi.

"So. A rotten little thief tries to invade us, does he? Well, Ilsiger slime, this is your last climb!"

And Hanse heard the sound of the guard's sword clearing its scabbard on his back, doubtless to come down on Shadowspawn's neck. Or wrists, or forearms; it didn't matter. He was helpless and absolutely vulnerable, on his stomach and clutching with both hands while his legs dangled.

That was when he was startled so that he nearly let go and fell, for his ears were assaulted by the loudest and most terrible yowling screech he had ever heard in his life. Wincing, scrabbling desperately, Hanse twisted his neck to look up.

He saw the Beysib guard all astagger, shocked by that ghastly sound; and he saw the red streak that was Notable on the pounce. The cat began eating holes in the Stare-Eye's arm and the poor worse-than-disconcerted idiot forgot what he was about and struck at the cat with his sword. That cost him not just the pain as he struck his own arm, but his balance. With only a grunt he went right over Hanse and through the crenelation and down a hundred feet and more to a messy splat of an end.

Mignureal did it again, Hanse thought, wriggling onto the roof in double-time. *She knew, and Notable just saved my life. Twice, probably. But he also went down with the Stare-Eye...how'll I ever explain to Ahdio?* Then he was on his feet, ready to seize the taut rope stretching down and out and down, and the cat on the nearer merlon said "mrowr?"

Hanse could not control his chuckle. "I like you, cat! Want to hop on and ride me down? Careful now—you sink a claw into my shoulder and I'll tell Ahdio you're soft on mice!"

They went down.

The snake from the Beysa's apartment would be useful— it and its venom and a few physicians working away in quest of an antitoxin. As for the Beysa, the sand-viper in her bed had doubtless given her a lot of fun. As for the Ti-Beysa crown—the PFLS was made. Amid all the yammering chatter of PFLS voices, Hanse sort of faded into the shadows, fleeing all the praise and overblown encomiums. He was sure that there was no way the word was not going to get out. The theft and the blow against the invaders were enormous accomplishments. Someone would tell: Shadowspawn did it.

I've got to get out of this dam' town!

Mignureal went up the long, long hill with him, she leading the ass and he the horse.

"I've got to leave town," he had told her. "Maybe... maybe forever. You're coming with me, right?"

She stared at him for a long while, until at last she nodded. "Right."

Up at Eaglebeak, they tethered the two animals to fallen chunks of fine building stone and Hanse went to the old well. *If only I hadn't dropped all that coin down here*, he thought. *This is going to be a job among jobs. Gods, but I wish I had it out already!*

Since by choice he remembered only that he was Hanse, son of a barely-known mother and the never-seen father who had been only her casual acquaintance, he knew nothing about previous wishes. He was mightily surprised when the two laden, leathern saddlebags came floating, noisily dripping, up to his waiting hands.

Zip and Jing and a lot of others were mightily surprised, a little over an hour later, when a big leather bag came flying down, seemingly from the sky. It struck the hard-packed earth of a Downwinder "street" with an enormous crashing jingling noise . . . followed by a lot of little jingles as a flashing clinking rolling skittering mass of good minted silver splashed out.

"For Sanctuary," a voice called from above, and it was not the voice of Ils or even Shalpa, but of a thief on a rooftop. Getting that bag up there had been a lot of work, but it was worth it for the effect: "Shadows can go anywhere, into palaces and even into the hallowed and guarded precincts of Zip!"

"Hanse! You've just been elected second-in-command and Master Tactician! Come down, man!"

They waited a long time.

Much, much later than that, an aide ushered a sentry into the tent of their leader.

"Your pardon, General. Go ahead, Pheres."

"Sir, there's a man and a woman, both mighty young out here. Wrigglies. I mean Ilsigi, sir. On a horse and an ass. With a lot of silver coin in an old cracked leather bag— a big one. Threw back his white robe and hood to show me he's dressed all in black. Said he's a friend of yours? From Sanctuary? Right out of the shadows, he says. Sir."

The general stared, then smiled and rose from his camp-table to stride past the two men and out of the tent. "Hanse!" Tempus called.

GYSKOURAS

Lynn Abbey

Illyra needed no special S'danzo power to read the young man's past. He had been, and still was, a sewer-snipe. His face was marred by neglect and disease. He watched her, and her scrying table, with the desperate intensity of one who had been beaten, betrayed, yet still hoped for victory. She stood beside her table to stare him out of her shop, when he tossed an ancient, filthy golden coin onto the gray baize beside her.

"I need to know. They said you would know, one way or the other." His surprisingly deep voice made the simple phrases into an accusation.

"Sometimes," she replied, listening to the steady pounding of Dubro's hammer, her fingers poised over the coin.

They came to her in greater numbers now that Moon-flower was dead and her daughter had run away with the thief, Shadowspawn. Illyra could not think of the immense woman who had defended her right to *be* S'danzo in Sanctuary without feeling a storm of grief as immense as the old woman herself. She wanted to tie a knot across her doorway, turn her back to the Sight, and give way to her grief, but they came with their coins and *demanded* and she did not know how to turn them away. Dubro helped, intimidating the ones he sensed danger in, but he had let this one through. Her forefinger brushed the gold. "If the answer can be known, sometimes I can know it." Gathering her skirts over one arm, she settled behind the table and gestured for him to sit on the stool. The gold was still on the baize and the silk was still tied around her cards when he began his story.

"I killed a pig last night. By the White Foal—for luck. I need lots of luck."

Illyra felt the first lies drift between them. Sanctuary was swollen with Beysib stomachs and Ranke, tearing itself apart with wars and assassinations, was a fading presence in this corner of its once-great Empire. Even sewer-snipes should know enough to sell a pig for Beysib gold and use the gold to buy luck.

"I—I took the blood to a place, a special place. It's mine, and Vashanka's. I gave Him the blood."

She set the cards aside and suppressed a shiver. Unlike many S'danzo women sitting in their rooms throughout the Empire, Illyra did have the Sight. An un-Sighted S'danzo woman survived by listening to her clients without laughing; she used the cards for mystery. Illyra used the cards for inspiration and guidance when the Sight came to her; she had no need for inspiration as this youth unburdened himself.

"It was like a wind. It was hot and cold; wet and dry all at once."

"Then it could not have been a wind," she told him, though she Saw the truth of his memories swirling around her. It was not like *her* Sight to be out of her control this way; she sought to rein it in.

"It was a wind. And the blood—the blood was covered with sparks.

She Saw the secret place in his mind: an altar abandoned to the marshes and discovered by the snipe who prayed there without knowing what it was or had been. Blood sacrifices made on its mossy stones—not pig's blood but men's blood: Beysib blood and bits of flesh he'd hacked from their corpses as offerings in his own private worship. Illyra felt the unholy wind whip around him while the rest of the marsh froze motionless and saw the blue-white flames dance on the blood. She heard the shrill giggle of a child's laughter as the congealed mess on the altar was absorbed into the flame; then the Sight was gone and there was only the ragged, scared youth—who called himself Zip and tried to hide his true name even from himself—staring at her.

"So, what do you see. Did the Stormgod hear me? Does Vashanka favor me? Can I bind Him to me? Sell me a potion to bind the Stormgod!"

She meant to send him away. The S'danzo had no use for gods and were happiest when the gods had nothing to do with the S'danzo. It didn't matter that she could answer his questions. He had focused her Sight on the god and she wanted him, and all that was in his memories, gone before *it* noticed her. Yet she could still hear the laughter and didn't that mean, answer him or not, that the damage was already done?

The youth mistook her hesitation for imminent betrayal. "Don't give me *suvesh-talk*." He reached across the table to grip her wrist.

"See the priests if you want to talk to the Stormgod," she replied icily, extracting herself with a swift, small movement he had never seen, or felt, before. But for the blacksmith, whose hammer rang in the sunlight beyond her shop, she'd have been a sewer-snipe herself. She knew his type of brazen pride—and knew, as he did himself, that any whim of fate could squash him, without warning. He had stumbled into something vaster and more dangerous than he had ever imagined. As much as he lusted after the excitement and glory, he feared it.

"What do the priests know?" he said, as if any priest would have spoken to him. "Nosing up to the snakes. They don't know anything about Vashanka."

"If you know so much more than the priests, you certainly know more than a S'danzo fortune-teller." She pushed the gold coin back to him.

"A half-S'danzo fortune-teller who knew when that damned fleet would arrive could talk to Vashanka if she dared." He ignored the coin and met her stare.

Anything that survived in the gutter of Sanctuary was dangerous. Zip had already violated her home with his visions; would he be any more dangerous with the truth about his prayers, sacrifices, and altar—or any the less?

"Keep your gold and everything else. Vashanka is no more."

He sat back as if she'd struck him. Surely he'd heard the rumors, lived through the storm that saw Vashanka's name struck from the pantheon archstones? Perhaps he hadn't quite believed that the Rankan Stormgod had been vanquished in the skies over Sanctuary, but he should have learned to contain his horror if he expected to survive.

"I give Him blood at my altar . . . and He takes it!"

"Fool! Leave the gods to the priests. You find a pile of rotting stones in the mud by the White Foal and you think you can lure Vashanka to your cause. Vashanka! The Stormgod of Ranke—and with the blood of a *pig!*"

"He hears me! I feel Him but I can't hear Him! He's telling me something and I can't hear him!"

"You don't want to know what hears you. Could Ranke have built a temple to Vashanka, lost it to the White Foal, and all Sanctuary forgotten it was there except for you?" She was standing, leaning over her table, screaming in his face and unmindful of everything except the laughter *he'd* left in her mind. She couldn't See what he had raised yet, but it was getting clearer the longer he sat there with his sacrifices and memories battering against her.

232

"Get out of here! Vashanka does not hear you! No god yet born hears you! Nothing hears you! May the dung rise up and swallow you before anything listens to you again!"

She did not believe the S'danzo had the power to curse, but the sewer-snipe did. Zip backed up until the sunlight from the doorway fell around his feet, then he turned and ran, not noticing, or perhaps not caring, that he had left his gold coin behind.

"'Lyra! What happened?" Dubro called to her from the doorway. He took a step to follow the youth, then turned back and rushed to catch Illyra before she collapsed over her table. He carried her in his arms like a sick child, berating himself for not sensing the danger in the young man, while she whispered broken phrases in the ancient S'danzo language.

The rat-faced sewer-snipe had forced her to See what should not be Seen and what she should not dare to remember. Each breath and heartbeat solidified the images and knowledge. Illyra worked frantically to blind herself to what had happened, before it spread like poison through wine and condemned her as surely as it had condemned the young man. She bound the knowledge in the form of one of the great black carrion-birds that flocked above the Charnel House and, with a wrenching sob, set it free.

"'Lyra, what's wrong?" her husband asked, stroking her hair and swabbing her tears with the corner of his sweaty tunic.

"I don't know," she answered honestly. A shimmering blackness of her own devising hung in her memories. The fear remained, and a sense of doom, but the vision itself had been seared away; the sound of a child crying was all that remained. "The children," she whispered.

Dubro left his forge in the care of his new, anxious apprentice and followed Illyra through the Bazaar to the Street of Red Lanterns. Children were an inevitable by-product of life on the Street, and even if most of them wound up in the gutters, a few of them enjoyed a healthy, sheltered childhood within the Houses themselves. Myrtis, madam

233

of the fortresslike Aphrodisia House, kept the boys as well as the girls, and had apprenticed one youth to Dubro in exchange for sheltering the couple's twin son and daughter.

The Street was quiet and drab in the afternoon sunlight. Illyra let go of Dubro's hand and told herself that there was no danger, that the blackness in her mind was a nightmare she could release and forget. She thought nothing of the young woman running toward them until she fell to her knees before them.

"Shipri be praised, you're right here! He was sleeping with the rest—"

The woman's hysteria rekindled Illyra's anxiety and her Sight. She Saw the room where Myrtis, frowning, leaned over a cradle; where chubby blonde Lillis cowered in a shadowed corner; and where her year-and-a-half-old son had stopped crying. Following the certainty of her vision she raced ahead down stairways and corridors.

"You've come so quickly," the ageless madam said, looking up from the cradle, a momentary wrinkle of confusion on her brow. "Ah, but yes, you do have the Sight, don't you?" The confusion vanished. "You know as much as I, then." She made room for the child's mother at the cradle.

The little boy lay rigid in some sudden, paralyzing fever. His breath came in sporadic gasps, each holding the possibility that there would be no others. His tears were drying on his dirty cheeks. Illyra brushed her fingers across one rivulet and shivered when she saw that the darkness was in the tears themselves.

"It is like no disease I know of," Myrtis disclaimed. "I would send word to Lythande, but the Blue Star is beyond my call now. We can summon Stulwig or some other—"

"There's no need," Illyra said wearily.

She was seeing everything twice: once with her own eyes and mind, then a second time with the Sight. The strangeness should have been overwhelming, but because the Sight itself was involved, there could be no surprises. Dubro pushed aside the curtain and joined them. She glanced at him and Saw the completeness of his being: his boyhood, his manhood, his death—and quickly lowered her eyes. Again she made a raven of Vision and set the knowledge free, but the new darkness it left within her was insignificant compared to the old.

Because she would only look at her shallow-breathing son whose shape and fate was the same in both visions, Illyra was left alone with him. She sat on the rocking stool and felt the square of window-light move across her shoulders, then the first chill of twilight. They brought her a thin broth, which she ignored, and wrapped a heavier shawl around herself as the night air thickened. She moved as little as Arton did in her arms.

A fresh wind carried the weather through Sanctuary: an almost silent storm of thin clouds passing swiftly before the moon. It was midnight, perhaps, or somewhat later, when a moon-cast shadow broke free and came to rest on the headboard of the cradle. Illyra bowed her head and allowed the raven to return. Sight decayed and reformed without darkness. She Saw Zip's face, his benighted altar, and the mark of a Stormgod in her son's cloudy tears.

She did not know yet how to save Arton, though Sight and sight were the same now and a path of silver-edged importance was emerging where there had been only blackness. Her plan was still unformed when she drew the borrowed shawl tightly around herself and went, unseen and without light, through the back passages of the Aphrodisia.

It was well past midnight, for the Street had become quiet and the moon had set. Fog crept up from the harbor, emphasizing the silence, the darkness, and the dangers. Illyra, who disliked the city and traveled its streets as seldom as possible, walked confidently toward the garrison barracks where her half-brother was in command of the guard. In the back of her mind she recalled all the gossip of the Bazaar: how Sanctuary was more dangerous than ever now that so many gangs, mercenaries, and soldiers were taking an interest in it. She recalled as well that no S'danzo had ever used the Sight as she was using it to walk the streets in utter darkness, utterly alone and utterly safe. She could have distrusted its unfolding powers, conceived as they were as her son lay touched by some unknowable Stormgod, but, flush with the confidence of the Sight itself, she dismissed her thoughts and stepped deftly around the silver-traced offal.

"Ischade?"

Illyra turned, recognizing neither the name nor the hoarse voice whispering it. Her Sight touched on a ragged beggar.

"Why do you walk tonight?" the man asked.

As she had Seen with Dubro, she Saw with the beggar-king—and much, as well, about the necromant, Ischade, he had mistaken her for. She stepped back from him, and he from her, although in the darkness he could not have seen her but only sensed that she could see something in him that even Ischade was blind to. The new aspects of Sight were quickly becoming familiar to her; she continued on her way without needing to mold her Vision of the beggar-king into a raven to be rid of it. And when the watch at the barracks challenged her, she used what she had learned to Look at the torchlit face until the man, cowed by his own utter nakedness, stood aside and let her into the common room.

"Cythen?" Illyra called, knowing the woman was in the smoky room.

"'Lyra?" The mercenary rose from a group of men and, putting a firm, authoritative arm on the S'danzo's shoulders, pulled her into an alcove. "'Lyra, what are you—"

Illyra Looked into the other's face. Cythen cringed, then her anger flared, and this time it was Illyra who looked aside.

"Are you all right?" Cythen demanded.

"I must see Walegrin."

"His watch starts at dawn; he just went upstairs to sleep."

"I've got to see him, now."

Cythen tugged at a worn amulet. "'Lyra, are you all right?"

"I've got to see my brother, Cythen," Illyra's voice trembled with Sight and from her determination that she would speak with Walegrin before dawn shed light on Zip's altar. She waited in the officer's upper room while Cythen roused an unhappy Walegrin. He came into the room as a green-eyed death-wraith full of threats and fury, but she met him calmly with the Sight in her eyes.

"I need your help," she informed her stunned, superstitious half-brother. "My son, whom you have made a Rankan citizen, has been stolen."

"The guard patrols the Street of Red Lanterns; it is as safe as the palace itself." He defended the ability of his men even as he bound a bronze studded greave to his shin. "Did you report it to them first? Have they searched?"

"There is nothing for them to do."

Walegrin set the second greave aside and stared at her. "Illyra, what's wrong with you?"

Now that she was with him, Illyra found that the Sight was not so clear. She Saw him carrying her message, but she couldn't See him bringing the guard to Zip's altar to destroy it. "There was a young man who came to me this past afternoon with a story about an altar by the White Foal and the spirit of the Stormgod he sacrificed to there...."

"Arton...sacrifice?" It was outlawed, but it happened.

Illyra shook her head. "That young man—they call him Zip, usually—brought his filthy, unspeakable demon into my life. He touched me with it, and when I refused, it reached out to touch my son. Arton cries black tears."

"Poison—Zip?" He had the other greave strapped on and was smiling as he pronounced the snipe's name. "We've needed something clean on that one. Something that wouldn't fan the fires higher. And Beysin women, some of them, can make cures in their blood. If they cure a Sanctuary child, then that will bring quiet, too—"

Illyra hammered both fists on the table. Neither he nor the Sight would move as she wished. "You aren't listening to me! There's no poison in Arton's blood, Half-Brother. Spirits seek him. Godspirits raised on a White Foal altar.

237

What could you do for Arton that I have not already done? What could bare-breasted Beysin women do while the spirit of a Stormgod sits on its altar, waiting for another chance? Destroy the altar; I'll save my son."

Walegrin assessed her with one eye, then the other, and left the breastplate lying on the table. "Illyra, my men struggle to contain the Maze. There is more murder and intrigue in this town than one man can imagine, and you would have me stomp through the White Foal marsh, looking for a broken-down pile of stones. If it's only the altar you care about, then tell Dubro—he'll do it with his hammer."

"I have not told Dubro."

He raised an eyebrow, having believed that the pair had no secrets between them, and was about to ask more questions when she turned toward the fireplace.

"I don't know why I've come to you for help." She turned and studied the room. "The Sight ends, and I don't know what to do now."

"You can wait here," he said, almost kindly. "I'll make my report in the morning. Or, I'll guide you back to the Aphrodisia, and Arton and you can wait there."

The silver clarity of Sight was gone and she could not, of course, guess when it might return. The preternatural confidence it had given her was fading. She had too many terrified childhood memories of the barracks to linger there, and so accepted his offer. Walegrin called Cythen and two others to be her escort. They each carried torches heavy enough to serve as weapons. Once, they were delayed by the sound of a fracas in a blind alley. "PFLS," Walegrin muttered as the combatants scattered but to Illyra, illiterate and Bazaar-bound, the expression made no sense.

Myrtis welcomed the mercenaries with cups of fortified wine. Illyra escaped to the nursery where, as she expected even without the Sight, her son's condition had not changed. Dubro had taken the unconscious child from the cradle and was hiding the mite in his arms while Lillis, exhausted and worried beyond understanding by her brother's behavior, sat wild-eyed on the floor, clinging to Dubro's leg.

"You have been following some S'danzo intuition?" Dubro asked with accusation.

"I had thought Walegrin might help." Illyra let the cloak fall back from her shoulders. "He will try, though I'm not sure if he will help or hurt in the end. We'll pray it is enough."

"Do you pray?" her husband asked as if speaking to a stranger.

"To the one who wants our son—yes."

In time the sky grew rosy, then bright blue. Arton grew no worse, though no better. Despite their anxiety, Illyra and Lillis both leaned against the smith and dozed. Those children who normally made a noisy shambles of the nursery before breakfast were bundled off to some distant part of the house, and the family waited in silent isolation.

A black bird, not so great as the one Illyra had made of her Sight but undeniably real, cawed noisily outside the window. Illyra awoke and hoped it might be the Sight returning to her. Before she could know one way or the other, there was a furor in the hallways which ended with the appearance of the Hierarch of Vashanka, Molin Torch-holder, at the nursery entrance.

"Illyra," the priest said, ignoring everyone else in the room. Not knowing any other response, Illyra knelt before him: the priest's power was real even if his god was not. "How is the child?"

She shook her head and took Arton from Dubro's arms. "No better. He breathes, but no more than that. How do you know? Why are you here?"

Molin gave a sardonic laugh. "I had not expected to be the one answering questions. I know because I make it a point to know what is going on in Sanctuary and to find the patterns by which it can be governed. You went to the garrison. You said your son had been 'taken.' You spoke of spirits and of the Stormgod, but you did not mention Vashanka. You wanted your brother to deal with the altar, but you were going to deal with rest.

"They say you have the legendary S'danzo Sight. I'd

like to know exactly what you've been Seeing." The priest did not seem surprised when Illyra's only response was to stare forlornly at the floor. "Well, then, let me convince you."

He took her gently by the arm and guided her toward a tiny atrium where the rook was already perched in a tree. Dubro rose to follow them. Two temple mutes, armed with heavy spears, convinced him to remain with the children.

"No one has betrayed you, Illyra, nor will betray you. Walegrin does not see the larger picture when he tells me the details, but you—you might see a picture even larger than my own. You have the Sight, Illyra, and you've looked at the Stormgod, haven't you?"

"The S'danzo have no gods," she replied defensively.

"Yes, but as you yourself have admitted, something has touched your son, and that something is involved with known gods."

"Not gods, godspirits—*gyskourem*."

"Gyskourem?" Molin rolled the word across his tongue, and the rook tried its beak on the sound as well. "Spirits? Demonfolk? No, I don't think so, Illyra."

She sighed and turned away, but spoke louder so he could still hear what no *suvesh* had heard before. "We have Seen the past as well as the future. Men begin the creation of gods. There is a hope, or a need; the gyskourem come, and then there is a god—until there is no hope or need anymore. When they begin, the gyskourem are like other men, or sometimes demonfolk are summoned as gyskourem, but when they are filled then they become gods truly and they are more powerful than any man or demon. The S'danzo do not hope or need, lest we call the gyskourem to us."

"So Vashanka is not the son of Savankala and Sabellia. He is the hope and need of the first battles fought by the first Rankan tribes?" The priest laughed from some secret bemusement.

"In a way. It could be so. That is the pattern, although it is very hard to see so far back as for a god such Vashanka," Illyra temporized. The man was Vashanka priest, and she was not about to tell him of the birth or death of his god.

"But not so hard to see forward, I should think. My god has fallen on hard times, hasn't he, S'danzo?" Torchholder's tone was harsh and bitter, causing Illyra to turn to face him, though she feared for her life. "Don't pretend, S'danzo. You may have the Sight, but I was *there*. Vashanka was ripped from the pantheon. Ils was there, but I do not think that he or his kin can fill Vashanka's void. And there *is* a void, isn't there? A hope? A need? The Rankan Stormgod: the Might of Armies, the Maker of Victory, isn't here anymore."

She nodded and picked nervously at the fringe of her shawl. "It has never happened before, I think. He was changing, growing, even when he was tricked and banished. There is a great web over Sanctuary, High Priest; it was there before Vashanka was banished, and it's still there now. There is much to be Seen and little to be understood." She spoke to him as she would any other querent and for a moment he looked properly chastened.

"How much hope does it take, S'danzo? How much need? Can the god of one people usurp the devotion of another?" The priest seemed to ignore her then, digging deep into the hem of his sleeve, producing a sweetmeat for the rook, which flew tamely to his wrist for the treat. When Molin began again his voice was calm.

"I came here with the Prince, thinking to build a temple. The talk in Ranke was of war with the Nisibisi, and it was not a good time for an architect-priest. I would rather lay the foundation for a temple than undermine the walls of a city. It should have been quiet. Vashanka's attention should have been drawn to the north with the war and the armies, but He was here, almost from the beginning, and I never understood that.

"Now, the war goes on without victory. The troops are disheartened, rebellious, mutinous. They have slain the Emperor along with all of his family, and mine, which they could find. Now, the war belongs to Theron, and it goes no better for him, perhaps because it was not that the Emperor was a bad war-leader but because in a forgotten backwater of the Empire a Rankan god has been banished.

"I've been left with a cesspool of a city to govern because no one else is interested or able. My temple was never built, and will not be built now. My Prince, the only legitimate heir to the Imperial throne, lives in perpetual innocence, and there are two thousand Beysin in Sanctuary, not counting snakes, birds, and fishermen, who are planning to wait here with their Empress, their gold, and their revolting customs until their goddess bestirs herself to win a war they couldn't win with their own hands and weapons back home!"

His voice rose again, and it frightened the rook, which promptly bit the hand that fed it squarely between the thumb and forefinger.

"Lately I've begun to understand that I will not be going back home," he said more softly, binding the wound with fabric from his sleeve. "Or, rather, I've been forced to accept that Sanctuary—of all the forsaken places in creation—is going to be my home until I die. I will not have my dream of dying in peace in the temple where I was born. Do the S'danzo think much of their birth-homes? I was born in the Temple of Vashanka in Ranke. My substance is one with that temple. Some part of me: my eyes, my heart, whatever, is as it was when I was born and belongs more to that temple than to me. But now, look, the bird bites me; blood flows and new skin is formed. Sanctuary skin, Illyra. For me it will always be a very small part, but for you—isn't Sanctuary within you even as the S'danzo Sight is within you?"

He had drawn her in to look at his wound, and played her with his best arguments as he would have done had she been the Emperor himself. His eyes stared into hers.

"Illyra, if you won't help me, then I can't help Sanctuary, and if I can't help Sanctuary, then it doesn't matter if you save your son. Use the Sight to look around you. There is hope, need; there is a great vacuum where Vashanka reigned—"

242

Illyra jerked away from him. "The S'danzo have no gods. It does not matter to us which of the gyskourem becomes the Gyskouras, the new god other men bow down to."

"Before Vashanka was vanquished I made a grand ritual for Him, to consecrate his worship here, to establish Sanctuary in his eyes and, in truth, to control Him. A Feast of the Ten-Slaying and the Dance of Azuna. The girl was a slave trained in the temple in Ranke, and Vashanka was the Imperial Prince Kadakithis himself. It was, perhaps, the greatest of my offerings to the god, and my worst. The girl, remarkably, conceived, and a boychild was born not two weeks before . . . before Vashanka was lost. That child is about the same age, I would guess, as your own son.

"He is a strange child, much given to anger and ill-humor. His mother and the others who care for him assure me that he is no worse than any other child his age, but I am not so sure. They say he is lonely, but he rejects all the palace children brought to him. I think, perhaps, he has needed to choose his own companions—and then, this morning, I heard of your son . . ." He paused, but Illyra did not complete his sentence. "Shall I give you an old Ilsigi coin like the boy gave you yesterday? Do the S'danzo only speak to gold? Is your son to be the companion to Vashanka's last son? Is he the new god I must serve, or is he the Gyskouras of some other hope which I must destroy?"

"Why do you ask these things?" Illyra repeated helplessly as the priest's words stirred the Sight within her.

"I was high priest and architect for Vashanka. I am still high priest and architect for the Stormgod—but I must know whom I serve, Illyra. And, if I must, I must try again to bring the Stormgod into an understanding with his people. I could take your son out to that altar and make a sacrifice of him; I could bring him to the palace and raise him as the god's son instead of the one I have there now. Do you understand the choices I will have to make?"

Illyra Saw the high priest's choices, all of them, as well as the gods watching nervously as gyskourem were drawn to Sanctuary's maelstrom of hope and need. The web of

243

confusion she had Seen around the city was focused on the place where Vashanka had been and, for the moment, all other magic and intrigue were controlled by the hopes and needs which the emergent Stormgod must take into himself.

She put her hands over her ears and was unaware of her own screaming. When she was aware of anything again she was lying in the dirt of the atrium and Myrtis's cool hands were holding a damp cloth to her forehead. Dubro was glaring down at the priest with mayhem in his eyes.

"She is a strong woman," Torchholder informed the smith. "Stormgods do not choose weak messengers." He turned to Illyra. "I had not named Vashanka's last son; I had no name that was right for him. Now I think I shall make a naming ceremony for him and call him Gyskouras—at least until he chooses a different name for himself. And, Illyra, I think your son should be at that ceremony, don't you?" He summoned his servants with a snap of his fingers and left the atrium without formal farewells, the great rook shedding feathers as it struggled to clear the steep rooftops of the Aphrodisia.

"What did I tell him?" Illyra asked, taking hold of Dubro's hand. "He isn't taking Arton? I didn't say that, did I?"

She would never surrender her son to the priest or the gods, not even if there was the silver of true Sight in Torchholder's request. Dubro would never understand and, above all, the S'danzo did not acknowledge the interference of gods. They would leave the town, if they had to, sneaking out at night the way Shadowspawn and Moonflower's daughter had, since the Torch had already decreed that no one would leave Sanctuary without his permission.

While she'd been with the priest, Myrtis had gotten the little boy to swallow some honeyed gruel, but when she put the child back in Illyra's arms the madam made it plain that she did not expect him to survive and, with the high priest showing such an interest, she certainly did not want him surviving or dying at the Aphrodisia.

"We will take him with us," Dubro said simply, gathering up his daughter as well and leading the way out to the Street.

They could not have remained much longer at the Aphrodisia in any event.

Through years of labor Dubro and Illyra had amassed a small hoard of gold which they kept hidden where the stones of Dubro's forge became the outer wall of their homestead. But with the Beysib, and all the gold they brought with them, not even gold was as valuable as it had been and they could ill afford another day of idleness. A squall rose out of the harbor while they were walking, a sudden, damp inconvenience that should not have been remarkable in a seacoast town except that the raindrops striking Arton's face did not wash away his clouded tears but made them darker. Without saying why, Illyra clutched her son tighter and raced ahead through the storm-quieted Bazaar.

It took several days, even for the gossips and rumor-mongers of Sanctuary, to discover the coincidences: The recurrent, violent squalls; Molin Torchholder's unprecedented visit to the Aphrodisia House; and the S'danzo child who cried silent, storm-colored tears. The story that someone had smuggled an *unfriendly* serpent into the Snake-Bitch Empress's bedchamber had lent itself easily to lewd embellishment, while the tale that half-rotted corpses were walking the back alleys of Downwind was more frightening. But when the fifth storm in as many days dumped hundreds of fish, some as large as a man's forearm, on the porch of Vashanka's still-unfinished temple, interest began, at last, to grow.

"They're sayin' it's our fault," the apprentice said when the fire had been banked for the night and the stew was bubbling on the fire-grate. "They say it's *him*," the youth elaborated, glancing fearfully at Arton's borrowed cradle.

"It's the time for storms, nothing more. They forget every year," Dubro replied, digging his fingers into the boy's shoulders.

The apprentice ate his meal in silence, more frightened of the smith's infrequent anger than of the unnaturalness of the child, but he laid his pallet as far from the cradle as possible and invoked the protection of every god he could

remember before turning his face to the wall for the night.
Illyra took no notice of him. Her attention fell only on Arton
and the honey-gruel she hoped he would swallow. Dubro
sat frowning in his chair until the lad had begun to snore
gently.

A single gust of wind churned through the Bazaar, then,
with no greater warning, the rain thundered against the walls
and shutters. Illyra blew out her candle and stared past the
cradle.

"Tears again?" Dubro asked. She nodded as her own
tears began to fall. "'Lyra, the lad's right: people gather
by Blind Jakob's wagon and stare at the forge with fear in
their eyes. They do not understand—and *I* do not understand. I have never questioned your comings and goings;
the cards or your Sight, but 'Lyra, we must do something
quickly or the town itself will rise against us. What has
happened to our son?"

The huge man had not moved, nor had his voice lost its
measured softness, but Illyra looked at him in white-eyed
fear. She searched her mind for the right words and, finding
none, stumbled across the room to collapse into his lap.
The Sight had revealed terrible things, but none hurt her as
much as the weariness in her husband's face. She told him
everything that had happened, as the suvesh told their tales
to her.

"I will go into the city tomorrow," Dubro decided when
he had heard about Zip's altar, Molin's god-child, and the
Stormgod's demise. "There is an armorer who will pay good
gold for this forge. We will leave this place tomorrow—
forever."

Another gust of wind whipped through the awning and,
beyond that, the sound of a wall, somewhere, crashing
down. Dubro held her tightly until she cried herself to sleep.
The little oil lamp beside him guttered out before the squall
had abated and the household tried to sleep.

Illyra did not know if she'd heard the crash under the
awning or if she only awoke because Dubro had heard it,

had shoved her aside, and was already wading into the storm and mud. By the time she lit a candle from a coal in the cooking fire, Dubro had retrieved the young man whose visit had precipitated all their misfortune.

"Thinking to steal, lad?" Dubro growled, lifting the sewer-snipe by the neck for emphasis.

Mustering his courage, Zip twisted his leg for a kick where it would hurt the smith most and found himself thrown face-first onto the rough-wood floor for his unsuccessful effort.

"What did you want? Your gold coin?" Illyra interceded, grabbing her shawl and twirling it modestly around her as she rummaged through her boxes. "I've kept it for you." She found the coin and threw it onto the floor by his face. "Be thankful and begone," she warned him.

Zip grabbed the coin and scrabbled to his knees. "You stole Him. You cursed me and kept Him for yourself. His eyes were fire when I called Him back to me. He doesn't need me anymore!" The young man's face was torn and bloody, but the edge of hysteria in his voice came from something deeper than physical pain. "This is not enough! I need Him back." He cast the coin aside and produced a knife from somewhere around his waist.

Maniacal rage was not unknown to Illyra who had, more than once, said the wrong words to a distraught querent, but then she had been behind a solid wood table with a knife of her own. Zip lunged at her before she or Dubro comprehended the danger. The blade bit deep into her shoulder before Dubro could move.

"He'll take me back with this," Zip said in triumph from the doorway, brandishing his bloody knife before disappearing into the storm.

Zip's knife had left a small, deep wound that did not, to Dubro's eye, bleed heavily enough. They would need poultices and herbs to keep the cut from going to poison, and that would have meant Moonflower, if she'd been alive. Without Moonflower they had only their instincts to guide them until morning. Caring for Illyra was more urgent than chasing Zip. The frightened apprentice was sent to the well for clean water while Dubro carried his Illyra to their bed.

The apprentice had just set the water on the fire-grate when the doyen of the S'danzo in Sanctuary darkened the doorway. Tall, raw-boned, and bitter, she was not the eldest of the *amoushem,* the scrying-women, nor certainly the most far-Sighted, but she was the most feared. Her word had prohibited Moonflower from bringing the abandoned, orphaned Illyra into her home. S'danzo and suvesh alike knew her as the Termagant and even Dubro shrank back when she made the hand-sign against evil and entered the room.

Illyra pushed herself up from the pillows. "Go away. I don't want your help."

With a loud, disdainful sniff the Termagant turned away from Illyra and plucked at the blankets in Arton's cradle. "You've brought us all to the edge of death, and only you can bring us back—only you. You See the gods, but do you ever close your eyes to look around you? No. Even Rezel—and your mother's Sight was better than your half-blood will ever be—knew better than this. Suvesh pray and meddle with magic, but they are Sightless creatures and no one notices them. When a S'danzo woman opens her eyes . . . Even the mightiest of gods don't have the Sight, Illyra; remember that."

The crone looked away, unwilling to say more. Illyra slumped back against the pillows, her rage and fear dampened by doubt. Rezel had never troubled to tell her toddling daughter about the S'danzo ways. Moonflower had tried, but with the Termagant herself threatening and cursing from the shadows, Illyra had learned dangerously little about the people whose gifts she used.

"I have not sought gods or gyskourem," she whispered in her own defense. "They found me."

"There're demon ships sailing the harbor; black beasts rampaging through the Maze, and the wretched storms besides. The suvesh are making themselves a war god, Illyra, and the gyskourem they draw to Sanctuary will stop at

nothing to become that god. It is not the time for S'danzo
to be using cards and Sight for them."

"I have not used the Sight for them. I have not had the
Sight since just after my son was touched..." She would
have continued, but the herbal infusion had begun to steam
and the Termagant moved swiftly to make a poultice with
it that took Illyra's breath away when it rested against her
shoulder.

"Fool, you cursed the suvesh, not the gyskourem that
drove him," the crone whispered now that Illyra alone could
hear her. She glanced at Arton's cradle, her disdain replaced
by naked concern. "Does *he* have the Sight?"

Illyra would have laughed, had it been possible. Men
did not inherit the Sight, and girl-children did not know if
they possessed it until well after Lillis and Arton's age.

The Termagant noticed Illyra's half-smile. "*S'danzo* men
do not have the Sight. Who is to say what *he* might have.
You care little enough for the S'danzo—and, maybe I did
wrong to mis-See danger in you, to try to keep you and the
S'danzo separate. Know this then: it has been many generations since a new god was made from the gyskourem,
and never have they taken the place of so powerful a god
as Vashanka. But if gyskourem are to become a god, they
must first be drawn by need and sacrifice; then they must
become Gyskouras—become one with a chosen mortal. It
will be so, even with the new Vashanka.

"They have chosen your son as Gyskouras. Through him
they have Blinded you. Gods have never been a threat to
us but this one, this Gyskouras—who was your son—will
have the Sight, and will be invincible."

"But the Gyskouras will be Molin Torchholder's child
in the temple...."

"Many men hope and sacrifice, Illyra, but there can only
be one Gyskouras. It is not yet decided. One child or the
other must die before the Gyskouras can emerge to be among
men before becoming a god. You have loved your son. If
you can't free him from the gyskourem web, then kill him
before it is too late for us all—S'danzo and suvesh."

She pressed the clothes against the wound and, knowing that their sting would keep the young woman speechless for some time longer, turned to her husband. "You must avenge her," she said to Dubro as she began the first of four silken stitches which would hold the wound shut. "You may wait until she recovers or dies, or you can kill him outright for the insult to all the S'danzo. She will pay, but so must the suvesh who did this to her. None of us who use the cards are safe if this is unavenged."

Dubro shook his head. "If I had caught him before he left, he would be dead, but I cannot hunt a man to the death, old woman. I will send word to the town garrison. They'll be glad enough of a reason . . ."

"No." Illyra struggled to sit up. "No, let him go. Let him have my blood on his altar. If it will free Arton, it's small enough price. Let him be the Gyskouras of the new Stormgod."

"He attacked a S'danzo seer; his destiny is not for gods or gyskourem to decide. The S'danzo have no gods to protect them—only vengeance!" The woman raised her hand over Illyra's face and found it caught there in Dubro's bone-crushing fist.

"She is but half-S'danzo, old woman. You and the rest cast her out before. If she does not want vengeance, then you shall not give it to her." Dubro released the old woman and shoved her through the door into the abating storm. He frowned as he wiped the tears from his wife's cheek.

"Shall I go to the barracks?" the apprentice asked into the silence.

"Not yet. We'll wait and see what happens."

Illyra slipped into sleep, but Dubro sat, staring, in his chair. At dawn he awoke his wife and told her his intentions had not changed. He would sell his forge to the armorer and quietly buy a wagon. They would be gone from Sanctuary by sundown. His wife did not argue and pretended to go back to sleep. The Termagant's medicine had done its work well; the wound was cool to the touch. Once Dubro had left, she was able to dress herself, invent chores for the apprentice, and sit on the bench beside the forge to wait anxiously for her husband's return while Lillis played in the dust at her feet.

She was dozing, almost oblivious to the ache in her shoulder and the clamor of the mid-morning bazaar around her, when a heavy shadow fell over the forge. The storms came this way: darkness, then wind and rain. Pushing herself to her feet, she told the apprentice to tie the wooden shutters closed before even looking up at the sky. The Bazaar became deathly quiet as Illyra, and everyone else, looked at the cloudless sky. Nothing could be heard but the frantic calling of great flocks of birds seeking shelter. Evening stars appeared on the horizon, then the white-gold disk of the sun could be seen in the sky—with a black disk sliding over it. Someone nearby shouted that the sun itself was being devoured. The Bazaar, and the city beyond it, which had endured more of natural and unnatural disaster in the past weeks than it cared to remember, succumbed to widespread panic.

Illyra clutched the children to her and sat transfixed as the sun shrank to a glistening crescent of light. Then, just as it seemed it would vanish forever, a halo of white fire appeared around the black sun. It was too much—in a single unfeeling movement she dragged Lillis and the apprentice inside, where they cowered on the floor beyond Arton's cradle. The darkness became a storm that swept water and mud through the open doorway. Gusts of wind lifted the awning, beat it against the stones of the forge, then bore it away. Lillis and the apprentice whimpered in terror while Illyra tried to set an example of courage she did not feel.

The storm had begun to die down when Illyra realized her son was crying aloud. Letting the apprentice hold onto Lillis, she crawled to the cradle and looked into it. Arton had thrown off his blankets and wailed mightily, but his tears were as dark as the storm itself. She gathered him into her arms and was assaulted by something which was not Sight and yet which showed her the ravening gyskourem, fueled by the ambitions and sacrifices of men like Zip, pushing aside Arton's mortal spirit, making him and themselves together into the Gyskouras of the new Stormgod. There was Sight as well, or at least empathy. She felt her son's terror and knew that in mercy and love she should take his life before the gyskourem did, but there was something beyond that: a glimmer of hope and sacrifice that might yet succeed. Ignoring the pleas and screams of the apprentice, she wound her shawl around herself and Arton and went through the doorway into the storm.

The wind carried more smoke than rain as Illyra made her way through the overturned carts and stalls. Damage and injury were everywhere, but in the chaos no one had the time to notice a lone woman picking her way carefully toward the gates with a bundle in her arms. Fewer dwellings had been leveled in the town, but great plumes of smoke were rising in some quarters. Gangs ran through the streets, some to rescue, while others went to wrest fortune from the misfortunes of their peers. Illyra thought of Dubro, somewhere in the tangle of streets himself, but she had no time to search for him as she continued on her way to the palace.

It was not like the last time she had made her way boldly through the streets of Sanctuary. Her path was not etched in the silver clarity of Sight, and she could not have confronted the palace guards with the Sight of their destinies. But the palace, well-lit by lightning from the storm, was the largest building in Sanctuary, and the guards, busy consoling aristocrats and arresting looters, had better things to do.

Within the palace walls Illyra moved with the frantic courtiers, searching for something she could not name. Her shoulder throbbed from the strain of carrying Arton. The sense that was not quite Sight led her to a half-enclosed cloister. There, sheltered from the wind, rain, and casual glances of the palace residents, she crumpled into a corner. Tears were flowing down her cheeks when exhaustion mercifully closed her eyes and sent her to sleep.

"Barbarians!"

Illyra awoke to the echo of a shrill yell. The storm had passed, leaving in its wake brilliant blue skies and only a faint trace of smoke in the air. Her shelter had become the scene of a private quarrel between a pair she could see quite well but who could not, thanks to the patterns of bright sun and contrasting shadows, see into her corner. It was just as well: the woman was Beysib by her accent, though she seemed dressed in a modest Rankan gown, and the man was Prince Kadakithis himself. Illyra clutched Arton tightly to her, almost glad that he was once again motionless and silent.

"Barbarians! Did we not open our court while the storm still raged to hear their complaints? Did we not personally assure them that the sun has vanished before and *always* returns? And that the storms, whatever exactly is causing them, have nothing to do with the sun? Haven't we let them move their filthy belongings into the very courtyard of this palace?

"And did I not drape myself in great wads of cloth and pile my hair on top of my head so that they might think of me as their *proper* Empress?"

Illyra gulped as Kittycat shook his head. "Shu-sea, I fear you misunderstood my lord Molin."

The Beysa Shupansea, Avatar of Mother Bey and Absolute, if currently exiled, Empress of the Ancient Beysib Empire, turned her imperial back on the Prince; and Illyra, despite her awe and fear, was inclined to agree with his judgment. True, her hair and dress were Rankan-aristocrat beyond reproach, but she had painted her face with Beysib cosmetics, and the translucent, shimmering green from hairline to neckline only emphasized her Beysibness.

"Your high priest makes entirely too many points," Shupansea complained, tossing her head. A curl sprang free from her elaborate coiffure, then another, then, with a flash of rich emerald, a snake eased down her neck and under the shoulder of her dress. Sighing, the Beysa tried to entice the serpent onto her forearm.

"His point, Shu-sea, was simply that as long as the towns-

253

folk of Sanctuary think of the Beysin and, most especially, of you, as invaders, as people totally unlike themselves...well, it makes a sort of unity among them that never really was there before. All their violence is being directed at your people rather than at each other," the Prince explained. He reached out to touch the Beysa, but the emerald snake hissed at him. He pulled back his hand and sucked briefly on his fingertips.

Shupansea let the snake slide into a flowering bush. "Molin this...Molin that. You and he talk as if you love these barbarians. Ki-thus, they don't love you and your relatives any more than they love me and mine. Your own Imperial Throne has been usurped, and the agents of the very man who sits on it in your place are sulking through the alleys of this horrible little city. No, Ki-thus, the time has come not to show them how benevolent we are—but how merciless. They have pushed us to the very edge. They won't push us any farther."

"But, Shu-sea," the Prince said, taking her hands in his own now that the snake was gone. "That is precisely what Molin has been trying to tell you. We *have* been pushed to the very edge; we weren't very far from it to begin with. Your Burek clan is here in exile—hoping Divine Mother Bey will finish off your usurping cousin. I don't even have that hope. All we have is Sanctuary—but we have to convince Sanctuary that there's some reason to have *us*. Talk to your storyteller if you won't listen to me or Molin. Every day that passes—every storm, every murder, every broken flowerpot—just makes it that much harder for us."

The Beysa leaned on the Prince's shoulder, and for a moment both were silent. Their lives, the minutiae of survival for a prince or empress, were beyond Illyra's comprehension, but not the weariness in the Beysa's shoulder; she had felt that herself. Or the anxiety in the Prince's face—the look of a man who knows he is not quite up to the tasks he knows he must perform; that look crossed the face of everyone sooner or later.

The sudden empathy freed her Sight from whatever had

held it in bondage just as the Beysa wrested free of the Prince.

"So—I will wear all this cloth, and my women as well— and we will all look like clan-Setmur fisherwomen. This is not the gentle land of Bey; I have been cold to the bone since we arrived. But, Ki-thus, I will *not* take you as my husband. I am the Beysa. My consort is No-Amit, the Corn-King, and his blood must be sacrificed to the land. Even if your violent barbarians would accept your death at my hands, I will not take a man I love as No-Amit only to cut his heart from his breast twelve months later."

"Not No-Amit—Koro-Amit, Storm-King. Like you said: you're not in the gentle lands of Bey anymore. Nothing has to be the way it has always been. Sanctuary may not be much, but if it's ours no one will question what we do with it.

"Besides, no matter what you think of what Molin says— you've seen that child down in the temple. You've seen his eyes when *he* starts the storms, and you've seen them when the storms that he hasn't started are rattling the rafters. Even your great-uncle Terrai Burek says we've got to make that child think he *belongs* to us and not to whatever else is raising the storms around here."

The Beysa nodded and sank onto a damp stone bench. She reached out, and the beynit serpent began a spiraling climb up her arm. "I am the Avatar of Bey. Mother Bey is within me, guiding me; She is real for me, yet I am not like that little boy. I hear him in my sleep and Bey, Herself, is disturbed. Always She has taken the conquered Corn gods and, yes Stormgods into her bed, and always She has absorbed them into Herself.

"But this time we have not conquered the people of the Stormgod; the Stormgod was conquered without us, and we do not know what will rise in his place. Bey doesn't know. If I must take a Koro-Amit to appease this new god, then it will be the boy's true father: this Tempus Thales. I must believe that Mother Bey will take him to Her—and when it is over, I will still have you."

Both the Prince and Illyra blanched; the Prince for his own reasons, Illyra because the Sight revealed Vashanka, Tempus, and the child together in one twisting, godlike apparition.

"Molin will kill me if he finds out that not only am I not that little demon's father but that Tempus is. And, Shu-sea, if half the stories of Tempus Thales are true, when you cut out his heart he'll just grow a new one. I'd rather you cut my heart out than think of you bound to Tempus and his son. I never foresaw what would happen when I sent Tempus to take my place at the Great Feast of Ten-Slaying—but I won't run away from it now."

Illyra Saw, however, both the truth of the Prince's confession and the holocaust which would follow Tempus's ravishment of Shupansea—if that Sight were allowed to happen. Visions of war and carnage gripped her, but the Sight showed a single, silver path that led out of her corner.

"I can help you," she announced as she stepped into the sunlight.

The Beysa screamed, and the Prince, unmindful of the agitated serpent on her arm, pushed her behind him to confront Illyra alone. Calmly, patiently, and with the certainty of Sight around her, Illyra told the Prince that they had met before—when he had taken Walegrin's oath and almost immediately given Walegrin's gift, an Enlibar steel sword, to Tempus. Kadakithis, whether he truly remembered Illyra or not, was sufficiently impressed with her display of S'danzo prowess to take Arton in his own arms and lead the way to Molin Torchholder as she requested.

They found the priest not far from the nursery, giving orders to the frightened women who were the child's nurse-maids. He looked first at the Beysa and the Prince, then at Illyra, and finally at the bundle in Kadakithis's arms. Illyra looked at the huge black bird preening its wings above the doorway and remembered she had Seen something like this before, at the Aphrodisia House—just before she had left to find her half-brother, who worked for the priest—and had forced herself to forget it.

"You have won," Illyra acknowledged. There were other parts of that vision as well. "I cannot watch Sanctuary be destroyed. I will not see with my eyes what I See in my heart. I should have given him to you before. He is dying now; it may be too late. . . ."

"I could have taken him," Molin reminded her gently. "I have neither Sight nor, at the moment, a god. Still, it did not seem right that I could help that child in there become what he must become if Sanctuary is to survive if I stole your son from you. I had to believe that somehow you would understand and bring him to me. If I could still believe that, then I do not think it could be too late. Take your child in your arms again and come." He turned and ordered the door to the nursery to be opened.

Chaos reigned in the nursery. Torn pillows lay everywhere. Feathers clung to the nursemaids, and the weary-looking woman who appeared to be the child's mother was inspecting a deep-purple bruise on her arm. The child himself turned to glare at his visitors and discarded a half-empty pillow in favor of a short wooden sword. He charged at Illyra.

"Gyskouras! Stop!" Molin thundered. The boy, and everyone else, obeyed. The little sword clattered to the marble floor. "That is better. Gyskouras, this is Illyra, who has heard your crying." Though he held still, the boy met the priest's eyes with a cold defiance no one else would have dared. "She has brought her son to be with you."

Illyra pulled the blankets back from her son's face, unsurprised that his eyes were open. She kissed him, and thought he smiled at her, then she knelt down an allowed the children to see each other.

The child whom Molin had named Gyskouras had eyes which were truly frightening when confronted face-to-face, but they softened when Arton smiled and reached out with his hand to touch the other's face. The gyskourem were gone; even the shifting images of Vashanka and Tempus were gone—there were only Gyskouras and Arton.

"Will you leave him here with me?" Gyskouras asked.

"My mother will take care of him until my father gets here."

He took no notice of the Prince and, fortunately, for the moment Molin was taking no notice of him. Illyra set Arton, already struggling from his blankets, onto the floor and stood up just in time for the room to contain an eruption of a different sort, as Dubro, Walegrin, and a half a dozen Beysib guards squeezed through the doorway. But by then Gyskouras was showing Arton how to hold the sword. The smith could accept, even if he could not wholly understand, that his son belonged here now, and however painful and unpleasant the consequences might be, things were better than they might have been.

A FISH WITH FEATHERS
IS OUT OF HIS DEPTH

Robert Lynn Asprin

"You there! Back to the Maze! There be no easy targets on the wharves!"

Monkel, head of the clan Setmur, turned in astonishment to look for his comrade. A moment ago, the Old Man had been walking quietly by his side. Now, he was six paces behind, shouting angrily down a narrow alley between two of the buildings that lined the edge of Sanctuary's wharves.

"And don't come back!" the Old Man finished, kicking dirt toward the alley dramatically. "The last bravo we caught got cut up for bait. Hear me? Don't come back!"

Now Monkel was at his side, craning his neck to peer down the alley. The gap was littered with barrels and crates, and shrouded with shadows in the dim light of early evening. Still, there was some light . . . but Monkel could see nothing unusual. No figures, not even a glimpse of furtive movement greeted his unblinking gaze. If nothing else, though, Monkel had learned to trust his friend's judgment in detecting danger in this strange new town.

"Makes me mad to see trash like that on our wharf," the Old Man muttered, resuming their walk. "That's the trouble with money, though. As soon as you get a little extra, it draws scum who want to take it away from you."

"I saw nothing. Was someone there?"

"Two of them. Armed," the Old Man said flatly. "I tell you again, you'd best learn to use those funny eyes of yours if you're going to stay alive in this town."

Monkel ignored the warning, as he did the friendly jibe at his eyes.

"Two of them? But what would you have done if they had answered your challenge and attacked you?"

A flashing glitter appeared as the Old Man twirled the dagger he had been palming.

"Gutted them and sold 'em at the stall." He winked, dropping the weapon back into its belt scabbard.

"But *two* of them . . ."

The Old Man shrugged.

"I've faced worse odds before. Most people in this town have. That kind isn't big on fair fights. Besides, there are two of us."

Monkel was suddenly aware of his own knife, still undrawn in its belt scabbard. The Old Man had insisted that he buy it and wear it at all times. It was not the sort of knife used by men working nets and lines, but a vicious little fighting knife designed for slipping between ribs or slashing at an extended hand or fist. In its own way, it was as fine a tool as a fishing knife, but Monkel hadn't even drawn it.

A wave of fear broke over the little Beysib as he suddenly realized how close he had just been to being embroiled in a knife-fight. The fear intensified as the knowledge settled on him that, had the fight occurred, it would have been over before he could have reacted. Whether he was alive or not at the end would have depended entirely on the Old Man's skill.

The Old Man seemed to read his thoughts, and laid a reassuring hand on his shoulder.

"Don't worry," he said. "What's important is the spotting, not the fighting. It's like fishing: If you can't figure out where they are, you can't catch 'em."

"But if they attacked..."

"Show 'em your back and they'll attack. Once you spot 'em, they won't. They're looking for a victim, not a fight. If you're sober and facing them, they'll fade back and go looking for easier pickings. Thieves...or assassins. They're all the same. Just keep your eyes open and you'll be safe. You and yours."

Monkel slowly shook his head, not in disagreement, but in bewilderment. Not a year of his life had gone by without the passing of a friend, relation, or acquaintance into the shadow realms. Death wore many faces for those who challenged the sea for a livelihood: a sudden storm, an uncharted sandbar or reef, the attack of a nameless monster from the deep, or even just a careless moment leading to an accident. The head of clan Setmur had seen them all before reaching manhood, much less assuming his current position of leadership, and he thought he was accustomed to the shadow of death which haunted those of his profession. "We pay for the catch in blood," was an idiom he had used as often as he had heard it.

Violent death, however, the act of murder or assassination, was new to him. The casualness with which the people of this new land fought or defended themselves was beyond his comprehension. That was what frightened him the most; not the violence, but his newfound friends' easy acceptance of it. They no more questioned or challenged the existence of random violence than they did the tides or sunset. It was a constant in this Old Man's world...a world that was now his own as well.

The Old Man's comment about assassins was not lost on

Monkel. Too many Beysib were being killed—so many
that not even the most callous citizen of Sanctuary could
pretend it was random violence. Someone, or perhaps a
group of someones, was actively hunting the immigrants.
Clan Burek was being hit harder than his own clan Setmur,
and the theories to explain this oddity were many: the Burek
were richer and drew more attention from the local cutthroats; they were more inclined to venture into the town
at night than the fisherfolk of clan Setmur; and their arrogance and pride made them more susceptible to being lured
into fights against the Beysa's orders. While Monkel acknowledged these reasons and agreed with them to a limited
extent, he felt there were also other factors to be considered.
His lessons from the Old Man in basic street survival, which
he had, in turn, passed on to his clan, had much to do with
Setmur's low casualty rate. And perhaps most important
was the local fishing community's acceptance of the clan,
a phenomenon Monkel had grown to appreciate more and
more as time wore on. As a result of his appreciation, he
had privately decided to expand his duties as clan head to
include doing everything in his power to further the friend-
ships between his people and the locals, whether it involved
endorsing a boat-building project or simply accompanying
the Old Man on his weekly visit to the Wine Barrel, as he
was doing tonight.

The Wine Barrel had changed, even during Monkel's
brief time in town. Much of the new money in Sanctuary
was being funneled into its only readily expandable food
source—the waterfront. The fishing community was en-
joying an unprecedented affluence, and it was only to be
expected that a portion of that wealth would be spent at
their favorite gathering point and tavern, the Wine Barrel.

Once a rickety wharfside dive, the Wine Barrel had been
upgraded to near-respectability. Chairs purchased secondhand from a bordello had replaced the mismatched benches
and crates that once adorned the place, and years of grime
were beginning to give way to a once-a-month, top-to-
bottom scrubbing; still, some of the old traditions remained.

As Monkel followed the Old Man into the tavern, he noted several of his clansmen scattered through the room, all sitting with other Beysib, but there unchallenged nonetheless. There was one table, however, none of them sat at . . . in fact, no Sanctuary fishermen sat at without an invitation. That was the table that exploded with noise upon their entrance.

"It's about time, Old Man!"

"We already drank your share. You'll have to order more."

"Hey, Monkel. Can't you get the Old Man to walk any faster? The streets are dangerous to those who dawdle."

Sitting at *their* table were the elite of Sanctuary's fishing community, the senior captains of which the Old Man was the unofficial leader. It was no different from the other tables, but because they sat there, the service was quicker and their drinks arrived in portions noticeably larger than those served at other tables.

Of all the Beysib, Monkel was the only one accepted as an equal at the captains' table, partially because of his status as head of the Setmur clan, but mostly because the Old Man said he was welcome.

Prior to their relocation to Sanctuary, a Beysib scout ship had picked up the Old Man and his son Hort and fetched them back to the Beysa's court for interrogation. Once it became apparent that the Old Man would not willingly yield any useful information about their planned destination, the majority of the court had turned their attention to Hort, who was both more talkative and more knowledgeable about the politics and citizenry of Sanctuary. Only Monkel had continued dealing with the Old Man, plying him with specific questions only a fisherman would ask: questions about tides and reefs, the feeding patterns and nature of the native fish. The Old Man recognized them as the questions of a working man as opposed to those asked by the military or the politicians, and began to trade information for information. Their mutual respect had grown into a cautious friendship, and Monkel had made a point of protecting the Old Man from the curiosity and jibes of his own countrymen. Now they were in Sanctuary, and the Old Man was returning the favor by helping Monkel and his clan settle into their new home.

The next round of drinks arrived, and Monkel started to reach for his purse. The Old Man caught his eye with a glare of stern disapproval, but the Beysib merely smiled and withdrew a small coin barely large enough to pay for his own refreshment. Though poor by comparison with the royal Burek clan, the Setmurs were still substantially wealthier than their Sanctuary-raised counterparts. Soon after his arrival in town, the Old Man had warned Monkel against needless displays of money . . . such as buying a round of drinks for the captains' table. Rather than a gesture of endearing generosity, he had been told, such a move would be interpreted as an attempt to flaunt his financial superiority, hindering rather than advancing his acceptance by the local fisherfolk. Normally a bit tight-fisted by nature, Monkel had no difficulty following this advice, though the Old Man still tended to fret at him about it from time to time.

The cheap wine favored by the other captains was distasteful to Monkel, who was used to the more delicate, subtle texture of Beysib beverages, but he drank it anyway to avoid appearing overly critical of the tastes of his newfound friends. In a compromise with his own palate, he merely sipped cautiously at one glass while listening to the fishermen gossip.

The Sanctuary fishermen were a close-knit community, caring little for the affairs of the "city folk," and it showed in their conversations. From discussions with his clansmen who had more contact with clan Burek, Monkel had obtained a wealth of rumors speculating on whether or not the Rankan Emperor was dead and the effect it would have on Prince Kadakithis, currently the object of their own Beysa's affection. None of this was even mentioned at the captains' table . . . their conversation, instead, centered on the movements of various schools of fish, and occasionally touched on the unpredictable winds and storms which seemed to spring from nowhere to threaten the fishing fleet even at anchor. There was also still talk about the solar eclipse, though Monkel's assurances that such phenomena were not unheard of in the chronicles of the Beysib Empire had kept the fishing community from joining the town's panic at the time.

Monkel entered into the "fish" discussions wholeheartedly enough, particularly those concerning the deep-water species he was familiar with, but remained silent during the "storm" speculations. He had his own opinions, of course, but was more than reluctant to voice them, even here. There was a stink of sorcery over the harbor these days, but Monkel had been raised a fisherman by fisherfolk. He knew better than to stir their superstitious nature unnecessarily.

He was lost in these thoughts when he suddenly noticed the conversation had stopped . . . in fact, all talk in the tavern had stopped as the assembled fishermen stared at the front door. Since he was sitting with his back to that door, Monkel had to turn in his seat to see what it was they were looking at.

It was Uralai of clan Burek, resplendent in her guards' uniform as she nervously surveyed the Wine Barrel's interior. She caught sight of Monkel as he turned, and strode through the silent tables to where he sat.

"Monkel Setmur," she said formally, "the Beysa wishes to see you in the morning for a report on the progress of the new boat."

Monkel started to reply, but the Old Man cut him off.

"Tell the Beysa we'll see her tomorrow afternoon."

Uralai's eyes glazed for a moment, which Monkel saw at once as a sign of anger, a signal the Sanctuary fisherman would not recognize. He hastened to intervene before things got out of hand.

"We will be taking our boats out before first light tomorrow. Assuming the Beysa is not planning an early audience, we'll have to see her in the afternoon after the boats are back at the docks."

". . . Unless she wishes to reimburse us for a day's catch," the Old Man added with a smile.

Uralai bit her lower lip thoughtfully for a moment, then nodded once in a sharp, abrupt movement.

"Very well, I will so inform the Beysa."

With that, she spun on her heel and headed for the door.

"Wait a moment!"

Monkel rose and started after her, overtaking her just inside the entryway.

"What is it, Lord Setmur?"

"You can't... you shouldn't be walking these streets alone at night. It's dangerous."

"I was told to find you, and this is where you are. It left me little choice if I was to carry out my assignment."

"Perhaps... if I walked you back to the palace."

Uralai arched one graceful eyebrow, and Monkel flushed at her unspoken barb. She carried her two swords crisscrossed over her back and was trained in their use, while Monkel had only his knife.

"Please don't misunderstand me," he stammered. "I was not meaning to imply a supremacy at fighting. It's just that we of Setmur have found that many confrontations can be avoided when we travel in twos after dark."

"And after you see me to the palace? Then you must return through those same streets alone. No, Monkel Setmur. While I appreciate your concern, of the two of us I think I am better suited to survive an unaccompanied journey."

With that, she headed out into the night, leaving him to return to his drink.

"You shouldn't let yourself be bullied that way," the Old Man chided as Monkel resumed his seat. "You were ready to give up a day's fishing just so we could see the Beysa, weren't you?"

"I think the original summons was for me alone," Monkel growled, his mind still on Uralai.

"Of course it was. That's why I thought I'd better deal myself in. You're a good man, Monkel, but too honest for your own good. There are a few items in our expenses that will require a fast wit and a glib tongue to justify."

"Have you been cheating the Beysa?" Monkel said, attentive once more. "That's a fine way to treat a visitor to your shores. Would you do the same thing to your own Prince-Governor?"

"In a minute," the Old Man smiled, and the others at the table joined in the laughter. In Sanctuary, even honest folk had an eye open for anyone with more money than business sense.

Of all the assembled captains, only Haron held herself apart from the laughter. She peered thoughtfully at the young Beysib for several moments, then laid a hand softly on his knee and leaned forward.

"You care for that one, don't you?" she said softly.

Monkel was surprised at her perception. Haron was only a few years younger than the Old Man, and her age-softened features combined with her mannish attitudes had made her almost indistinguishable from the male captains at the table. She watched for and saw different things than the others though . . . like Monkel's reactions to Uralai. He hesitated then gave a small nod of agreement.

"Hear that, boys?!" Haron crowed, slapping her palm loudly on the tabletop. "Our Monkel's in love! That should settle the question of whether or not he's as normal as the rest of you!"

The head of the clan Setmur was shocked and embarrassed by the outburst, but it was too late to do anything to prevent it. In a moment he was the center of attention, being alternately congratulated and teased by the captains.

"Is she any good in bed?" Terci said with a wink . . . a gesture Monkel had never been sure how to interpret.

"You'll have to bring her down here some night. We'd all like to meet her."

"Fool," Haron scoffed, dealing the speaker a good-natured cuff. "Can't you see anything? She was just here. That little guard with the big tits. It was as clear as seabirds circling over a school of feeding fish."

Writhing under the cross-examination, Monkel deliberately avoided looking at the other Setmur clansmen in the room. He knew they would be staring at him in amazement and/or disgust. Sex was a private subject among the Beysib, seldom discussed and never bantered about publicly.

The Old Man eyed Monkel in quiet speculation.

"A guard from the royal clan Burek?" he said.

Monkel nodded silently.

"What does that mean?" Omat interrupted, half rising and leaning across the table to join their exchange.

"It means Monkel has about as much chance of winning her as you would have of sparking Prince Kittycat's courtesans," the Old Man informed him.

"How do you figure that?" Haron demanded. "They're both Beysib, aren't they? Monkel here's as good a man as any I've met. No one at this table knows the sea as he does. Why shouldn't he have her if he wants her?"

Though warmed by the compliment, Monkel had to shake his head.

"You don't understand. Things are different for us. If she had not been on my boat for the pilgrimage, we would never have met. I couldn't . . ."

"It's not that different at all," the Old Man grunted. "She's richer and used to hobnobbing with royalty. Marrying a fisherman would be a real come-down."

Monkel surpressed a start as Haron hawked noisily and spat on the floor. Of all the local customs, this was the hardest for him to accept. Among the Beysib, a woman's saliva was more often than not poisonous.

"That's a lot of bird dung, Old Man," she announced. "Just goes to show how little you know about what a woman looks for in a man. Ignore these wharf-rats, Monkel. Tell me, what does *she* think?"

Monkel gulped half of his drink, then kept staring into the glass, avoiding her gaze.

"I . . . I don't know. I've never told her how I feel."

"Well, tell her, then. Or, better yet, show her. Give her a present . . . flowers or something."

"Flowers," Omat sneered, waving his one hand. "The woman's a guard. What would she want with flowers? What would you do if a man gave you flowers, Haron?"

"Well, what do you suggest for a gift? A sword? Maybe a brace of throwing daggers?"

"I don't know. But it should be something she couldn't or wouldn't get herself."

The argument raged on for hours, until Monkel lost it in the memory-deceiving depths of his fourth or fifth glass of wine. Only two points remained in his mind: he should not discount the possibility of marrying Uralai until he knew her thoughts on the matter, and that he should announce his interest with a gift... an impressive gift.

"Are you ill, Lord Setmur? Or didn't the fleet go out today?"

Startled, Monkel spun about in his crouch to find Hakiem standing less than an arm's length behind him. He recognized the Beysa's local adviser from his visits to court, but had never realized the oldster could move so quietly. Of course, Hakiem *was* a product of Sanctuary's alleys.

"I didn't mean to unsettle you," Hakiem said, noting the Beysib's alarm. "You really shouldn't sit with your back to the mouth of an alley. It can draw the attention of those more bloodthirsty or greedy than curious."

"I... I stayed ashore today."

"I can see the truth in that. You are here and the boats are gone."

Hakiem's weathered face split in a sudden smile.

"Forgive me. I'm prying into matters which are none of my business. I was a tale-smith before your Beysa invited me to join her court, and old habits die hard. My storyteller's instincts say that when the head of the Setmur fishing clan remains ashore while his boats work the fishing ground, there is a tale lurking somewhere nearby."

Monkel regarded his visitor with skeptical eyes.

"Has word of my absence been reported to the palace? Did the Beysa send you to inquire after my health, or did you really come all this way in search of a story?"

The ex-talespinner nodded approvingly.

Robert Lynn Asprin

"Information for information. A fair trade. I see you are rapidly learning the ways of our town. No, I didn't come looking for a story, though in the past I've walked further on that quest. I am here on my own in attempt to insure with my presence that the Beysa is not overcharged too outrageously for the boat you're building."

He quickly held up a hand, stopping Monkel's protests before they could begin.

"I am not accusing you specifically, Lord Setmur, though we both know the expenses you reported to the Empress yesterday were inflated. I expected it would happen when I recommended your project to the Beysa, and so far the exaggerated charges are well within acceptable limits. Since you are usually out with the fleet, you have no way of knowing that I visit the wharf every day to create the illusion that work and expenses are being monitored. I like to think it will help my countrymen to keep their greed in check, thus avoiding the scandal of an audit or the challenge which would certainly result if they were left to find the upper limits on their own."

Monkel dropped his eyes in embarrassment and bewilderment. Along with random violence, he still had difficulty comprehending the easy way graft was accepted, if not anticipated in Sanctuary.

"My encounter with you today is a chance meeting spurred by my own curiosity upon seeing you ashore at this hour, nothing more," Hakiem finished. "Now for your half of the bargain. What, besides illness, could keep you from the fleet? I trust you have not chosen a wharfside back-alley for a sick-bed."

In response, Monkel held up a small stick with a length of fishing line wrapped around it.

Hakiem frowned for a moment, then followed the line with his eyes as it extended down the alley. A fine fishing net was hanging there as if for drying, and scattered on the ground under it were pieces of bread and fruit.

"It looks as if . . ." Hakiem fixed Monkel with a puzzled

stare. "Fishing for birds? For this you abandoned your duties with the fleet?"

"It will be a gift . . . for a lady. I thought it would impress her more than something I had simply purchased."

"But aren't the beyarl sacred to your people?"

"Yes, but I was hoping to catch . . ."

Monkel's voice trailed off, but Hakiem had heard enough to finish the thought.

". . . one of Sanctuary's birds." The oldster seemed vaguely troubled. "There is no law against it, probably because no one has thought to try it before. Are you sure, Lord Setmur, that such an undertaking is wise? Wild things are usually best left wild."

Monkel laughed. "That's a strange thing to say to someone who makes his living pulling creatures from the sea."

"Catching and killing for food is one thing. Trying to tame . . ."

Hakiem broke off speaking and laid a hand on Monkel's arm. Monkel looked, and jerked his line in almost the same instant, a reflex not unlike setting a hook.

A piercing scream and a flutter of wings announced his success as a dark bundle of feathers struggled vainly to escape the net's folds.

"Got it!" Monkel exclaimed, rising to his feet. "My thanks, Lord Adviser: your alertness has speeded my success."

Hakiem shook his head as he turned to go.

"Do not thank me yet," he said darkly. "This tale's not over, if it has even begun yet. I only hope its conclusion is to your liking."

Monkel heard none of this, for with the urgency of youth, he was already moving to secure his prize . . . or rather, what he felt sure would be the means to his prize.

As the days stretched into weeks, Monkel had more than one occasion to question his choice of gift for Uralai. The bird staunchly refused to be tamed.

Closer examination of his catch had shown a bird unlike

any Monkel could recall having seen, though admittedly he had spent little time studying land-birds. It was roughly the size of a raven, though its vaguely hooked beak would lead some to think of it as a hawk, and black as the sea at night. Dominating its features was a pair of bright yellow eyes which seemed at once soul-piercing with their analytic coldness, and smoldering with an ill-repressed fury that one normally only sees in a death match with a blood enemy.

When Monkel gave the bird the freedom of his quarters it began methodically breaking every item vaguely fragile and several he had thought beyond damage. When he packed the few remaining valuables away, the bird countered by leaving its droppings on his clothes and bedding and gouging and splintering his furniture with its beak.

As to Monkel himself, the bird's attitude varied. Sometimes it would flee in terror, crashing headlong into the wall in its efforts to escape, and at other times it would fly in his face, screaming its outrage while contesting his right to even enter the room. Mostly, it would play coy, letting him approach with outstretched hand only to flutter away to wait again on another perch . . . or better still, climb onto his hand momentarily, then use its beak in a slashing move to draw blood from his hand or face before taking to the air.

The bird thought it was terrific fun. The thoughts of Monkel himself, with an increasing number of scars and half-healed wounds adorning his features and appendages, are best left unrecorded save to note that he often found himself wondering if the bird was edible. At this point in their duel, simply killing it would have been an insufficient expression of his frustration.

The final breakthrough was triggered by a conversation with one of his clan members. Clan Setmur was growing more and more concerned about his attempts at bird taming. Not only was it leaving him in a perpetually foul mood, it was drawing unwanted attention to the wharf community. Whether his friends at the captains' table had let the news leak or if Hakiem was not as retired from storytelling as he claimed was inconsequential. What mattered was that it was now common knowledge on the streets of Sanctuary that one of the Beysib fishermen had caught a black bird and was trying to tame it. Curiosity seekers appeared in a surprising array of rank and status. Barflies and S'danzo seers, petty criminals and self-proclaimed emissaries of the crimelord Jubal all were asking questions with varying degrees of subtlety regarding the bird and its trainer. Once, a dark mysterious woman reputedly never seen by the light of day was heard to make inquiries.

To one and all, clan Setmur claimed ignorance, but, as a normally quiet private people, they were distressed at this sudden notoriety. Having failed in their efforts to convince Monkel to abandon his task completely, they instead plied him with every bit of advice they could think of to bring his project to a successful and, above all, *speedy* conclusion.

Thus it was that Monkel was approached by Paratu, one of his cousins, as their ship approached Sanctuary after a day's fishing.

"Have you considered treating the bird like a person?" she said without preamble. "Perhaps it resents your attitude."

Monkel found himself smiling in spite of himself.

"Whatever led you to that idea?"

In response, Paratu gestured toward the city.

"I was recalling what you told us when we first arrived at this hellhole . . . about dealing with the residents of Sanctuary. You said we shouldn't think of them as animals. That if we treated them as people, they would respond as such and everyone would benefit. Well, your advice worked, and it occurred to me that, like the people, the bird is from the city. Maybe the same approach would work for you now."

"There's one problem with that, Paratu. The bird *is* an animal."

"So are the people," she said, staring at the town. "They respond to respect, and I frankly doubt you could find more than a handful that are any smarter than your bird."

Monkel had laughed openly then, but later gave the suggestion serious consideration.

Starting that very night, he began talking to the bird...not with the simple commands of a trainer, but open conversation as one would have with a close friend. He spoke of his previous life, of his fears in coming to this new land, and of his achievements thus far in his period of clan leadership. He told the bird of the elegance of the Beysa's court and of Uralai's beauty. Once he got started, talking to the bird became an easy habit, for, in truth, Monkel was a lonely man made lonelier by the pressures of leadership.

To his amazement, the bird responded almost immediately...or, to be accurate, it stopped responding. Instead of flying in terror or slashing at his face, it would sit quietly on his hand, head cocked to one side as if hanging on his every word. Soon, he became bold enough to set the bird on his shoulder, where it was in easy reach of an ear and an eye. The bird never betrayed this trust. If anything, it seemed to glory in its new perch and would flutter quickly to Monkel's shoulder as soon as he entered the room.

After a week of this, Monkel tried taking it outside and, in a final test, would transfer it to other people's shoulders. Through it all, the bird remained well-mannered and tolerant. Though suspicious of its sudden domesticity, Monkel decided it was time to make his presentation. If he waited much longer, he knew he would have grown too attached to the bird to give it up.

"You'll see. She's very beautiful, just like I told you."

The bird regarded Monkel with an expressionless yellow eye, ignoring the sweetmeat he was offering as a bribe.

With an inward sigh, the head of clan Setmur twisted in his chair to peer down the palace corridor once more, then resumed staring out the window.

He had considered presenting his gift to Uralai in the Beysa's court, but his confidence sagged and he decided to wait and catch her coming off duty. He still had lingering fears about the reliability of the bird's manners, and while a mishap while presenting it to Uralai would be embarrassing, the same slip in front of the Empress would be a disaster.

"You'll like it here," he murmured, more for his own reassurance than for the bird's. "It's definitely a step up from fighting for gutter scraps. I'll bet any beyarl—those are our own holy birds—would envy the treatment you'll . . ."

A soft footstep reached his ear, and he looked again to see Uralai approaching. All of his fears and insecurities ascended to his throat in a tight knot, but he steeled himself and rose to meet her.

"Good evening, Uralai."

"Monkel Setmur. What a pleasant surprise." Her voice was nearly musical when it wasn't speaking for the Beysa. "And what a lovely bird."

Buoyed by her warm reception, Monkel hurriedly blurted his mission.

"The bird is a gift. I . . . want you to have it."

"Really? I didn't know they sold pet birds in this town."

Uralai was studying the bird as Monkel took it on his hand and extended it toward her.

"They don't," he said. "I caught it and tamed it myself."

"Why?"

Monkel was growing uneasy. When he had rehearsed giving the gift to Uralai, he had not anticipated a prolonged conversation, and his discomfort increased as the talk progressed.

"I wanted . . . I am an unsophisticated fisherman and, try as I might, I could think of no better way to express my admiration of you than with a gift."

"That wasn't what I meant," Uralai said, "though you have certainly achieved your goal. What I was trying to ask was why you chose this particular gift."

"The bird is native to our new homeland. Its spirit and the town's are one. If we are to survive here, we must also become one with that spirit. We must not cling to our old

275

ways and customs, but rather be open to change and local ideas . . . such as your not being offended by the admiration of one from a lower clan."

"You speak quite well for an unsophisticated fisherman."

Uralai took the bird on her hand and moved it up to her shoulder. It hopped obediently onto its new perch. Monkel held his breath. A new awareness washed over him of how easily the bird could go for her eye.

"Your idea of becoming one with this miserable town is hard to accept. I will have to think about it further. However . . ."

She laid a soft hand on his arm.

". . . accepting your admiration is not as new as you seem to think. Remember, you are the head of your clan, while within my own, my status is less . . ."

The bird turned and loosed a load of dung down the front of her uniform.

Monkel rolled his eyes heavenward and fervently wished he could expire on the spot.

"Don't worry." Uralai's laugh was only a little forced. "It's a wild thing, like this town. It doesn't know how to behave politely. It's a wonder it's as tame as it is. Tell me, how did you do it? Was it very difficult?"

"Well . . ."

Before Monkel could continue, the bird moved again. This time, it hopped onto Uralai's head where it repeated its earlier misdeed in sufficient quantity so as to dribble some onto her face.

"You did that on purpose!" Monkel exploded, grabbing for the feathered fiend. "I'll . . ."

The bird launched itself out the window and disappeared with a scream that was more triumphant than apologetic.

"Good riddance!" Monkel shouted. "I'm sorry, Uralai. If I had thought . . ."

Uralai was shaking with silent laughter as she wiped the droppings from her face and hair.

"Oh, Monkel," she said, using his name alone for the first time, "if you could have seen yourself. Maybe I should have accepted your escort the other night. You're becoming as violent as those people you drink with. Now, come. Walk with me and tell me about the taming of your departed gift."

It was more than an hour before Monkel took his leave and floated home on a headier wine than any served at the fisherman's tavern. The gift had succeeded beyond his wildest hopes in opening communication with Uralai. What was even better, with the bird gone, he no longer had to worry about having unwittingly visited misfortune upon her house.

The bird was waiting for him when he arrived home, and no amount of cursing or thrown rocks would entice it to leave.

A SPECIAL NOTE FROM THE EDITORS
TO THIEVES' WORLD READERS:

We would like to take a moment to thank our readers for their continued support over the last five years.

The fan mail we have received is of Homeric proportions, which has created a problem at our end. For years we have tried to answer each letter individually, and as a result have countless sacks and drawers of unanswered mail. We've read it all, but replying is biting heavily into our writing (for pay) time. In desperation, we are converting to a word processor and a computerized mailing list, and armed with the weapons of modern technology we will tackle the backlog. If you have written us without receiving an answer, do not give up hope! We're working on it...even if the response is several years late.

As an added bonus in appreciation for your patience, your address will be included in our private mailing list. This will be used for an infrequent newsletter, giving advance information about future volumes and announcements of new *Thieves' World* spin-off products.

Again, thank you for your support. The series wouldn't still be going without you!

Robert Lynn Asprin
Lynn Abbey

November 1984